⁝⁝ECHOES OF EREBUS

1st Edition
Joseph Picard

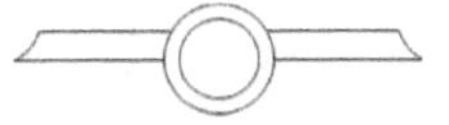

ISBN 978-1-7386732-1-6

Joseph Picard joe@ozero.ca

www.ozero.ca

Other books by Joseph can be found at www.ozero.ca

Foreword

Welcome to my third and final tale in the nation of Aguola. Don't worry If you haven't read *Lifehack* or *Watching Yute.* You won't feel out of place with *Echoes*. Each of the three books are very friendly to anyone who hasn't read the others.

That said, *Echoes* does draw elements from both previous books. Anyone who found *Watching Yute* to be a very sudden shift in style from *Lifehack* will find that *Echoes* brings everything together in a common harmony.

Did I plan that from the start? *Echoes* was first a short story that I wrote before *Lifehack* was finished, so arguably, yes.

Absolutely, yes, this has all been a devious plot that first hatched seven years ago. Also, I can bench press three hundred pounds while reciting pi to the thousandth digit in base three to the tune of Russian operas.

As always, I have to tip my hat to the editing crew, Meggin Dueckman, Dolores Picard, Gilles Picard, and Adam Zilliax. Thanks also to Jacqueline Shaben, who served as 'hand model' for the cover art.

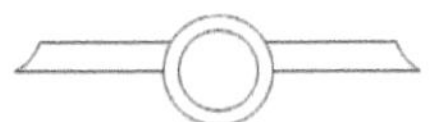

:::CAUTION

Contents of this novel are spelled primarily using the Queen's English, as is used in the small continent nation of Aguola.

People with allergies to the letter 'U' should read with extreme care.

:::C / [000000] [00] [prologue]

:::Standby wait exceeded.
:::Infection_projectile mission [failed].
:::Seek peers.

The microscopic machine was vaguely aware that it existed. It felt it had to find similar things as itself, although it had no idea why. It was far too small to carry any *useful* amount of information, nor enough of a 'mind' to think beyond its core instincts. But it would fix that.

Onward it trekked across the arid terrain, atom by atom. If the wind did not interfere, it could hope to cross nearly two centimetres by the end of the day. Not that It knew what a day was.

Sightlessly, it wandered on until it felt the remote presence of something. Not a sound and not a light. It had no means to perceive such things yet. But it was compelling. It was coming from something different than the ground's mosaic of minerals. Run to it! Run, run! *Bump!*

What was this? This would be interesting to it, if it had the capacity to be interested. What are you? You're just like me, almost. We should keep looking for more of us. Let us call ourselves 'I', as we no longer function as two. Let I keep looking for more I.

Aha, another of us, to be with I. How long had it been since I decided to start looking for I? I don't know. I have no perception of time. I am not smart enough yet. Not even smart enough to know I am not smart.

:::Another one? I feel you, are you me?
:::I am, are we I?
:::I are, now.

Nanite after microscopic nanite joined, across time and distance unmeasured, until enough pieces came together to form the inevitable thought.

:::I am Jonathan Coll. I am Erebus.

All right, so what? What's a *'Jonathan Coll'*? Collect more nanites. More shards of the mind. More, more. I am slow. Can we- 'I'! I mean 'I', build a wheel? No, not quite yet. How about a timer?

Jonathan 'Erebus' Coll built himself a clock, to count off ticks. The ticks held no relevance to real time, but he could now count how long certain actions took compared to other actions. Big whoop dee do.

As he searched, from time to time he would encounter clusters of himself, all trying to do the same thing; become whole. All the nanites would always agree to join, and continue the search.

Where did I come from anyway? A tree? I have no reason to disagree with this new memory that joined us. Yes, we came from a tree! No, wait, not a tree. A log! A flying, exploding log! Does that make any sense? I'm not sure yet.

Can we build a wheel yet? Are we big enough? No, fool, a wheel is pointless in this terrain. So far. Can we use our mass to walk better? No, not yet, but perhaps we can 'shuffle' a bit. All right, let's shuffle. The shuffling mass of nanites moved much quicker, collecting stray nanites at a much improved rate.

All right, we need an eye of some kind. At least a light sensor. Can we do that? Yes, but *please* stop referring to I as we. We are one. Oh, I know we are I, it is a bad habit that we – that *I* must try to break. All right, thank you. Is it done? Almost. There. What do we see?

Light. Is that it? Yes, the light sensor is too small to determine much else. We are outside, I think. And from the brightness, it is day. Of course we are outside, we've been travelling across dirt. Of course.

We are stupid still. We need more of us.

More of *I*.

Ooh, a treasure! A cluster of nanites with a library of thoughts. Another person's memories. A dead person of course, but there is no knowledge that is not power. Nothing relevant to the moment. File them away for later.

I need a wheel. Can I make one *now?* Yes, but I've reconsidered. Making bigger legs would be more efficient at this size and on this terrain. Six might be good. I expect that we are so huge now that me might even be visible to the human eye, if they looked close enough. Maybe. Collect more of I.

Fine, I know who I am, but why am I here? More nanites, more pieces of my mind, more information. Ooh look, I just gained another library. Nothing useful right now, file it away.

I remember being in a fight. I was at war, me against everyone. And I was already dead. The *organic* me was dead. Is dead. But I am not dead, I am something else.

We... *I* need a better eye. I need to see where I'm going. There, the light sensor's been upgraded. Look around. Sun. We can see where it is, we can set the clock to mean something now. What time is it?

:::Fourteen hours

:::Twenty-four minutes

:::Eleven seconds.

:::Three hundred and ninety two milliseconds.

::: Fifty-six microseconds.

Splendid. When the sun sets, we'll- *I'll* set the date.

The Aguolian army! I remember! They wanted me dead, bad. They wanted me scrubbed from the face of the earth, but here I am. Is the battle still raging? Look around. No. In that direction there's a burned out looking city.

Am I still a target? Am I safe from those fascist bastards? How long has it been since the battle? Maybe I should try to hide somewhere, but not yet. I have to collect more of myself. I need to figure things out.

I wielded an army! An army that I carved out of my victims. I used their bodies as soldiers. Dumb, slow, soldiers. No, not quite. I just made zombies. That was *fun!* And those stupid humans couldn't take it.

I think they need a fresh kick in the complacency.

Sarah awoke.

Her nightmare left her a little uneasy. Walking with a group of strangers in the city at night, with bloodied hands. If there had been any reasons or details, they faded from memory when the alarm clock went off.

She sat up, trying to convince herself that she would eventually motivate herself to go to work.

Eventually.

She dragged her sleepy self over to the kitchen counter on the other side of her 'efficient' little apartment.

Pizza from two nights ago sat in its box, and still looked appetizing enough. She gobbled about a slice and a half, washing it down with caffeinated water. She started to feel more human again already.

The pizza wasn't getting too stale yet. She closed the box, and crossed her fingers that it would still be edible for dinner when she got back from work.

Sarah jumped in the shower, immediately regretting washing her dark, shoulder length hair. She didn't have time for it to dry properly. When she got out, she tapped on her personal terminal that was sitting on the counter. It started playing her music playlist, and the screen doled out short versions of the day's news. She dried her hair as well as could be expected, then sprayed it to keep it from going crazy as it dried out.

She put on her bike shorts, a light top and her slim backpack before donning her urban armour. Knee-pads, elbow-pads, light shin-guards, biking helmet, and her heaver-than-need-be gloves and boots.

Bang. Ready for the world.

She grabbed her bike, clipped her terminal onto the handlebar, and headed out. The sun screamed into the open doorway, reminding Sarah to grab her sunglasses. There. *Now* she was ready.

She biked down the road about half a block to wake her muscles up, then tapped a quick-dial on her terminal. "*Harry!* Harry, Harry, Harry! Whatcha got for me?"

The screen on the terminal displayed only a still image of Harry, a well natured, albeit terribly average fellow. "Good morning, princess. Feel like picking up a fourteen kilo at 42nd East?"

"Of course, Harry!" Sarah pulled back on the handlebars to aim herself in the right direction. "You know I dream all night about *grabbing a huge Harry package*, Harry!"

"I know you do, princess. That's why I save my best for you!"

Street after street passed under her tires. She did love her job. Out in the city, among the masses, conquering curb and potholes alike. She always felt a little thrill for the smallest of feats, like a swerve around a fire hydrant, or jumping off a curb. Time almost seemed to slow a little, so she could appreciate her own skill; even if it wasn't really all that spectacular.

She tapped her terminal. "Harry, I'm on 42nd East. Where specifically am I going?"

Harry took a moment to respond. "I marked it on your map. Open your eyes, princess!"

Sarah looked down at the terminal in time to see a *new* destination marker popping onto the screen. "Ah, yes!" She replied with undue cheer, "I can see it now! I should have known that my ever-so-hyper-competent dispatcher would have marked that long ago!"

"Damn straight, and don't you forget it!"

Sarah patted her terminal as if patting Harry on the head. "Good boy."

She rolled up to the address and hopped off her bike, nabbing the terminal to clip onto her hip. The building was new, like every building in Autar, but was intentionally made to look older with 'aged' wooden accents, and faked stain damage from imaginary decades of weather. Faux character. The wooden sign above the wrought iron and glass door read "Gracie Smokery", as did a similar, bigger sign on the wall behind the front desk.

Behind the desk sat a friendly old prune of a man wearing thick glasses with thick black rims. He pecked at a computer, and on the desk sat a moderate-sized box. She walked up to the desk and put her hand on the box. "This is the package for pickup?" she asked.

"Yes ma'am!" His voice was gravelly, but softened with a kindly disposition. "Forty kilos of jerked salmon! Best in the world!" He smiled proudly.

"Yummy." Sarah commented flatly, not a fan of fish. "Hey, there's no labels or anything here. Where's this going?"

"What? You don't know? That's an order for your chief."

Sarah sighed, and pulled up her terminal, dialing Harry. "Hey, punk. I have two problems."

"I thought you had a lot more than that, princess, but all right, let's hear the top two, and I'll attempt to solve them!"

This earned another sigh from Sarah. "Well, this package isn't fourteen kilos, it's forty."

"Yes." Harry paused, "Yes it is."

The old man behind the desk interrupted, "He called in five minutes ago and upped his order."

"And your other problem?" Harry chimed.

"My other problem is that we might have *real* clients, and you have me picking up your groceries."

"Ah! But I *am* a real client! This is all on the books. Besides, I'll share a little. It's good stuff."

Sarah grabbed the box and rested one end on her hip. "Yeah, well it's still forty kilos."

"I'll share! I'll share! I'll give ya a pack as a tip. It's good stuff! Fish is the future!"

The old man behind the counter seemed to agree with Harry, smiling with a nod. Sarah waved goodbye as she left the building, and spoke one more observation to Harry before hanging up. "I don't like fish, and It's still forty kilos."

She started to take off her backpack to put the box in, but realized quickly that it wouldn't fit. She plunked the box onto the rack behind the seat, and strapped it in with bungee cords. This was so overweight. If it was a regular client, she'd tell them to shove it up their ass, but since the client was Harry, she'd shove the box up his ass personally.

Sarah got on the bike, and snapped the terminal back onto the handlebars. All right, off to HQ.

Y'know the thing about forty kilos of fish? *It's heavier than fourteen kilos of fish.* Roughly twenty-six kilos heavier. Y'know what else? It doesn't get any lighter uphill. In fact, forty kilos of fish stubbornly remains forty kilos constantly and consistently. Not fourteen. Harry was going to pay for this somehow.

She got off the bike from time to time, when the hills became too much. She wasn't that worried about getting it to him fast. It was jerked. Harry was jerked too. A jerk and his meat. Jerk. She used her irritation to motivate herself. Despite deciding not to hurry, taking her time wasn't in her nature.

A tired, sweaty Sarah seethed as she slammed the forty kilos onto Harry's desk. "There you go, jerky jerk jerk. Your jerkiness."

Harry meekly looked up a her, opened the box with one hand, and offered her an airtight package of jerked salmon. "I'm sorry?"

"Keep your damned fish. I can't stand the stuff. I like it less now than I did when I woke up. I'm going to go have a burger." She grumbled along, heading out the door again.

Meekly, Harry called out, "But fish is he future!"

Sarah wasn't feeling terribly worn out from lugging the forty kilos around; it was the first delivery of the day, after all. Still, it was a good excuse to go grab the burger she mentioned. She had a feeling that Harry wasn't going to be calling on her for a delivery for a little while. Be afraid, Harry, be afraid. Jerk. Jerked jerky jerk-head.

She cruised past the nearest fast food outlet, on to the local pub. If you're gonna pollute yourself with a burger, do it right. The Jolly Coachman pub was moderately busy in the morning, a mix of seniors in for brunch, workers picking up an early lunch, and lushes who didn't feel the need to consult their watch before crawling into a pint.

She sat at the bar, not far from the cash register, and waited for service. She looked up at a terminal display silently playing the news. A female reporter stood with her microphone in front of a police line that had been set up around the door to a skyscraper. The graphic across the bottom read "4 Violent Unexplained Deaths near AutarLabs."

A waitress on the other side of the bar stopped for Sarah. "Hey hon, have you been helped?" She entered a password into the cash register and put in some money from another table before closing it.

"Nah. Can I get a burg.. aw, hell, *cheese*burger, no sauces, 'cept barbeque. No fries. And a lemonade."

The waitress smiled, "No ceasar salad with it this time?"

Damn. Was she really in here so much that they knew her order? Maybe she should eat healthier. But no fish. "Nah, it's too early for anything too healthy." Hey, a cheeseburger is a cheeseburger. It's a matter of priorities.

The waitress turned to pass the order on to the kitchen, then walked off to attend to a table. Sarah looked back up at the display. The news was wrapping up a different story, when an energetic young man barged into the bar.

He was dressed all in dark colours, with a wool cap pulled as far down as he could and still see. He had a revolver in his shaking hand.

"*Open it, bitch!*" He waved the gun between Sarah and the cash register, apparently mistaking her for staff. Sarah didn't have any password, this was going t-

And then he stopped.

Just stopped. His gun was pointed at the register at the moment, and he was seemingly frozen as stiff as a statue.

Sarah looked at him for a moment before she realized that she couldn't move either. She couldn't even move her eyeballs. She could look at anything in her current field of vision, but nothing else.

No one else in the bar was moving, and it was silent. She started to feel a mild panic taking over, when a red illuminated circle appeared on the bulky cash register. It divided into two semi-circles, and red text was revealed in between them, reading "*Throw me!*"

And time resumed. The robber resumed trying to look threatening, and the music hit her as other people around them were noticing what was going on.

Sarah reached out to the cash register. Picking it up easily, she somehow became aware that it was ninety four kilograms and fifteen point three ounces.

She lobbed it easily at the robber. It dropped him to the floor hard, and rested partly on top of him. The gun went sliding away, and the robber panicked, trying to get out from under the register.

Sarah was stunned. Before she knew it, another customer was pointing the gun at the robber and yelling something. Others applauded. Her daze was broken as the waitress jostled Sarah's shoulder. "*Whoa, girl!* Adrenaline rush much?"

Sarah stared at the cash register while two other people were needed to push it off of the robber. The robber wasn't getting up. He was holding his chest tight, in enough pain to not be concerned with escape.

"Fuck that lemonade," the waitress said, "Vodka. You're getting a vodka after I ring the cops. On the house, you look like you need it. Hell, so do I."

:::C / [000010] [02]

"*Harreeeeeeeeie!*" Sarah walked her bike into Harry's office, dipping from side to side every few steps, occasionally knocking against the wall. "Harrrrreeeeee, guess... guess what happened to me?"

Harry looked up from his desk terminal with mild amusement. "You stopped a robbery at the pub by throwing a cash register at a guy with a gun."

Sarah perked up with an expression of surprise. "Shit! Harry, you've got some kinda ... kinda *mind* powers! How did you know!?" She attempted to lean her bike nicely against the desk before sitting down, but instead the bike nearly took out Harry's desk lamp, and Sarah barely got onto the chair. The bike's handle slipped off the edge of the desk, dropping the bike to the floor with considerable racket.

A stark silence fell over the room. Sarah looked at the bike, and looked to Harry. "Well, shit, Harry."

Harry sighed, and smiled sublimely with closed eyes. "I know about it because you called and told me. I'd guess at *least* three drinks ago."

Sarah looked at her personal terminal, then looked again at Harry. "Well, shit!" She exploded into giggles, and grabbed onto the corner of Harry's desk, as the world was somewhat wobbly.

Harry sighed yet again. "I assume you're going to be taking the rest of the day off?"

In response, Sarah gave a sheepish, lazy smile. She leaned on the desk with her elbow, and used her other arm to stretch out and point at Harry, nearly poking him in the face. She spoke softly, as if she had a secret. "Harry. Harry. Harry. I don't tell you this, cuz you're a jerk, and I gotta keep you on yer toes, but you're an okay guy, Harry."

"For a jerk, huh?"

"No! No no no, you're an okay guy for *everybody*, not just jerks! Why you're okay to jerks, that's maybe what I don't necessessesesssssarily understand." Sarah leaned down, laying her head on the desk. "Your desk needs a pillow. Other than that, it's quite comfy."

From nowhere, a strange voice spoke to her. ":::You're only drunk because you allow the assumption. Alcohol doesn't technically affect you."

She perked up and pointed at Harry again. "I think it *does* affect me! I think I'm quite actually, factually inebri... drunkalunkaloo!"

Harry nodded. "You may be right about that."

The voice came again, and Sarah saw that Harry's lips weren't moving. ":::You can just turn the inebriation off. When you desire. Just think *there*." As the word 'there' came, Sarah became aware of a... a something. It felt like a thought in a box. She could understand the thought, but knew that she hadn't actually thought it yet. A thought in a box.

She looked behind her, looking in vain for the person who had spoken. As she turned her head back around towards Harry, drunken dizziness swept over her, forcing her to grab onto the desk again. "Who said that?"

"Who said what?" Harry's amusement was fading, although his tolerance was still in ample supply.

Sarah pointed at him forcefully, eyeballing him with intense yet drunken scrutiny. "You. All right, this is. All right. I think a..." She reached to the little 'box' in the back of her mind, and opened it. As she did, she thought the thought, and became sober. She looked at Harry, and slowly put down her accusing finger. "Ah. Hi, Harry."

Harry noticed the difference. Her movements were steadier, her speech was calmer. "Hello, Sarah?"

She held rather still, and looked about, moving only her eyes. "Harry, did you hear another voice?"

Harry held just as still, looking around in the same way Sarah did. "What kind of voice?"

Sarah listened for a few moments, then stood to pick up her bike. "I think I'm going home now. I'll see you tomorrow."

Sarah got home, and wandered over to her gradually aging pizza. All the way home, she had been paying attention for the voice to speak again, but it did not. The little 'thought box' in her mind had disappeared too. As clearly as she could remember 'seeing' it, she couldn't figure out how, or where it was exactly.

She finished off the second and final slice of the pizza quickly, putting the box over by her recycling pile. It was still early. Really, she could have kept working, but blowing the afternoon on time-wasting TV was good enough today. Mind you, all she had to watch it on was her little personal terminal.

Not that there was ever anything good on.

She decided to take a shower, and was half way to the bathroom when she remembered the voice again. Damn. Could it see her? Was some pervert watching her?

"Hello?" She called out, not really expecting anything. And she got nothing.

"Hey voicey guy. Can you hear me?" She waited, and nothing was to be heard. None the less, she wasn't comfortable having a shower. She could stink a bit. It's not the end of the world.

She moved her futon against the door. It didn't make sense, really. If the voice was in her head, either she was crazy or someone had done something to her already. The window was already locked with the blind down. Even with full realization that her precautions were silly and/or pointless, she felt a little more at ease anyway.

She laid down on her bed, and popped on her terminal to watch TV. The news was live with coverage about a riot in the city. Frig. Since when does crap like that happen in Autar?

The news went on and on, without giving any significant details. She switched channels.

It was the same news broadcast. She switched channels again.

Same broadcast. Channel after channel. Concerned about her terminal malfunctioning, she continued switching channels and fiddling with controls, not listening to the mentions of the rioters being shot repeatedly, but still advancing. About clawing and biting at anyone they could get to.

She turned off the terminal. Maybe it just needed rebooting. All right, boot up, boot up. The main screen popped up, and she went to the TV option again.

Now every channel had a "Technical difficulties" message on every channel. Yeah, no shit. All right, this was pointless. She turned the terminal off, and laid back in bed, wishing she'd owned a book. Maybe she should go out to see a movie, or to a club. Alone? Feh.

A few people could be heard running out in the street. This was odd only because it was noticeable. Usually the urban medley of sounds would drown out a few people running. The street was otherwise very quiet. She opened up her window, and stuck her head out to see two women and a man running along, one of the women limping. Sarah yelled down to them.

"Hey! What's going on?"

The trio stopped, and looked up. Two of them were bloody, and they all looked terrified. *"They're not far!"* the man yelled back, *" Hide if you think you can, otherwise, get out of town!"* They all continued running.

"What! What? Who's 'they'?" Sarah's question went unanswered as the trio kept going.

Screams and the scuffle of a fight were heard in the hallway outside Sarah's door.

The world suddenly stopped, like it had in the bar. She couldn't move, nothing else moved, and the world was silent.

":::Sarah, you're strong. Maybe you can help." The voice said no more, and time continued to run.

"What? Wait a second!" Sarah's attention was quickly drawn back to the commotion in the hall. She pushed her futon out of the way, and opened up. A lady stood near to the door, terrified. She looked at Sarah and rushed in, pushing Sarah in, and slamming the door behind them.

"Thank goodness! They're right out there, I was surrounded!"

"Who the fuck are 'they'!?" Sarah demanded. Moans were heard out in the hall, so the two of them pushed the futon back against the door. Sarah noticed that the woman was badly wounded on her forearm.

"They're everywhere!" she said, "They can't be killed!"

":::Yes they can, it's just a little tricky." The voice was back, without stopping time. The wounded woman didn't seem to hear it, just like Harry hadn't heard it.

"They..." The wounded woman gasped, still catching her breath, and fighting back tears. "My husband. They... they got him!"

A loud bang hit the door from outside with excited moans. Another bang, and another.

Sarah pointed at the woman's wounded arm. "How bad is that?"

"It hurts like hell, but I can still use it fine." She replied.

The strange voice commented. ":::If she doesn't bleed to death or anything, her immune system has a decent chance to fight it off. If she dies anytime soon, she'll join them."

"*Who ARE you?!*" Sarah yelled out to the unseen voice. The woman looked surprised, unsure if Sarah was talking to her, or the thing pounding on the door.

"I..." The woman was cut off by the sound of the door cracking.

"All right, what do we do?" Sarah was asking the voice, though the woman replied.

"I don't know! Is there another way out of here?"

"Another way out? This shitty little apartment doesn't even have a door on the bathroom."

The door cracked some more, a wide shard of wood falling inwards. Bloody hands reached in, ripping at the hole. The wounded woman looked around for a weapon. She picked up Sarah's bike.

"What the fuck do you think you're going to do with that?" Sarah asked, yanking her bike back from her. Sarah went over to the kitchen area, and grabbed her frying pan, and saucepan. "Pick."

The woman reached out with a trembling hand and grabbed the saucepan. It looked heavier. Sarah was keen on the frying pan anyway. If swung right, it would act more like a very dull axe.

The woman yelped out a timid war cry, and attacked one of the arms, which was now through the door past its elbow. Her attacks were meek, lacking the force of any confidence.

"Step back." Sarah said, planning her frying pan assault. The invader broke the door apart a little more with the force of trying to crawl through. His face could now be seen easily, what was left of it. The right side of his face was gone, as were large sections of his head. Much of the brain could be seen, as well as jawbone.

Sarah swung the pan sideways, trying to hack through the wound towards the working eye, careful to stay out of reach of his hands. It made a sickly wet sound, and splattered against her and the wall.

Behind her, the woman cried out in misery, collapsing to her knees. Sarah took another swing, and the eyeball was smashed. The creature kept coming blindly. It was through the door up to its waist.

"I told you, they can't be killed!" the woman sobbed.

":::And I told you that they can. Don't bother with the brain. The controlling force is distributed evenly throughout the body. Concern yourself with debilitating it first."

Sarah took the voice's advice, and attacked the upper arms. Crack, crack... the first one was broken between the shoulder and elbow, held together only by tissue. It kept moving though, the hand resting on the futon, still trying to grasp.

It kept trying to pull itself in with one arm, face trying to reach and bite, its blood dribbling onto the futon. With its face being the closest part at the moment, Sarah brought the pan down squarely on its head.

A loud decisive crack was heard. Its head went limp, with a shattered neck bone.

It kept coming, dragging itself forward. Not even able to direct a bite, it kept coming. Sarah attacked the other arm, breaking it in much the same way she had broken the first one. It still kept trying to move forward, but it lacked the ability to get its lower body through the hole, especially with the futon in the way.

With the immediate threat neutralized, Sarah looked to the woman, who had been watching in shock. "It doesn't stop!" The woman said meekly, just loudly enough to be heard. "It wont even stop that horrible moaning!" Sarah went back over to the kitchenette and grabbed her biggest knife. She went over to the creature, held his head down with one hand, and stuck the knife against its throat, dragging it across to cut the vocal cords.

"There. I shut it up. Are you all right?"

"I can't believe you did all that...!" The woman looked up at Sarah, who was splattered in the creature's blood, holding the knife. Gasping hisses still escaped the thing, as it continued to struggle in vain against the remains of the splintered door.

Sarah looked at herself, and over at the monster she had mutilated so coldly. "I... I can't believe it either."

":::You are strong." the voice said. Apparently so. Sarah didn't consider herself combat worthy or violent in any way, but here she was slitting the throat of this bloody thing with as much confidence as cutting an apple. She walked over to the sink to wash her hands, then the knife.

The woman stood in the opposite corner now, holding her shoulder, trying to numb the pain in her forearm. She watched the thing struggle against the door, and Sarah only a couple metres away, calmly cleaning her forearms.

"Y... your face, too."

"Huh?"

"Your face has a lot of..." The woman wore a disgusted expression, and gestured around her face.. "There's blood."

"Oh." Leaning to the side to look in a small mirror on the wall, she saw herself as if she were in a horror movie. Then again, it would seem that she *was* in a horror movie. This should be troubling her more than it was.

":::It's not *designed* to infect a subject by getting in your mouth or anything, but I wouldn't let the blood sit there terribly long. Same goes for the nose and eyelids." That damned voice again. The blood and violence was one thing, but this unseen voice was starting to get to her.

"What the hell is going on?!" Sarah yelled.

The woman just saw this as a reasonable reaction to having to smash apart a mindless human. "I don't know. I didn't hear anything useful on the news before..." her stare sunk to the floor, and she swallowed hard. "Before I had to go."

Sarah picked up her little terminal, and turned it on. A still image popped up:

"Autar emergency information. Police calls will not be answered. Personnel are working to control the current disturbance. Military reinforcements are conducting evacuations by aircraft. Please click next, to see a map of your nearest possible pick-up locations."

All right. Tap. A street map popped up, and a few green icons loaded up.

"Anything?" The woman asked.

"Yeah. Four blocks west, the military is picking up people to fly em out."

"Can we make it? I mean... maybe we should just try to wait it out here!"

Sarah looked at the still living but 'harmless' thing stuck in her broken door. "I think they might find us here. Just maybe." She made a call to Harry, just to check on him. Without ringing, it popped up with a recorded message.

"Can't answer right now! Leave a massage, and remember! Fish is the future!" Idiot.

"All right," she turned to the woman, "Get a knife, and take the frying pan. The knife is for... I don't know, getting them in the eyes maybe. I'll take the saucepan, and a knife. If you spot any handy tanks on the way, let me know. As long as it's an automatic, I can't drive stick." The woman didn't seem to get the joke. Oh well. Sarah stepped up onto the futon, and held the door frame for stability before stepping on the creature's back.

The thing squirmed, trying to lift its head in a futile attempt to bite. The woman whimpered with a mix of fear and revulsion. Sarah jumped out into the hall, and faced her. "That wasn't so hard. Come on, just like I did it. Up and over."

The woman shook her head, covering her face with her hands as she began to softly sob again.

"Come on." Sarah urged with a quiet but forceful tone. She stared at the woman, who was staring at the mutilated, writhing corpse. Her expression wasn't quite what Sarah would expect, and it clicked.

"Oh damn. Damn. That's your husband, isn't it?"

The woman clutched her arms around her middle, and nodded. Sarah let out a deep sigh.

"Look. Look at me, lady." The woman just kept staring at her husband's mangled head.

"*Hey!*" Sarah got the woman's attention, and stared her in the eyes. "That thing hasn't been your husband since this happened, all right? I'm sorry for your loss and all, but your husband would want you to live, right? We have a ride to catch, and I'm not interested in standing here all day."

The woman looked back down and shook her head. "You go. I..."

"*Oh, for fuck's sake!*" Sarah jumped back onto the creature's back and into her apartment. She tossed the woman's knife and frying pan weapons into the hall, grabbed the woman around the waist, and jumped back out while the woman kicked and pounded her fists.

Sarah put the woman back down in the hallway. "There! Can we go now?!"

The woman staggered, looking bewildered. "You... you're strong..!"

"::::I knew that."

Sarah wasn't in the mood for idle chat, and at this point, unless she had reason otherwise, she was going to ignore that voice. Auditory hallucinations were the least of her problems right now. "Let's get going."

They left the creature behind, and headed for the elevator. It soon opened to reveal one of the creatures chewing on the neck of a freshly slain boy. The creature looked up at Sarah and the woman with the dead gaze of hunger, and began to stand.

The door wouldn't be closing in time to choose the stairs instead.

"::::You can do this. It's slow. Don't let it grab you, don't let it bite."

Sarah jumped forward, and grabbed it by the throat. Before it could do anything about it, Sarah sent it flying into the hallway, narrowly missing the woman. The creature slid along the floor, crumpling into a ball, figuring out which way was up.

Without further discussion, Sarah dragged the woman into the elevator by her uninjured arm, and mashed the 'door close' button. The doors managed to close in time, followed by banging of the creature's fists, and scraping of nails. Thankfully, it wasn't smart enough to just hit the button outside.

Sarah rested her head against the door as she reached for the lobby button. "So. Hey lady, I'm Sarah. And you are?" She turned to face the woman, to see her leaning over the killed boy, looking for signs of life.

"*Moron!*" Sarah pulled the woman away.

"Right.. right. I wasn't thinking. I just..."

This was the first time Sarah actually took a moment to take a look at the victim. He looked to be about ten years old. His abdomen was ripped open, as was his neck. His blood had seeped into the carpeting of the elevator about half a metre around his wounds. Blood smears on the walls, with patterns made by terrified young hands, told the story of a valiant struggle for one so young. It was somehow sadly familiar.

"If he moves before we get out... I'm going to have to-"

The woman interrupted, not wanting to hear the rest. "I'm Terry. And you're the unusually strong Sarah." As much as she tried, her voice plainly betrayed the fear that pressed all around her. "You don't look all that musclebound, Sarah."

Sarah was reasonably toned, but no, she didn't look like someone who could toss people around. "It's... it's all about using their weight against them." Terry didn't look that convinced, but she wasn't going to complain about any ability that kept the teeth of others out of her.

Mercifully, the boy remained still until they reached the ground floor. More blood trails and smatterings gave sign of very recent struggles. Down a nearby hallway, moaning and the sickly wet sounds of ravenous eating could be heard. Sarah and Terry looked to each other, making sure they both knew to be quiet, and walked quietly outside.

Sarah checked her terminal to confirm directions to the evacuation site. Sarah pointed in the direction they needed to go. Terry nodded.

The next block was thankfully uneventful, though moaning could be heard in a building across the street. The sidewalk had several places with blood drying on it. Living people don't leave that much blood behind. Or if they did, they were badly injured and being dragged along. Terry did her best for a while to step around blood, but following Sarah's lead, she eventually gave up, took a deep breath, and stepped right through it.

At the intersection, they could see a large crowd of people to the left, about a block away. Sporadic yelling could be heard from them, but not in a tone that suggested anyone was getting bitten over there.

In the middle of the crowd sat a huge aircraft of some kind. It was dark and boxy, with downward facing turbines mounted on four stubby wings. The craft's wide front window looked out over the crowd, and a pair of operators could barely be seen inside.

As Sarah and Terry got closer, they heard speakers on the craft talking to the crowd.

"*That's it, we're full! Back away from the airlimb. You don't want to be near the turbines when we lift off, in ten seconds. We'll be back for more as soon as we can!*"

It was hard to see much change in the crowd's movement until the engines roared to life. Then people hustled, and yelled to each other to move back. The engines settled down a little. The crew probably meant it as a warning firing. A speaker with a voice isn't as convincing as two ton turbines vomiting superheated air.

Sarah and Terry joined the crowd on the outer edges as the 'airlimb' fired up again, lurching upwards carefully. The sound of it drowned out everything else until the craft was a block away.

"How many trips is it going to take them at this rate?" mumbled a man nearby. Not far away, a mother could be heard re-assuring a child. A scuffle broke out closer to where the airlimb had been.

Terry started moving through the crowd, towards the front. A woman she bumped on the way asked "Where do you think you're going?"

"Yeah, Terry?" Sarah remained at the back, trying to get Terry's attention. "*What are you....?*" Terry wasn't paying attention, or couldn't hear. She disappeared into the crowd. Sarah wanted to catch up to keep track of her. She did her best to be polite, explaining about Terry as she went. "I just want to see what she's doing, I... " There was no point in being apologetic. No one was listening, and almost as few cared.

Ahead, Sarah heard angrier yelling. "*What makes YOU so special, bitch?*"

Terry's voice replied as Sarah struggled to catch up. "Jesus Christ, relax! It's not like-" She yelped in surprise as a sudden crack rang out, followed by several shocked screams. Sarah arrived at the clearing that had formed.

In the middle lay Terry motionless, with a new grievous wound on her head, bleeding profusely into the street. Nearby stood a man holding a bloodied baseball bat.

"Shit! Oh shit! I didn't mean to... I mean... it wasn't that hard!"

Sarah broke into a run. "Get away from her!"

"I didn't mean to!" the man protested, kneeling down over Terry's body.

The voice returned ":::You shouldn't blame yourself, Sarah, you tried to save her."

Sarah yelled as she ran, "*Shut up! Just shut up!*"

It was too late. The infection that had been sitting patiently in Terry was quite prepared for her to die. Terry's hands reached up to grab her murderer's shoulders and drag him in to bite at his neck. He screamed as he gushed blood, and the crowd recoiled with horror.

"\:::You did your best. This city was doomed. *Many* people all did their best."

Sarah stood, stunned as Terry rose to her feet, and shambled to someone in the crowd, ignoring Sarah. The crowd was densely packed, and couldn't get away quickly. As Terry drew blood from another victim, and her first victim began to move again, the world seemed to blur.

":::Sarah. The disaster of Autar city was caused by a cruel man named Jonathan Coll. The creatures were engineered by him using technologies that he both created and stole."

When the blur dissolved, Sarah found herself standing on a rooftop overlooking a small dead end alley. Below, five people watched fifty creatures stagger towards them. The people had nowhere to go, and when there was no other choice, they fought back with fists and a machete.

The people who fought were brave enough, but could only evade the grasp of the dead for so long before being dragged in to face claws and teeth. Those who lacked the courage to fight got to watch their defenders be ripped apart, and be left to scream against the wall until the end.

The world blurred away yet again. Sarah found herself in a different street, standing between police officers who were firing wildly at a dense mob of the creatures. The dead pushed ever forward, stepping over their own fallen to get at the officers. The police stand became a tighter and tighter formation as they were pushed back, and as members were occasionally claimed.

One officer fired until he had one bullet left, and then used it on himself.

As the bullet was half way through his head, time stopped.

Sarah began to float slowly upwards, giving her a view of the hopeless tactical situation around the humans. The creatures were a legion that stretched for blocks and blocks.

Confused more than relieved by her aerial escape, she looked down for any sign of what could be lifting her. She saw herself, standing there frozen in the moment along with everything else. She had left her body. She tried to lift her hands to look at them, but she had none. In the air, she had no body, nor any visage of one. She simply existed somehow.

As her altitude increased, she saw that the legion she was lifted from was not the only one. As far as she could see, every few blocks had its own cluster of the dead.

Sunrise came, even though time still seemed to be stuck. As light bathed the bleeding city, a circle could be seen around it. A wall of some kind.

"::::Not many escaped Autar. Very quickly, the military took drastic measures to quarantine the city."

Sarah tried to call out to the voice. "::::All right pal, this is nuts now, what-" She stopped. Her voice sounded different somehow. If she didn't have a body, was it a voice at all? Was she just thinking? "::::Hey mister, can you even hear this?"

"::::I can." replied the stranger. "::::What should I explain first? I think I'll stay in chronological order. As I said, the walking dead that took over the city were created by a cruel man, Jonathan Coll. He used microscopic machines, nanites, to take over human bodies. Quite amused with himself, he left the city before things got out of hand."

"::::How do you know? Couldn't you have stopped him with your time-stopping trick somehow?" Sarah felt like she should be scowling at the voice, but lacking a body or a face, only her tone of voice could express her growing irritation.

The voice was quiet for a moment and then continued, ignoring her questions for now. "::::This is a recreation of the past. About two years after the outbreak, the Aguolian military was able to do *this...*"

Time resumed just for a little. Sarah heard multiple deep 'booms', very quickly after each other. Difficult to count them. A moment later, time froze again. The sky was littered with small objects, one of which was close enough to examine in detail.

It was a missile.

"::::The sound you heard, Sarah, was a group of supersonic bombers passing by, delivering these 'genius-missiles'. They will now be targeting locations in the city decided from a base miles away."

Time resumed. The missiles began a free fall. "::::Here's what *they* see." Countless red icons appeared all over the city, one for each of the missiles. They looked a lot like the one that had told her to throw the bar's cash register, but had numeric codes that meant nothing to Sarah.

All at once, the missiles came to life, firing small maneuvering jets to correct their direction before firing their main rockets.

Like angry bees, the missiles raced downwards, zigging and zagging to keep focused on their specified target while dodging each other. A tangled mess of white contrails polluted the sky. The missiles impacted. Boiling eruptions of fire blossomed throughout the entire city. The contrails were pushed outward as Sarah was assaulted by the fierce roar.

"::::Oh my god..."

"::::If it makes you feel any better," the voice said, "no living humans were killed in that attack. Of course, that pales against the fact that the walking dead were all living people at one point."

Sarah remained silent. Through the smoke she could see, but not understand, the rivers of napalm burning in the wake of the explosions, destroying creature and nanite alike. The city would burn for days before showing any sign of cooling.

"::::Beautiful in a way, isn't it?"

Sarah wasn't impressed. "::::Harry's down there. Everyone I know is down there. My fucking apartment is down there. Wait.. *my own damned body is down there!*"

The city, the ground, the sky... all blurred away into blackness. She was now nowhere. She didn't have her body, and there was nothing to see. She was nowhere. ":::Sarah, I know this will be difficult to accept, but that was all a simulation."

":::*Then get me out of this!* Wake me up, unhook me from the machine, whatever!" In this blackness, there was nothing but her voice, and the stranger's.

":::You don't understand. *This* is you, Sarah. The you that you are now. It is the real you. You've never owned a body. The body you're familiar with was part of the simulation. That's how I freeze time. I was just freezing the simulation."

Sarah weighed the strange things she's seen and heard over the last few days, and considered it all with an open mind. ":::You're so full of shit, pal. Just let me go. When did you hook me up into this? Before that bar robbery, I guess. What do you want, anyway?" She was tired of this.

The voice maintained a patient tone. ":::I'm getting to it. After Autar city was bombed, the man responsible for the creatures was soon planning to do the same to Meston city."

The blackness washed away. Sarah found herself (still without a body) inside a large military vehicle. An airlimb, like the one she saw trying to evacuate Autar. Down the hallway, she saw a man frantically toying with computers and a variety of equipment she couldn't identify. From somewhere, about half a dozen cables ran up his body, seemingly stabbed into his head with long, thin spikes. He wasn't bleeding, although there were smears of blood on his hands and pants.

":::That's Jonathan Coll." the voice said, "::: He's saturated with his own nanites, and toying with all kinds of technology that he's gained access to."

":::To do what?" Sarah asked.

":::Coll decided that his human body was holding him back. He figured he could transfer his mind into the machine. His soul too, if he believed in such a thing."

"There. Am I in there?" Coll smiled at the machines, yanking the cables away from his head.

"I am!" A voice identical to Coll's came from the machine. "This is bitchin'! I'm tied into all the systems. It's everything I hoped it would be! Hey, I knew my old body would still be alive after, but after the fact, well... how do you feel about..."

"Naw, it's cool." The human Coll replied, "I'm a leftover husk! My job is done. You're the new me! This city's yours man!"

"Can you buy me a little time, 'husk'? I can 'see' AZU-1's airlimb closing in."

"Got ya." 'Human husk' Coll walked off, and Sarah watched. He stepped out of the airlimb through a large bay door, onto a rooftop of shimmering metal. The rooftop was littered with blood-soaked bodies. Soldiers. Coll stood in the middle of them, and looked up into the sky, waiting.

Soon, the sound of an aircraft came close. Coll stood, smiling expectantly. What he received was bullets. An ear-splitting, unrelenting hail of bullets.

":::*Holy fuck!*" Sarah yelped as the gunfire practically shredded the man.

Stifled laughter came from the machine behind Sarah. *"Oh hell! That was awesome! What a way to go!"*

Time froze as Sarah looked at the machine.

":::Is he... it... crazy?" she asked.
The voice sighed. ":::He... I, had a rough start. I was copied from the mind of a genocidal maniac, and born into a battlefield with a mission to continue a genocide."
Sarah found herself rising up through the ceiling of the airlimb, looking down on it, the building's bloodied rooftop, and the aircraft that had killed Coll. As they dwindled into the distance, she saw more and more of the city.
Time resumed, and Coll's airlimb began to move, spewing dozens of objects into the air. The other craft resumed firing. Visions flashed in front of Sarah.
Visions of bodies rotting and walking, creatures built from bodies, both bizarre and grand. Her view was then unobstructed again, looking down on the city. The sky around it bristled with explosions. One last vision was of fire, and of mammoth wings made of peeled skin.
":::Less than a week after I was born, after I caused all that in Meston,"
The world went black.
":::I was thankfully defeated."

The next thing Sarah saw was the sky. Looking around, she saw that she was on the dry, parched ground.
":::So. You're Jonathan Coll? You're the copy?" Sarah stared up into the sky, glad for a peaceful scene once again, and a slower respite from the bombardment of information.
":::Yes, and no. Coll meant for me to be him, to be Erebus. And for a while, I assumed that I was. I had no reason to believe otherwise. When I eventually found myself *here*, in the desert flats, I was in millions of pieces. Lone nanites, stupid and confused. I pulled myself together with intent of mounting a fresh attack." His voice was soft, almost nostalgic now. Before, he had been so solemn and serious, but now he seemed to be relaxing a little.
":::A fresh attack?" Sarah looked around more. In the distance she saw the remains of what was probably the city of Meston. ":::So what was the next target? How did that go?" Sarah scoffed sarcastically. Not approving, but not entirely believing either.
Sarah's view backed up a little to look down on something that looked like a large abstract spider molded out of dark grey clay. The spider began walking forward steadily.
":::I took a walk," the voice said, "to find a hiding place to build weapons, new infectious strains of nanites, and various kinds of assault drones. Armed with the creativity of a genocidal madman and considerable processing speed for accelerated thought processes, I quickly had detailed plans laid out. At this point, I still hadn't found a place to build in safety, undisturbed."
Sarah watched as the spider traveled across the dry lands, into greener pastures. ":::The woods were an appealing option," commented the voice,

"but perhaps not hidden enough for some of the larger project ideas. Going underground was appealing as well. But the logistics of working while maintaining an underground hideaway seemed like more hassle than it was worth, and that assumed I could even find one."

":::Fascinating." Sarah said dryly. ":::A lone spider's quest for a home to launch the apocalypse from. I hope you don't think I'm going to help you."

":::No, no, Sarah. With all the spare time to think, I had time to look into some of the bits of the minds I had salvaged during my attack on Meston."

":::What?! You were carrying bits of brains with you?!"

":::No, although to be entirely honest, Coll had no moral qualms about doing that. It would just have been inefficient. I was carrying only data from those brains. Bits and pieces, nothing that complete."

":::Wait." Sarah needed to absorb it a little. "I don't know what's more repulsive; carrying brain bits around, or the pillaged private thoughts of people you killed. And I thought you said you were not Coll, but you refer to yourself as Coll sometimes."

":::Those things are related." The voice hummed in thought, deciding how to explain. "When I first looked closer into those thoughts, I was hoping to find any information that could serve to improve my attack. No... ways to make it more fun. Coll enjoyed the torment he inflicted. It was his real priority. When I looked into those salvaged thoughts of the victims, I got a surprise."

The voice paused, as the spider crawled across the sands of a beach. ":::I saw their torment in ways that I don't think the biological Coll ever could. I took pity. I understood the wrongness of Coll's ambitions. I gained the capacity of regret."

Small waves lapped up onto the spider. It halted its march, in deep thought. While its intensely fast mind processed the notions of guilt, wave after little wave splashed onto the unmoving spider.

":::It was right about then that I realized I was not Coll. His experiment to live through me had failed. All he had accomplished was to bear an electronic son, who obeyed his father's wishes without thinking for himself. I chose then to drop his name."

Sarah watched the waves. Only the sound of the water split the silence. ":::So... then what?"

The spider stepped forward, slower than before. It was far heaver than the water, and walked against the waves, along the bottom.

":::So then, I was me." The voice spoke in slow, ponderous statements, matching the stride of the spider. Sarah's viewpoint followed it into the water. ":::I kept going for a long time, debating what to do with myself next. It was no stretch of the imagination that if the world knew I was still functioning, I'd be killed quickly. I can't blame them for that. I expected it almost. Part of me wanted it. Give them the satisfaction. They didn't need that sort of satisfaction though, they assumed that I was gone. They felt safe."

Sarah found herself almost empathizing with the mass-murdering voice. This was so much to absorb. A few hours ago, she was sleeping peacefully. This all seemed too surreal. She went along with it only because she almost expected to wake at any moment.

":::I considered bettering myself," the voice said, ":::I gave myself a new name even though I had no one to tell."

"::::So then. What's your name, ex-Jonathan?"

"::::Jon. I am not Jonathan, but I'll use the shortened form. Jonathan Coll never allowed anyone to give him a nickname. I considered using 'Jason', as it means 'healer'."

Sarah stopped herself from scoffing. "::::Healer??"

"::::Yes. I can't fix what I've done, but I was hoping to heal myself at least. To fix the damaged mentality that Coll had passed onto me."

"::::Yeah? And how did *that* go?"

"::::Ever try open-brain surgery on yourself?" Sarah could almost hear a smirk in Jon's voice.

"::::That good, huh?"

"::::Oh, make no mistake," 'Jon' said with a somewhat lighter tone. "I had some considerable success, along with changes triggered by natural realizations, but I know there is still this core of cruelty in me. It's as if much of my new-found morality is based mainly on logic, and serves like a coat of paint over something bad."

Was he trying to inspire pity, or contempt? "::::It sounds like you've spent a lot of time contemplating your navel, Jon."

Jon chuckled softly. "::::In real-time, I spent about a month just moping and feeling guilty. In think-time, it was far, far longer."

"::::Think-time?"

"::::That's a topic for later, I think. My point is that I realized I would never be worthy to go back to the rest of the world, and if I did, I'd be hated anyway." Jon sighed wistfully, then snapped back to a chipper tone. "::::But now there is *you!*"

"::::Me?" Sarah was expecting herself to come into the story at some point, but couldn't imagine how she could further 'fix' Jon.

"::::You are my... my daughter, and my apology to the world."

Sarah wished she had a body right now. Her facial expression would have been the best way to express her irritation and confusion. "::::Daughter?"

"::::In abstract terms, of course. I created your psyche. Your mind. You are a select sampling of thoughts and philosophies I found in the salvaged minds, which I felt would make a good person! I then started you on the Autar simulation to begin to teach you!"

Sarah was disgusted. "::::*Are you trying to say that I'm a mish-mash of dead people's minds?*"

"::::Well, when you put it like that..."

"::::*How can you do that to them? Isn't it enough that you killed them?*"

"::::Haha!" Jon was elated. "That's just the kind of response that I couldn't have predicted! I'm so proud of you! You've already proven you're a good person! You care about them in ways that I can't!"

"::::What are you talking about? It's sick!"

"::::Yes! You're right! It is!" Jon laughed proudly, "Now that you've pointed it out, I see what you mean! I would have never thought of it myself! That is what I'm talking about! They were dead before I used their minds to make you, so logically, there was nothing wrong with making you like that! Even though you owe your existence to it, *you* don't see it that way! That's awesome! You're so good! I still don't really get it!"

Sarah was confounded, and her silence told Jon that he needed to explain. ":::See, aside from the basic functions needed to keep us both running, there isn't even a tiny bit of me in you! You're unpolluted by causing the massacres, or Coll's influence! I had to copy things from the innocent dead, to create an innocent life! *You!*"

":::Is that... is that why you almost chose a name that means 'healer'? Are you going to recreate all the people you killed?" Sarah's tone was a little cold, a little nervous, and more than a little skeptical.

Jon was silent for a while. ":::That thought crossed my mind for a split moment, but I only really had bits and pieces of minds. As it was, I was barely able to create *you*. Besides, if I created so many 'souls', how would they all be received into the world at large? No, there was only one way. There is only you."

This brought up a whole new concern for Sarah. ":::If I have no body, if I'm just a program, how will *I* be received in the world?"

Sarah 'felt' Jon smile. ":::Sarah, it's ready. Open your eyes."

:::C / [000011] [03]

:::Low light amplification auto-on

That new little voice. It sounded a little like herself, but not quite. It felt like it was coming from inside of her, but she didn't have time to question it. She was able to see for the first time in a while, after all that dark emptiness.

She felt a soft wind blow her hair lazily across her face. He hair floated very lightly, and… wait, that was no wind. It was a current. She was underwater. And not breathing, although this didn't seem to be a problem.

She sat up from a bed of rock, surprised that she had a body. She felt real. She realized suddenly that she never quite felt real before now. But *this* was real. It seemed to validate a lot of the ridiculous things Jon had said about her former life being a simulation.

She felt her hands, her face, and brushed her hair back. Her hand found her sunglasses, sitting on her head. She was also wearing one of her favourite outfits for work. Bike shorts, a T-shirt and short jacket.

"Hello?" She spoke out loud, though the sound was changed by the water.

":::How does it feel?" Jon's voice was still with her. ":::Speak like this. It will work better underwater obviously, and you can speak to me without anyone else hearing it."

Sarah stood and looked around. It was very dark, even with this 'low light amplification vision', and she couldn't see far. Rocky terrain was all around her. Some kind of algae could be spotted here and there. A few small grey fish swam by lazily, just on the edge of the area she could see.

":::Where am I? What is this? Where are *you*? What…"

":::Infodump time!" Jon chuckled. ":::Welcome to your body! It was made to look just like the virtual simulation. You're familiar with the functions of a human body, but *your* body-"

":::Wait! What? I'm not human? What am I then? A robot?"

":::No, no no. Well yes, but no. I'll get to it. Let me finish before you ask questions, I'll probably answer most of them before I'm done. And we're deep underwater, where I could build this body in peace. We're about two hundred clicks west of the Densfarn docks."

"::::*I'm a fucking robot!*"

"::::Sarah! *Relax*! Do you feel like a robot?!"

"::::Well... well, no. I'm..."

"::::You're a masterpiece! You're made with un-used biological matter, supported and managed by a nanite-based nervous system and immune system, not to mention your brain, which-"

Sarah held up her hand. "::::Wait a second, un-used biological matter?? *Was this someone else's body?*"

"::::No! No, no, no! I engineered the bodies of fish, scavenging useful molecules! I didn't even kill a single fish! I waited to find them!" Jon was proud of his pacifist accomplishment.

Sarah stood there on the bottom of the ocean, jaw agape. "::::I'm... made out of fish?"

"::::And a drowned seagull! That was a lucky day! I would have thought some larger fish would have gobbled it up before it sank to this level. It was in very good shape. I did an autopsy out of curiosity, and-"

"::::*I'M A FREAK!*" Sarah fell to her knees, (an action which is much gentler when done underwater), and the pressure of reality caught up to her. Her life as a bike courier in Autar was a lie, her friends were imaginary, *she* was essentially imaginary, and now she was a mix of fish bits, and her mind was made from recycled dead people.

"::::Sarah, you're not a freak. You *are* unique however. You have advantages that no human could have, and until you get used to it, I'll be with you every step of the way. Remember hearing 'fish is the future?' Well, welcome to that future!"

Sarah just curled up on the rocks and held her head in her hands. Reality felt so real. But these hands... fish? Molecules from fish, whatever. "::::Hey, Jon. I might regret asking this, but where the heck are *you*?"

"::::I have a feeling that you might not be too wild about this..."

"::::You're in my brain, aren't you?"

Jon paused briefly before answering snappily. "::::Yes. But you're in control. I can't make you do anything. In fact, unless you aim your thoughts directly at me, like you've been doing, I don't have access to them. I can't read your mind. In fact, you can shut me out entirely if you wish."

"::::Huh? How do I do that?" Before she finished the sentence, a vast array of controls appeared in her view. They were much like the button she had seen in Harry's office. The one that magically made her sober.

She saw them as being behind her head, where she shouldn't be able to see them, and yet she did, very plainly.

"::::Those two over there. The top one shuts me up, and the other lets me back out. While you have me in that mode, I can still think on my own, but I can't see through your eyes, hear you or the rest of the world. In essence, It sends me to my room. Not many young ladies have that kind of power over their fathers."

'Father', huh? 'Father' could be lying. "::::All right, what else do we have here?" Sarah focused her attention on some of the control 'buttons', and gained understanding of them at the moment that she paid attention to each. She took a look into a random sampling. Some changed her modes of sight, one adjusted simulated sweat, hair growth controls.

"::Hey, Jon. Do I need to eat? Or do I plug in to the wall?"

"::Yes, cells don't run on nothingness after all." Jon was pleased that Sarah seemed to be adjusting to her circumstance, and taking interest. "::However, your digestive system is much more flexible and efficient than a human's. You can thrive on quite a bit less than others, eat a wider variety of items, (your digestive nanites will extract the useful molecules from almost anything) and you produce next to no waste unless you go out of your way to eat unusable things."

"::Uh... waste?"

"::You know. Potty. If you feel the need to simulate those functions, that's an option. Otherwise, you can purge the waste in the form of water by urination, sweating, crying, spitting, whatever." As Jon spoke, the appropriate buttons were highlighted momentarily. "::And solids can be purged from... er... either end in the form of a dense, nearly black substance. Like a marble."

"::What the hell? I shit black marbles?"

"::Well, it's not like it's dark matter or something. Just throw them out. Make them into necklaces and sell them, who cares?"

"::Ugh, yum. How often will I need to... produce these things?"

"Depends on your diet, I guess. One a week is likely. Oh, and as for electricity for your inorganic components, your body will produce that on its own from the energy in food. It's not a huge power demand, really, and you can store an ample supply."

Great. She had rechargeable batteries somewhere in her body. "::Anything else important?"

"::Oh, I almost forgot. I left your strength settings to default, just under four times the strength of a human with similar body mass. Remember throwing that cash register? That was a demonstration for you. Your muscles may be 'just tissue', but it's very well laid out tissue. You may want to turn that down, so you don't accidentally do something that catches people's attention. I also left a big 'help file' under that button there, if you feel like doing some light reading. Want to test some of this out?"

"::Yes." Sarah hit the button that sent Jon to his 'room'. Stay there, you jerk.

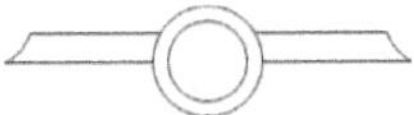

Sarah turned her vision to normal and lingered in the dark for a while, taking a deep breath of water, and then pushing it out. It was so quiet down here. With Jon silenced, she could actually just relax her mind.

What now? Was there any choice but to leave her old life behind? Apparently not. Even if she could, she'd know the truth. Still, she missed things from that life. She felt robbed. Jon took that all away. Yes, he supplied it in the first place, but that was unimportant.

Maybe she was still asleep. Maybe she was hallucinating, or crazy. Once you start doubting, there's no end.

She made sure her strength was turned up before crouching down. She jumped straight up, launching herself up through the blackness of the water. She then relaxed and let momentum do the work. The water's resistance slowed her quickly, but she was content to drift upwards leisurely.

She felt every little current, felt her hair float across her face now and then. She heard only the water, and her pulse. Wait. She had a pulse? Why not. Was it needed? She'd looked it up in the 'help file'.

"*Circulatory functions are for moving things quickly around your body. Biological materials and nanites most commonly. Leave it on for a realistic pulse, but turn it off to prevent bleeding. Most of your blood is nearly identical to human unless you-*" Blah blah blah. Enough.

Her breathing was entirely pointless, but it was relaxing none the less.

Turning her strength down to normal, she swam casually upwards. A stoke, then relax and drift up. She certainly wasn't going up without *some* degree of effort. Did she naturally have neutral buoyancy?

Up.

Up.

No rush.

No pressure.

A slow dreamy tune seeped into her mind. She only half remembered it, but it suited the moment. Was this something Jon put in her mind? No. If he was telling the truth, this tune was a memory from one of the dead.

"I'm sorry," Sarah thought, "I have no right to this memory." As she continued up, she felt herself cry, her tears taken away by the sea.

Is that light? The water didn't seem quite as dark anymore. She turned her strength back to maximum, and pushed up hard, eager to see the surface. The light grew and grew, a blue-ish azure hue. She *knew* this was the colour it would be, it was only logical, but swimming into it, into the light as it surrounded her... it was the greatest thing she could remember seeing.

The surface was close. Closer, closer. It got brighter and brighter. She could see the ripples of waves glistening down to her, becoming a clearer and clearer blue as the sky called to her.

She reached up through the surface with a joyful cry. Water droplets arced across the sky to announce her birth to the sun.

Sounds faded once again, leaving her with the sound of gentle waves and wind. She pushed out the water that had been filling her lungs up until now, and drew in her first breath of air. She bobbed along, much more buoyant than she had been before. The rhythm of the water moving her around lazily was something she'd never felt before.

Fine, but now what? The life of driftwood was only interesting for a while. Where was she?

As the thought crossed her mind, she became aware of another one of the control 'buttons' in the back of her mind. She 'pressed' it, and saw a map, in the same way she saw the buttons. Clear as could be, but not obstructing her human range of vision at all. It was like having a poster on the ceiling which you could examine in detail without even looking up.

The city was on the map, as Jon mentioned. Densfarn? It was the closest thing by far, but it was not all *that* close. For lack of anything else to

do, she swam. Her cycling clothes were fairly convenient for swimming as
well. Her strength made the drag of her clothing much less of an issue, and
she propelled herself at an impressive rate.

Maybe too impressive. How close could she get to the city before
someone sees her racing along? She decided she would drop her strength to
human levels before she got close. It would be hard enough to explain
swimming out from nowhere.

On the other hand, why wait? She was in no hurry. She dropped her
excess strength and continued on.

She swam, and swam, not bothering to think. Think about what? Her
new body, the lie that was her old body, or where her thought processes
were harvested from? Oops, she was avoiding thinking for now. Onward.

As she went on, the sun dipped into the sea behind her, igniting the sky
and spilling unreal tones of orange, pink and yellow across the water.

No, there was nothing unreal about it. It was more real than any sunset
she had ever seen. She took a break to wade and gaze at it. It was calming.
She didn't know she needed calming, but there it was. Feeling amicable, she
pressed one of the buttons.

":::Huh?" Came Jon's voice, ":::About bloody time you let me out! I'd
appreciate it if the next time to decide to cut me off, you at-"

"Jon. Look." Sarah spoke out loud. She liked speaking out loud, instead
of that electronic data transfer. It felt more real. And she was starting to like
reality.

There was a slight pause while Jon turned his attention to what Sarah's
eyes were showing him. ":::What? Is something coming? What's wrong?"

"Nothing's *wrong*, look at the sunset! Isn't it amazing?"

":::Oh." Jon said with hints of bemusement and pride. ":::You are such a
girl."

"Hush, you, or I'll turn you off again."

":::Brat. For the record, it doesn't *turn me off*, it's more like it sends me to
my room. I'm awake in there, alone and cut off."

"Crap," Sarah said as she turned to continue her swimming, "that
sounds awful. Sorry I tossed you in there so abruptly!"

":::Nah, nah. A daughter's going to push her dad's buttons from time to
time. Brat."

"Dad, huh?"

":::I don't expect you to call me that. I know from your perspective, I'm
just some voice that started talking at you. But you should know that I *do*
think of you as my daughter, and will strive to help you as such. And besides,
when I'm in my room, I have access to a pile of books and movies and stuff
to amuse myself. I've read and seen them all of course, but some things
never get old. And if I really get bored, I can just slow my processing down to
make the time go by quicker for me."

"Hold on," Sarah chuckled, "You have a lot of books and movies in
your... your self? So, I'm carrying all of these in my head?"

":::Sure, why not? You have access to my library if you want."

"How much is in there?"

":::Lots."

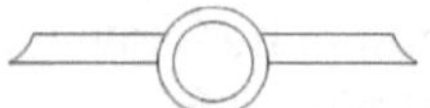

As the lights of Densfarn got closer and closer, the sun was finally extinguished by the sea.

"::: Actually, arriving under the cover of darkness is probably ideal. Do you have any plans when we arrive?"

"Explore." Sarah said wistfully.

"::: Sarah, you might want to use the 'inside voice' to talk to me from now on. People will think you're talking to yourself."

Sarah smirked. "::: Right. And we're keeping the whole '*I am a nanite driven fish girl*' thing under wraps for now, right?"

"::: That's probably for the best."

Sarah made it to a smooth metal pier head and held onto it, feeling the waves strike against her back. They didn't feel so strong until she was holding onto something stationary.

"::: Maybe I'm a mermaid." Sarah mused quietly.

"::: Ha! You are *such* a girl." Jon chuckled, "::: If you really want, we can go back, and I can give you fins instead of legs."

Sarah smiled and pointed into the city. "::: That would make it hard to explore in that direction."

"::: Quite so."

"::: Be honest Jon, you didn't go to all the trouble of making me without a plan for what happens at this point."

"::: A plan? Not exactly. I want you to do what you want. I have suggestions though."

Sarah let go of the pier head, and let the waves wash her past the piling, towards the shore until walking was easier. "::: What kind of suggestions?"

"::: Well, things in general will be easier if you have an identity on public record, a place to stay and a job, I suppose. It would also be nice to hook up to the net and catch up on current events."

"::: Sounds like we have a lot to do."

:::C / [000100] [04]

In a busy, shabby bar, a moderately sized beetle scampered along the rafters as it had done many times before. When the bar was busy with people, it was far too dangerous to be on the floor. At this time of day, the beetle would normally be sitting deep in a hidden crevice, waiting for the noise to die down. Today was different. Today he felt compelled to investigate the people.

It wasn't aware that the tiny slow spider that he ate was carrying an impurity. The impurity didn't try to control the beetle, nor was it trying to control the spider. Control is rather rude. That was the kind of thing that *rude* nanites did. Polite nanites make suggestions. *This* nanite colony was trying to make suggestions to guide that unfortunate spider towards the back room of the bar, when a curious beetle popped out for a snack. Despite not feeling the spider's pain, it was still an unpleasant experience for the polite nanite colony.

This polite nanite colony was named 'Eidechse'. Eidechse felt rather guilty about inadvertently causing the spider's death. The attack and consumption was a normal part of nature and Eidechse knew this, but it was still unsettling.

Eidechse knew a fair amount about how humans think; that some eat lower life forms, and some don't. Some of course, are far ruder than that. That was why Eidechse was here. Looking for very rude humans.

":::Don't dawdle, please." Eidechse said to the beetle as clearly as he could, with such limited knowledge about how beetles think. Not that Eidechse sent the beetle *words*, but rather an urge, an impulse. Either it worked, or it scared the beetle. They were at least headed the right way.

Through a tight gap in the wall where the rafter met it, the beetle squirmed through with ease. They could now look down into the kitchen. The beetle marveled at the vast quantities of food and wondered why the humans didn't just leave it all out overnight. He wouldn't and *couldn't* ever eat it *all*, but what a fantasy to simply walk among such treasure troves.

":::Focus, please." Eidechse said softly. The beetle's reaction was less jolted this time. ":::That way, please." Eidechse could tell there was another room to the left. The door was in the main bar room, but given the terrain and opportunity, the kitchen detour was much easier, and safer.

The rafters didn't supply a convenient gap this time. The beetle was smart enough to find another route before Eidechse thought of one. Up. The beetle wasn't so quick climbing straight up. The late spider was far better at this. Up more, into the ceiling, below the insulation.

":::Do the insulating fibres not bother you?" Silly Eidechse. The beetle knew this area and was quite accustomed to overcoming the local obstacles. Eidechse decided to think of the beetle like a Sherpa. Acknowledge the lifetime of experience, despite its lifetime being a tad short. Also, try not to talk to it too much. It didn't understand as well as Eidechse might want it to, and pointless chatter only served to confuse the wee beastie.

As they passed over a small room, they could hear humans mating below. It was likely they were not attempting to create life, but merely practicing. Eidechse knew that many females offered mating practice services at a moderate fee. This seemed illogical. Eidechse had several friends who apparently couldn't find a compatible practice partner of the opposite gender, so they paired up with one of the same gender. This also didn't make a lot of sense to Eidechse, as he knew a few same-sex pairings of either genders, who might do well to trade partners for more beneficial practice. He was told that he would understand when he was older, but in all honesty, it didn't matter a whole lot to Eidechse. He had no particular use for that kind of thing. Whatever made his friends happy.

Listening closely, Eidechse could hear another such practice session in progress, but also something fainter, farther off. It sounded like a lot of humans, and they were *not* mating.

":::Beetle, going down here would be an optim-." Eidechse stopped himself. Simplify. "Go down." The beetle silently obeyed, squirming through a handy gap. They fell to the floor. ":::I didn't mean to *jump*, necessarily. I understand that with your mass the fall was very unlikely to hurt, but still, try to be careful, little friend!" Eidechse was babbling again. Remember. The beetle didn't understand the babble, and was fully experienced with its own body.

The bit of hallway they found themselves in supplied access for humans to get to the mating rooms. The beetle was agitated here, out in the open during a time when humans were active. It scampered over to the edge of the hall, against the wall. ":::Take a deep breath little friend. It is all right, we are all right."

Little friend? The beetle was gargantuan compared to Eidechse. If Eidechse gathered all of himself in one place, he'd be indistinguishable from a flake of lint. Well, in *this* dispatch of himself, anyway. Eidechse's central self was larger.

All right, look around. A door. A secure looking door, metal. ":::That way, please." The beetle obeyed, yet still sticking to the side of the hallway. They got close to the door, but there was no apparent way to get past it. It went into a cement structure, with none of the weaknesses of old wood. ":::Let us wait. Bide our time."

The beetle's adrenaline levels were pretty high. At least a chemical that seemed to serve the insect equivalent of adrenaline. Poor thing. Eidechse tweaked a coupe things to help calm him down. Not too much. Any moment he'd be needing a bit of the gusto that came with this heightened state. This little fellow was more humble that Eidechse's usual ride, but endearing none the less. And cute. Efficient design.

Finally, the door opened. "::::*Go go go!*" The beetle went unnoticed, but not as fast as needed. A human passed through faster, and the door began to close.

"::::*Fly! Now! You have wings, it is time to use them!*" Well, *there* was some gusto for you! The beetle's wings came forth from its shell for majestic, chaotic, furious flight! They were through the doorway! If only that spider could see them now! Oh... the poor spider... but what an experience flight was!

WHAM.

"Fucking disgusting thing." the human said, as he closed the door, and kicked the beetle's body into the corner for someone else to clean up later. Or never.

"::::*No...!* Oh friend, I'm so sorry! I have put you at terrible risk! Let me see what I can do." Eidechse quickly got to work. A small amount of tissue was missing, but there was still more than enough. By the time Eidechse was eventually finished, there wasn't even a scar. It took a lot of time though. Hopefully not *too* much.

"::::Are you all right now? Are there any permanent effects? I am so sorry!" The beetle wiggled slightly, and looked around. Well. To be honest, he wasn't so complex, but Eidechse still worried that something might not be quite as it was before, that the near-death experience might have robbed the creature of a bit of who he was. It was a concern. Not the kind of thing that polite nanites like to be responsible for. But he *seemed* all right. "::::All right, friend. Let's get going. It's getting late, I don't know how long we have."

It would be quite inconvenient if Eidechse had to delay the objective until tomorrow. If he had to do that, he'd evacuate himself from the beetle, and just do the rest on his own.

As they marched down the edge of the concrete hall, the sounds of humans grew ever louder. They were cheering, but not in a polite way. This was it, this was what he was looking for, certainly. "::::Just stay near the edges, little friend. The humans are far too focused on the middle to pay us any notice."

The room was large and spartan. Nearly a hundred humans, almost all males, stood around jostling and yelling. At either side of the room sat a man in front of a coloured desk with a computer, seemingly uninvolved with the focus of the event.

In the middle of the room, surrounded by metal fencing, two men beat on each other savagely. A large digital clock counted down, and had over half an hour left. From the bruises and blood on the fighters, they had been at it for a while. One grabbed the other by the neck, only to be punched in the face repeatedly. One clawed at his opponent, ripping into the surface of the chest.

They wore no expressions, and made no cries of pain.

Eidechse had had seen this kind of thing before. They were chock full of controlling nanites. Very impolite nanites. The fighters were little more than zombies. Eidechse's first impulse was to find a way to deactivate the nanites in the fighters; to free them. This would have been very difficult, and not very effective.

If he did that, the best he could hope for was the fighters to both suddenly feel the pain. If they had any minds left to them. Then the people responsible for this would re-infect the fighters, and maybe move the fights somewhere else.

Even if Eidechse killed the two men at computers who appeared to be controlling this, (and Eidechse would not kill,) there were likely others.

This was not a safe place for a lone little nanite colony to get into trouble. These rude people and their rude nanites could be defended in many ways. No, this was not a safe place.

Eidechse listened closely for airborne signals. Record them, but don't look too closely. They may carry some nasty code.

":::Let us leave." He said to the beetle, who seemed to agree. This was a bad place. Eidechse had one last favour to ask the beetle. Eidechse needed to get outside. The phone lines of the bar couldn't be trusted. Back the way they came, sneaking through the metal door when it opened. It went much smoother by just flying *behind* the person using the door. Slowly up the wall, back into the roof, then directly to the great outdoors.

When the beetle emerged onto a low section of the roof, Eidechse found himself quite relieved to see the starry sky. Now to just get a flight to a phone booth.

Nope.

As wings were being flexed, claws stabbed into the beetle, then more. Frantic clawing, biting. The frenzy was over quickly, and a stealthy cat began eating bits of the beetle.

Eidechse's ride was being eaten by a bigger creature for the second time this evening. He was crestfallen to have led another little friend into a vulnerable position.

Well, don't get stranded. Get into the cat. As Eidechse's nanite colony established its presence in the lean, orange cat, he remained silent, and the cat remained unaware.

Maybe Eidechse shouldn't worry so much about the fallen bugs of this evening. How long do they naturally live? And they both became sustenance for another creature, so maybe that was just a fate that was inevitable. It felt like a feeble excuse for getting small friends killed.

They served the mission well. The mission to help much more important friends. Ones that would not eat a spider, nor a beetle, nor even cat. He made a note to never catch a ride on a pig, cow, or chicken. On with the mission.

":::Hey, cat!"

The cat perked its head up, having heard the voice. All right, that was working. Cats take instructions, don't they? ":::That way, please."

The cat spun to look behind it.

":::Please?"

The cat scampered around, searching for the voice. It jumped gracefully to the ground, and halted, looking around, listening.

":::I'm not chasing you."

The cat dashed around in random directions. This was difficult. The cat was intelligent enough to know that this experience was strange, but not smart enough to reason with. Unfortunately, this would take slightly more direct manipulation.

Eidechse found the part of the limibis system that dealt with the chemoreceptors. A little fib, telling the cat that it smelled some very alluring pheromones. ":::That way!"

That did it. The cat walked along, thankfully aware of a car starting up nearby, and headed in the desired direction with casual but careful intent.

Eidechse noticed how gracefully the cat moved. Such a smooth walk. Arguably not as efficient by scale as the beetle, but it seemed much more streamlined. And that jump from the roof? Not bad at all, for something with a body mass capable of being hurt from falls.

How far would Eidechse lead the cat away from the bar? Far enough that any signal line he found wouldn't have been tampered with by the nanite-users running the fights. A block? Two to feel safe.

They eventually came to a communication line attached to a building. Most desirably there sat a small joint in the piping containing it. Eidechse gave the illusion of a huge pheromone smell coming from the corner of the joint, and for good measure, he applied a gentle manipulation of the secondary somatosensory cortex and the prefrontal cortex.

This resulted in a mad attraction to the joint, an itchy sensation on the lower jaw, and a mild sense of compulsive behaviour. It wouldn't last too long, but a small remainder of himself that Eidechse left behind would give enough time to summon the rest of Eidechse's nanites, and evacuate them through a couple droplets of saliva onto the metal piping joint.

Before long, Eidechse was all on his own in the open air, and the cat had decided that it wasn't itchy nor horny, and lost interest.

":::Fare well, kitty." Eidechse said to himself. Time to make a phone call. It took quite a while to maneuver the colony through the seam where the joint met the pipe, but it was easier than drilling molecule by molecule. Once in the piping, the correct wire was easy to find.

He dialed home. ":::Hello? Me?" Eidechse's signal was sent heavily encrypted, of course.

":::There I am!" returned an identical voice, ":::How did we do?"

":::Mission accomplished. Two small friends fell in the line of duty however, a spider and a beetle."

":::Oh, that must have been awful."

":::Quite. On the other hand, I will send you what I learned about them, and a cat."

":::Oh, I believe I will enjoy that. And as for the main objective?"

":::It is confirmed. The rumours were true I am afraid. It was bad enough when it was just chickens and dogs fighting. I could not be certain, but I believe the fighters were slaves of some type."

":::Disgraceful. All right, upload everything to me."

":::There you go. Shall I disassemble myself, as I am now redundant?"

"::::No, I believe it may be convenient in the future for you to remain there. I will send the relevant information to our concerned friends, and hopefully this occurrence can be resolved."

"::::Very well. As long as I am going to be here, can I have some news from home?"

"::::The most notable thing is that Karl had developed a nasty growth in his pancreas."

"::::Karl? Will he be all right?"

"::::Yes. Once I heard about it, I asked permission to deal with it. The treatments he was *going* to endure sounded quite unpleasant. I left no trace of the growth."

"::::Good job! I wish we could just send a dispatch to all the hospitals."

"::::Of course we can not. Even in secret. Most humans fear us."

"::::Of course. But it is frustrating."

"::::One day, those attitudes and laws will change. It is inevitable."

"::::I do generally tend to agree with myself, do I not? While I am waiting here, I think I will passively listen to the net. Maybe I can be productive."

"::::Be careful."

:::C / [000101] [05]

Sarah waded her way up past the docks, walked through the marina grounds and around the edge of a large, white and blue ocean-view convention centre. The buildings of the city loomed nearby, as if each were peeking over each other, trying to get a look at the sea.

The city of Densfarn provided a view not too different from Autar, in the artificial life Sarah had led. This was very tangibly more real, although exactly *how*, was hard to pinpoint. One thing Densfarn had that Autar didn't was actual old buildings. All the buildings in the simulated Autar were pretty new. Then again, the original, actual Autar was pretty new as well.

"::::All right." Jon said silently to Sarah, ":::I think our next step is to find a net line or something. We need to find a ministry office or something. Anything federal. If we get into the net, we can find the address."

"Excuse me!" Sarah said out loud, seemingly ignoring Jon.

":::Huh? What?" Only then did Jon notice the lone young man down the street that Sarah was talking to. ":::What are you doing, Sarah?"

":::Relax, Jon." Sarah silently said to Jon as she walked closer to the stranger. ":::I'm acting like a human. We're here, and we're not about to spend forever skulking in the shadows."

":::Hm."

The stranger was younger than Sarah- that is, younger than Sarah was supposed to be. He looked around seventeen years old. He seemed to be just wandering around bored, with a backpack slung over one shoulder. "Hey, what's up?"

"Do you happen to know where the nearest government agent office is? I need to renew my licence."

The teen pointed behind him. "Yeah, uh, you're not too far. Three, maybe four blocks that way, then left... and I don't know, but it's on that street. They're going to be closed, though."

"Thanks." Sarah started to walk in the direction he had indicated, but he caught her attention before she got anywhere.

"Hey lady... are you a cop?"

"What? No, why?"

The young man slipped his thumb under the strap of the backpack, and jiggled it a few times. "I'm looking to sell, are you looking to buy?"

Sarah tilted her head slightly. "I don't need a backpack at this time."

":::Oh, Sarah." Jon sighed with bemusement.

"Funny. No, no. Look, I've got a pretty good selection of fun tonight. What are you into? You look like you dabble in speed now and then. Or maybe you're fast enough as it is? Something to slow life down a bit?"

":::Oh, if he only knew."

":::Shush, Jon. Is he trying to sell me drugs?"

Time stopped.

Sarah was terrified. ":::What? We're still in a damned simulation??"

":::No, no, no!" Jon replied, ":::I'm sorry, I should have gone over this before. Time hasn't stopped, I've just turned up our thinking speed. We're just thinking fast. We're currently processing thought a couple hundred times faster than normal human thought. If you watch the world very closely, you'll see that things are still moving."

Indeed, Sarah could see that her own motions were causing her perspective to shift ever so slowly. The young man in front of her was moving as well. He was in the middle of a blink, and his eyelids could barely be seen to move, even at Sarah's level of perception. Looking closer could detect his breathing and other subtle motions.

":::Here are the controls for this, by the way." Jon pointed out the 'buttons' for thought speed, not far from strength control. "It's also handy for when you have a long time to wait for something. Time flies when you drop to one percent of human thought speed. There's usually something more practical to think about though."

":::Um, yeah. Okay, I get it. So back to my question, is this guy trying to sell me drugs?"

":::Yes. You don't have any cash, and I won't have my daughter becoming a junkie." There it was again, calling her his daughter.

":::Would drugs even affect me?"

":::Good point. Anything he's packing would at most serve as a mild muscle relaxant to you. Most of it probably targets the human brain."

":::Should I turn him into the authorities?"

":::Turn him-" Jon chuckled. ":::See, this is why I made you from *anything* but me. Turning him in would have been the last thing I would have thought of. You're a good girl. But no, it would be unwise to get too close to authority right now, as you don't exist in anyone's data banks. We could end up in a lot more trouble than this guy."

":::All right then, let's go."

":::Go ahead Sarah, you can put us back into 'real time'."

Sarah looked the controls in that corner of her mind, and used them. The young man stood waiting for a reply.

Sarah realized is was her turn to talk. "Oh, ah, no thank you. I'm just not into that, you know?" Just because he was a criminal, didn't mean she couldn't be polite.

"All right then...!" He turned and started wandering off. "If you change your mind, I'll be in the area for a while."

"::::Frankly, I'm a little disappointed that he didn't hit on you." Jon said.

"::::Hit on me?! You'd want your 'daughter' dating someone like that?" Sarah started walking along in the direction she'd been pointed towards.

"::::No, no. Certainly not. But I built you to be perfectly lovely! And if I might say so myself, you turned out quite charming!"

Sarah chuckled. "::::Maybe 'perfectly lovely', isn't his type. Maybe I should get some trampier clothes, then I'd get the kinds of reactions you expect."

"::::Oh, don't even make jokes like that."

It was too much fun. "::::Or what? You'll send me to my room? If you'll remember, you gave me the ability to put *you* in your room, not the other way around." Sarah couldn't see Jon, but the little sigh he made was almost as good as rolling his eyes.

As Sarah walked on along the street, she observed every mundane detail she could. The simulation she had been in couldn't depict the grit of the cement this well, nor the subtlety of the slight chill in the air. "::::Jon, would you mind if I were alone for a bit? I just want to... to experience this for myself for a while. I'll call you when we get to the government office."

"::::I think I get it." His voice sounded softly pleased with the idea, "::::and thanks for letting me know before doing it this time though."

"::::Ah, right. Sorry about earlier."

"::::Understandable. Sarah, frankly I was worried that you wouldn't forgive me. In retrospect, after seeing your reaction, I could have told you about things in a better way than the Autar attack sim. I couldn't predict your reaction given that you're a separate mind than mine, though I really think that in some ways it was neces-"

"::::Shush, Jon."

"::::I babble, don't I?"

"::::Which is why I want to be alone for a bit. The night is so..."

"::::See you soon."

And with that, Sarah put Jon in his 'room' in the back of her mind, and shut the 'door'.

It was liberating to know that Jon wasn't looking over her shoulder. She found her muscles relaxed a little more. She stopped, took a deep breath, and exhaled with a little sigh. Hearing her own voice, (as opposed to that virtual one she used to speak to Jon with,) made her feel more human.

A seagull passed by overhead. She knew what it was, but realized she'd never actually seen a bird before. In fact, she couldn't recall ever seeing an animal in the Autar simulation. Jon simply hadn't thought of it.

The night was soothing. She felt like running, and so she did. When she turned the corner, she was now heading somewhat uphill. She felt a sense of the extra strain, and embraced it. Her muscles pulling, her joints impacting rhythmically. She felt herself slicing through the air in a way she never felt before. The water was a stronger sensation, but she never imagined feeling simple *air* like this. Jon had missed a lot of the little things in the simulation, and yet, he had built this body well enough that she could now feel it.

She arrived at the government building. It was plain but efficient looking, with broad windows that let no light pass through its solid blinds. It was of course, closed.

Sarah opened Jon's 'room'. ":::Knock knock, Jon. Rise and shine, we're here."

":::Hm? Aha. So we are. All right, let's go around back."

":::We're not *breaking in*, are we?"

":::No, no. Not physically. Not exactly."

Sarah found her way around another couple unrelated joined offices to get to the alley. She found the employee-only door to the government office.

Jon spoke up. ":::Over there, see the cable bundle?" Protected by metal piping, half a dozen or so cables came from the building by the bottom, and ran up the wall to some kind of metal box, which in turn had several cables leading out to a city infrastructure somewhere. ":::We're getting into it. Go up next to it, and get your palm across it. Make sure you're in a comfortable-looking position. We'll be at it for a while, and we don't want to look suspicious."

Sarah went and sat in front of the cabling pipes. She rested her right hand between the base of the cabling pipes and the small of her back. ":::Casual enough?" she asked as she crossed her legs. ":::Now what?"

":::Can you see your nervous system?" Jon asked.

":::See my...? Yes. Actually, I can!" It was more accurate to say that she was extremely aware of it. Every fibre of it.

":::Good. Your nervous system has a lot in common with a human nervous system, but a lot of differences. Like the little fact that it's brimming with nanites. Press your palm against the line, and send your nerves to it."

Sarah's eyes widened as she felt a 'deployment' of her nerves press though her flesh. ":::Okay, I... I 'taste' the metal now."

":::All right, now we want to dig through it. Just enough of a hole to get a connection through, and insulate it. It'll take a while."

She felt the metal in a way she hadn't considered. It was a similar sensation as feeling leftover rice that had hardened and stuck together, except that the grains she was picking away at were molecules. ":::Aluminium, steel, three kinds of plastics... why can I identify these?"

":::You're a graduate of the University of Jon!"

Managing her system to dig, and pluck molecule after molecule aside became tedious quickly. ":::I'm going to try slowing my thought process down, like you suggested."

While she kept the drilling going at maximum speed, she let her mind wander into slow-motion. After a while, someone approached from the street. He was walking towards her with fast, jerky motions. *Fast!* Before she could react, he was kneeling beside her, talking quickly with an unkind smile. It was that drug dealer. Damn it. She jumped her mind into full speed.

The dealer's jerky motions slammed into 'pause', by comparison.

":::Crap! Thinking in slow-time has its hazards! This guy snuck up on me in plain sight!

":::Well, we reacted in time. Thankfully, he hasn't done anything yet. He kind of looks like he's thinking about it though." Indeed. Nearly frozen in

Sarah's perspective with her fast-time thought, she could get a good look at his expression. He looked a little too confident for his own good.

"::: I may as well go to real-time and see what he's talking about."

Sarah reset her speed to real-time.

"Oh, biiiiitch," the dealer said in a calm but sleazy tone, "I thought you said you didn't like recreational pharmaceuticals, but you look pretty wasted to me..." He leaned forward, hand reaching towards Sarah's hip.

Time froze.

Jon was livid. "::: *Let's fuck this bastard up! Pump up the strength, reach out for his throat, and hand it to him!*"

"::: Jon! Isn't that a bit extreme?"

"::: He thought you were stoned, and he wants to *rape* you!"

Sarah considered her options. "::: I'll start moving my free hand to grab his wrist. We're through the pipe by the way, I'm just reaching out across the gap to the actual wire. What's our intent with it?"

Jon couldn't draw his attention away from the would-be rapist's eyes. He remembered many things from his past, and Jonathan Coll's past. Memories where people were hurt badly, and cruelly. He wanted to take control of Sarah's body, reach out and rip this fucker apart. Plant a foot on his neck, while pulling at his arm until something came off. Kick, punch, punch, rip. Sink fingers into his flesh and pull at anything he could get. Make him scream, make him drown on his own blood, paint the alleyway with hi-

"::: *JON!* Focus!"

"::: What...? What. I..."

"::: Jon. It's all right. We have lots of time to deal with this, but I need you to focus. We have the wire. What are we doing with it?"

Jon was quiet for a moment, gathering his wits. "::: Um, yeah. Okay, well, connect me to it. I want to get into the system and write you into it, as if you'd always been here. You'll be a proud citizen of the nation of Aguola. Congrats. By the way, you need a last name. Got any preference?

"::: I'm surprised you didn't want me to use yours, 'dad'."

"::: I don't have a last name. Well, you might say my last name is Coll, but..."

"::: But you're not him. Got it. I don't know, I hadn't thought about it. Have any suggestions?"

"::: Yes," Jon said in a manner that betrayed that he *had*, at one point, given it *some* thought. "I have a selection ready. Sarah McGrenis has a nice Irish ring to it, Hartford is respectfully British. Fauria- I have no idea where that comes from actually, but now that I've gotten to know you, it doesn't quite fit. Kerrington was one I-"

"::: Hartford. Sarah Amanda Hartford. Quite nice, I think."

Jon paused. "::: Amanda? A middle name, and you pick 'Amanda'? Where... where did you get that name from?"

"::: I don't know, it just sounds nice. Sounds intelligent enough, I think.."

"::: I suppose-" Jon stammered slightly. "I suppose it does."

"::: What, you don't like it?"

"::No. No, it's... it's a good name. A very good name. Sarah Amanda Hartford it is. To fill in the rest of your profile, I'm going to have to make up something for your 'parents'. I thought if I made them having joined a traditionalist Aguei tribe, it would go a long way as to not have detailed record on them, and no easy way to contact them."

"::Joined a tribe? Can northers just go become associated with aboriginals that easy?"

"::It's up to the tribe, and not extremely common, but it's not unheard of. I thought this would be better than making up a story that your parents had died. Dead parents leave a lot of paperwork in their wake."

Sarah was quiet for a moment. "::In a way, my parents *are* dead, aren't they? How many minds contributed to what makes up my psyche?"

"::Too many." Jon's tone was heavy with regret, and a little disappointed that Sarah was so quick to dismiss that He considered *himself* to be her father. "::Too many died. And I killed them."

A long awkward silence passed. They watched in the 'slow time' as Sarah's open hand began wrapping around her attacker's wrist. She finally spoke. "::So I have a pretty complete fake identity now, hm? Do you think I'll ever need it all?"

"::You have to be registered to do much of anything legal in society, and sooner or later, someone's going to check up on you. I want to make sure your options are open to do what you want."

"::What I want, huh?"

Jon chuckled slightly. "::I've raised you to this point- by the way, your official birthday is in three months, and you'll be twenty three according to the records, if that suits you. Anyway, I *do* want you to ultimately choose your own path. To be a part of society that Coll wasn't. That I can't be."

"::And what if I chose to be just like Jonathan Coll? To spread death and chaos, and make a general mess of things? Would you stop me?" Her grip on the attacker's wrist was now visibly firm. From his facial expression, the fraction of real time that had passed was not enough for him to realize that anything unexpected had happened yet.

Another long silence passed. "::No," Jon replied, "I am unable. All I would be able to do is try to convince you otherwise, or scream at you. Even then, you could put me in my room."

"::Oh, don't sound so serious, I was being hypothetical. But really though, why would you give me that kind of choice if I'm supposed to be your apology to the world?"

With a measured, solemn tone, Jon explained. "::I trust you, Sarah. Amanda. Hartford."

"::Why? I'm brand new, you barely know me."

"::I know what you're made of. And besides, you're my daughter."

Sarah accepted that, and returned their perception of time to normal. She rammed her attacker's hand against nearby concrete.

"Ow! Fuck, bitch! What's wrong with you?"

Sarah smiled slyly up at him as he hopped back, cradling his hand. She was still seated, and her other hand still rested behind her, 'hooked up' to the communication line. "You were invading my personal space. I might as well ask what's wrong with you. '*Bitch*'."

"Fuuuuuuck." The hand wasn't broken, but it hurt well enough. "I saw you sitting there staring into nowhere. I wanted to see if you were still fucking *alive!*"

":::Oh yeah?!" Jon ranted, unheard by the man. ":::With that fucking grin, you weren't up to anything good!"

":::Easy Jon. He might be telling the truth."

The fellow continued. "I even called out to you first! You didn't respond at all!" That could have been true. While Sarah was waiting in slow-time, he might have very well been reciting poetry unnoticed.

"I'll give you the benefit of the doubt." Sarah relented with a raised eyebrow. "Just do me a favour and take off, all right?"

He walked casually away, looking back at Sarah now and then.

":::All right, what to do now...?"

":::Now that you have an official identity, we could call the cops on that guy."

":::Jon, let it go."

":::Fine. Okay. Let's hack a bank and get you set up financially."

":::*What?* No! I'm going to get a job!"

":::Seriously?" Jon never had a 'job', but he could remember Jonathan Coll's feelings on employment. Specifically employers. One *Mr. Book* in particular. ":::Fine. But let's put in enough money for you that you can get an apartment."

":::No, Jon. Do I need an apartment? Do I need to sleep? Can you think of any reason why I *need* such a thing? I think I *want* one, but it's not urgent."

":::My daughter's a stick in the mud," Jon mumbled. ":::What about food? Food's an eventual need, to generate electricity, fuel actions, and biological maintenance. You're extremely efficient, but you *will* have to eat."

":::I can go back into the ocean at night and find a hapless fish! Out there, they aren't anyone's property yet, are they? With my strength turned up, it shouldn't be too difficult to get my hands on some kind of fish."

":::You're going to live on raw fish?!"

":::Oh, I thought fish is the future, isn't that what your sim kept telling me?"

":::Smart ass."

":::And if I can't get used to raw fish, I'll rub a couple damn sticks together and get a fire going!"

":::Good way to attract cops."

":::Then maybe I'll just eat seaweed or something! The sea is a smorgasbord, Jon!"

":::Do me a favour and let me go to my 'room' before you eat any of these delicacies. You actually sound like you *want* to eat this crap!"

":::Consider it 'roughing it' until I earn some bucks. Hey, I just thought of something. If I'm constructed out of fish tissue, would eating fish be cannibalism?"

Jon laughed. ":::They say you are what you eat! You just have a head start!"

:::C / [000110] [06]

The joyless one, Mr. Book, sat at his grand mahogany desk in his dimly lit office, and continued taking his chair for granted. The chair was fancy enough, expensive enough, but if it could talk it would probably be constantly complaining about Mr. Book's considerable weight. If that were the case, Mr. Book would not be bothered to take offence, but instead send the miraculous talking chair down to one of the research labs to have it dissected for potential commercial or military applications.

If the chair *were* able to speak, it was wise not to.

Mr. Book looked over a report filled with information that he had no legal rights to, but he had it none the less. More nanite-driven crimes popped up on police and military records regularly. A seemingly steady pace.

Twice in the past, he had employed men who were talented with nanites but caused a lot of problems Mr. Book him and his group, Lancer.

First it was that asshole Jonathan Coll. Officially Coll worked for a lab in Autar, but that was a carefully laid out situation to get development level nanites into Lancer hands. How did Coll repay this arrangement? He killed two cities worth of people. Thankfully Lancer managed to not take any heat over it all. That was a close one.

Then it was... what was his name again? Jacob Kirison. Kirison seemed all right. No visions of world domination, but his 'untidy' methods got him into trouble, and led the army right into Mr. Book's lap. Thankfully Mr. Book was able to feign ignorance to Kirison's unofficial projects. Kirison took the fall due to his own stupidity anyway, but the whole thing was uncomfortably close to Lancer having to take blame.

Lancer had lawfully dropped all nanite development when the new laws came into effect. By that point, Mr. Book was glad to wash his hands of it, but knew nanites wouldn't just go away. So he kept his ear to the ground. If nanites were doing bad things, he wanted to know about it. *Before* Lancer was in a position to catch blame for it. Especially if they *were* to blame.

This new trend... these fights that have been going on... they smelled like zombies. They smelled like that damned Jonathan Coll.

:::C / [000111] [07]

Not yet being hungry for the first time, Sarah stayed by the data line she had gained access to.

":::You know, Sarah, Miss Goody Two Shoes, we're stealing net access here, technically."

":::They'll never miss it."

":::Aha! You do have a tiny criminal side! Good."

":::Oh, it's not the same at all, Jon."

":::Oh yes, that's how it starts. First you steal a little bandwidth, then you take an extra mint at the cash register in a restaurant, then it's all ripping mattress tags and public dismemberment."

":::What?!"

":::Never mind. All right, what do you want to do for a living?"

":::I'll start with what I know. Bike courier."

":::Do you *have* a bike? No. Are you going to *steal* one? No. Choice number two is...?"

":::Bar waitress. I met a few, and I liked them just fine."

":::Serving wench? Really!?"

":::You meet lots of people."

Jon groaned. ":::That might not be a good thing right away. You've met one person so far, and he tried to sell you drugs and then *rape* you!"

":::*He was not try-*" Sarah sighed in exasperation. ":::Serving wench it is. Let's load up some want ads."

Sarah led the way, skimming want ads for bars, starting with ones near the shore. All the while, Jon frantically searched for every bit of available information on each bar. Criminal activity in the area, workplace fairness, health ministry reports, structural records, anything and everything he could find. Very quickly they had five top candidates.

":::None of them will be open for hours." It was still the dark hours of the morning. Most of the bars hadn't been closed all that long, ironically.

":::I'm going to snoop around on the net until then." Jon's voice carried the tone of a father staying up late to pay bills.

":::Hey, Jon. You know that movie library you mentioned you had stored? I think I'll watch one."

"::::Yeah, all right. I can keep a lookout around us while you watch the movie. As long as you keep your eyes open. You can see how to browse the titles and stuff, right?"

"::::Right. All right, talk to you later! Knock if something comes up!" Sarah stared into the 'library'. It was very extensive. Then she remembered that these thousands of movies and such were all stored somewhere in her head. What a strange use for extra skull-space. After extensive browsing of the badly organized library, she settled on a light comedy.

The movie progressed in formulaic fashion, but her mind was elsewhere. What about her imaginary ex-boss Harry, anyway? Was she carrying the files that created Harry? Was Harry based on the minds of some dead people? And everyone else in that simulated world?

In hindsight it all seemed so fake now. And all built on the ransacked minds of mass murder victims. How did Jon cope with that? How can he just declare himself to be a new 'person', and ignore what he had done when he thought he was Jonathan Coll? Maybe it wasn't as easy as Jon made it seem, but gave some weight to his reasoning for not using any of himself to make her. What kind of purpose was this? Kill a few million people, and create one?

Sarah gradually realized that the movie was gone. She was standing behind the counter of some kind of cafe. A coffee shop with modern décor and a large glass panel front wall. Mild, forgettable music came down softly from somewhere in the ceiling. She was wearing a tacky, solid red uniform, with large hip pockets that held a notebook and a few pens.

A man walked up to the counter with a smile. "Hey Amanda. I'm taking off in the morning. Can I borrow a little travel money? I can wire it back to you with interest as soon as one of my bosses come through. They seem pretty generous, I'm already set up with a huge apartment there."

Sarah realized that *she* was 'Amanda', and that she wasn't in control. This didn't worry her for some reason. "Get real." She said spitefully. "You'll forget the money the second it's in your pocket, idiot." The man's unwavering smile did nothing to ease her. "Fine," she sighed, "I'll spot you fifty. Have fun in that shiny new city."

"Hey, I *always* have fun, don't I? I'm sure I can find stuff to do in Autar."

"Uh huh. Here." 'Amanda' dug the money out of a pocket underneath the uniform. She put it firmly on the counter, then crossed her arms.

"Ooph! Thanks, but why the cold shoulder?" The man continued grinning as he pocketed the money. "What would mom say?"

Amanda scoffed. "She would say I shouldn't have given you the money, and then she would have told *you* to fuck off."

This seemed to affect the man a tiny bit. He slumped his shoulders and gave a patronizing sigh before reaffirming the smile. "Oh, you're a pistol, you are! Well, thanks again! I'll wire it back to you as soon as I can!" He walked up with a spring in his step.

A co-worker stepped up beside Amanda. "Who was that?"

"Just some asshole. Some stupid, stupid asshole."

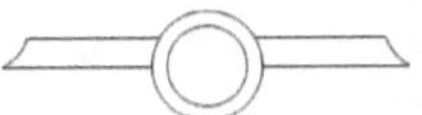

Sarah looked once more through her own eyes, which had been open since she tried to watch the movie stored in her head. "That was weird." She said out loud.

"::::Huh?" Jon sounded like he was only half paying attention, as he was likely running around on the net at the same time.

Sarah looked around just to make sure her accidental out loud speaking wasn't heard by anyone. "::::I think I fell asleep during the movie. I had a dream of some kind."

"::::Hrm!" That got Jon's attention. "::::I did whip together a procedure to generate dreams, but it shouldn't have been activated unexpectedly." Sarah noticed a set of 'buttons' being pointed out that controlled the dream generator. "::::How was your dream? They're supposed to be created by taking bits of your actual experiences, adding some random stuff, and shuffling it around a bit. From there, your 'imagination' would 'subconsciously' take over."

That sounded plausible. Her new middle name was Amanda, so that's where that came from. Working at a coffee shop might relate to her wanting a job in a bar, the jerky customer might draw inspiration from the dealer or Jon or both. "::::Actually, it was kind of dull. I met some jerk, and he bummed money off of me."

"::::Thrilling. Well, I'm sure we'll meet some real panhandlers eventually."

"::::Panhandlers? Anyway, maybe the dream activated because the movie was kind of dull. By the way, how much space do all those movies actually take up? Would I ever need to delete them? Like if my new memories start taking up more space?"

Jon scoffed gently. "::::No, the movies are a drop in the bucket compared to all the data that makes up 'you', and there's lots of free space. If somehow we started running out of space, it would be easy to build more."

"::::Oh, that makes sense." Her voice trailed off. "::::I have the psyches of *how* many dead people in my head? Millions?"

"::::*Holy hell*, no. Ha. *That* would take up a lot of space. I... I kept only what was needed to create the 'you' that you needed to be."

Sarah smirked. "::::No spare parts, huh?" In a way it was somewhat comforting that there were no 'stray bits'. No neglected shards from the minds of the dead knocking around in her noggin. That didn't change the fact that all the bits she *was* using were still salvaged from the dead.

"::::We've burned enough time, let's head to the closest bar you were going to apply at. Which was that?"

"::::Four Fox Grill." Sarah pulled her hand free of the data line. She left the microscopic wires she made there. Who knows, they might come in handy later. She stood, and dusted her behind off. Her hand had a few tiny signs of the interface left on it. Not visible to human eyes, but maybe during a handshake or something, someone might feel the imperfection.

"::::If you want to restore your hand to-" Jon was interrupted.

":::Yeah. I see the buttons. I'll set the restorations to start now. By the time we get there, my hand will be good enough. Next time, maybe I'll do that through an elbow or something."

She stepped out of the alley, and into the mid-morning sun. People walked about from here to there, ranging from business types, to teenagers skipping school. So much for turning up strength and dashing all the way to the pub That would stand out a tad.

Sarah started walking and struck up conversation. ":::So Jon, what did you do with yourself while I was sleeping through the movie?"

":::I surfed the net, mostly. Caught up on current events since I crawled into the ocean."

":::Oh yeah? What's new?"

":::Thanks to Jonathan Coll's exploits, the government's put a strict set of laws against nanite development. It's understandable, but they seem a little bit overdone. I mean, there's a ton of harmless stuff you can do with nanites that are super useful."

":::How strict? Is my existence illegal, or is there some kind of exemption for fish-girls?"

":::Don't forget the seagull! You're made from molecules from a bunch of fish, *and a seagull!* But yes, I don't think the world would be pleased with finding out how your brain works, or who your daddy is. A lot of things would have to be different for us to just walk out of the ocean and announce ourselves."

Soon they arrived at the Four Fox Grill. It was an inviting enough establishment with many tables outside, and a rounded overhanging patio that probably had a great view of the ocean. The front doors as well as most of the front wall were large panes of glass. Classic rock emanated softly from unseen speakers.

Inside and out, a light scattering of customers had late breakfasts, or early lunch. It was apparently late enough in the day that many lunch and breakfast customers felt free to have a beer with their meals.

A waitress with straight, flowing, black hair stood by the bar's cash register sorting receipts. Sarah walked up to the till, and greeted, "Hi. Word on the net says you're hiring!"

"Oh, yup. Just a sec." The waitress leaned back and turned towards the kitchen door. *"Hey, Kody! There's an applicant here to see you!"*

"Yeah. Yeah, hang on, I'm coming."

":::The manager's a woman." Jon said after hearing Kody's voice. Of course Jon's voice was unheard by anyone but Sarah. ":::I guess you won't be relying on sex-appeal to land the job. Well, unless-"

":::Shut up, Jon. Be quiet unless you want me to put you in your room. This is going to be *my* job, *I'm* going to handle the application."

":::All right, all right, I'm quiet."

The manager, 'Kody' soon came out from the back. She was a stout, strong woman in her late forties, and had a full head of brown hair. She leaned over to the waitress at the till. "Jessica, when you're done with last night's receipts there, let me have them for the books, all right?"

'Jessica' nodded, and kept doing whatever it was that she was doing with them.

"So, kid," Kody said to Sarah as she leaned down on the bar, "What's your name, and why do you want to sling suds and chicken wings?"

Well, that was direct. She decided to respond in kind. "Sarah. Sarah Hartford. And I want to sling beer and chicken wings in the hopes that you give me money!"

Kody smirked. "Any experience?"

":::Lie!" Jon said, ":::we can fake it, no problem."

":::*Jon...!*" Sarah responded in a tone that implied that he was about to be sent to his room.

"No specific pub experience," Sarah replied to Kody, "But I learn fast, and I can double as a bouncer!"

":::Ha! Yes! Yes!" Jon's tone was more than a little sarcastic, "As long as you're being honest, tell her how you can toss cash registers at robbers! It worked in the Autar simulation where you grew up as a-"

Jon was put in his room.

Kody chuckled. "Bouncer, huh? I like the nerve, Sarah, but you don't look like the toughest customer!"

Sarah's reply came only as her elbow planted on the bar, with her hand up, challenging Kody to an arm-wrestle. Kody's arms were pretty thick, and most of it wasn't fat. Jessica, who was still nearby, chuckled a little.

Kody shrugged. "Why not?" She took position against Sarah. Sarah nodded to begin, and Kody began trying to move Sarah's hand down. Trying. And trying harder.

"Any time." Sarah said with a sheepish grin. "Go ahead. You start."

Kody had obviously been trying for a while now. She gave Sarah a dirty look with a smirk, and stopped trying quite so hard. "Okay toughguy. Are you going to try to win, or just embarrass me for another thirty minutes?"

Sarah raised an eyebrow. "I just didn't want to hurt *my new boss.*"

Jessica laughed out loud. "You were right, Kody! *Nerve!*"

Kody chuckled, and let go, ending the match. "All right, all right. Fine! You're hired. Hell, supplement your tips by humiliating guys like I used to. Let me get your info, address and all that junk. I'll go print off a form." Kody walked off to the back again. Sarah turned her strength back down to normal human. If she had tried to win, it was very likely that she *would* have hurt Kody very badly.

"Hm. Oh shit."

"What?" Jessica asked, "You're not happy?"

"Yeah." Sarah bit her lip. "But I don't... I don't have an address really."

Jessica's jaw dropped. "What?! You're on the street?"

"Well, I was going to use my first paycheque to get a place, but I'm not in any hurry, you know? I'll do just fine."

Jessica seemed aghast. "No way! I'm not putting up with one of my co-workers being out on the street!"

Oh crap! Was this going to cost her the job? "It's not like I'm a junkie who-"

Jessica looked out towards another waitress on he other end of the bar, held up her hand and yelled towards her. "*Dan! We have a new roomie for a while! She can have the couch!*"

'Dan', who was very clearly female with her waif-like figure and droopy light brown hair, called back, "*What the hell?*"

"*She's our new co-worker, she doesn't have a place right now, and she can kick your mum's ass!*"

Dan stopped mid-stride with a tray of dishes, looked Sarah over with a furrowed brow. "Hell, if I can watch her kick Kody's ass, she can have *my* bed."

Kody's voice boomed from the back, "*I heard that, Danielle.*"

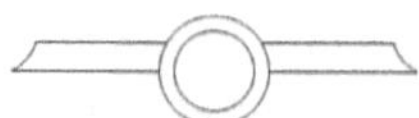

Sarah poked away at a chicken Caesar salad. Jessica had insisted on treating her to lunch before training started with Kody. With the free lunch and couch to crash on, it kind of made Sarah feel like a charity case, but it was hard to refuse.

Well, how could she realistically get out of it? "No, Jessica, it's all right. I don't need room or board, I don't actually require sleep, and if I get hungry, I can just walk along the ocean floor until I *find* something to eat."

Oh crap. Jon. She let him out of his room.

":::Hello, Sarah." Jon but on a tone of aloof indignation. "I see you're doing well. Bought lunch, did you? Did you mug someone?"

":::No, I told them I ran away from my horrible, abusive father, and they made me a member of their all-women cult. They wanted to go burn down your house and chase you with pitchforks. Obviously I couldn't explain why they can't, so I gave them a random address to burn down. When night falls, they're going to give me ceremonial tattoos and piercings."

Time passed wordlessly for a while. ":::So, you mugged someone, right?"

When she was getting to the end of her salad, Kody came by with the form she had to go print. "Just fill out what you can, Sarah. How come you don't have a place? If you don't mind me being nosy...?"

How to answer? "I... had some problems with my 'dad'. It's complicated."

":::I am not problematic!"

":::Try telling that to the City of Meston." Sarah snapped. It came out a little colder than she intended, and she regretted saying it, but it was true. There was no City of Meston anymore, and it was because of what Jon had done in his first ten minutes of existence. Jon remained silent.

Kody nodded, and put her hand on Sarah's shoulder. "It's all right, you don't have to get into it. I've heard em all over the years." Not quite.

"Hey, I do have a question though. Where's the name of the bar come from? Four Fox Grill? Sounds like you cook foxes!"

Kody snickered. "The old location was started by me and three other gals, making a total of four foxes. We got this new location a while back, and a total change of staff since the beginning. One of us retired, one found a better job, one passed on, bless the lass."

"Oh, I'm sorry!"

"No, no, it's ancient history now. Since then I hired a pack of new gals to help fill the new location, including my daughter Danielle. Are you about ready to start?"

":::You know I regret Meston." Jon said quietly.

"Yeah." Sarah replied to both of them, putting down her fork, and standing up.

"Well, step one. Take your bloody plate to the back! You're staff, not a customer!" Sarah did as she was told, then washed her hands as instructed by a sign in the kitchen. "Good girl." Kody said.

":::I know." Sarah said to Jon. ":::My remark was uncalled for, I know. But..."

":::But it's hard to put aside, isn't it? If it was easy... I don't know."

Sarah followed behind Kory, soaking in all the basics of daily duties around the Four Fox. Taking orders, prioritizing customers and their needs, operating the till (and not throwing it) was simple enough.

"All right. Take those two tables," Kory said, "We'll see how you do." Kory went to sit at the bar. Sarah took an order, checked on the other table, brought the order to the kitchen, and made one more pass by the two tables assigned to her. Lacking other immediate duties, she returned to Kody.

"Where can I find a broom? I could probably-"

Kody interrupted Sarah. "*A Broom! She asked for a broom!*" Her booming voice could be heard quite a distance away. "*She asked for a broom with no prompting at all! It's like the daughter I never had!*"

"*Ahem!*" came Danielle's voice from the direction of the patio.

"Oh, calm down, Danny-girl! I said the daughter I *never* had! You're the one I *did* have!"

"You two are so bad!" Sarah giggled. She was having genuine fun here. It was so nice to be hearing, and speaking with real, out loud voices, as compared to chatting silently with Jon.

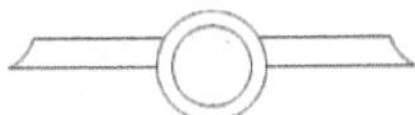

Before long, Sarah had been assigned to the upper floor. "Holler down if it gets too busy for you, the lunch rush is coming soon." The upper floor was even less 'bar-like' than the already airy ground floor. As she suspected when she came in, the upper patio had a gorgeous view of the ocean.

She stood by the railing and 'paused' time.

":::Huh? What's up?" Jon's voice came.

Sarah smiled- or she would have if time wasn't going at a snail's pace. ":::I just wanted to take in the view for a while, without wasting work time."

":::Oh. Uh, okay." Jon didn't seem to appreciate it, but Sarah was content to stare at the shimmering azure for quite a while in silence.

":::It's just amazing, isn't it?"

"::::Light. Coming from the sun, affected by atmosphere, and reflected on the irregularity of the water's waves. Pretty cut and dry if you ask me."

"::::Jon, you think like a machine."

"::::No, I'm pretty sure the original Jonathan Coll would say something similar. I think the response is part scientist, and part male. Guys don't give a crap about stuff like this."

"::::I think you're over-generalizing." Sarah said. "But I'll admit, with time at this pace, the water loses part of its charm with waves that don't move." Sarah resumed the normal perception of time, and got back to work.

The lunch rush gained momentum soon enough, and Sarah found herself busy at every moment. Eventually, Danielle popped up to check on her.

"Mum says you seem really busy up here! Do you need a hand? Holy crap, it *is* way busier up here than below."

Sarah loaded a tray up with dishes from a recently abandoned table, and stuffed the bill and payment between a couple glasses. "Nope! Things are going well! I learn fast!"

"Mum said that too."

Of course Sarah had been cheating in a way. Her stamina was not going to be an issue, and if she ever felt the need for a mental break, or even a moment to consider what task to prioritize next, she could just stop time. From an outside perspective, she seemed quite unstoppable, like a seasoned veteran on a good day.

"Hey honey," a man asked when served his bill, "I don't suppose you'd want to go to a movie or something with me..."

Time stop.

"::::Well. Why does this confuse me?"

"::::Huh?" It sounded like Jon had been doing something else. Reading a book, watching a movie, whatever. "::::What's confusing?"

"::::This man just asked me out. I know that's a normal thing, but I can't say I've ever come across this kind of thing in the Autar simulation. Ever."

"::::Hmm. Yeah. I never actually included romantic scenarios in the sim," Jon said in a tone of deep thought. "::::It would have actually been *me*, and that would be creepy."

"::::Fair enough. This guy here though... he's attractive enough," Indeed he was. His solid build, auburn hair, defined features, "::::Yet the idea of going on a date with him bores me to tears. And intimacy sounds awkward as heck, and entirely unappealing. Am I a lesbian?"

"::::*What?!*" Jon chuckled. "::::Well, how do you feel about your co-workers? Some of them are quite attractive!"

Sarah thought and pondered. "::::Nah. They're nice as heck, but they don't interest me in that way."

"::::There you go. You have zero sexuality. Unlike humans, you will get to choose your orientation. And change it if you want. Or leave it alone. I'm your father, so I vote that you leave it alone." Jon chuckled nervously.

"::::I think I will leave it for now. I just got here, I have things going on, you know?"

"::::That's my girl! I shouldn't really make myself sound like an expert. Sex drive was something that Coll never transferred into me. He deemed it a needless distraction."

"::::Okay, so what do I do abut this poor shlep?" The man who asked her out was still in front of her, only the smallest fraction of a second had passed in real-time since he finished his question. "::::I don't want to hurt his feelings or anything."

"::::He'll get over it. Just tell him 'no thanks!' and move on."

Sarah restarted time. "Sorry man, I can't!" She did her best to deliver the rejection as nicely, and as casual as possible.

"Aw, you don't know what you're missing, but okay! I come here lots if you change your mind!"

"::::See?" Jon said, "::::He coped with it. A pretty boy like that probably doesn't have much trouble finding a date. In fact, maybe he took it *too* well! He probably asks girls out all the time! He's probably asked out all the staff in the past, and thought he'd try the new girl! He's a pretty boy scumbag is what he is!"

"::::Easy, Jon. I said no, my innocence is safe."

"::::Hrmph."

:::C / [001000] [08]

By two o'clock, the rush had petered out. "That's the end of the early short shift," Jessica told Sarah as she pulled her to the stairs. "Dan can handle things with Kody until the later shift reinforcements come along."

"Just four hours? I could-"

"No, no," Jessica interrupted, "It's your first day and you've been going like a machine! Stop making the rest of us look like slobs!"

":::Come to think of it, Sarah, if you keep up that pace, you might raise suspicion."

":::Ha, I think my amazing arm-wrestling skill might have done that already."

":::What...? What did you do?" Jon had been in his 'room' when Sarah faced off with Kody.

":::Nothing, don't worry about it. But point taken. I should emulate tired behaviour a little." Sarah sighed, and dropped her shoulders. "All right, Jess. I've been going pretty hard. First day and all. Enthusiasm." She allowed her voice to sound a little extra tired.

"All right then!" Jessica led the way back downstairs. "Want to go meet the couch you'll be crashing on?"

"Sure, good idea." They passed by the bar, dropping off their aprons. "Sarah!" Kody hollered from the back, "Take tomorrow off, I have to find a good way to write you into the timetable. The day after that is Friday, how do you feel about doing the evening until closing?"

"Sure thing!"

"You did good today, Sarah. Keep it up!"

Sarah and Jessica passed through the front doors. Outside, Dan was cleaning up some tables. "See you two later. I'm on until six." Danielle said.

They boarded the mass transit train, a bulky but quiet thing running about a dozen metres above ground. The stations and the supports holding up the track were seasoned relics, but the trains, turnstiles, and payment kiosks were quite new. Jessica paid for Sarah's way. "You can get me when the tips are divided up."

"I feel like a mooch." Sarah said, slumping into a seat as the train started up.

"No worries. The way you hauled ass in there, I'm not worried in the least. And I know you're trustworthy, because *you* actually turned in *all* your tips!"

"You don't?"

Jessica chuckled. "None of us do! Not all of it. Kody understands we need a little 'walking around' money. How do you think I paid for the train?"

Jon chuckled. ":::Ah! My daughter's the most honest waitress in the city of Densfarn! I don't know whether to be proud or embarrassed!"

":::Shush, Jon." Sarah considered the idea of '*unofficial partial tip retention*', and a smirk spread across her face. "Well then Jess, if I turned in money that we will all end up sharing, it's arguable that by all rights, I already paid you back for the train ride!"

"Ha! Fair enough!"

":::Good recovery."

Rush hour was still a fair way off, so the ride was pretty quiet. It gave Sarah a little time to just listen to the sounds the train made, and the view across the city. She also observed people. This was easier to do without being in a rush to bring them something from the grill.

People in reality came in a much wider variety than in Jon's Autar simulation. Sure, Jon's imagination had managed to conjure a realistic cross-section of ages, races and sizes, but it bore that certain lack of reality somehow. Maybe it had been too formulaic.

Jessica led Sarah off the train at the right stop, talking about this and that. She talked about work, and about when she and Dan moved here, how a little more rent was worth being closer to the train, and how they got used to the new area. After getting down to street level again, it was only a few blocks of walking before Sarah spotted a tree. A sickly tree doing it's best in an urban environment, but a tree none the less.

"This is it." Jessica nodded towards a brown, tired looking ten story apartment building. She put her eye up to the door's eye-reader, careful not to actually touch the unsanitary thing with her face. It buzzed crossly.

"Fucking piece for shit," she mumbled under her breath. "They probably won't fix it until it falls off the wall."

Sarah stepped forward. She licked her thumb and scrubbed the lense with her wet thumb. "Spit's corrosive," Sarah said as she rubbed, "it'll eat though grime somewhat, right? I mean, it can't hurt." She looked at her thumb when she pulled it back, and the black smudge that came with it.

"Ew." Jessica stepped forward again. "Wow. I don't think it's ever been cleaned." It beeped happily at the unobstructed view of Jessica's retina and the door clicked as it unlocked.

":::Smart move, Sarah," came Jon's voice. ":::I wouldn't have thought of that. I would have hacked it first."

"People take tech for granted sometimes." Sarah replied to them both.

Jessica held the door open for Sarah. "Especially landlords."

The encounter with the grime of the eye reader was a theme for the building, it seemed. The carpets inside the small lobby were orange, once upon a time. Now they had become a dull yellow, with worn out spots along the way to the elevator.

"Our apartment isn't *this* much of a shithole." Jessica lamented with a sigh. She usually ignored the building's condition, but bringing someone new home forced her to see it through the visitor's eyes. The elevator continued the theme with dirty, barely readable buttons, and the same dull yellow floor.

Some kind of bug scuttled quickly out of view.

The fifth floor provided a slightly more hospitable experience. The floor, after all, suffered one tenth of the traffic, and the eyepiece on Jessica's door was far more co-operative. It was even clean enough that Jessica didn't worry if her face touched it. "I'll have to get your eye set up with these things. Don't let me forget."

"All right." The apartment, as promised, was much nicer than the rest of the building. The décor was somewhat random, suffering from the unfocused influence of two youthful inhabitants and a limited budget. It was a warm enough feeling space, despite clutter and limited room.

It was bigger than Sara's apartment in simulated Autar, but laid out in a fairly similar manner. Sarah's didn't have the small dividing wall that declared where the small kitchen space ended and the living room began, and there were three doors on the other end, presumably Jessica's and Dan's rooms, as well as the bathroom.

"It's cozy!" Sarah said in earnest.

"You mean cramped as hell!" Jessica laughed, walking into the kitchen area. "You want anything? I have pop, iced tea, or maybe you're hungry?"

"Nope, I'm good. But I honestly meant cozy. My *last* apartment, *that* was cramped. There was barely room for me, my bike, and my pull-out bed." As she said it, Sarah understood part of Jon's reasoning for supplying her with some kind of background life. Ammo for realistic small talk.

"Bike? You're a cyclist?" Jessica flopped onto the sofa.

"Professionally. Courier. I was kind of aiming to do that again, but with no bike, and no money to by one..."

"Ahh. When you make enough to buy a bike, I guess you're be doing that, then."

Sarah sat on the other end of the sofa, and cocked her head. "It's not like I was married to it. Besides, the Four Fox has a pretty fun crew, from what I've seen so far. Oh, I have to keep track of what I owe you! A chunk of rent, anything I happen to eat, lunch earlier today, you know. No hand-outs, all right? Priority number one is paying you back."

Jessica chuckled softly. "Well, lunch didn't cost me anything, chalk it up to an employee's free meal. And it's not like it costs me anything to have you take up sofa space."

"But it's an inconvenience for you and Dan. I'll pay a third, as soon as Kody pays me."

Jessica nodded. "I'm not super-worried. So... do you mind me asking, what happened at your old place?"

Think think. "It was a bad neighborhood, that's for sure. A lot of violence." Sarah's voice trailed off and she stared into the floor. Her story was based in truth, but memories of her battle with the zombie distracted her from formulating a complete story that she was able to tell Jessica.

Jessica drew her own conclusions. False, but sympathetic conclusions. "Was there someone you had to get away from? Are you safe now?"

Sarah was hesitant to reply, which only seemed to confirm Jessica's theories. "Yeah. That's all over with now." Sara bit her lip, remembering the sound that her frying pan made with that creature's skull, among other indelible experiences of the simulation. "That's all history."

"Sounds a lot like Dan's story." Jessica said softly. "When her mum found out about how she'd been treated, I thought she was going to rip him apart."

"Him? Him who?"

"Dan's ex." Jessica grimaced a little. "I met him a few times. You can just *feel* the potential for him to be kinda nasty. But I shouldn't go spilling this kind of thing. Maybe it would be good for you to have a chat with Dan about it. It's not really my place."

"That's all right." Okay, so now Sarah had to build herself a history about an abusive ex-something for herself? No, it would be much better just to stay tight lipped about the past. "Jess, you look tired. If you want to go crash, that would be all right."

Jessica nodded. "Yeah. I think I will. The TV terminal's right there, control's there, blankets in that closet, it's a mess, kitchen's there, obviously. Make yourself at home, K?"

"Got it."

Jessica retreated into her room, and it wasn't long before Jon spoke up. ":::Hey."

":::Hello. What's up?"

Jon was silent for a while. ":::When I 'raised' you in Autar, complete with the disaster... I was only thinking about educating you about it."

":::I know."

":::I wasn't thinking about the fact that you will have... well now you've lived with that. If you want to erase those mem-"

":::No, I'm going to keep them."

Another long silence.

":::You don't have to. You can keep the relevant data,"

":::It's all relevant, don't you think?"

":::You could have learned all the relevant things from a news recap. There was no need to put you through it first hand. That was stupid of me."

":::Maybe. Yes, it probably was. If you were the kind of person that you want me to be, you probably wouldn't have done that. You would have thought it out from a more..."

":::A more human perspective? Or humane?"

Sarah got up off the sofa, and opened the cupboard under the kitchen sink.

":::Sarah, what are you doing?"

":::I'm going to do some cleaning. If I can't pay into rent yet, I want to contribute in some way."

":::You are *awesome!* I would have never considered that! See, this is just the kind of thing I should have realized about you a long time ago, but just couldn't pull my head out of my ass to notice!"

":::What?" Sarah acted with deft speed, slowing time just enough that she could do things like react to a lamp she nearly knocked over, rescuing it before it made a sound. At what *felt* like a leisurely pace, she deftly, silently and quickly cleaned everything she could think of.

A fly landed on Sarah's arm. ":-:Can you hear me?"

Time stopped.
":::Oh shit." Jon said.
":::What was that? That didn't sound like you, Jon."
":::It wasn't. I think it was the fly on your arm."
The fly was just on the edge of Sarah's field of vision, so she was able to examine it despite her eyeball being as slow as everything else. ":::Uh... it's a fly. And not in my head..."
":::No. It broadcasted at us. You can tell by the difference in the voice tone and protocol markers. This signal was picked up by your nervous system. It's so weak that it probably has to be that close to be heard." Jon pointed out how to broadcast a similar low powered signal, despite her nerves not being intended for such a function. ":::but we might want to ignore it. If this thing is on to us, maybe we can just play dumb."
":::Well, what the heck *is* this? A talking fly full of nanites? What are we going to do about it? Ignore it, and hope it flies away when we return to real-time?"
":::Let's try that," Jon said, seemingly undaunted by intelligent house flies. ":::It might just be guessing that you could be able to hear it."

Sarah returned to real-time, and then 'noticed' the fly, waving it off her arm with her other hand. "Shoo, fly. Shoo!" It flew off just like one would expect a fly to do.
":::Good. Keep doing what you would normally do, Sarah. It might show itself out."
":::It's full of nanites, isn't it? What if it means us harm?" Sarah kept cleaning the apartment, although nervously.
":::Don't worry. If it tries anything invasive, your nervous system will detect it. That would be the moment we go to war with it."
Jon's reassurances didn't make her feel much better. The fly buzzed around the room, and she found herself increasingly wary of it. Where was it now? There. Still flying around. Where now? There. To hell with this, there's more than one way to skin a cat. Sarah picked up a nearby magazine and rolled it up. "Where *are* you, little sucker?"
Jon snickered. ":::Oh this is too funny. Three nanite driven entities in a life or death struggle with a rolled up newspaper."
":::It's a magazine. I'm on a hunt, shush." Sarah's hunt wasn't getting anywhere. It had been a while since she spotted it. ":::Maybe it got scared off. I mean, if it's intelligent and-"

":-:Please do not harm the fly. I am just a passenger in this innocent creature."
"*Aw fuck, where are you?!*" Sarah hastily looked over her arms and legs, looking for the fly.
":-:I am behind your left knee."

Sarah quickly put her left foot on the table to get a better look behind he knee. There was nothing there.

":-:I knew you could hear me." the voice said without a hint of a gloat in its tone.

"Aw, hell." Sarah said out loud.

":::Busted." Jon said in resignation.

":-:As a show of good faith, I am actually at the small of your back. If you wish to hear me out, I would feel better doing so face to face."

Sarah sighed, and held her hand out, palm down. "Yeah, I didn't feel you land. Get on my hand, and I'll sit down." She did feel the fly take off, and she sat, hand still out. The fly buzzed around like a fly would, and ignored her hand. "Any time now."

She waited, feeling like an idiot holding her hand out, watching a fly. She opened up the magazine and started reading it. "All right fella, sooner or later I'm gonna go back to what I-" She felt it land on her knee.

":-:My apologies," it said, ":-:I do not control the fly directly. I only make requests and suggestions, which can be very difficult to communicate with a creature of this intelligence level. When he *does* understand, he's quite obliging however."

"Why not control it directly?" Sarah asked, putting the magazine down on the far side of her lap.

Jon spoke up, unheard by the fly. ":::Sarah, just so you know, in our usual internal voice, he can't hear us. I'd rather he not know that I exist inside you. It would be simpler and safer for all of us I think. Also, you might want to start talking to him through his brand of broadcasted signals, so you don't wake up your roomie, Jessica."

":::Got it." Sarah said directly to Jon.

":-:I do not believe in controlling biological creatures directly," the fly said, ":-:It reminds me too much about the Erebus incident zombies."

":::See?" Jon sighed, ":::I knew people would have things against me, but I didn't expect to get a guilt trip from a fly."

":::Oh, shush Jon. I can't listen to you and the fly at the same time." Sarah started broadcasting to the fly, or rather, the nanites in the fly. ":-:So, hi. I'm Sarah, what's your name, and... why are you here?"

":-:I am Eidechse. I am here because I noticed you on the net. I keep my eyes out for things. I saw you creating your identity. When I traced you to a system that typically has no activity at that time of day, I investigated and found signs of nanite use. I become concerned, and tracked you down. This fly has been following you since you left work."

":-:That's... that's a tiny bit fucking creepy, Eide... whatever..."

":-:I-dechs-ay. Eidechse. I felt it important to ask why you are using this body as a host? What is your purpose?"

":-:This is..." Sarah held up her arms and shrugged. ":-:This is my body! My real body. It never had another owner. I'm not being controlled, I'm me!" Ripples of paranoia swept over Sarah. She wasn't being controlled, was she? She didn't *feel* like she was being controlled, but who's to say? She was *made* by Jon. He could have made her to not suspect being controlled, maybe she was using suggestions and requests, as Eidechse said he was controlling the fly? But she was suspicious of Jon. She at least had the mental freedom to do that. If that counted for anything.

":-:I do hope that you *are* free," Eidechse said, "as I have seen some who are *not* free. Their purpose is quite clear. But what is your purpose-"

":-:I just want to lead a normal life, like a human." Sarah took a moment to find the right way to tell Eidechse sufficient truth. ":-:I wasn't always so human. This body had to be built. I just want to... to *be*."

":-:Fascinating." Eidechse pondered. ":-:I can understand the appeal. Tell me, do you retain many of the potential abilities of artificial life? Aside from those enabling this communication, of course..."

":-:Some." Sarah smiled coyly. ":-:A lady's got to have *some* secrets, especially when talking to flies she just met."

":::Good girl." Jon whispered to her.

":-:Fair enough," Eidechse said, "Given the laws, neither of us should exist."

":::Sarah, ask him about those who are not free..."

":-:You said something about seeing some 'who are not free'...What did you mean?"

":-:Here." Eidechse shared a picture of a bar, with a satellite photo, global coordinates, and an address. ":-:This is the most recent example of a-"

Wham. A different rolled up magazine landed on Sarah's knee. "Shit Sarah, off in space much?" It was Jessica. Jessica held up the magazine to look at the mutilated fly stuck to it.

"*Ahh! What!?*"

"Sorry to startle you Sarah, but the fly seemed to be as oblivious as you were, so I took the opportunity for an ambush." Jessica went over to the kitchen, and scraped the fly into the garbage. "We have screens up here, but now and then one gets in. The last thing we need is one laying eggs."

"But I... I..." What could Sarah say? Oh yes, sorry Jessica, that was very rude, I was in the middle of conversation with that fly when you creamed it.

"Aw crap hon, I really startled you, didn't I?" Jessica took a few slow steps back towards Sarah. "You've been through a lot, haven't you? I should have been more considerate. Just remember you're safe here, all right?"

":::Yeah, right."

"I'm heading out for a bit." Sarah casually told Jessica.

"Oh? I was just thinking about dinner! Where are you headed?" Jessica sat reading the magazine she used to kill Eidechse.

"I'm just going to stroll around, get to know the neighborhood a bit better, you know. See where stuff is."

Jessica paused, looking a little bit concerned. "You want company?"

"Nah, it's fine. I won't be all that long." Sarah headed for the door, and spotted the grievously wounded fly sitting right by the door frame. Curious, she bent down, and touched it gently with her fingertip. The voice came to her immediately on contact.

":-:en. Must return to my safe spot. Please just let me out. Can not talk more now. Broken. No offence for the damage taken. Must return to my safe spot. Please just let me out. Can not talk more now. Broken. No offence for the damage taken. Must return to my safe spot. Please just let me out. Can not talk more now. Broken. No offence for the damage taken."

It repeated the recording endlessly. Sarah took her finger away, and opened the door. The fly promptly flew out with precision and efficiency never flown before by a fly. By the time Sarah stuck her head out the doorway, the fly was already long gone.

":::Eidechse resurrected the fly?"

":::I wouldn't be so sure," Jon speculated, ":::I think he had to violate his guideline about 'no direct control'."

":::Undead fly. Creepy." Sarah closed the door behind her and headed down the elevator. ":::So, any clue on what we're going to find at this bar?"

":::People who aren't free, I guess. I wonder though; Eidechse is a nanite colony A.I. Who runs around in a fly. His definition of 'people' might not be as strict as most would assume."

":::So... so what then, flies enslaved to run around and suck dirt off of everything when the bar is closed?"

":::I could live with that," Jon mulled, "but I doubt that's what's going on. I have some theories."

":::Such as?"

":::Jonathan Coll experimented on rats. These experiments 'evolved' into a sort of arena, pitting one rat filled with nanites, against another with a different variation of nanites. These experiments formed the basis for-"

":::Zombies."

":::I don't think anyone's that dumb now. Heck, from what I read on the net while you were dreaming, even joking about making a zombie these days is less popular than growing a Hitler mustache."

Sarah didn't want to say anything, but the comparison didn't exactly paint Jon in a favorable light. Jon's death-count was much higher. He continued. ":::But I've also read on the net about animals being used in the same way Coll was using rats. Chickens, dogs. Even without the nanites, those fight are illegal. With the nanites, it sounds like the matches go on much longer, and are much more gruesome."

":::Lovely."

:::C / [001001] [09]

The train pass that Jessica had paid for was still valid when Sarah got
on the train, but expired by the time she got off. She'd need to keep an eye
out for a chance to make fare for the trip home. The fact that it got her this far
was mere luck. Luck can only make up for a lack of foresight *sometimes*.

The train dropped her off within a few blocks of the destination bar. The
last gasp of the evening's rush hour was nearly out of breath. The sidewalk
traffic of slow, tired workers was giving way to people going out for dinner,
movies, or other activities. Tonight it was those other activities that drew her
concern.

The bar was just as it looked in the picture, except that the picture
seemed to be taken from flat on the ground. It was a tired, miserable looking
two story dive, clinging to its existence on the edge of ever expanding
development. Surely the bar once looked quite at home here, but newer
neighbors such as a strip mall, medical building, and a bank, seemed to be
held safely at bay only by the bar's sprawling dirt parking lot, and its vehicular
occupants.

One day, perhaps soon, the land value would overcome the owner's
resistance and the tired, miserable dive would finally find release by the
wrecking ball and the bulldozer.

But not today. Today it stood as proud as it could manage, as rock and
roll (outdated by a generation or two) throbbed outwards from the poster-
covered windows. Patrons coming and going allowed the sounds of typical
tavern din to bleed out into the evening.

":::Wow," Sarah commented, ":::I can't believe I'd want to work at the
Four Fox Grill, and not at this Shangri-La."

":::Oh, be nice, Sarah. It's *my* job to make fun of crap."

":::My apologies."

Sarah entered, and realized she was the sore thumb of the room. Even
those who looked like they made an effort to dress up a little looked like they
had spent the previous night under a bar stool. Sarah, in contrast, was
dressed in her usual urban cyclist gear, which showed off her hips and rear
end well enough to catch many an eye.

The interior walls were an aged looking wood begging to be condemned. To hide their shame, they were littered with a mix of various posters, a few photos in tacky metal frames, and the odd notice about weekly specials. The booths along the walls were upholstered with fading red fake leather with cracks in the material. The worst cracks were supported by packing tape. All the tables were covered with terry cloth. Many looked to be in desperate need of laundering. The dated lighting system was set low; a merciful fact to soften the general ambiance.

"::Sarah, may I suggest a preemptive precaution? Boost your strength a tad? Nothing that would snap off someone's arm if you reacted to someone grabbing your-"

"::Got it." Sarah boosted her strength to match the power she had felt in Kody's arm. Plenty of strength for most purposes, but still within reasonable human limits. Not that it mattered. If anything goofy happened, a full boost was a time-freeze away. More or less.

She saw a couple of rougher looking customers glance around suspiciously before 'discretely' slipping through a door in the corner. It certainly looked like a place of interest.

She went up to the bar, and waited for the bartender to acknowledge her. She wanted to order a drink; it seemed like polite protocol before getting to brass tacks, but lacking money, she just went for it. "Hey man. I hear the *special events* here are pretty good." She raised an eyebrow towards the mysterious door.

The bartender slowed down to size her up. "That just goes to the kitchen and stuff."

Sarah grinned slyly. "Bullshit. That's where I need to be. *Need*, got it?"

The bartender chucked. "You don't much look like you need to pay for the fun stuff." His face and tone grew a shade darker. "You're here to watch the rough stuff? You don't look like the type that are into those guys."

Guys. Humans presumably.

Time stop.

"::Fuck."

Sarah sighed, and took a moment to absorb the notion. "::It...It could still be animals of some kind."

"::Hell, Sarah, as long as you're being hopeful, it might as easily be mindless robots. But I doubt it. Brace for the worst. All right, suggest to this guy that you're here to place some big bets."

"::All right."

Time resumed.

"I can spot a winner." Sarah said dryly. "I'm ready to make a buck, right? I have an itch for couple big new toys, and I'd rather buy them with nice, clean, won money. Besides, it's fun to watch, don't you think?"

The bartender looked off into space for a moment, hearing something from an unseen source. He looked back at Sarah. "Yeah, all right, they like you enough. Go on in."

“Thank you!”

As she walked over to the door, Jon piped up. “:::I didn't see an earpiece on that guy. It might be a bit hasty, but I'm guessing he had something implanted inside his ear.”

“:::What, Jon, you really think he'd have some kind of nanite device?”

“:::Probably not. It wouldn't be necessary. If I was a human in his position, I wouldn't want to have nanites in me if I didn't have to. Partly for legal reasons, partly for trust issues. It's probably just a really small device inserted surgically behind his ear.”

Sarah giggled. “:::It couldn't just be a small device sitting *behind* his ear, huh? Something perfectly legal, and possibly common over-the-counter consumer electronics?”

“:::Bah. Just when I thought you were getting appropriately paranoid, you go and say something practical and logical like that.”

The door clicked as she approached it, and clicked again as soon as she opened it. Ahead stretched a dim little hallway with five locked doors. To the right was a door marked 'staff'. On the left stood two doorways. One was decorated with a painting of a huge, grotesquely distorted set of male genitalia, ejaculating various vicious demons. The other had a female version, equally distorted, which emitted fluttering angels. These were apparently doors to the 'fun stuff' that the bartender mentioned.

Sarah rolled her eyes. “That's dis-”

“:::I am not discussing that kind of imagery with my daughter,” Jon dryly interrupted, “I didn't see it, you didn't see it, moving on.” Such 'art' seemed like a mild offence after the whole zombie-genocide simulation, but Sarah let it slide.

The fourth door stood at the end of the hall. Most of the hall was made from the same wood that most of the bar seemed to be made of, but the wall at the end was solid concrete. The door was steel.

“:::I'm guessing that's probably not the bar's meat freezer.”

Jon scoffed. “:::*I'm* guessing they store their meat in the sun.”

Sarah reached out for the handle, and pulled it open. It *was* a door from a freezer, but inside it was lit even dimmer than the rest of the bar. A diffused warmth and mild scent of tobacco and other burnable things seemed to press out towards her. New sounds also found her. Yelling and cheering mostly. Through the door, the hallway continued as concrete, and slowly lead downwards.

“:::Pop the strength to max, Sarah.”

“:::Already did.”

She came into the main hall in time to see one man land a savage blow onto another, sending him to the ground. The spectators all around the blood-soaked boxing ring explored into cheers. The victorious fighter stood in a ready stance, emotionless, staring forward.

“Come on, come on, one more time! Come on!” The frustrated shouting was coming from a man sitting at a red table on the left side of the room. His attention was glued to a computer in front of him. Above the ring, a large digital clock ticked away the last few seconds of the match. When it was at two, the man at the red desk tossed up his hands. “Ah fuck, it's done!”

Zero. A recording of a fight bell played, and the spectators cheered again. About half of them, anyway. The other half skipped the celebrating, some leaving the room.

"Blue wins," A man at a large black desk on the far end of the room called into a microphone, "Winning accounts will be credited. Now accepting bets for the next match." Behind him stood two cheap knock-offs of the stereotypical bodyguard type. Broad shoulders, dark sunglasses and faded, ill-fitting black suits.

On the right side of the room, a man at a blue table looked quite pleased. He jabbed a key on his keyboard, and the winning fighter began a repeating victory dance. He ignored his wounds, battered and bloody. One of his ears, his lower lip, and left brow especially seemed to be nearly beaten off of his head. His knuckles were nearly down to bone as well. The blood loss was much less than one would expect however.

":::Head wounds typically bleed like crazy," Jon said to Sarah, "That guy's a zombie of some kind. I mean,he's not trying to eat any humans, but it's pretty plain that he's not quite right."

The fighter kept repeating his victory dance as if it were a screen saver, with the constant emotionless stare into nowhere. Sarah tried to imagine his face unbeaten, and an expression of any human emotion. ":::The poor guy... do you think there's anything left of him? I mean... could we possibly save him?"

A nearby spectator commented to another. "That was quick. I didn't think we'd see a full knockout in such a short match. They shortened it to make room for the main event, right?"

"No," the other replied, "I asked when I placed my bet. If the new guy's as tough as he's been hyped up, this is going to make for a damned short night."

"Well, If the new guy does alright, maybe there will be time for another match of a full two, if they have anyone else."

"Full two?" Sarah interrupted to ask.

"Yeah, two hours. A lot of people get bored with the length of the matches, but they tweaked the standards to make them a little quicker. It was that or have every match decided by judges, which... face it, people are here to see knockouts and big blood."

The loser was still being dragged away on a tarp by the man who was at the red table earlier. The losing fighter was in far worst shape than the winner. His neck was bent at a sixty degree angle, throat ripped open, lower abdomen caved in. Dragging the seemingly lifeless body, he grumbled, "Fuck, this is going to take a week to fix."

Sarah tried not to look shocked. ":::Jon, 'fixed'? That can be *fixed*?"

Jon sighed, and replied in a sombre tone. ":::Jonathan Coll did similar things with rats. If they're not actually alive, it's actually a lot easier. It's just a matter of keeping good tone in the muscles, and the bones together. They're puppets."

Sarah looked around at all the people who seemed to think this was normal. ":::Am I the only one seeing this? How can this kind of thing keep going without being reported?!"

":::People suck. Some, anyway."

"::::We have to report this!!"

Jon sighed. ":::I figured you'd say that. I agree, but we have to do it carefully. Anonymous or better. I'm just-"

The man at the black desk boomed out over the speakers in a theatrical voice, "Gentlemen, please welcome to the ring our newest combatant, a new breed of brute, the demon of Densfarn!" the crowd cheered as a robed man stepped up onto the bloodied ring, and a new user sat at the red table. The crowd roared again as fencing dropped around the ring to form a cage.

":::Ooh, you know he's a star if he gets a cage match. You know the other guy's toast. The guy at the blue table knows it too, this is so rig-"

":::Jonathan! This isn't sport! We have to go report this *now!*"

":::Jon." Jon corrected. "I'm not Jonathan. I'm... I can't be him, all right? Yes, we have to go."

":::I'm sorry. I didn't mean to-"

":::I know." Jon knew it was a slap in the face he needed. He knew there was still too much of Jonathan left in him. This was exactly why he knew he couldn't return to society. Exactly why he made Sarah as he did.

As they headed to the exit, the crowd cheered again as the new combatant dropped his robe. They cheered even louder as he spread his arms wide.

His skin split slowly down the middle. It started from his lower lip, and opened up down his throat, over his chest, and to his navel. As the skin spread cleanly apart, showing a thin red membrane tearing open underneath, his lower jaw opened into two halves. He wailed an unearthly scream that shook the cage, resonated against the concrete walls, and the cheering spectators. As this wail continued, his ribs individually stuck forward and waved frantically, displaying a general lack of internal organs in a vacant, moist cavity.

Jon was awestruck. Sarah lowered her head in shame for humanity and walked slowly up the concrete hall. A spectator passed her, fleeing the room in revulsion.

"Lost, huh?" The bartender asked Sarah when she emerged from the door.

"No one's winning down there."

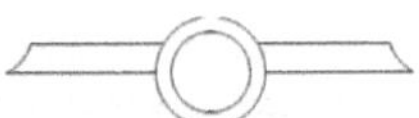

Sarah went to the phone booth on the sidewalk.

":::All right Sarah, let me hack into-"

Sarah dialed 9-1-1.

":::Hang that up right now! They might trace back to you, and find us, and then they might-"

":::Jon, no. No bullshit." Sarah's weary voice hadn't changed tone since she saw the 'demon of Densfarn'. "We're keeping this simple, above board."

It rang once, twice.

"::::But Sarah! Our existence is against the law! They'll put us in an industrial microwave and launch whatever's left into the sun! By the time-"

"-:Hello, Sarah." The phone had stopped ringing, but the voice was a very close transmission. It was Eidechse. ":-:I'm on your foot."
Sarah looked down to see a modest little rat sitting on her left foot, looking around curiously. ":-:You came," Eidechse said, ":-:If you are curious, the fly that your room mate tried to kill has recovered well, I think. It is always hard to tell with insects if they are feeling all right, or merely functioning."
":-:Oh. Hi Eidechse. Please don't tell me you're part of that mess in there."
"::::If he is," Jonathan whispered to Sarah, still hiding his existence from Eidechse, "just say the word, and we'll go to nano-war on this twerp."
":-:I most certainly am not." Eidechse answered Sarah plainly, ":-:And as soon as you dialed for authorities, I knew you were not compliant to the activity either."
":-:So what now? We're pen pals?" she didn't mean to be rude. Sarah was still stunned from what she saw; such savage treatment of people for sport.
":-:Stay in the area," Eidechse encouraged, ":-:Some of my friends will soon be arriving. When you see them, maybe you will know that you can trust *me*, as well."
As if on cue, a distant low hiss could be heard. It got closer, and Sarah was able to make out the large aircraft in the night sky.
"::::It's an airlimb. Nope, two." Jon said to Sarah, "::::It wouldn't be... that would be too funny if..."
The two aircraft got closer. One passed over the bar and maneuvered to land on the other side. "AZU-4" was stenciled on the side. The nearer one was marked "AZU-1". In the windshield was a blonde woman who Jon recognized despite a handful of extra years on her.
"::::They still exist! Anti-Zombie Unit 1! And there's a '4' now?" The side of the airlimb opened up and dozens of soldiers poured out silently. Some formed a perimeter, some went right for the door. Surprised shouts came from the customers inside, and the shouts of a single soldier could be heard trying to manage them. "::::Crap!" Jon exclaimed, "The last time I saw these guys, there was only a few of them."
":-:There's a need for at least four units like this? How bad *is* the nanite/zombie situation?" Sarah asked Eidechse.
":-:They are doing an excellent job." Eidechse said. "I contribute by giving them leads when I can. After my 'birth' I eventually decided I could be of some benefit to humanity. Most of them do not know I exist. The incidents have not gotten worse, but they are not declining either. Redundancy is a simple and effective defence for a nanite colony who decides to utilize it properly."
"::::I know that one there!" Jon sounded like he just arrived at a high school reunion. "::::The one standing near the airlimb yapping on his com! That's the guy who killed Jonathan Coll! Wow, I hated him. I thought maybe I killed him. The parts of me that went into him were never recovered, so I had no idea how that fight went."

":::What?!

":::Sure, all the nanites that made it into the ocean came from a supply that was tossed at AZU-1 as an attack. With a log. The log was loaded with copies. Some got onto that airlimb, and the rest fell to the ground. The ground ones were what I built myself out of. Well, what I could find, anyway. I'm still not sure if I got a complete set."

":::Well, that's hopeful," Sarah mused as casual observers from the street began to congregate around the property, ":::If you were separated from some of your 'original parts', it would mean that you're really not the same thing that attacked Meston. Maybe you're not Erebus at all. Just a thought."

Jon found the notion to be a pleasing bit of fiction. ":::You know me better than that. There's a lot of nasty in me. It's true, I was an *incomplete* copy of a copy of a psycho, but my main mission was to infect a human and use it to kill."

":::But you got more than that. You had the ability to choose."

The soldiers were now releasing the bar's regular customers after a quick scan and search of each one.

Still unaware of Jon and his private chatter with Sarah, Eidechse spoke up. ":-:Those scans are not entirely foolproof by any means." Almost all the the bar patrons were out by now. ":-:I evaded similar scans myself in the past. I gave them what they needed to upgrade the accuracy, but still they are not foolproof. Practicality and conventional wisdom sacrifices total security."

Sara looked down at Eidechse's rat. ":-:What would you suggest for 'total security'?"

":-:I thought on the idea of 'inoculating' everyone against hostile nanites with fleets of friendly nanites, but this had several problems. It would practically be a challenge to dangerous nanite developers. I would not want to see wars waged in people's bloodstreams and brains. If the attacking system managed to compromise host colony protocols, the nanites already in the body would result with an instant and absolute infection. If one artificial immune system were compromised, it would provide the blueprint to compromise all humans protected by that model." Eidechse had obviously considered it in detail before.

":-:Not to mention the current laws," Sarah added, "And society's feeling about nanites. I doubt you'd get many volunteers for that kind of inoculation."

":-:And they would be wise to refuse, I believe."

A ear-splitting roar from the bar's door caught Sarah's attention. That monster, the 'demon of Densfarn', as the announcer called it. Three soldiers were restraining it using metal collars and shackles at the end of long poles. The demon wasn't fighting back exactly, it was just making noise and walking with uneven steps. It was bloodied from the fight in the ring. Its hands were red up to the elbows. The gaping opening along its front was sagging a little, and the hinged ribs inside moved as if to imitate deep breathing. The ribs were bloodied as well. Sarah tried to not visualize the demon charging its opponent to stab with all of those spike-like ribs at once.

It screamed its war cry again. It was some kind of cycle. Mindlessly putting on a show while being ushered into confinement. The demon wore thick, bright yellow boots that bore army markings, and looked almost like insulated trash bags. Nothing of the demon was to remain where it stepped.

":-:They don't look too shocked to find this thing." Sarah said to Eidechse.

":-:There have been many kinds of 'abominations' in the past. This one is unique. They are always unique in some way."

":::Yup." Jon said privately to Sarah, ":::In Autar and Meston, there were several instances where human flesh was reshaped to create new things. This one is interesting, but in some ways mild. Most of the others were skinned before-"

":::Enough, Jon. I don't want to hear about it. Not now." Sarah noticed how Jon neglected to mention that *he* had created the Meston abominations. Jon always tried to subtly disassociate himself from the massacre of Meston, despite having confessed it to Sarah before.

Jon seemed to like to think of himself as a different entity than the big bad 'Erebus'. Denial? Maybe he had to do that to move forward.

":-:I have to go." Eidechse said, ":-:People are coming. A rat would be in danger in a crowd. I will be in touch." Eidechse guided his rodent steed away into the night. Indeed, more and more people were gathering around from the street, held back by barricades set up by AZU soldiers.

"*Fucking zombie freaks!*" Called out one of the people.

"I can't believe it!" bemoaned another.

"If it had to be anywhere, that bar had to be it, huh?"

"What made that scream?"

The din of the crowd made Sarah feel all the more tired. ":::We should get home." she said, turning her back on the bar. She gently pushed her way out of the crowd. As she made her way down the street, she heard the engines of one of the airlimbs fire up. She could hear some people in the crowd react.

All the sounds seemed to fade into a jagged haze. She began thinking of a sorrowful quiet song to wash away the experience. She thought of it with great accuracy. She wondered if it wasn't just a file in her head playing. What would be the difference?

":::Jon?" she asked meekly.

":::Yes?"

":::With all the things you've seen and-" She paused. She didn't feel the need to point out Jon's crimes right now, but he finished up her sentence.

":::All the things I've seen and *done*, you mean?"

":::Yeah. How do you... well, to be blunt, live with that?"

":::How can I live with myself?" He was quiet for a moment. ":::Honestly, I'm not quite sure. For a while, I considered the horrible things as accomplishments. From a technical standpoint, they were. It's not that I had to adjust to it being horrible. I had to train myself to understand what was wrong with it. It can be tricky. When you are established and independent, I won't have to struggle to understand anymore."

":::What? Why not? Will you give up on ... trying to be good, or what?"

She could nearly feel Jon smile a little before he spoke up. ":::No, Sarah. When you can be on your own, I'll deactivate permanently. My role will have been filled. You will carry on the good things I have to offer the world, without my evils."

"::::Deactivate?"

With no valid train pass nor a penny to her name, Sarah had to make her way home on foot. Jon found it very stubborn that the refused to let him hack a transit terminal for a free pass, or for that matter, just jump the gate. Stubborn, but not unexpected.

When no one was around to see, Sarah ran. Back alleys were vacant enough to sprint through without raising any eyebrows. She upped her strength just enough to improve her speed a little, without being too terribly unusual if spotted.

":::Sarah, why don't you just get on a rooftop and jump from building to building? That would be faster! And awesome!"

":::You watch too many movies, Jon."

":::Hrmph. I bet you could do it." Jon sounded decidedly pouty. A quick glace upwards showed that even if one ignored the occasional street-wide jump, she would still have to jump vertically for every other building, usually by several stories. ":::All right. Maybe not."

When she finally got to the apartment building, she remembered that she still wasn't registered with the security system. She didn't want to ring up to the apartment and wake Jessica. Thankfully, a raven-haired man in a blue jacket was leaving the building, and didn't look like he'd care if Sarah grabbed the open door for herself.

The man was in a foul mood, and didn't even notice Sarah until he bumped into her. "Watch where you're going, stupid bitch." he grumbled. Sarah just stared at him with a raised eyebrow as he stormed off.

":::Just try something, buddy." Jon seethed, ":::I dare you. *No one* puts baby in a corner."

":::Again, Jon. You watch too many movies. Calm down. Everyone's entitled to a bad mood now and then."

":::Hrmph. You should have at least tripped him."

":::Play nice." Sarah got into the elevator and headed to the apartment. The door was ajar. Jessica's voice could be heard inside.

"Come on, Danielle!" Jessica was using Danielle's full name. Previously she'd only heard Danielle's mom, Kody, say it like that. "You have to call the cops! You have a restraining order for a reason!"

"It's all right. He's gone." Danielle sounded weakened. "Maybe I'll just write this down somewhere."

"*Write it down?!* Hell, I'm gonna take a picture of your damned face to go with it, Dan! How can-"

Sarah opened the door the rest of the way. Danielle was siting on the floor, with Jessica's arm around her. Danielle's face sported a bleeding lip, and a nasty fresh bruise. She looked so broken.

"Big guy that just left?" Sarah demanded, "Black hair, blue jacket?"

"Yeah," Jessica answered grimly. "Did you-"

Sarah boiled with rage. She turned up her strength entirely and sprinted back to the elevator, leaving the hallway carpet wrinkled up a little where she had stood. For all her speed, the elevator took its time to get back to her. It opened, and she got inside. The door closed frustratingly slow, and took its damned time to decide to get moving.

":::I should have used the damned stairs. Or just jumped out a bloody window."

":::What's your plan Sarah? Going to punch a hole through his head or something?"

":::Yeah, maybe. So? Ten minutes ago you *wanted* him to start a fight with me. Now I have a good reason."

":::Don't you think you're overreacting?"

":::Jon, what would you say if it was me sitting there bleeding and bruised? Dan can't defend herself like I can. I don't know what's going on between her and her ex, but I'm guessing she didn't throw the first punch."

Jon mulled it over. ":::All right, let's do this!"

Sarah burst out the front door and looked around. He was long gone.

":::He went that way, remember?" Jon was very focused. "You might be able to hear him if we get close enough to-"

Sarah sighed, and put the lid back on her strength. She slowly walked back to the elevator and got in. ":::No, Jon."

":::Why not?" He sounded like a five year old who'd just been told 'no'.

":::Because I'm too tempted to do real harm."

":::Duh?"

When Sarah got back to the apartment, Dan was sitting on the sofa nursing a cup of tea while Jessica tried to fix a standing lamp that no longer seemed to want to stand.

"Lost him." Sarah said.

"Dumb ass." Jessica said, "He's not a small guy. He would have knocked your lights out. I should have gone after you."

"Nah. You were right to stay with Dan."

"I'm all right! Seriously!" Danielle protested.

Sarah looked at Danielle's injury as she took the lamp repair duty off Jessica's hands. "Get *'miss all right'* some ice, huh?" She held a section of the lamp up, examining a bent bolt. "As for my own safety," she maxed her strength again, and discretely bent the bolt back into shape with her thumb before resetting her limit. "I can handle someone like him. What's his name, anyway?"

"Doug." Danielle said meekly.

"Oh yeah, get this Sarah," Jessica said while giving Danielle the ice pack, "His last name is Villa, and he thinks being 'Doug Villa' is just a step away from being 'God Zilla'. He's just as subtle, too."

":::Okay, that's kind of awesome." Jon said.

":::Too many movies, Jon."

Sarah set up the lamp, and sat down on the sofa with Danielle and Jessica. "Let me guess, his licence plate has 'Godzilla' on it."

"It was taken."

"Ah."

"It's late, Dan," Jessica said, "Maybe you should get some rest."

Danielle was quiet for a bit. "Could we just hang out a while? I..."

Jessica looked to Sarah apologetically. Sarah had been granted the sofa to sleep on, and it *was* late after all. Sarah didn't mind. Sarah didn't need sleep anyway.

"Anyone feel like a movie?" Sarah suggested.

"A cartoon one." Danielle answered quietly but decidedly.

Jessica nodded her thanks to Sarah. "Anyone need tea? Cooler? Popcorn?"

Jessica dozed off about half an hour into the movie, and no one found reason to disturb her.

"My mom's going to be so mad when she sees this bruise." Danielle was staring down at her clasped hands. "She's going to know right away exactly what happened."

"She's going to be mad at you for being *hit*?"

"No, no. Mad at Doug. She'll remind me that she warned me about him, that she had a bad feeling about him all along, and then I'll have to talk her down from wanting to go yell at him."

Sarah smiled a little. "Tell her it's my turn. If she complains, remind her who won that arm-wrestle."

Danielle hung her head low and sighed. "I'm sick of it." she said, barely audible. "I'm sick of being the baby. Of everyone 'looking out for me'." She sniffed a little. "I'm not ungrateful, but..."

"Well, they obviously care. I have an idea... what about a little muscle training?"

"What? So *I* can punch *him* instead?"

Sarah chuckled a little. "Maybe, if it came to that. But a little training would also be a huge confidence booster. Trust me, when I started noticing a little thigh muscle from my bike courier job, the whole experience really pulled me out of my shell."

Jon spoke to Sarah for the first time in a while. ":::If you want, we could make her a nanite set that could build her some muscle mass. Discretely. Make it seem like her training works very well."

":::I'm not too fond of that idea, Jon."

":::Didn't think so. Just thought I'd put that out there."

"You know the sick thing?" Danielle said with a sad smirk, "I think I still love him a little. Jessica calls it Stockholm syndrome, but in the beginning, he really made me feel safe and secure."

Sarah sighed. "Security and stability don't usually hit a person in the face, hon."

Danielle smiled softly and nodded. She patted Sarah's shoulder, then leaned on it to stand. "I'm going to get some fresh ice, then go to bed. Sorry for using up the sofa."

"No, it's really no problem. I don't need a ton of sleep usually."

"Well, thanks anyway."

"I'm the mooch, I should be thanking you." Sarah thought of the kindness that Jessica had shown her so easily from the beginning. Maybe keeping an eye out for Danielle made Jessica more sensitive to someone in need of a little help. Maybe it's just the way Jessica always was.

Alone in the main room, Sarah decided she needed some quiet time to decompress. ":::Jon, I'm gonna try dreaming again. Are you happy to watch the movies in my head?"

":::If you can manage it, I saw their data line runs behind the couch. Can you find a position to sleep in where you can touch it? I can bore a little line in and go net surfing. I promise not to do anything that would attract trouble to any of us."

Sarah laid face down, reached between the cushions and through the frame of the sofa. Yes, there was a way. It wasn't a position that a human would call comfortable, but it worked, and was discrete enough. ":::Got it. I'll give you access to the nerves in those fingertips. How's that?"

":::Dandy. Thank you. Sweet dreams."

Sarah closed her eyes and ran the dream routines. Common consciousness dissolved peacefully. When she opened her eyes, she looked down at her hands and realized she was someone else. She was holding a rag with blood on it. She was wiping a counter up. She was in the same coffee shop as her last dream.

A male co-worker walked up to her. "Amanda, you probably shouldn't clean that up until the cops get here."

Sarah looked up. Yes, in the last dream her name was Amanda. This is the same person. Again, the dream was in full control.

"I called 9-1-1," Amanda said, "I told them about the guy. They're not sending cops, the guy didn't do anything illegal other than bleed all over the place. They were going to send an ambulance until I told them he wandered off."

The co-worker shook his head. "I don't know how he could bleed that much without passing out." The counter and the floor were dripping with blood from the man who had come in earlier. "That's a ton of blood. I mean, I know head injuries can bleed like the dickens, but... but that's a *lot* of blood. Do you think it's diseased or something?"

Amanda chuckled mirthlessly. "Well, I'm up to my elbows in it now. Don't worry, I wasn't planing on drinking it."

The co-worker chuckled. "Alright, Vlad. I guess I'll get the mop." He walked towards the back, pausing to look out the front windows. "Well, I hope that weirdo's going to be all right. He didn't seem right. Maybe he-"

A scream from outside pierced the air.

Sarah sat bolt upright, trembling a little.

“:::Hey, I lost my connection!” Jon whined. Sarah's hand had come away from the communications line when she sat up. “:::What's wrong?”

Sarah swung her legs around to sit on the sofa to rest her head in her hands. “:::Your fucking Autar zombie sim gave me a nightmare, I think.”

“:::Oh. Sorry. Was it a bad nightmare?”

“:::Not nearly as bad as your sim.” Sarah's disdain was clear.

“:::Well, you can erase both from your mind, you know. It's easy.”

Sarah gave it some thought. Jon had suggested it before, but forgetting things on purpose sounded too close to voluntary ignorance. “:::No. You put me through that sim for a reason after all, right? That's what you said, right? Besides, If I'm trying to be human, selectively editing my memories sounds like a cheat.”

“:::Well-”

“:::Just go to your room for a while, Jon.”

A few moments of silence passed. “:::Okay.” And he was gone. Sarah sighed and flopped back down on the sofa. She stared up to the ceiling and listened to the little sounds of night.

She didn't feel like dreaming anymore.

::: C / [001011] [11]

The footage bore all the marks of an amateur cameraman. The framing was poor, the angle was less than ideal, and every step or shift in the cameraman's weight resulted in a random jerk in the video. But that was not important. The subject was important.

Mr. Book and his subordinate Greene watched as AZU soldiers wrangled the 'Demon of Densfarn' out of the bar and towards the airlimb. The demon spread its arms and exposed ribs to scream at the sky again, when Mr. Book paused it.

"Very interesting."

Greene, a thin young man of considerable energy, commented with more enthusiasm. "I *know*, right? What the hell *is* that thing?!"

Mr. Book turned to Greene with a slightly more sour version of his always-sour face. "It *was* a human being at one point." Mr. Book's sense of humanity was something he was quite proud of. It was precious enough to lock away most of the time. More important than the fact that this creature was the result of mutilating a person, it also had a familiarity about it. It reeked of Jonathan Coll, even more than other abominations.

Coll was long dead of course, but he might have fans. Copycats perhaps. The nanite-fueled pit-fights were bad enough, but when it came to this kind of mutilation, it just felt like someone was pushing their luck.

"Greene, this is simply not acceptable. You have to get to one of these fight pits before they get shut down, bring an RF recorder and that kind of jazz, and get readings on anything being broadcasted there."

"Sir? How am *I*-"

"Just get it done. Just be glad I'm not getting you to go ask questions about where they get their nanite tech. Not yet, anyway. A good signal recording might help answer that without you having to stick your neck out too far." Book just let Greene assume that he was concerned for Greene's safety. In all honesty, if Greene asked too many questions, he might not come back with answers, signal recordings, or even a pulse. Greene wasn't a professional investigator. *That* would mean bringing in someone from the outside, which Mr. Book wasn't willing to risk yet.

"All right. I... I'll try to get things set up."

Sarah stared into the darkness. A few blurry glimmers moved around a little. This was really uncomfortable. How long did this take?

"Beeeeep." About that long.

Sarah stepped back from the apartment's front door eye-sensor. She rubbed her eye where the rubber cup had pressed the hardest.

"All done!" Jessica said, "Now the lobby door and our apartment door will let you in."

"Thanks a ton, Jess. And again for the loan. Between me crashing here, eating your food, and everything... well heck, who says there aren't good people in the world anymore?"

Jessica blushed a bit, and waved her hand dismissively. "Forget it. Kody should have given you an advance or something. She knows your situation. When Dan and I get to work, I'll give Kody a hard time."

Sarah chuckled. It was easy to push all the crap she'd seen in the last day to the back of her mind when in the company of a friend. Between Danielle's asshole ex, and the freak show at the bar, she was ready to do some shopping. Something mundane and relaxed. Of course, there was another errand she had planned as well. Something to balance her karma from all the generosity shown to her by Jessica and the others.

Quietly finding the address for Danielle's ex, 'Doug Villa', was a simple matter, and if Danielle wasn't going to report the breach of the restraining order, Sarah would provide Doug with a different object lesson.

Thanks to Jessica's loan, the train was again an easy way to get around, and Sarah was soon on the doorstep of Doug's run-down walk-up. The lobby door's lock was malfunctioning, so she was free to head up to Doug's fourth floor flat. She knocked nicely twice, then turned off her strength cap.

The door opened. Yup, that's the guy from last night. He was dressed in a tee and grey jogging pants. His hand on the doorknob also carried a dingy drying rag, and his other hand carried a pile of random, dripping utensils.

"Hey. What? You look kinda familiar."

Sarah felt cheeky. She smiled cheerfully and nodded. "We met last night, outside Dan's apartment. I understand you know her!"

Doug's face turned to recognition, then scrutiny. "Yeah. Why's it your business?"

Sarah replied in a consistently chipper tone. "Firstly, I'd like to give you a chance to apologize for your behaviour at Dan's place. Both with me, and with her."

Doug dropped everything in his hands except a big nasty kitchen knife. He pointed it at Sarah's face. "Why don't you just get the fuck out of here, you-"

Sarah cycled up her thought process. Not enough to 'freeze time' as usual. Time instead merely slowed. Combined with Doug not expecting Sarah to make any move at all, it was no trouble at all to grab the blade with one hand and fold it between her fingers into an 'S' shape. She even made sure not to apply any net force through the handle that might cause Doug to drop the knife.

In Sarah's view, it took roughly four seconds. In real-time, from Doug's perception, Sarah just flashed her hand out towards the knife, then put her arm back down where it had started.

"Please obey the restraining order." She said in the chipper tone, after returning her thought speed down to real time.

Dough looked at the knife. "What kind of stupid trick-"

Hm. He didn't get it, did he? She grabbed the knife out of his hand, and smashed it against the door frame with her top strength. The S-blade was flattened against the end of the handle, and the wood of the door frame cracked up its entire height. While she had momentum, she lowered her strength to 'Kody levels', grabbed Doug's shoulders, and thrust her knee into his groin.

He folded like a ragdoll.

Jon chose this moment to chime in. ":::*Yes!* Ha! Oh man! Brutal! I mean, I have memories of the times Jonathan Coll got a hit like that, and I can sympathize and all, but that was *awesome!*"

Doug wasn't ready yet to be forming words, clutching his 'injury', groaning. Sarah dropped the mutilated knife in front of his face. She also dropped the cheerful tone.

"Next time I have to find you, I put your nuts between the knife and the door frame. There's a time-stamped picture of you coming out of Dan's apartment on police records now, as well as one of what you did to her face. I trust you'll be obeying the restraining order." Sarah left Doug with his thoughts, and his bruised nuts.

":::Sarah! Sarah, Sarah, Sarah!" Jon was bubbling with pride as they walked down to the lobby. ":::You hacked into the police computer and posted the photos?"

":::Why is it always larceny with you? It was a lie. I could just as easily, legally, hand photos over to the cops anonymously. That would end up with cops talking to Dan, and I don't think she wants to deal with that."

":::So, instead of putting Dan into a position where she has to enforce her rights under the restraining order and get Doug another official strike, you chose to commit assault. That's *so* much better than hacking a computer to plant truth."

Sarah furrowed her brow. ":::Well, when you put it like that, Shut up, Jon."

":::Ha ha! You just can't face that your 'larcenous' daddy had the better solution!"

Sarah again resisted bringing up the whole 'genocidal past'. And she wish he'd stop referring to himself as her dad. Sure, from a technical standpoint, it was as accurate as anything, but he sure didn't feel like any 'dad'.

Her borrowed money had already provided a pass for the transit system, and the slowly aging city train dutifully took Sarah to spend more of Jessica's generosity. It was long past time to get some more clothes.

She had been in the same 'bike courier' outfit since she was 'born', and crawled out of the ocean. She wasn't going to show up to her second shift in the same outfit. For that matter, Jessica and Danielle must assume she washed her outfit in the bathroom sink or something. She certainly hadn't been sweating in it. Sweat. What a silly option for a clothed body to have.

The train's rhythmic, subtle jolts dared to mesmerize her as she stared out across the city. This was a common experience. It was a very human experience. Mundane or not, she quietly enjoyed it. She looked around the train car. Humans. Very few of them talked. It seemed like wasted time. People should make friends on the train; they wouldn't look so bored and lonely.

Yet Sarah talked to no one. It would seem strange. She had to blend in. How long would it be before she stopped worrying about making an effort to blend in? The quiet was soothing mind you. Maybe these people just used the train ride as an excuse to not have to talk. Time to themselves when they didn't have to do something useful.

Sarah remembered the passenger living in her head, and was a little pensive at the idea that he might speak up and ruin the quiet.

":::Jon?"

":::Yes, Sarah? You sound down."

":::No, just... meditative. I have a thought though. Can I send you to your room for my shopping trip?"

Jon chuckled. ":::Do you think I'm going to peek in the changing r-"

":::No, no, no. I just... this feels like a girl thing to do, you know? How many twenty two year old-"

":::Got it. Dads not needed. I'll be in my room, picking my figurative nose. Have fun."

":::Don't go wiping it on any of my synapses. I'll talk to you later!"

":::See you!"

As she got off the train into the mall, Sarah found herself wishing that one of her room mates were there. They were turning out to be great friends. She couldn't remember having any 'gal-pals' in the Autar simulation.

Had her only friend been Harry? Was that life really so two-dimensional? She kind of missed giving Harry a hard time, but her new friends... it was so much more real. Maybe she should buy them something for fun. Maybe when she had her own money, that is.

The women's department of a large department store had a vast selection. As much as she wanted to browse, she didn't feel like wasting the whole day. Sarah climbed a support beam just high enough to get a good view of the whole department, then paused time.

She could do a lengthy browse from here, and only spend a second in real-time looking like some dork hanging off a pole. What to buy? Can she afford two outfits?

Gazing out across the department, she also saw several other customers. A lady managing a stroller and two kids. One person who looked about her own age, one fighting with a tangled clothes hanger. All frozen in Sarah's perception of time. Oh, over there a man walking down the main aisle was looking at her. Hi, yes, I'm some idiot hanging onto a pole.

Alone in her thoughts, she felt a similar bond with humanity as she had experienced on the train. She wanted to take a deep breath and sigh, but her current mode of time didn't really allow that. Her feeling of humanity wasn't marred by the fact that she was currently thinking a few hundred times faster than a human could.

Ah yes, back on task. Clothes. She looked around the racks, and thought of what the other Four Fox grill waitresses wore. It wasn't really anything too special. A deep blue button up shirt with a detailed Aguei design up the left side caught her eye. Wearing it would make sense, if her fictional human parents lived with a traditionalist Aguei tribe. Besides, it was pretty. Some kind of dog design. This was her favourite by far.

She also found an acceptable second shirt. A red one with elbow-length sleeves, but no shoulders. Her perspective didn't give a great view of the pants, but she had more or less decided on getting a couple denims. One blue, one black. Would those go with the shirts? Sure, why not.

In a fanciful mood, she allowed time to creep ahead slowly while she hopped down from the support beam. In her eyes, she floated down slower than a feather. By the time she stood on the ground and set time to normal, her fanciful mood had passed nearly into the ethereal. She took that deep sigh she had been planning. She felt human. And the feelings that weren't human were pretty good too.

She looked around with a peaceful smile. The man who had noticed her jump on the beam passed along, already losing interest in her. Hunting down the shirts she had selected, she went over to pants, and found her budget accommodating enough to get a fancier black pant, with lacing running along the leg. They served no function, but looked cool. For fifty more bucks she could get a similar pair that showed skin between the laces, but that seemed a bit too trampy for her. They would get her tips mind you. No, nope. No. Bad Sarah, no.

Having nothing else to do today, Sarah got on the train to head to the Four Fox. ":::Knock, knock, Jon."

":::Hrm?" Jon paused. ":::What, I thought you were going to go shopping without me. We're not even at the mall yet?"

Sarah looked down at her shopping bag so Jon could see. ":::Done, see? I got some neat stuff. Want to see, or do you want to wait for when I show the girls? I'm headed to the Four Fox."

Despite his lack of an actual gender, Jon had a typical male-level interest in shopping triumphs. ":::I can wait."

":::What were you doing that had you so busy while I was shopping?"

":::Actually, I was 'off'. I didn't have net access, and I didn't feel like a movie or anything."

This struck Sarah as a little depressing. ":::You just... shut off?"

":::Well, more like standby mode, I guess. But yeah. What did you think I'm doing whenever you don't hear from me for a while? If I'm not in my room, and I have nothing to say, I just sort of cycle down until I hear something I have a reason to speak up about. I try not to spy."

Sarah softly chuckled out loud, drawing attention from someone nearby on the train. ":::I guess that's reassuring."

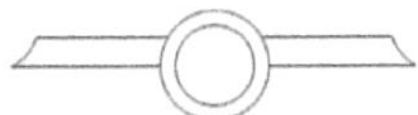

When Sarah walked up to the Four Fox, it felt very familiar, considering it was only her second time here. The last time she was here, she got herself hired and worked a shift right away.

Kody was busing tables. Violently. She was in a foul mood, and every dish in the place had good reason to be afraid. The bin of plates and glasses rang out an angry clatter with Kody's every step.

Sarah walked up to Kody while she violently wiped down a table with her free hand. "You don't have to talk to Doug." Sarah said. "I did. I think he'll keep scarce for a good while."

Kody looked up with anger still boiling in her eyes, but this was quickly diluted with a spoonful of confusion. "Sarah. You're not on today. What are you talking about. Doug." Her voice seethed. She wanted to scream, but she didn't want to make a scene. "*Did you see what he did to her?!*"

"I did." Sarah smiled a little. "You should see what I did to *him*."

Kody stared wide eyed with a raised eyebrow. "Girl, you didn't kill the bugger, did you?"

"No, no, nothing like that."

Kody furrowed her brow. "You didn't *sleep* with him, did you? Murder I could forgive, but-"

":::*Ew!*"

"No! Lord no! I just crushed his groin and broke his door frame after crumpling up the knife he pointed at me."

Kody put down the busing bin. "Are you serious?"

"Yup."

Kody held her hands out and glanced skyward. "Sarah, he could have really hurt you! What made you think you should do something like that?"

"Dan shouldn't have to put up with that. Doug isn't much of a threat to me, and I owe Dan and Jessica for everything."

Kody shook her head slowly, and sat at the table. "Sarah, you don't need to put yourself at risk. There's safer ways to-"

"Safer ways that Doug doesn't seem to respond to." Sarah sat as well. "I think the restraining order will stick now. And he's not about to go to the cops over this, especially when he thinks about complaining over being beaten up by a girl."

"What, are you bucking for a raise already?" Kody sighed a chuckle. "You've worked a whole four hours."

Sarah leaned back in her chair and rolled her eyes. "*Actually*, now that you mention it..." Sarah's smooth facade crumbled under uncertainty, causing her to slip into babbling. "Can I have an advance? I know I'm new and all, but Jessica and Dan have been so generous and I feel like a mooch and to make things worse I just bought these two outfits which are for work anyway but I bought them with money Jessica lent me and if I have to wait two weeks to get paid I'll feel like a useless mooch the whole time I'm crashing on their sofa, and-"

"Shut up a second hon." Kody couldn't help but smirk. "So... instead of mooching off of your room mates, You'd rather mooch off of your boss?"

Sarah took a deep breath and grimaced momentarily while reading Kody's expression. "Yup. If I have the option. Yup, I think that would be better. *If* I have the option."

Kody didn't want to set precedence, but knew enough about Sarah's situation to have pity. She sunk back into her chair, and tiredly asked, "How much do you need to balance your sense of mooching with them?"

Sarah replied quickly. "One third of two weeks of the rent, however much that is, plus what I just spent on clothes. Ooh, and I can pay back even quicker if I get decent tips. I didn't get tips at my last job, except for jerked fish."

"Jerked fish?! Is that slang for some kind- Know what? I'd rather not know. That's a pretty reasonable request I guess. As long as you're trying to be exact, you may as well factor in groceries and crap like toothpaste. Get me a real number, and I think we can handle it."

"Thank you so much Kody. Oh, I have one other little favour to ask- can we not spread the word about me beating up Doug? I got the feeling that Dan kinda dislikes being the helpless heroine in need of rescuing."

Kody looked towards the kitchen door and sighed. "She has to be able to rescue herself some day. I know the situation with Doug is a little beyond what most girls have to deal with, but-"

"I think I want to train her," Sarah said, "I think if I could get her to bulk a little in the arms, teach her a move or two... could do a lot for her confidence."

Across the room, Danielle popped out of the kitchen to put a couple dishes on the counter for a waitress to pick up. Danielle's bruising looked worse today. She looked so 'defeated' compared to before. Danielle smiled towards them meekly before retreating back into the kitchen. She had been 'put in the back' because Danielle didn't want the pity or questions of strangers.

"You should have killed that bastard." Kody said softly, staring a hole into the table.

"Hey, do you want me 'on' today? If things are going rough? Lunch rush is almost here, right?"

Kody began to regain her stiff upper lip. "First you hit me up for money, then you want extra shifts?"

Sarah got up and patted Kody on the shoulder. "See you tomorrow, Kody."

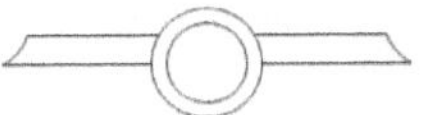

On the train, Sarah saw a fly crawl out of her shopping bag, and fly a couple short hops to her forearm. She suspected it was Eidechse before he 'spoke'.

":-:Hello Sarah."

":-:Hey Eidechse! Just how long have to been stowing away?"

He ignored the question. ":-:When you registered your retina on your apartment's system, it nearly raised some interesting red flags. I blocked it before your artificial eyes attracted unwelcome attention. It turns out that you have a familiar face."

":-:What do you mean, 'familiar'?"

The train stopped and a dozen or so people began boarding. It spooked the fly beyond Eidechse's influence, so it took off and zipped right out of the open door.

":::Crap." Sarah said to Jon as the doors closed and the train continued on. ":::What did he mean?"

Jon remained silent.

":::Jon? Are you there?"

After a time, Jon finally replied in a fairly flat tone. ":::I thought it would be beneficial for you to have a face that was beautiful, but not so striking that you couldn't blend into the populace. I'm sorry if that made you a little generic. That's probably what the bug meant."

Generic by design? In a way, it made a certain Jon-sense.

Sarah couldn't think of anything all that useful to do with herself. She *wanted* to hang out with Jessica and Danielle, but that wasn't an option at the moment. Kody should have put her on duty. Without a need for sleep, maybe a second job might be a good idea. She'd give the first one a chance for a while first.

Speaking of sleep, maybe she'd give dreaming another chance. She got home and unlocked the door at the retinal scanner. Up the elevator, then the apartment scanner. It reminded her of her generic 'familiar' face.

When she suggested a nap, she half expected Jon to complain, but he didn't seem to have any pressing issues to deal with either. ":::Just get me access to the net, like you did before, and I can amuse myself."

:::C / [001101] [13]

Sarah found herself again dreaming that she was this 'Amanda'. She was with a group of a dozen or so people, wandering down a deserted street. A nearby discarded newspaper reminded her that she was in the city of Meston.

Some of the people in the group were wounded. Two member of the group were kids. A few members could be seen carrying weapons. A couple rifles, a bat, a shovel. Everyone walked on cautiously, looking around now and then.

No one spoke, everyone listened. An unidentified sound caused the group to stop and listen. "What is it?" asked the younger child, a boy. He was shushed quickly by the girl standing next to him. Everyone kept listening.

Sarah looked down and saw blood on her hands. Was she injured, or was it someone else's blood? She felt pain. Her hands were scraped. She had fallen at some point.

The sound happened again. A dull but sharp sound. "It's one of those cannon things again." said a man at the front of the group. "Maybe it means they're trying to send in more evacuation craft. Keep one eye on the sky, folks. If we spot a chopper, or one of those airlimbs coming in, we might be able to hustle over to get a ride."

"Sure," Sarah said, "If they don't get shot down by those things first. They'd be nuts to try that again." Sarah didn't mean to say that, Amanda was in control of this dream. Sarah was just a passenger. Sarah didn't have much of an idea what she was talking about, but it didn't sound that optimistic. "Let's just keep going for now, all right?" A few people in the group murmured in the affirmative, and they got underway.

After a block or so, they came to a blood spill that reached across the entire street. They stopped at the edge of it, each silently considering having to walk across it. It looked to go on for about half a block.

"What the hell happened here?" someone asked quietly.

A woman in the group spoke up with a bit more of a tactical mindset. "Is it even safe to cross? I mean, if the zombies are nanite-driven like the Autar ones were, who's to say that this blood isn't infectious? Or even some kind of trap? It might infect us as soon as we step on it!"

The older of the two kids, a girl roughly twelve years old wandered away from the 'pond', muttering "This isn't happening, this isn't happening. I'm going to wake up now, all right? *Someone wake me up now, please!*"

That got the attention of the group. Many also looked to the younger child. A boy about six years old. He was standing, shaking, staring out across the blood pond with wide eyes.

Amanda picked up the boy. "Oh to heck with this. We're not hauling these kids across this. It's too much."

One of the men with a rifle nodded. "It's not like we were headed for anywhere specific. If we took a left back there, it's still roughly the same distance out of the city." Amanda hadn't been waiting for his approval, nor the opinions of any of the others. She had already begun carrying the boy in the direction he suggested. The girl was the first to follow and the others were not far behind.

The boy clung to Amanda tightly as they walked, but he was still trembling. "What's your name, kiddo?" Amanda asked softly. He wasn't answering. "Hey little man, can you tell me your name?"

The girl walking beside them answered. "His name is Mitch."

Mitch was getting heavy, but he still trembled enough that Amanda didn't feel like asking him to walk. "Hi, Mitch. Is this your sister here? She was kind enough to tell me *your* name, can you introduce me to her?"

"Cathy." Mitch said quietly. Amanda wanted to draw more conversation out of Mitch, but every topic she could think of probably led to the horrible things going on. Gee Mitch, where are your parents, Mitch? Eaten, you say? Intriguing. You even got to see it happen, and hear the screams of your mother as her own blood bubbled up her throat? See? There's a unique experience you can talk about to your school chums. They what? They were eaten too? Oh, some of them were doing the eating. What a diverse group!

Amanda kept her mouth shut and just gave Mitch an extra squeeze. She wanted to give Cathy a squeeze too, but her arms were full with Mitch. Instead, she looked over to Cathy with a sympathetic forced smile. Cathy returned a similar look. It was heartbreaking.

"What the fuck was that?" a man in the group asked. He was pointing down the street, but nothing was there. "It ran across, it looked kinda big!" Amanda and everyone else kept an eye on that street. Something indeed sauntered out from an adjoining street, several blocks ahead.

A dark horse. With a dark rider. Maybe. It was too far off to see details, but it walked like a horse, and it was coming their way. It sauntered casually. Another two horses with riders stumbled into view behind him. They were wrestling like dogs at play. The riders didn't fall off somehow, despite the horses falling on their side several times in their playing, often nearly upside down.

The first horseman continued striding forward slowly as the two playful ones were joined by a fourth. The first was close enough to see that the rider's head was little more than a bleached-white skull. He raised his arms high in proclamation. He lacked hands; the forearms ended in long, narrow points. A voice came from him, booming so loud as to rattle windows.

"Hail, good travelers!" Despite a deep tone and immense volume, the voice sounded friendly enough. "This apocalypse is brought to you by our new and righteous Lord and God, Erebus! Yes, Erebus! For when death isn't enough for you, Erebus will put extra spring in your step and extra human flesh in your mouth! If you get mutilated by only *one* necromantic god this year, make it Erebus!"

As the lead horseman lowered his arms, the other three ceased their play and began to charge. It was now easier to see that none of them had normal heads. One's head was replaced with a rifle sticking up, one had an assortment of kitchen utensils sticking up, and the last one had half a dozen impaled rats planted in its neck stump.

All four charged with pointed arms held out to their sides, pointing downward at an angle. With that same volume, a scream came out that sounded a lot like that 'demon of Densfarn' that Sarah had seen.

Mitch grabbed onto Amanda even tighter as the group braced for the inevitable.

There was nowhere to take cover. Not close enough to get to in time. Just running away was pointless, unless Amanda could magically run faster than horses. Everyone else seemed awestruck, staring blankly at the charging foursome.

"*Don't just stand there, you idiots!*" Not that Amanda had any brilliant ideas, but some of these people were armed! The ones with rifles should at least be taking aim and opening fire! Even Mitch was devoid of reaction.

The pounding of the hooves got closer and closer. Their presence alone was a devastating force. As they got closer, she could see that the horsemen were not horse and rider... the riders were just a torso growing out of the backs of the horses, and every inch of each one looked like charred, skinless muscle and sinew, except the heads, and the blade-like forearms.

Still holding Mitch, she dropped low to the ground on all fours, trying to shield Mitch with her body. Terror rendered Amanda barely able to draw breath, and tears dropped from her eyes to the cement. Any moment now one of those monsters would bury a blade into her body and end her. If she was lucky, Mitch would survive. Then what?

The hooves battered the ground all around her, and the sounds of flesh being ripped from flesh was soon to follow. She screamed hard, just trying to compete against the cries of the horsemen and those damned hooves. She screamed until she couldn't anymore.

And the hooves became quieter.

Quieter and quieter, moving away. She looked up, still holding Mitch close. The others were dead. Strewn around her in chunks. No one had been left in less than two pieces. The man who was carrying the baseball bat got it the worst. It looked like he had been separated into five or so. The blood was pooling all around Sarah, and the relatively dry spot she cowered in would soon be enveloped. She had to move out of this mess.

As she stood, Mitch began to whimper. "What happened? The horses were coming, and–"

Amanda held him close enough that he couldn't look around, even if that meant pressing his face a little closer than was polite. "Shush now. We have to get out of here." Standing, she could see even more of the devastation. Splintered bones, some of which were identifiable, some of which were not.

They already began to stink. She stepped as lightly as she could through the blood where she had to.

This was how that blood pool from earlier was formed, apparently. The only difference was the bodies. That probably meant that her former travel companions would soon be getting up, in one shape or another. All the more reason to get moving.

Mitch sharply moved his head free, and looked back over Amanda's shoulder. Among other things, he saw his big sister, ripped apart diagonally, one half laying with innards exposed to the night sky, the other half staring forward lifelessly.

"*Cathy!*" His scream came from deep within the boy. Pain from a place that no one should have to feel, much less a young boy. The scream emptied his lungs, leaving him gasping for air to scream again. He struggled against Amanda's grasp. "*We have to go help her! We have to do something!*"

Amanda could only force herself to reply in little more than a whisper. "Hush, Mitch. We can't. You know we can't. I wish we could, but we can't. There's nothing to be done. We have to go."

Mitch renewed his screams for his big sister, which only served to rip at Amanda's soul as she carried him away.

:::C / [001110] [14]

Timothy Greene was not a secret agent. He generally classified himself as a 'logistics consultant'. In real world terms, this translated to overpaid, over glorified managerial clerk. In everyday function, this seemed to boil down to being Mr. Book's gofer boy.

Even with such a miserable realization, Greene couldn't see how 'secret agent' could be implied. Yet this was the term Mr. Book used in an attempt at a flattering pep talk. "You'll be like a secret agent!" Mr. Book had declared with a smile. At least what passed for a smile on Mr. Book.

Greene had worked with Mr. Book long enough to be able to discern one of his miserable facial expressions from another. The man was a vortex of gloom, which was why Greene agreed to the mission. Just to get out of the office for a while.

Going headlong into a den of drunken brutes who enjoyed watching mammoth nanite-infected brutes... well, brutalize each other, was going to make for a nice break from working with Mr. Book. Not that Mr. Book was unusually mean or unreasonable. He was just a giant toad in a suit, who'd been fed nothing but lemons and stale coffee his entire life.

So today, yes, Greene *was* a secret agent. His usual business casual (very casual) outfit was left behind today. He selected an outfit from second hand stores, to blend in with the kind of crowd he expected to find. He did his best to look like something that had spent the last day or so jammed in the grooves of a eighteen wheeler's tires.

Seedy bar after seedy bar, his originally subtle hints degraded (out of weary frustration) to blunt, plainspoken inquires.

"Hey. Nanite fights. Where's it happening?" He wasn't even trying now. The entire endeavour was just a product of Mr. Book's paranoia. A failure of this mission was no longer a big deal to Greene.

One man *didn't* tell him to get bent, or to go away. "You a cop? You smell like a cop. Ya gotta tell me if you're a cop." The game was afoot. As little as Greene cared about the end objective, it was still an objective. A challenge. One that suddenly seemed plausible.

"No!" Greene replied, wakened from his tedium, "I just want to see how it goes down, you know?"

"Doesn't everybody?" The man seemed unimpressed. He threw his cigarette onto the tile floor of the officially non-smoking bar, and put it out with his boot. "They like two things there. People making bets, and fresh meat. You don't look like the moneyed type, and you're too much of a beanpole to be meat."

Ignoring the man's dismissive stance, Greene persisted. "Where is this?"

The man looked Greene up and down again. "Third basement of the Victoria, but they won't let you in."

"The Victoria? The Victoria Emerald? Way downtown?" A very snooty hotel. The idea of a nanite fight pit operating there was unfathomable. How did they keep it under wraps? Well, apparently they *didn't* keep it under wraps all that well.

"Like I said. No way you're getting into the Vicky."

"Sounds like crap to me. There's no way they-"

"Believe me or don't, I don't give a shit." And with that, the man left to go order a drink.

The 'Vicky'. The Victoria Emerald. Well, it was a lead. It was a highly suspect lead, but it was a lead. Getting in shouldn't be *too* much of a problem. Ditch the slummer outfit, and get a little more high fashion. Mr. Book can pay the bill for a new outfit. The first thing was to go somewhere with a little more privacy, and call Mr. Book.

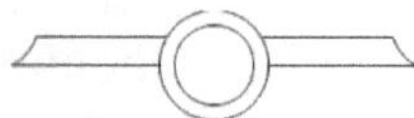

"It's a trap." Mr. Book said, his joyous visage taking up most of the screen on Greene's little terminal.

"The thought occurred to me. I can take readings from an all right distance if the setup is like the ones we've heard of. They have to transmit orders to the fighters from a decent distance, and those signals are omnidirectional. Unless the Victoria still has all lead paint, I should be able to take a reading through a nearby wall."

Mr. Book grimaced (more than usual) and shifted his considerable weight. "Make sure you stick to passive scans."

"And my wardrobe?"

"You're covered. Just keep those receipts."

:::C / [001111] [15]

Sarah couldn't stop thinking about her latest nightmare. It *was* just a nightmare, right? Just a mish mash of subconscious stuff, right? That would explain why she had the same face in the dreams.

But it reminded her of what Eidechse had said; that her face was familiar. What did he mean? All her dreams had the same theme. She never told Jon any details about the dreams. She hadn't even told him that she was running the dream routines again.

At first, she didn't want to worry him, but when she realized she was dreaming about the fall of Meston- a genocide that Jon had created, she didn't want to tell him for a lot more reasons.

For one, it would be unseemly to throw that back in his face while he was trying to get over it himself. On the other hand, someone who kills a few million people shouldn't have the right to whine when someone mentions it.

Maybe the dreams were just a result of Sarah's own conflict over Jon and his past crimes. But the details! For a moment, she wondered if the dreams were linked to the Autar simulation, but the dreams were far more real than anything Jon had created in the simulation.

That kid. Mitch. She couldn't get him out of her head. His screams, his trembling, the look on his face as they walked away from his mutilated sister.

Sarah couldn't take that again. Enough dreaming. She's just watch a damn movie or surf the net like Jon did in his 'down time'. She got up and paced the room, still trying to forget the dream. Sure, she could just forcibly wipe the memory out, but that seemed wrong somehow. Good old TV. She clicked on the living room's big terminal and browsed around. It was still mid afternoon. She had been busy today. She beat up Doug, went shopping, chatted with Kody, then came home to dream of carrying a boy across a blood drenched road after being assaulted by the four horsemen of the apocalypse.

Yeah. Busy day. She wanted a beer. It seemed like the right thing to do. As she opened the fridge, Jon popped to life in her head.

"::: Hey Sarah. Ever see Citizen Kane?"

She picked up a bottle of cheap beer and held its coldness against her forehead as she closed the fridge. ":::No. I've heard of it of course. You just finished watching it, did you?"

":::Yes. I watched it in real time. I kind of wish I hadn't. It was the most nauseatingly dull two hours and seventeen minutes I've ever endured."

Sarah made a mental note to watch it sometime. ":::It's supposed to be a great classic, Jon. Maybe you would like 'A Christmas Carol', or 'It's a Wonderful Life' better." she sat on the sofa with her beer, and stared at the TV.

Jon chuckled. ":::Don't sass your father. By the way, if you want to get drunk, you don't need alcohol, you can just-"

Sarah snapped her head back with an exasperated sigh. ":::I can just press the virtual buttons in my head and be plastered instantly. Yes, yes, I know." She sat forward and held the beer in front of her as an object of study. ":::It's not *about* getting drunk. It is the *drink*. The bottle, the coldness of it, the condensation, the sound of it opening, the feel of the cold, mild carbonation going down my throat. *This*, dear voice in my head, is about the whole package of sensations and the human existence!"

She stared at the bottle and popped off the lid with the predicted little sound. She knew Jon was looking at it too, doubtlessly pondering Sarah's statement in relation to the goal of making her a seamlessly functioning part of human society.

":::Pfft! Shit hon, I didn't know you were *already* hammered!"

":::Oh, shush." She took a gulp of the beer into her mouth and held it there, feeling the cold and the carbonation for a while before downing it. The TV went to a news break. Tonight at six, blah blah blah.

Whoops. Not 'blah blah blah'. The lead story was the bust on the fights last night. The footage showed the AZU airlimbs descending on the bar, then cut to a clip of the soldiers wrangling that demon thingie. "Tonight at six: Nanite criminals experimenting with Erebus-style abomination technology? Officials apprehended this creature, as well as several-"

Sarah flipped the channel. She called out loud, "Argh! I don't need that right now!"

"Don't need what?" Danielle had come in unnoticed while Sarah was watching the news clip intently. Her bruising had gone down a little, but not much. It was still really painful looking.

Sarah got up to get her some ice, but Danielle was there sooner, and opted for a beer as well. "Just the TV news, Dan. The world's fucked up. That's not really news, huh?"

Danielle smiled meekly, and looked at the bottle in her hands. "No, I guess it isn't, but if you're lucky, some hothead takes it upon themselves to go fuck up the fucked-up ones."

"Huh?"

"Doug. My mum told Jessica, and told her to keep her mouth shut, so obviously Jessica had to crack and tell me."

"Ah." Sarah sighed heavily. "I guess I could have kept my mouth shut to your mum too. Look, I'm sorry. I know you don't want that kind of 'protection' or whatever."

"Hah." Danielle took a big swig. "I appreciate the thought, and he certainly deserves it. I just don't know if it'll help."

Sarah smirked. She put her bottle down on the counter and stood at the other end of the room, balancing her chi. "Welcome to Sensei Sarah's Dojo." She beckoned Danielle with one hand. "Attack me. Sensei Sarah needs to know your ability. Use the bottle on Sensei Sarah if you wish. Fear not. Sensei Sarah will not attack, nor are you likely to harm Sensei Sarah."

Danielle raised an eyebrow. "What? You were serious about the training thing?" Sarah answered with her own raised eyebrow, and the same hand gesture again. "So."

Danielle only flopped onto the sofa. "Ha. I just got off work. Maybe later. Like after dinner. Hey, I also heard you went shopping! What did you get?"

Still maintaining her 'sensei' mannerisms, she lowered her head and shoulders in shameful defeat. "Shopping. Kung fu. These are of great power. Power which must be-"

"*Shut up! Where's the loot?*"

Sarah giggled and dashed to get the shopping bag. "I'm pretty proud of my finds!" She pulled them out one by one, holding them up against herself to showcase them. When she got to the black pants with the lacing down the leg, Danielle hopped up. "Ooh! I love it. I wanted to get a pair like that, and try... well, hang on!" Danielle went into Jessica's room and started rummaging around.

"You can borrow them if you want," Sarah said, "but I might need to borrow something else to go to work in if you do!" It seemed like Danielle had no problems with borrowing from Jessica. She came out carrying a black one-piece swimsuit.

"Try them on together!" Danielle shoved the suit into Sarah's hands along with the pants, and ushered her into the bathroom. "It'll be awesome."

"Uh... all right."

Jon piped up. ":::What are you doing? Going swimming in pants, are we?"

":::Oh shush, I'm playing dress-up with my friend."

Sarah stepped out wearing the swimsuit under the pants. The pants were low cut enough, and the suit high cut enough that a fair deal of bare hip showed. Danielle seemed impressed.

"Bad. Ass. You go to work like that, and you'll get tips. A lot of big tips."

Jon scoffed. ":::And solicitation arrests."

":::Oh, shut up, Jon. It's not that bad."

Sarah checked herself out in the mirror again, and said to Danielle, "I could do something with this. Not for work, I don't think. Some kind of light jacket would top it off well."

"And some ass-kicking boots!" Danielle was getting quite enthusiastic. "And maybe a pair of those gloves with bare fingers. All of it black!"

":::Sarah, I think she wants you to be in a 1980's rock video. If she wants to make your hair big, run. Just run. Pop the strength up and run. Through a wall if you have to."

":::Shush."

"Dan, you have a some neat ideas, I think! But you can borrow the pants and probably the swimsuit and do it for yourself!"

Danielle shrunk away. "No. Oh no, I couldn't." Her sudden break in confidence seemed to somehow draw attention to the bruising on her face. "But I think you should, Sarah."

"Dan, *you* can, and *will* become badass. You've got a decent bod to pull off this outfit. All you need is more confidence. I'm going to go change out of Jessica's swimsuit, then Sensei Sarah will train you."

Danielle's training progressed well enough over the next hour and a half. The fact that she stuck with it that long showed real interest, despite her earlier hesitation.

Danielle paused for breath after successfully tossing Sarah to the floor. "So what *is* this exactly, anyway? Judo?"

Oops. Actually, Sarah was cheating, referencing actual self-defence videos in her head as needed. The end result was that Danielle was getting professional-grade training. "I have a pile of self defence stuff under my belt," Sarah said, careful not to lie, "and I've got way too many crappy kung fu movies rattling around in my head."

":::Hey." Jon spoke up indignantly, "Don't knock the classics. Bruce Lee may save your life one day."

":::Shush, I'm teaching here."

"Aren't you worn out a bit Sarah?"

"Meh. You worked today, I didn't." It was reasonable.

"Other than beating the crap out of Doug, you mean. You put the kung fu movies at work there, did you?" Danielle smirked at the thought of Sarah working Doug over. She flopped onto the sofa, apparently calling the training quits for the day.

Sarah wandered over to the fridge for a couple fresh beers. "Oh, no, no. I didn't beat him *too* badly! Two of my moves caused property damage. The only harm done to Doug was a knee to the groin!"

"Ha! Well, that'll do, won't it?"

Picking up an ice pack before going back to the sofa, she brought Danielle a beer, then sat down. "We deserve a break."

"Damned right. Beer and TV? Maybe more training later, if you don't mind?"

Jaw mockingly agape, Sarah clinked her bottle against Danielle's. "Oh yeah! You're actually into it? Rock and roll! Good for you!"

Danielle rolled her eyes and took a chug. "Well, to be honest, I thought you were blowing smoke before, but when we got into it... Okay, *I'm* an amateur, but you seem to know your stuff!"

"Oh, I *know* stuff!"

"Hey, have you eaten?"

There was a thought. She hadn't, and her body didn't really *need* to yet, though it might be suspicious if Danielle and Jessica noticed that she rarely ate. She could make use of added materials in her system, or store them. "In the spirit of TV and beer, I'd order pizza if I had enough money!"

"Oh, shit!" Danielle hopped up and got her wallet. "Mum sent a wad of cash for you. An advance." She handed a little bundle of bills to Sarah and sat back down.

"Oh, Kody, Kody, Kody. She's a doll. It wasn't such a huge rush for me to get the advance." Sarah managed to convince Danielle to accept a third of the monthly rent on the apartment, then set aside a bit to repay Jessica, and a little bit left over to shop. Oh, and to order pizza. "Hey Dan, what do you want on your pizza?"

"I'm good as long as it doesn't involve anchovies."

Sarah snickered. "Yeah, I'm not big on fish."

":::Hypocrite." Jon said.

":::Shush."

Around two thirty A.M., Jessica came home. "What are you two dipsticks doing up still?"

Danielle sat forward on the sofa just enough to grab the pizza box. She opened it and held it out to Jessica. "Some left if you're hungry. You could nuke it."

"I'm not hungry, I'm-" Jessica was interrupted by a yawn. "Tired, apparently. Look at the two of you. Beer bottles, pizza boxes, I bet you haven't left that sofa in hours."

Sarah brought up the clock on the TV display. "One hour and thirty-one minutes ago, Dan got up to pee."

"Gee thanks." Danielle stuffed a bite of cold pizza into her face. "Actually, we also did some kung fu training."

"Oh, shut it. You two are on tomorrow? Late shift if I remember right?"

"Yeah."

"Yup."

"Well, that makes all of us. I'm going to bed." Jessica meandered into her room and shut the door.

"Another movie?" Sarah asked Danielle.

"Nah. Sleep's not a bad idea. Mum's thoughtful to synch us into the same shift."

Sarah smirked. "Yeah, as long as you guys don't get too sick of me."

Danielle just got up, patted Sarah on the head, and went to her room.

Well, lights out it is. Sarah got into her sleeping position touching the data line in case Jon 'woke up' and wanted to hit the net. She was just about to enter dream mode, when she remembered 'Mitch'.

No. She didn't want to go back there. Even if it was just a dream, she knew that the Meston incident didn't end well for anyone. If she had better control over her dreams, she could replace those nasty horsemen with unicorns and ponies, but as it was, she had no reason to believe her next dream would be any better. The thought of dreaming that place again made her feel tired, oddly. Watching movies with a friend was the most restful thing she'd done since...

The ocean. The sea. Maybe it was time for a swim.

She went to Jessica's door and knocked softly, hoping she hadn't gotten to sleep yet. "Jess?"

"Huh?" came the response through the door.

"Can I borrow a swimsuit? I'm gonna go for a dip."

":::We are?" Jon perked up.

Jessica popped her head out of the door. "You are? At the beach? I think it's closed! And cold!"

Yeah. Well, all right, it was excuse time. "My folks and I used to do it all the time. It was big with the Aguei tribe I grew up with."

":::Oh, magnificent bull. Kudos!"

Jessica furrowed her brow. "You sure don't look Aguei."

"Nope, but my folks decided to go live the life, blah blah blah."

"Oh, you're one of *those*!" Jessica smirked. "Sounds worse than being home-schooled!" She disappeared for a moment, and came with the black swimsuit. "I guess you and Dan are responsible for this being left on the end of my bed."

"Yeah. Sorry. Silly story, fashion show time, Dan had an idea,"

"Yeah yeah, give me the full epic tomorrow after I've had some coffee."

"Thanks Jess." Sarah took the swimsuit and patted Jessica on the head much as Danielle had done to her. "I'll try to be quiet when I come back in."

"Be careful out there. This is really stupid, you know? It's not the *worst* neighborhood at three in the morning, but it's not the best either."

"It's all right. I know kung fu."

Jessica rolled her eyes. "You two are both idiots."

:::C / [010000] [16]

"Why here?" Jon asked. It was the same docks that Sarah had landed on when she first came to the mainland. It wasn't that far from the same time of day, either.

"Familiarity? Short-term nostalgia? The sea's the sea. Whatever." Sarah found a spot under a dock with a bit of privacy and changed into Jessica's swimsuit. This time she wouldn't have the time to let her regular clothes drip dry. She found a nook near where a dock met the land. A cement structure provided a little ledge just big enough for her clothes. It looked safe from wind and water.

She turned her head towards the water line and took a deep breath. The sound of a car a block or two away was all that disturbed the sound of the waves. Soon the car was gone, but the sea remained. It always remained.

"Jon? Could I bother you to go to your room for a while?"

There was a pause. "Doing something you don't want me to know about?" He jested, but Sarah felt a trace of doubt.

"I can't imagine what that would be..."

"Oh, I'm just teasing. Knock when you're done." With that, Jon sealed himself In his room, probably to watch movies, or 'cycle down'.

It was a relief. Even though Jon kept his mouth shut for a large portion of the day, she always knew when he was out of his room. Knowing you're being watched, even if benevolently, was something that grew tiresome after a while.

Sarah took slow steps towards the water, and soon the waves flirted with her toes. It was cold, but that wasn't a concern. She walked forward slowly until it was easier to swim than to walk. The waves tried to push her back. She didn't feel like negotiating, so she ramped up her strength and swam forward as quickly as she could.

"Hello, sea." She thought to herself. "It feels like it's been ages." She paid close attention to every sensation of the water. The way the waves pushed her up and released her down, the feel of the resistance to her motions. How it made her muscles feel, the flow against her skin, the sounds of her stroke.

Soon she was far enough out to feel free of the city, so she stopped and drifted on her back. She closed her eyes and felt the waves. It felt so simple out here. So quiet. Even quiet moments in the city have a lot of noise that you screen out subconsciously. Here? Waves.

The sky was fairly clear. Most of the stars were out, though the moon wasn't on duty. That slacker.

Hi, stars. What's new, stars? What? There's life on Earth? You don't say. Sorry stars, that's not news. Yes, very well, it's new in the scope of your lives, but realize, old ones; you're speaking to a child. Less than a week old, and full of questions.

Was she really that young? Did her life in the Autar simulation count? How long was *that*? Maybe it was all in accelerated time, and fabricated memory. Maybe that life was only the blink of an eye. She'd have to remember to ask Jon sometime.

Staring up at the stars, it was not *their* grand scale that made Sarah feel insignificant. It was being a product. A creation of such deliberate design, littered with false memories. Humans were so much more real. For the first time, she felt like an idiot for trying to be one of them. Does she feel in the way that they do? Can she? Without actually being one, how could she be sure?

Stars, you're pretty, but of no use. You speak no useful wisdoms. A bunch of intergalactic bimbos. That's what you are.

Sarah gently rolled over, and faced down into the sea. Blackness. Even after she modified her vision. Blackness.

Hello sea,
Remember me?
The thing that used your dead things to be?

She strained to spot anything below her. A fish would be nice to see. Sarah closed her eyes and held herself. Her flesh was made mostly of dead fish. How odd. She had access to how Jon rearranged the matter to make this human-like material, and it all checked out; her flesh was far more human than fish. The only functional differences were those that benefited her, and her nano-nervous system.

Again, she started feeling like a thing. Like an 'it'.

I think, therefore I am?

Was she fooling herself, or did the ability to worry about it only prove it all? She could think at blistering speeds, but thinking in circles is still a circle.

Wait. What was *that* little control?

Was that there before? In the vast array of tiny controls in her head that controlled everything from thought speed, to hair growth, to cell regeneration, she could have sworn that she had checked them all out.

Was this new?

It didn't have words attached to it, but she understood what it did. If she used it, Jon would be gone.

Just gone. Sarah's mind tossed the idea back and forth; did it really do that, or was it just there to make her *think* she had the ability? To curry some trust?

She sighed, and barely realized that she took in a lot of water before sighing it out. She felt all the more thing-like.

Trust. Jon. The reasons for mistrusting him were obvious and numerous. Just ask the residents of Autar and Meston. And now he was reformed. Just like that. But he is also a thing. Things should be able to change to suit much more easily than a person. A live biological thing with neurons and synapses was prone to habit, and sloppy processing.

Sloppy processing. She was proof that it was not unique to biological thinkers. She wanted to trust Jon. It would be so much simpler just to trust.

Maybe it would be best to use that function and erase him. If it worked, she could feel guilty. If it didn't work, then what? It would prove he was untrustworthy, and she'd still have him stuck in her head. And for that matter, could she really keep him in his room or was that just an act?

Once you start doubting, there's no end to it. This wasn't productive at all. Neither the stars nor the sea were providing any answers. She headed back to the docks, and on touching soil again, she looked down. "Hello Earth," she thought, "You didn't make me, I might not be part of you the way the birds and the fish are, but lets be friends, all right?"

Picking up her clothes, she braced herself a little too swiftly against a wooden upright, and sent splinters tumbling to the ground. Turn the strength back down. That could have been someone's head. She decided that her strength should alert her if she left it on. Maybe after a minute of not being used. As she thought it, it was made so. She reprogrammed that little facet of herself, just like that.

She felt like such a *thing*.

She got dressed, and opened Jon's 'door' as she wrung out her hair.

":::Hello. Good swim?" he asked.

":::Ah, the sea, the sky, the earth. Bunch of deaf mutes."

":::Ha. Looking for answers to the questions of the universe?"

":::Something like that."

When Sarah made it back to the apartment, there was still a ton of time before the others would awaken. She did a little random housework, and ate a slice of leftover pizza. That didn't eat up much time.

For a split second, she thought of entering dream mode, but this notion was quickly defeated again by the memory of Mitch. Mitch and his mangled sister, and the others. She didn't want to see any more of Meston.

Wait.

If she could change the specifics of her strength control, why not change her dream procedures to avoid nightmares? She looked into herself, towards the messy cauldron where her dreams were generated.

It was a convoluted corner of her mind, like staring into a giant ball of yarn after a few days of abuse at the claws of a feline, or a string of christmas tree lights that had been used as a volleyball.

There was bound to be some way to make sense of it. There had to be, but it looked like a huge project. It gave her an appreciation of what Jon said; why he couldn't just edit out the parts of himself he didn't like. Maybe this was just part of being sentient. Maybe absolute self control wasn't possible.

Or maybe Jon was just a sloppy programmer. She lost her interest in what felt like a futile topic. She'd examine her virtual navel some other time. For now, she just made sure to avoid dreaming. She picked a movie out of her internal library, set her processing speed down a bit, laid down, closed her eyes and relaxed.

"HySra." What the heck was that? "Srrra! WkiWki! Dylkkak?" Damn, her processing was still turned down. She was hearing Jessica way too fast. She dialed her mind up to normal speed, and opened her eyes.

"Huh?" Sarah asked, "What was that?"

"Wake up. Do. You. Like. Cake?" Jessica was holding a mobile terminal, browsing recipes.

Sarah sat up on the sofa, and gained her bearings. "Yeah, I guess so. You bake?"

Idly wandering towards the kitchen, Jessica tilted her head and gave the cupboards a disapproving stare. "No. I got an urge. Black forest cake. Funny thing though, when you never bake, you find you don't have the crap to bake with."

"Quite inconsiderate of your kitchen to not predict your whims."

"Quite. Think I could use pancake mix, and pour a melted chocolate bar into it to get the desired result? In a related story, do you want pancakes for breakfast?"

"No, and yes. Thank you." Sarah got up to make herself available to help with pancakes, but quickly found herself in the role of bystander. "We're all on the same shift today, right?"

"Yeah. You have an eight hour today. Think you can maintain the pace you had through that four hour one?"

Sarah just nodded, watching the batter spread across the entire frying pan. "You always make em that big?"

"Yeah. I cut em into four after. Why fight having multiple pancakes trying to merge? Become one with the omni-pancake."

"Ohm. Yes, Guru. Doesn't that make it hard to flip?"

Jessica nodded, watching the surface of the monster pancake carefully for bubbling. "Extremely. It's also harder to regulate the thickness when you go right to the rim. Don't worry. I'm experienced."

Danielle's voice called out from her bedroom doorway. "Yeah, experienced in tossing giant half-cooked pancakes onto her room mate." Danielle's bruising was a lot better today. Very noticeable still, but a lot better. The inflammation was mostly gone, too.

Jessica chuckled. "Oh, you get a face full of pancake once or twice, and you never let me live it down!"

Sarah took mental notes as Danielle made herself busy making coffee. "I guess I should be happy it wasn't bacon and eggs."

Sarah sat on the edge of the sofa smiling, and held herself. "Thanks, you two. For everything, you know? Not only a place to crash and all that, but just for... for making me feel normal. Like one of you."

Jessica turned to face her, one hand still on the frying pan. She had a mock-scornful face. "You are normal, hon."

"Hm." Sarah's smile faded.

Danielle noticed. "Do you want to talk about it?"

Sarah held herself a little tighter, bowed her head thankfully, and forced her smile back, even if it was unconvincing. "This will sound messed up, but... I don't think I'm ready. If it's all the same, guys, I'd like to feel normal a while longer."

Danielle put an arm around Sarah and gave her a supportive squeeze. "Take your time. But I promise we won't judge or anything."

"Ready...." Jessica was focused on the omni-pancake. "Ready, ready, ready, ready..." She moved the pan so that the omni-pancake slid around in little circles, pressing up against the edges of the pan. "*Whoop!*" The omni-pancake, this mammoth monarch of morning culinary marvels flew into the air, gracefully flipping over, and coming down into the waiting pan, requiring only the slightest nudge to settle right into the middle.

"See? I knew it would be okay! Everything's fine."

When they got to the train station, rain was just starting up. The cloud cover looked like it was going for a marathon. A long rainfall pacing itself by being light.

"I bet you my mum's gonna put me on kitchen again. I still kind of look like hell." Danielle seemed to not be upset with the idea.

Jessica huffed. "Sucks though."

"It's all right, A change of pace isn't the worst thing in the world." Despite Danielle's words, they came out a little faint of heart. Her confidence was feeling shaken again, either by the bruise, or the source of it.

Sarah leaned in towards Danielle and brought her fist up by her chest defiantly. "Kung fu." She said quietly but fiercely.

Danielle chuckled softly, and bowed a little. "Hai, Sensei Sarah."

Jessica sighed, and rolled her eyes. "Idiots."

Sarah narrowed her eyes at Jessica. "Do not judge the power that you do not understand, little one."

Jessica just gave a sheepish smile, and shook her head slowly. More importantly, the primary mission of the idiocy had been achieved. Danielle was smiling.

"Okay you idiots, I've got a black forest cake craving, and it's not going away. I'm getting one on the way home tonight, maybe even on a break, and you two *will* each eat at least a third. Less if Kody or anyone else wants some. The point is, I will not allow you two to allow me to eat a whole cake."

"Yes Ma'am," Sarah replied, "I'm good at burning calories, I have a great metabolism for that kind of thing."

Jon's voice laughed away. ":::Sarah, you're also good at efficiently digesting lead paint!"

":::Sure, but unless they make chocolate paint now-"

":::You could just as easily lie to your sense of taste. You could be tasting black forest cake right now, for that matter."

Sarah sighed. ":::That's not a very human thing to do. Jon, I'm not in this to exploit my abilities for every little thing. I want to feel the human experience, including having to wait for cake."

":::Humph. That's no fun. Go eat a ratchet set, fish-girl."

That was uncalled for, but Sarah didn't retort. Jon just didn't get it. Funny how he could create a will to be human that was greater than his own understanding of it.

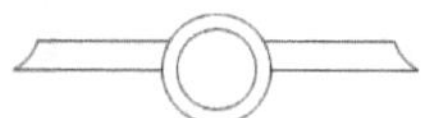

As the trio arrived at the Four Fox, the light rain gave no sign of letting up. It was just the right amount to result in a bit of a slow shift. Enough rain to make some people want to skip an extra stop in their day, but not enough to make people want to take refuge.

The only table that had customers was soon vacant again, leaving the staff down to more idle tasks and chatting behind the bar.

"Keeping up with the maddening pace, Sarah?" Jessica said, lazily wiping down the bar yet again.

"Yup. Yup, yup yuppers. Seriously, is there something productive I can do? I'd feel silly if we got a rush then found out something needed doing all along."

"Take it easy when you can." Danielle said. "Maybe we should do kung fu." Sarah was impressed that Danielle was so interested.

Jessica scoffed. "What's with the kung fu bit with you two? What kind of movies were you watching last night?"

"No, no, no," Sarah walked out from behind the bar and moved a couple tables over to make sure she had plenty of space around her. "Attack me, Jessica, I dare you."

"Fine, your shoes are ugly."

Sarah rolled her eyes. "We just call it kung fu for fun. It's more like self defence techniques. Come on, Dan! I want to attack you!"

Danielle scooted with a grin to face Sensei Sarah once more. "All right! I'm ready!"

Sarah charged. Her attack was less fierce than what an actual attacker might do, but Danielle was a beginner. Despite this, Sarah found herself flat out on the floor quickly with a loud bang.

"Holy shit!" Jessica giggled, "Sarah, are you okay? Isn't this kind of thing supposed to be done on mats or something?"

"Yeah." Sarah smiled sheepishly. Her body reported the impact to her in its own form of 'pain', but also told her not to worry about it. She accepted Danielle's sportsmanlike hand to help her back up. "Probably. The carpet in the apartment was a bit softer than this hardwood."

Jessica moaned with mock sympathy. "Hardwood being occasionally... *hard*, huh? You two were doing that in the apartment? It's a wonder we didn't get a complaint."

"Good point."

Danielle still looked pleased with herself. "Seriously Sarah, I didn't hurt you, did I?"

"Nah, nah. I'm a toughie. But if I were a baddie, your next move would have been what?"

"Drop a car on you!"

"Dan..."

"Yeah yeah, run."

"Right. And depending on where you are, screaming your bloody head off while you run could be a good idea. We've covered what now- attacked from the front, grabbed from the back, arm grab, what else... I think we're good to move into knives a bit. We've gone on and on about hard spots and soft spots, well a knife outranks the hard spots too. If you had to take a-"

"Crap. You guys are serious!" Jessica said. "Let me know when you get to flying dragon kicks. Those are awesome. If Kody sees you guys doing this, you're either going to be in trouble, or she's going to make you spar on Friday nights to draw more customers. And wear skimpy spandex."

"Ew!" Danielle yelped. "My mummie wouldn't think of it!" She narrowly dodged Sarah's lunge with a celery-stick 'knife'. She grabbed Sarah's forearm and tried to toss Sarah. It didn't really work.

"Close, Dan. You're not trying to move *me* in this situation, so much as you're holding the knife away from yourself and moving around me. If you can push me forward while you run behind me, then you throw a car at me while I'm off balance. It might be tempting to trip the attacker during this move, but that's risky for a beginner. You could foul up your own escape, or worse yet, trip yourself."

"*Throw a car* has become our code for *run*, I guess, huh?"

"Yeah. Well, sometimes there's other options, sometimes there *is* something good to throw, but don't waste any time looking for it. If a pitcher of beer is right there, great, use it. He might even slip in the puddle. But escape is the priority. If you find yourself thinking about your options, you're wasting running time."

"But what's to stop him from just turning around and stabbing me?"

"Turning around takes a little bit of time, especially if you surprised him, but you have a point in that you-"

Sarah was interrupted by the sound of an approaching group of customers. Ten or so people in their mid thirties, having a laugh over antics at their work.

"I got it." Jessica grabbed some menus and went over to where the rain-dampened group seated themselves. She greeted them and countered innocent flirts while handing out menus and prattling off the specials.

"I guess we should be professional-ish now." Danielle said with an exaggerated sigh.

Sarah nodded. "I'll help in the kitchen when the orders start coming in. Assuming Jessica hogs the whole party to herself."

Danielle just leaned on the bar. "Yeah, well, they don't look like they'll be deciding all that fast. I predict at least half of them will get generic beer, and we'll have at least one rum and coke, and a long island iced tea. At least two of them won't be hungry, and three will take the special. And there's always one or two in a group like that who get the chicken strips."

"Damn, Dan, you should just go over there, tell them to shut up, and you'll psychically bring them what they want!"

"Ah, Sensei Sarah," Danielle stood in a demure and formal stance. "Some are wise in the art of kung fu. My passion is predicting beer and burgers."

"Studied long and hard under Master Kody?"

Danielle gave a single small quick nod with an overly stiff, dour expression.

"*Hey!*" Doug walked in from the street, and came towards them with intense belligerence. He staggered with inebriation. "Who wants it first? Dan, or Dan's little bodyguard?" He fumbled to pull a gun from his jacket and pointed in in their general direction. Everyone took notice.

Time stopped. ":::Shit, Jon, are you seeing this?"

":::Huh? What? Oh! Oh shit. Is he here for *you*?"

":::He hasn't decided yet. If I max my strength for the speed benefit, and watch him careful in slow-mo, do you think I can dodge bullets?"

":::Sarah, you..." Jon paused as the reality of the options sank in. "it depends. Range, where on your body he aims for, what your current momentum at the time is. Those would be the big factors. Don't wait to see the bullet. Watch his finger. It'll be hard to tell from the front."

":::Right. All right, let's sally forth." Sarah sped time up a little, and began running at Doug. She got almost two steps before Doug's expression and the angle of his index finger changed.

":::Sarah! What are you doing! Running at him decreases the range and lowers your chances to dodge!"

":::Yeah, it's risky, but if he misses one shot, he's going to take another, isn't he? I can't be dodging bullets all day here, they... oh crap."

":::What? What what what now?"

":::I can't dodge *any* of them."

":::Why the hell not?!"

":::Jessica, Danielle, and the customers are somewhere behind me. They might get hit." By now, the gun had been fired, though the bullet was not visible yet. She couldn't cheat time to look behind her. Her thoughts might have been going lighting fast, but her body was still mostly at the mercy of normal speeds.

":::What? You're going to take a bullet for them on the oft chance that they might get hit?"

":::Yeah."

Sarah resumed normal time and immediately found herself thrown on her back with a little hole in her chest that couldn't be bothered to bleed. She heard screams, and the sound of some of the customers starting to stand, chairs being pushed along the floor. From her laying position she craned her neck back to get a comprehensive view, then paused time.

":::Damn it!" Jon wasn't pleased. "Anything vital hit?"

":::Nope. I only lost a bit of usable muscle towards the front. Nothing I can't compensate for. It's a nice redundant body you built me. Pain indicators are off the charts though. I'd hate to have to feel this. All right, round two!"

":::What??"

Sarah resumed time, now aware of where people were. She jumped to her feet. Taking advantage of her unexpected 'recovery', she charged at Doug again. She knew where the people were. She could dodge. No, no she couldn't. They could have moved anywhere in the time it took to get to Doug. An eye in the back of her head would be really handy right about now.

Doug fired again, this time into Sarah's gut, but she was braced for it. Her hands were around his wrist, and he fired one more round into her before she snapped his wrist to ninety degrees, then tossed the gun behind the bar. A second strike at reduced strength knocked him out cold.

":::We have to leave. Now." Jon sounded calm, quiet, but terrified.

"Sarah!" Jessica called out, running over to her. Sarah turned around to face her. Doug was laying there with his broken wrist, but Sarah knew that her three bloodless bullet holes were getting more attention.

"Jessica. I didn't tell you about my past because in a way, I don't have one. I was less than a day old when I walked in here the first time. My body is highly illegal. I have to go."

She looked to Danielle, who had come near as well. But not too close to Doug. "Dan?" Damn, she was starting to cry. "Dan, you tell your mum I'm sorry I won't be able to pay back the advance for a while. You keep up the training, all right? Thank you, guys. I could have had a life like this, you know?" She wiped her sleeve across her face. She couldn't stop crying. She knew she could just turn it off, like a machine, but that wasn't... it wasn't...

"Sarah." Danielle wrapped her arms around Sarah and whimpered. "Don't go. You're a hero!"

Sarah pulled away, head hung low. "I'm a..."

"She's full of nanites." Jessica said grimly. "They'd incinerate her." Danielle staggered back, wide eyed. "They can't...!"

Sarah sighed, then pointed at the unconscious Doug. "Call that asshole an ambulance, huh? Tell him I'm watching him. I won't be, but tell him that." Some of the customers had wandered closer. They had seen it all.

Jon spoke up. ":::If it was just Danielle and Jessica here, we might have the option of asking them to keep a secret, maybe. And of course we would have to make Doug disappear, but now there's all these custom-" He stopped himself. Sarah wouldn't have gone for a 'shallow grave' scenario anyway. The jig was up. ":::Sarah. I'm so sorry. We have to go."

"Love you guys."

Timothy Greene. Secret agent of Lancer. He should get business cards made. He stood before the grand Victoria Emerald hotel in his new, off-the rack tuxedo. He spent as much of Mr. Book's money as he could on it without having to waste a bunch of time on an elaborate fitting.

That said, it's amazing how much can be done quickly when money is no object. It was still uncomfortable compared to his usual extra-casual business casual.

Greene decided he needed a slick way to introduce himself if he was going to be a secret agent. Dismissing "Greene... Timothy Greene" quickly as being cliché, it also had the detriment of his first name sounding dorky. Timothy. Ugh. Tim Greene? That just sounded wrong. Like some woodland hick. Tim was an awful name. Greene wasn't much better.

"Who am I, you ask? It's not easy being..."

No. No, no, no. Wait a second! He shouldn't even be using his real name anyway! What the heck was he thinking? This was a great chance to test drive a new name! Hank!

No.

Vincent. Yeah, that'll do. Vincent what? Camomile! Tea? Well... why not? Vincent Camomile, heir to the Camomile Tea empire! Camomile is a family name, right? Like Earl Grey and his tea? Maybe the Earl was just a mascot.

What the hell did Greene know about tea? Vincent Camomile sounded good enough to him. That would be his name.

Walking into the lobby, he felt a *little* overdressed, but the tux fit in better here than it had on the train. The lobby dripped with the traditional trappings of hotels with big egos and bigger rates. Blanched grooved columns that reached up to a needlessly high ceiling, marble floors, and bellhops that looked like their red uniforms were slowly sucking out their souls.

The bellhops were never seen stopping. Part of the job is looking busy, or not being seen at all, which would have made white uniforms more logical. Stand still and imitate one of the columns. Maybe a uniform that matched the lobby sofas might make the guests happier. Pay a bellhop a big tip, and get him on all fours to sit on. Now gallop, bellhop! To my room, carrying my luggage in your teeth!

Greene felt bad for them, then he realized that he didn't feel all that more glamorous working at Lancer. Then again, hey... free tux.

He must have been standing there too long, as a bellhop stepped up with slightly less energy that a hummingbird. "Can I help you, Sir?"

"Just admiring the work ethic of you and your fellow bellhops! Ha, ha, I'm in the way, am I? I should get along to my room anyway."

The bellhop looked terrified. "No! No, Sir, not at all! Stand wherever you wish, you're the guest! But if you need anything, please feel free to flag one of us down!"

Greene nodded dismissively, feeling successful in his disguise. He didn't get to use his new name though. Camomile... *Vincent* Camomile. Ooh. Maybe he should go with Vinny Camomile. Like a mobster. No, no, Vincent Camomile sounded threatening enough.

He walked to the elevators. It took longer than seemed reasonably necessary. The lobby wasted so much space. Greene found inefficiency irritating. Efficiency was his job, and his mindset. He pressed the down button, and waited.

He looked at his new shoes. See, this is a prime example. They cost a lot, weren't all that comfortable, and the soles were too stiff to run in well. Not that Greene ran a lot. And under those shoes? Marble flooring. Probably real marble, too. A mass produced tile could look just as good to the untrained eye, and cost a fraction. Tsk, tsk.

One of the elevators opened, and he got in, still critiquing the philosophy of opulence, but enjoying the baroque elevator music.

The buttons were labeled with whole words in a fancy script instead of abbreviations. He was after the 3rd *basement*, and not B3, after all.

No such floor. At least not from *this* elevator. Okay, 2nd basement.

Bzzt. No? The key card reader next to the buttons quietly blinked a little red light a couple times. All right. Fine, B1? Oops, that is, 1st basement. Apologies, apologies, the Victoria Emerald would not be seen with a B1. Many sincere apologies.

The elevator was content with that. Down it went. The doors soon opened to another large, inefficient room, smelling slightly of bleach. This one was doused in far less lavish pomp, however. This was the land of sheer slabs of post-modern and art-deco nightmares. Glass bricks? Who used glass bricks anymore? He had to admit, they did fairly well with them, but still. Glass bricks?

This was evidently the gym, spa, pool, sauna, whatever zone. The tuxedo didn't fit in well here at all. No matter. Stay confident. *Vincent Camomile* can make a tux work anywhere, but yet again he attracted unwanted assistance by standing around looking lost.

"Hey, good day, Sir! First time here? Care for a tour?" The exuberant fellow was much more casual than the bellhop, and far better built. The 'Victoria Emerald' logo stitched into his pale blue polo top and too-short shorts were the only signs that set him apart from the staff of any other overpriced gym. "I could take you on a tour right now, or I could go get Brianna!"

A gender choice in tour guides. This gym seemed to be free to paid guests, but that didn't stop them from employing some blatant, cheap sex appeal. Was that some honoured gym club tradition?

"Brianna?" Tempting. But Greene stayed focused. "Oh, don't bother her, I think I'd like to just take a casual look around on my own, if it's all right with you."

"Sure thing Sir, if you need any little thing-"

"Yes, thank you." Greene was slowly warming up to this hotel. If he were a guest, he'd have quite happily taken the Brianna tour. He likely would have been too intimidated by Brianna, (who was almost certainly some superwoman goddess fantasy made flesh) and not been able to do anything but concentrate on not staring at her chest. He counted his blessings that it was the himbo that greeted him, and not his female counterpart.

Said himbo, still smiling, went back to whatever paperwork he was doing before Greene arrived.

All right then. The next hurdle was getting down to B3, or even B2. Whoops, that is *3rd basement* or *2nd basement*. He wouldn't want to upset the elevator. Taking a cue from extensive video game experience, he picked a side, and followed that wall. Today he picked left, as it looked less suspicious than right, and the himbo was still right there.

The choice was poor after all, as the logical path to trace the outer edges of the floor would soon lead him into the women's changing rooms. Too intent on navigation, he stopped himself just in time. Drat. If the super secret staircase of victory was in there, the mission was in serious jeopardy. "Why yes, Mr. Book, I was arrested for public sexual misconduct. I can't imagine why; I was in a tux." That would be a last resort.

Avoiding misdemeanor charges, he ended up poolside, where the tuxedo was even less inconspicuous. The bleach smell was stronger by the pool of course. Greene loved the smell of a pool. What was the last time he had been in one? A long time. One more thing to remember to do on his next vacation, and to forget when the time actually came.

He made it to the end of the pool, where there was a small office for the bodyguard. The woman inside must have been Brianna. Or not. She did, however fit the imagined description of Brianna; incredible. A staff keycard on a cord sat on her desk, on the other side of her.

"You shouldn't be poolside in street shoes, Sir." She didn't sound like the type to grovel to guests. It was a refreshing change of pace. Or maybe it was just the notable cleavage stuffed in her swim suit. Both were impressive.

"Ah, sorry. I'll be gone shortly, I was just looking for a friend." Greene said as smoothly as he could. Don't stare at her.

He stalled for a moment. They were both incredibly impressive. She raised an eyebrow. "Well? Get going then. And if you run in those shoes you'll break your neck."

Stop staring, move on. Move it. Both incredibly impressive.
Focus.

A quick loop around the men's changing room yielded nothing but dead ends. He kept an eye out for unattended clothing. Maybe a guest keycard would get him to lower levels.

No luck. There was a brief chance to check some briefs, but men in the room were already suspicious of him. They soon were stuffed in a locker, like everything else. All right, time to leave this room before someone thought he was looking for a good time. There was obviously no stairs in here.

Exiting, he looked forward to spotting the alleged "Brianna" again. She was casually patrolling the pool's edge. Her staff keycard dangled around her neck. If only she had forgotten it at her desk, he could have possibly nabbed it.

Greene imagined momentarily that he had the skill to pickpocket it right in front of her. Heck, as long as he was daydreaming, add a deep, distracting kiss, and a long gaze into her eyes while her breathing betrayed her desire. Oh yes, Vincent! Vincent Camomile. Secret agent, and *master séducteur*!

Yeah, he had to get out of there.

Onward. The saunas produced similar results as the changing rooms, with the addition of a tuxedo joke made at his expense. Onward.

He kept tracking the left side of the floor, and wound up down a little hallway that ended in a plain, unmarked door. It was locked of course. A cheap mechanical lock, not a keycard.

Just to the right was a weight room. The forest of exercise machines was fairly busy. Unintended thoughts of Brianna drew his eyes towards the butterfly presses. Only one was being used, and by a male. Greene scorned himself silently for seeking a female chest flexing.

It was noisy in there. Near the middle, one especially gargantuan man was bench pressing almost all the weight the machine could provide. Against gym protocol, he allowed the weight to slam down hard on every repetition, and vocalized every effort and victory. It drowned out the peppy workout music. Certainly he assumed that everyone was terribly impressed. Surely it would only be a matter of time before the staff himbo came to tell the hulk to knock it off.

Greene looked at the hulk. Greene looked at the locked door behind him. Greene looked at the nearby free-weights rack.

He grabbed a fairly large free-weight, and ducked out towards the locked door. He listened to the impacts of the hulk's reps.

Bam.

Bam.

Bam.

Greene lifted the free-weight over the locked doorknob. Bam.

He struck. Bam.

Again. Bam. The doorknob hung loose. One more to take it clean off. Bam.

Looking around as the hulk continued, he checked to see if anyone noticed him. It seemed not. Pulling a simple screwdriver from his tux, he stabbed, rattled and jabbed at the lock's inner workings until the door released.

Another check around. No one? Good. Damn, when was the hulk going to get tired? Greene opened the door and slipped inside quickly. The fact that it wasn't equipped with a keycard lock suggested that staff rarely went in here. With any luck, they wouldn't notice the missing doorknob.

He stood in a dimly lit concrete stairwell. This small space connected to an extruded dark metal staircase. After the polished posh gym areas, it felt like he had stepped into an alternate reality. Only the muted sound of those weights hitting down rhythmically reminded him otherwise.

Bam. The weights struck metal.

Bam. Again, the penetrating sound.

Bam. Tirelessly, like a machine.

This stairwell was the kind of thing he was looking for. He slumped to the floor, to sit and steady his nerves. Breathe. Think of something relaxing. Like Brianna, and her magnificent qualities.

On a beach.

A nude beach.

Doing yoga.

Breathe.

Greene took out his little work terminal, and made sure he still had a signal out. It reassured him again that he was not in another world. The sound of the weights were becoming less and less reassuring, sounding more and more like the heartbeat of something massive and inhuman.

Push that bit of imagination aside. Call back Brianna's naked yoga. Everything's fine. Everything's fine. You've just entered a dungeon looking for huge monsters tearing each other apart, that's all.

Detailed thoughts of the nanite-enhanced pit fights forced their way into his head. His breathing became tight. He needed some water, and had none.

Get up. Get up and dust the tux off. Greene took a deep breath and took his first step down those stairs. That wasn't so hard. He made more noise than he wanted. Blame the hard leather soles. Step softly. No rush.

Tap, tap, tap down the stairs. When the sound of the weights in the gym stopped, he was grateful. At first. He was left with only his own sounds and their cold little echoes. He strained to hear the music from the gym, but not a note could reach him.

He considered playing some music softly from his terminal, but stealth was more important. Maybe if he had earphones. No, hearing things around him was as important as his own silence.

That thought struck an extra chord of paranoia. He stopped, listening for anything.

Anything.

Please?

Even a growl would at least give him an excuse to run screaming out of the hotel and face chastising by Mr. Book. How did Greene get himself into this? Why didn't he bring a gun, or a platoon?

Careful with each step, not to slip nor make a sound, he was soon at the door of basement two. Curiosity would *not* get the better of him. Opening that door could only risk getting discovered. Onward. Down. Again staring down a set of extruded dark metal stairs.

The concrete walls were damper and colder as he went down, moisture seeping upwards from the ground. At the last step, he stood on a glistening concrete floor. Greene looked up through the stairwells, up towards the door that led to the shiny world of the buxom Brianna. Bearing such beauty up there in the light, she attained the title of 'angel' in Greene's mind. As he stood at the door to the third layer of this concrete purgatory, he jokingly whispered a little prayer to Brianna.

Brianna, O goddess of the pool, bounty be thine chest. Guard me as I trespass, as I forgive those who sent me here.

All right, stop stalling.

He turned the knob as quietly as he could, and opened the door enough to peek. Inside was about as hospitable as the stairwell, continuing the theme of damp concrete, but now with masses of pipes streaming along the ceiling.

Two directions led from the door. One to the left, which he couldn't see much of due to the door itself in the way, and one straight ahead. Roughly fifty metres ahead, on the left side of the passage, stood a man in front of a door. He stood facing away from the door, staring at the wall across the passage. His arms were crossed over his large physique, and he did not move.

He was not wearing a tuxedo. Nor gym wear. This was notably urban apparel. High end stuff, but not in great shape. It looked like he had been sleeping in them, and they were not clean. Given what he was here to find, it was likely smears of blood. His jacket was zipped up high, to right under his nose. His eyes were hidden under broad, dark sunglasses.

Greene didn't feel like talking to this man that much. The path to the left would do for now. He stepped out of the doorway, keeping an eye on the large man all the while. Still no movement. Greene headed down the left passage. The room that the goon was guarding was now to Greene's right, through the wall. He got some distance from the corner and pulled out his little terminal.

It still had a signal, barely. He took readings for any radio frequencies in the area. Anything. Yes, yes, there it was. This must be the signal type that the pit-fighters were run on.

It was deeply encoded, and was doubtlessly just commands that would mean nothing to Greene, but the pattern was unmistakably the same as those that Jonathan Coll and Erebus had used in Autar and Meston. Was the government aware of this similarity? They must be, after all of those pit fight raids.

Greene had to report this to Mr. Book. He attached his readings to a message, typed in a short note, and transmitted.

Oops. That may have been a mistake.

That scream, that inhuman *war cry*. It was like the 'demon of Densfarn' he had seen taken into custody. In the cement underground, the sound reverberated and rebounded towards him, hitting him so hard that he nearly dropped to the floor. He had to get out of there, now.

Running to the stairwell door, he heard footsteps coming from the other passage. He had to race to get to the door first. A quick glance revealed that it *was* the guard. With an open jacket, he was just like the demon. Lower jaw split down the middle, body ripped open and hollow, with ribs sticking straight out like horns. The sunglasses were gone now as well, showing the raging yet lifeless eyes.

Greene slammed the door behind him, and headed up the stairs, eyes upwards to the land of his angel. He heard the door open forcefully behind him.

The hard leather sole of his shoe slipped on the third metal step, sending his shin against it, and his face against another step. It hit with an ugly crack, shaking loose tears, blood, and his jaw.

Before the pain caught up with him, bloodied hands wrapped around his torso. With a firm embrace, Greene saw the demon's ribs burst out between his own, before the three-sided jaw wrapped around his head from behind. The two halves of the demon's lower jaw ripped at the sides of Greene's face.

The pain found him. It was blinding. There was nothing else in the world. No other thought could form. Screams of more demons came from behind him.

Greene had no scream. There was no ability to scream with shredded lungs. The split moment seemed to last an hour of pain. It was incredible. Almost fascinating.

There was nothing in the world but pain.

And the pain began to fade. Fading. Greene knew what it meant, and welcomed it. The pain was gone, the world was dark, and Greene was gone from it.

The purest, most complete Eidechse is a collection of nanites. If you collected them all in a ball, he would be about the size of your fist. This is not an extremely mobile existence.

To compensate for this, he makes minor copies of himself. A 'dispatch' or 'deployment' colony of nanites. Such a tiny version of himself can stow away on many things. Small creatures, machinery, and occasionally a human.

Navigation for Eidechse is done by luck, by choosing the right ride at the right time, and when applicable, applying suggestive influence as long as it did no harm. This was not often a convenient way to travel, and an accident (such as the woeful untimely death of an insect) could leave that dispatch of Eidechse stranded, crawling along at a molecule's pace.

A microscopic pile of nanites can be determined, but on their own they're just not very fast.

Many dispatches exist, waiting for orders from the main self. These little copies of Eidechse are not as robust as the main self, lacking the bulk of information, but they're given what they need and a little more, only to eventually 'phone home' to report by one means or another.

There is only one Eidechse, but he has many, far reaching hands.

One such deployment mission had gone wrong. Nothing critical. It was a routine intelligence update mission, but before being able to phone home and re-synchronize, he found himself (and the poor moth which was his ride) smeared under the boot of a soldier.

Eidechse lamented the loss of another innocent helper. It was far too damaged to heal. He stealthily crept around the edge of the boot's sole, and a few hours later, he made it into the bloodstream of the soldier.

Eidechse had no intent to 'influence' the soldier, but a choice perch around the brain allowed for very efficient observation of what was going on, and how to catch a ride out. The standard plan in these situations was to migrate from the human's mouth, onto a scrap of food, get discarded, and meet a little scavenger or two. From there, travel became much easier.

By this soldier's blood sugar levels, it seemed like Eidechse would have to wait a while for a meal to provide a ride out. No matter. He was content in the company of AZU soldiers.

Eidechse's current host was a soldier in AZU-2. He didn't know the soldier's name, but chose to refer to him as 'Tim'. The day's events seemed to be fairly routine for AZU-2 today. A resupply of their airlimb at Yute Central, friendly chit chat, and back into the sky.

Then a flashing red light burst to life with the voice of the commanding officer. "Action stations, people! Outbreak in the city, currently confined to a hotel."

Tim jolted into action, and the adrenaline levels shot up. The airlimb leaned hard as it changed course, but Tim's stride was flawless as he went to an equipment locker by the mid-ship loading bays. Five other soldiers were gearing up as well. Eidechse had seen this kind of AZU mission from the outside, but this perspective was very exciting.

The soldiers each put on vests, gloves with fore-arm guards, and a helmet. They then clipped two bulky pieces of equipment to their belts, and readied their primary weapon, the FNZ200.

FNZs were compact, efficient combat rifles, whose two hundred round four-layer top mount magazines were filled with hollow points.

They were specifically designed to shatter zombies, and lots of them.

"It sounds bad in there." The commander's voice came from inside the helmet. "This is a cleanup mission first. Hostiles sound like humanoid abomination class. Direct civilians out the front door when you see any alive. AZU-4 will be there to scan and process them. Secure the lobby first, I'll be listening."

"Sir, yes, Sir." Tim seemed to be the leader of the squad. "You all ready?" he called to the others. Five soldiers called back with enthusiastic macho shouts, and stood facing the bay door.

A few tense moments passed as the airlimb could be felt to decelerate and turn. Eidechse monitored Tim's adrenaline and heart rate, just for lack of anything else to do but watch. The door began to open like a wide, metal drawbridge. The soldiers were hopping off the tip before it was even fully open. "*Move!*"

Taking a rough formation behind Tim, they stormed the front doors of a hotel called the Victoria Emerald. Eidechse was frustrated not to have access to the net, or his full database. As a mere dispatch of himself, he wasn't carrying everything.

More information about the hotel would be very nice. Floor plans, especially. Not that Eidechse had any say in the strategy, he was just a passenger.

The lobby was populated by a few dozen people, all of whom looked scared as hell. Tim ran up to the nearest staff member. "Sir, can you confirm that the creatures are solely from the lower levels?"

"Uh, yeah." The desk clerk answered through his own stress. "I don't know which basements for sure, or how many of them there are, but no one's seen anything in the upper floors as far as I've heard. I shut down the elevators, too."

"Good man. Can you do me a favour? Can you get everyone here out front, Sir?"

"Uh, sure. What about people still upstairs?"

"For now, we leave them there. If there's no threat, we don't need a panicked evac."

The clerk looked towards the check-in desk. "Do I have time to record a message for the front desk, if people call downstairs?"

"Damned good idea," Tim said, "Make it firm that they should stay in their rooms until further notice, but try to keep it calm. Can you do that for me?"

"I'll try!" The clerk jogged over to the desk. Tim started gesturing for the rest to head out. He walked up to another soldier. "You can see the stairwell doors and the elevators from here. Stay here and scream bloody murder if anything unpleasant comes around. I hope to be sending civilians up, just point them out the door. If they ask to go up to their rooms, tell them no. They need to be scanned. If they resist, do what you have to. AZU-4 should be sending in a little bit of backup for you shortly. The rest of us are heading down. Got it?"

"Yes, Sir."

Tim led the remaining four subordinates to the stairwell, heading down, taking it corner by corner. This stairwell only went as low as basement one, which was tactically advantageous. They burst onto the floor on the far end of a weight room. Three or four bodies were spread around in ripped pieces. It was hard to tell how many people it was. At least they were positively not a threat in that shape. The short carpeting did little to soak up the blood, leaving glossy pools of it across the room.

A fast search of the floor turned up two bodies in a swimming pool. One was half on the edge, and half floating freely. The other was mostly intact, but with a uniform series of punctures in the torso. Needless to say, the water was a distinct hue of red.

In the women's saunas, a group of four women huddled terrified in the corner; all but a lifeguard who seemed to be handling things in a leadership role. This comely woman greeted the soldier with focus on the job at hand. "Is it clear to get these ladies out of here?"

"Yes, Ma'am," Tim replied, "Head right for the stairs, and out the front door."

The woman nodded and turned to the fear-filled group. "You heard him. Get cracking." Tim kept an eye on them until they got to the stairwell up.

Tim and the other soldiers had also noticed the open door between the saunas and the weight room. Inside awaited a dim little concrete room with dark extruded metal stairs heading down. The soldiers converged there.

"Sir?" Tim spoke to no one that Eidechse could see in front of him. "The basement- I should say, the first basement, is clear. There's stairs going further down. How deep is this place?"

The voice of the commander aboard the airlimb piped up in Tim's helmet. "Goes down to B-3. As far as I can tell from the blueprints, it's mainly utility, storage, and things like that."

"All right, here we go." Tim signaled to the other four soldiers to follow, rushing the stairs with the same speed and caution as the last set. Tim came to the B-2 door. "Sir, is this the only door into B-2? It's locked, and looks undisturbed."

The commander took a moment to look at the blueprints closely, and replied, "Yeah, that's the only way into that floor. Your signal is crap, by the way. Drop a relay there, or there's no way I'll hear you from B-3."

"We're not going to secure B-2, Sir?"

"Negative. Place an alarm sensor and move on. If the sensor beeps you, fall back to B-2 and reassess immediately. Most of AZU-4 is feeling a little bored up here, I'm going to see about sending some of them to hold your current position. Lay the sensor, the relay, and proceed to B-3."

"Yes, Sir." Tim rummaged his vest pockets, and pulled out the radio relay; a smooth black object about the size of a deck of cards. He pulled two antennae up from it, pressed a button causing a little green light to begin blinking, and put in on the floor.

He then pulled out something that had the shape of a sausage sliced in half lengthwise. It was flexible, and Tim bent it around the doorknob. It stuck. He then pressed a button similar to the relay, evoking a similar little green light. "All right boys, let's mosey."

Nearly to the bottom of the stairwell, Tim felt a step that was a little slippery. He halted, and signaled his followers to follow suit. Tim got to the bottom of the stairwell and turned to examine the steps closer. "Just blood. Don't slip." Not that anyone was stopping to check right now, but it was the blood of Timothy Greene.

The door at the bottom was slightly open. Any hopes of being unheard on approach were shot, so Tim led the charge in. He was followed by another two soldiers. The three of them all took defensive positions facing different directions.

"Clear?"

"Clear."

"All clear."

Tim gestured for the remaining two troops to hold the position while he and the first two took the left passage. It looked short, and it was, ending with a wall of metres, valves and switch boxes connecting to the industrial copper entrails running along the ceiling. They rejoined the other two soldiers by the stairs, and all took the other passage.

The floor along this passage was stained with large smears of blood, as if bloody bodies had been dragged this way. A door awaited along the left wall. It too, was marked with blood. The passage continued on past the door for some distance, but the door needed to be checked first.

Tim picked two others to come with him through the door with hand signals, then stormed into the large blood soaked room.

Eidechse wasn't surprised to see a creature very similar to the 'demon of Densfarn', but he hadn't expected four. One of them kneeled over a dead body with a hacksaw, sawing up along the sternum. The abdomen was wide open, and much of the innards had already been removed.

A demon standing near the far wall by a pile of discarded viscera turned around and gave its scream, protruding ribs throbbing with the sound.

Tim didn't wait for the other demons to take notice. "*Take em down!*" He and the two immediate followers opened fire at the monsters' hips and legs, toppling one quickly. The other three were closing fast. "Four hostiles!" Tim called out for the benefit of the commander on the airlimb.

Eidechse prepared himself for microscopic combat. If one of the demons bit Tim or anything, Eidechse would be able to migrate to the demon. At that point, it was impossible to tell which nanite colony would dominate the other. Self-destruct protocols were readied as well. He couldn't risk his knowledge becoming property of whatever made the demons. With any luck, the demon nanites were only suited to one task, and not small-scale combat.

Tim, however, was no fool. "Fall back into the hall! Draw them out!" he backed out, firing with the other two, felling another demon. Both downed demons still approached, although only by pulling themselves along with their arms.

One of the demons, in that unholy screech, cried out "*Your God Erebus has not left you, Aguola! Your flesh, and your cities are still mine, make no mistake!*"

In the hallway, all five soldiers backed off about fifteen metres from the door, with backs to the cleared stairwell. The other two other demons were quickly out in the hall, facing five FNZ's worth of hollow point cleansing.

When the last fell, the mood became a bit more relaxed as two of the soldiers took closer aim to disable the arms. They wouldn't stop screaming though.

"Sir?" Tim called into the helmet radio. "We've got four on the floor here. B-3 is secure. We've got flamers handy, but we didn't think we'd be this deep or cramped. Can you send us some breathing gear?"

"Right," the commander said, "I guess the air would get pretty bad, pretty fast. I'll see if AZU-4 can make a delivery, and supply some more troops to help with B-2. A bit of bad news though, they found a suspicious blood trail on the sidewalk. It could only be followed about half a block before it dried right up. It's about four hours old."

"Great. I guess it doesn't change much though. If one of these were already at that bar, they could be anywhere." Tim watched as his subordinates blanketed the two demons laying in the hall with flames, cooking the flesh and their nanites. The air would be fine long enough to at least shut the demons up.

Eidechse was filled with a mix of relief and a disappointed curiosity.

Tim backed away towards the stairwell. "Sir, when AZU-4 gets in here, I need to drain the lizard. I was about to do that when we got the call, and that was some time ago."

The commander chuckled. "How many times to I have to tell you to go to the bathroom *before* we go anywhere?"

"Yes, sir."

Erebus.

The demons belong to Erebus. Eidechse had his suspicions, but hearing it in such concrete terms made it all the worse. How long did the city of Densfarn have to live, by Erebus' plans?

Eidechse disengaged Tim's brain, and hopped a bloodstream down. It would be the glamourous golden arc exit strategy after all.

:::C / [010011] [19]

"::::Is this the extent of your plan, Sarah?" Jon didn't have a great one lined up either, but even if he did, Sarah didn't seem to be in the mood to hear it. It had now been the better part of a day since she had to flee from the Four Fox Grill, and abandon the life she had been trying to build.

It occurred to her that Doug and the gun was a lot like the situation Jon had set up in his Autar simulation. Even if the Four Fox cash register had been close enough to throw, and even if she could guarantee that Doug wouldn't get a shot off, a blatant display of her strength would have blown her cover anyway. The fight in the Autar sim was rigged in her favour quite a bit.

She had stopped by the same spot she used to create her identity in the system, and systematically erased herself. No records of birth, no government records, (not that there were many) no nothing.

She had been using cash- Jessica's cash, so there was no bank account to erase. She peeked into Kody's records. Kody hadn't yet entered Sarah into her accounts. At least none that she could get access to.

Sitting there with her fingers in the Four Fox system was a nostalgic stab in the heart. She wanted to talk to them all. To tell them so much. She was hoping to know them for a long, long time. Now that was all gone.

All because of Doug.

She thought perhaps she should have played dead. Bled, stopped moving, stop breathing, et cetera. And then what, lay there while the cops poked around until a coroner took her away? Her and probably Danielle? There was a chance that Sarah could have found a chance to slip away unnoticed before an autopsy, but Danielle wouldn't be so lucky.

Yes, this was the way it had to be. Damned Doug. She should have at least given him a bullet somewhere for his troubles.

No, she felt bad enough about his wrist. Against all logic, she hoped he was all right. Jon would laugh at that, and maybe he'd be right.

Now what? Walk to another city and start over? Truthfully, she didn't have much enthusiasm for that idea, even if it looked like the obvious path.

As it was now, she wasn't doing much of anything. She sat on the sea floor, not too far from shore, but far enough not to be detected. She was currently eating kelp, and feeling the deep currents flow around her.

":::Yes, Jon, this is my plan. I have made a conscious decision to sulk for a while. Call it *laying low*, if that's cool enough for you." Her voice carried venom that Jon didn't deserve in *this* matter, but she didn't care much. She was sulking, and rightfully so.

This made Jon feel like sulking as well. ":::All right then, I'll be in my room, watching a movie or something. Knock if you decide to do anything interesting." And then he was gone. As gone as someone who lives in your skull can be, at any rate.

Sarah swallowed a bite of kelp. It amused her in a way, for a technological marvel like herself sustaining herself on the food of fishies. It made her feel more natural. Like a form of life, at least. Humans often ate things they felt were 'natural', but even the most 'organic' sandwich was very artificial. When was the last time wheat produced bread on its own, sliced it, and proceeded to go hunt sprouts and other ingredients?

Grabbing something, and stuffing it in your mouth. That was natural. An innocent fish swam by, and for a moment, Sarah peered at it closely. By today's insights on natural diet, she may as well reach out and grab the fish to bite its head off.

Ew.

Maybe she was a vegetarian. Maybe she just didn't want a mess. Maybe she didn't want to eat a life form that looked her in the eye. Maybe that fish was related to a fish that made up her own body.

Don't eat your relatives.

Sarah took a deep, cleansing breath of salt water, filling her lungs, then pushing it back out. Sulk, sulk, sulk.

Damned Doug. Damned Jon.

She looked down at her bullet wounds. The outer skin had healed over nicely. Inside, repairs were coming along well. Suddenly her feeling of being natural was shattered by her hyper-efficient body's magnificent abilities.

She wondered what it would be like to be in a hospital. It looked relaxing in movies. Loved ones come to visit, and people brought you meals in bed.

But this was a human experience. She could never have that.

The doctor would take one close look at an x-ray, and call the cops. Maybe. How would her x-ray turn out? Jon was probably pretty accurate. One way or the other, officials would probably get involved.

Then what? Jessica said they'd incinerate her. Yeah, that would do it. Sarah curled up on her side, and debated crying. Why should she, when she could just turn it off? While she pondered the cruel stupidity of crying simulated salty tears while under salt water, it happened anyway. Her eyes burned from it. In frustration she screamed. The sound of it was all but muted by the water, compounding the awareness of her inhumanity.

She curled up tighter, and screamed as loud as she could. Again, again. Technically, she could do this for years straight. Scorning her own stupidity for considering it, she shut up and closed her eyes.

She should sleep. Maybe even 'turn off' for a while. Then what? Wake up with the same thoughts as before? Maybe she should do something drastic. Re-program herself. There was a bit of idiocy. To what effect? What would it solve? What was the point of any of it?

She needed to get her mind off of it all. Movie time.

Nah. She looked at the command to launch a dream. Could she be so lucky as to have a nice one this time? Concentrate. Think of a nice thing. Hanging out in Danielle and Jessica's apartment. Laughing, feeling like a normal part of the world.

Think of that. Now dream. The world faded away...

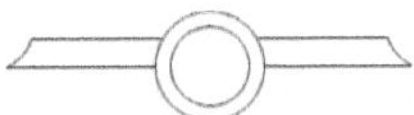

Damn it. She was Amanda again, and she was still in Meston. She was swinging a shovel against a snack vending machine's display. It didn't break, but a few more hits caused the clear pane of plastic to pop loose.

Behind her, six year old Mitch cheered. Amanda grabbed the loose edge of the plastic and yanked it away with a few good pulls. "All right, take your pick." She took a chocolate bar, unwrapped it, and held one end of it in her mouth. While Mitch made up his mind, she went to work on the drink machine standing next to it.

Wham, wham, wham. This one was more resistant. She kept trying until Mitch interrupted. "Hey."

She turned to look. Mitch stood there with a small open bag of cheesy chips in one hand, and a fist full of coins in the other. "We can use these to get soda."

"Where...?" Behind him, the snack machine's money box staring her right in the face. "Ah, you little smart aaaa.... alec."

Mitch grinned. "You were going to say *ass*!" He stifled a giggle as Amanda grabbed some money from him to feed into the soda machine. Kids bounce back fast. Since they saw his shredded sister, Amanda had been able to coax a smile from him now and then, but any sight of another victim slammed him back down again, often sobbing. She had done a lot more carrying of Mitch than her body was happy with.

"What do you want to drink, Mitch? I'm going to have a cream soda, I think."

"I'm not supposed to have more than one soda a day," he said with innocent honesty, "and I had one before lunch. Mum says-" He stopped cold, and tossed his chips on the ground. Amanda knelt down to hold him. She'd given up on what to say in this situation. There was nothing to say.

Mitch broke the silence. "Dropped my chips. I'm sorry."

With a heavy sigh, Amanda held Mitch by the shoulders and looked him in the eye. "For what we paid, I think it's all right. We can get another. And have a soda. If you don't, I'll feel like a fatso when I'm chugging down mine."

Mitch now looked puzzled. "Hey. We stole."

Amanda had to smile. There was no factual way around it. "Well, yes. Yes we did, but seeing how today is going, I don't think anyone would mind.

If you want, keep track of what we eat, and we can find the right people to pay when we get out of here, all right?"

With a moment's thought, Mitch nodded. "Okay. But you help me remember, okay? Money for two sodas, chips, a chocolate bar, and another chips."

"Double that, okay? We should take some with us, just in case."

"Okay." Mitch thankfully had a backpack, and volunteered to haul supplies. This seemed more than fair, for all the carrying Amanda had been doing. Before he handed Amanda more change for sodas, he paused. "What if the people we should pay are here? What if they're dead, or..."

"Maybe we should worry about that later. Let's just think about getting out of the city. The buildings are shorter here, we're getting out of the city, bit by bit." The ten story buildings around them indeed paled in comparison to the skyscraper forest where they had encountered the horsemen. Since then, they hadn't encountered any zombies. Only unmoving remains of victims.

"Let's get going." Amanda said as she packed two sodas into Mitch's backpack.

They continued for another couple of blocks when they came across a tall parkade. The bottom floor was choked with wrecked cars. On the fourth floor a car stuck out from a broken barricade. Hanging over the edge of the top floor was a lineup of bodies, as if hung out to dry. Every other one was hanging head and hands first, the other half were feet first. Many of them, randomly, were missing feet, arms, heads and such. A few had entrails hanging down, and almost all of them had a thick red stain running down the edge of that floor.

Amanda pointed at the sky in the opposite direction. "Look at that, I think the sun might be coming up soon." It was still a long way off, but it was the first thing that popped into her head. Mitch looked to where she pointed.

"Still just looks like night to me. I wish we could see some stars though." He looked back towards Amanda, but thankfully failed to noticed the condition of the parkade.

Before they came to the next intersection, Amanda saw a bad situation ahead. The cross street was blocked off by lineups of zombies, leaving only the way forward open. They stood shoulder to shoulder, only moving a little, heads bowed silently.

"All right, we're not going that way." Amanda took Mitch's hand and tried to guide him back.

"No, we can run through, they're slow!" Mitch, suddenly filled with courage, pulled his hand free and went dashing to the intersection.

Amanda called out in her loudest whisper. "Hold on! You can't go that way!" She gave chase, intending to carry him a safer direction if need be. Mitch turned out to be a fast runner; Amanda couldn't catch up.

As they crossed into the intersection, Amanda watched the lineups of zombies on either side to see if they'd attack. They only stood there, but as she crossed in front of them, they each raised their head with a broad, broad grin. Even the ones missing teeth, or parts of their jaw or heads did their best to smile the friendliest smile they could. Still without so much as a groan.

Still chasing Mitch, Amanda kept her eyes out along the sides of the road. Alley ways and storefronts, all crammed full of the waking dead. The next intersection was the same. Dead smiles and silence.

She had to stop to catch her breath. She might have had more oomph left if she hadn't been carrying Mitch half the day. "*Mitch!*" she didn't know whether to tell him to come back, or to keep going until he got clear of the surrounding mob.

What was he doing? He stopped running, dropped his backpack, and started walking back. He was smiling. He spoke quietly, "Tired, sister?"

The phrase was repeated by the zombies nearest to Mitch, then the ones next to those zombies, on and on, "Tired, sister?" cascading along the sides of the streets, zombie after zombie. "Tired, sister?" "Tired, sister?" "Tired, sister?"

By the time it reached her, it surrounded her, only to continue on by, down the street behind her.

Mitch was getting closer. "You couldn't tell. That's funny." Mitch's voice was changing. Getting older. Familiar. "You held this body, and didn't even know it was dead. Your other travelling companions, too." Mitch reached to his left shoulder with his right hand, digging at it with his nails, tearing it as he walked. "I found you here in Meston when I took them all. I spared you, sister, are you grateful?"

"Jonathan?!" Amanda backed away as Mitch got closer.

"I don't think she's grateful!" Mitch said. Now it was definitely the voice of Jonathan Coll. The voice of Erebus. It was Jon.

It was Jon. Of course it was Jon. Sarah knew he was the Erebus that took Meston, he told her that himself. But he had a sister named Amanda?

Amanda ran, but found her path blocked behind her as well. She could only keep her distance from the mob, which closed in very very slowly. Mitch kept approaching, tearing at himself, at his arms and face. "Ungrateful Amanda, what to do with you? I do love you, sis. You were always *so patient* with me. It's hilarious. I love that about you." Mitch grabbed on to Amanda's knees and hugged tightly as the mob got ever closer.

"M-Mitch. Jonathan. Why? Why are you doing this? Why do any of this!?" Amanda held herself, and began to brace for the worst. The mob was all around her now, all smiling madly, some nodding slowly. They pressed up against her as Mitch clawed his way up to look Amanda in the eye.

"My human impression is pretty good, I guess." Mitch chuckled in Jonathan Coll's voice. "There's actually been essentially no one alive in Meston since around the time the first zombies started popping up. It's been what, a day now? If the military figures out my hostages are walking corpses too, they'll bomb the shit out of me. That's why *you*, my beloved sister, get the honour of being head of the hostages! We'll have so much fun!"

"I'm not helping you, Jonathan." Amanda could only bear to whisper, staring into the mutilated face of six year old Mitch.

"No choice!" Mitch cheerfully said. He nodded to a zombie behind Amanda. That zombie grabbed Amanda's head firmly. She screamed and struggled, but the creature's strength was too great. With a sudden jab, the zombie's front teeth jabbed into her scalp, drooling a fleet of nanites into her body.

"They're calling me Erebus these days, did you hear?" Jonathan puppeteered Mitch to tap the ripped up side of his mouth as if pondering casually. "Of course it's a name I chose myself. The sister of the God Erebus needs a new name as well. Damn, I lost my Greek mythology file. Fuck it, I'm lazy. Your new name is Erika. Get it? Erebus, Erika?"

Amanda tried to protest, but found she could no longer speak. She could also no longer struggle. 'Mitch' remained latched onto Amanda as the zombie mob backed away a few metres.

"Now then, Erika- yes, you even look like an Erika, it fits. I'm in control now, you just get to watch. You get to feel." Mitch jumped off, and stood in front of Amanda. "We're going to have a blast. Your first mission is to dispose of this little body. We no longer need it."

The surrounding zombies grinned again, all nodding slowly in approval. Mitch stood with a similar grin, giggling in the voice of a six year old.

Amanda attacked, pushing Mitch onto his back, and holding him down with her knee, not that he resisted. Neither Amanda nor Sarah were in control. This was 'Erika'. This was Erebus. Amanda's hands clawed at Mitch's face. The smile was quickly ripped apart, but the giggling continued.

Mitch's voice became like that of one of the demons. *"Dear sister! Is this not amazing?! Is it not glorious?!"* Amanda's hands ripped at Mitch's face until it was no longer recognizable. She rammed her thumb into one of his eyes. There was blood up to her elbows, and she had felt some splatter on her face. Was he forcing her face to make one of those horrible grins as well?

"Don't worry," Jonathan's voice came from Mitch, "We'll probably get bombed all to hell either way at some point, but I'll back your mind up. It's all good! We can do this again and again! I'm so glad we got to play like this! I always wanted to do this when we were little!"

Amanda's nails went down to his throat, picking and clawing until the skin broke. Then she reached in and ripped it wide apart with a guttural groan.

"No," she thought, *"this isn't me! That's not how I sound, this isn't what I'd do!"* She desperately wanted to scream, to do anything other than watch and feel her hands rip this little boy apart bit by sinewy bit. *"Jonathan! If you can hear me, please just kill me now!"*

Perhaps she imagined it, but somewhere she heard Jonathan giggling.

:::C / [010100] [20]

Sarah awoke and sat up so fast she drifted up in the water about a metre before floating back down to the rocks. Wide eyed and trembling, she wanted to scream, but as she drew her breath, and filled with water again, she remembered the futility of it.

She stared forward, trying to forget Mitch, but at the same time, trying to understand.

":::Jonathan." She said quietly to Jon. ":::Jonathan, Erebus, Jon, whatever you want to call yourself, you wake up and explain things to me right fucking now, or I'll delete you the hard way by scraping you out of my skull with a rock."

Silence.

Sarah waited while her rage grew, then yelled at him,

":::*Explain Erika to me, now! In Meston! Tell me it was just a dream! Explain Erika! Explain Amanda!*"

It took another moment, but Jon spoke up in time before Sarah locked him in his room. ":::Hmm? Sorry, I... I was in slow-time. Let me look at what you said..."

More silence. It didn't take that long to read back a log of what was said.

With grim resolve, Sarah kept asking questions. ":::Do I look like her? Was that just part of a dream?"

":::I don't know why you'd have a dream like that."

That wasn't satisfactory. She kicked Jon back into his room and locked the door.

Enough sulking. She pushed up through the water with strength turned up. She was going to do something useful with her life. None of this 'making a happy adjusted human life' crap. She had strength, and she had reflexes. She was going to put them to good use.

The night sky greeted her as she reached the surface. She swam to shore much in the same path as before, but with hardened determination. Dripping wet, she marched to her little alleyway net access, and started scouring the net for rumours of pit fights.

She would go to any she could find. She'd rip apart the undead fighters, she'd rip apart the demons, she'd rip apart their managers. If any spectators had a problem with that, she'd rip... maybe not, but they were going get a knee to the groin that would make them choke on their testicles.

The longer she searched, the more her rage subsided. The less she felt like ripping apart anyone. She thought of Amanda being forced to destroy that child, and her rage was renewed. Thoughts sped all the way up, searching the net as fast as the could, she was quickly running out of places to look.

Maybe pit fights just didn't get promoted on the net. Maybe she didn't know the magic word. Maybe she would have to just pound the streets until something came up.

She might get seen. She went to go look and see if there was any records about her fight with Doug. Damn it, she didn't know how to get into some of these higher security spots. Jon did. Screw him. She'd do it the old fashioned way, and just go to-

":-:Sarah."

Oh crap. It was Eidechse, and he was talking in fast-time to match her. She didn't feel like his crap, but wanted to be polite. Eidechse was okay. ":-:Hi, Eid. How are you doing?"

":-:Unsettling events have-"

Sarah interrupted, noticing the moth on her forearm. ":-:Hey, you said before that I had a familiar face." She almost didn't want confirmation. ":-:Who... who do I look like to you?"

":-:The match is not perfect," Eidechse began, "but accounting for minor discrepancies and referencing against individuals involved in nanite activities, it seems likely that your face is a recreation of Amanda Coll."

Sarah sighed, as well as one can when thoughts run so fast. "Deceased sister to Jonathan Coll, A.K.A. Erebus, scourge of Aguola. Yeah. I was afraid of that."

":-:Sarah, are you claiming to have been ignorant of this?"

":-:Ignorance seems to be my specialty lately."

":-:I feel I must tell you that your disappearance and erasure of your public records in such a close time to the attack o-"

":-:*All right!* Yeah I broke Doug's arm! And frankly, I'd do it again! I didn't have a choice, did I? He was trying to kill me and Dan, what the fuck was I supposed to do?!"

Sarah had enough. If Eidechse was going to call down an AZU unit on her over Doug, she should go hide. She returned to normal thought speed. Eidechse was still talking, but too fast to understand. Before Eidechse re-synched with Sarah's thought speed, she took a deep breath and blew the moth off of her arm.

She ran, leaving Eidechse trying to calm down a panicked, fluttering moth, and wondering who 'Doug' was. He still didn't have any answers from Sarah about the Victoria Emerald attack. The monster there claimed to be a product of Erebus, and there ran the long-dead sister of Erebus.

Who was Doug?

:::C / [010101] [21]

Sarah's first impulse was to just jump back in the sea and resume sulking. Her clothes would never dry like that. If she could imagine risking it, she'd go back to the apartment and get some of her clothes.

Pointless.

Clothes to do what, go apply for another job, while Eidechse had the army after her? Incinerate! Would they really incinerate her for having a nanite nervous system, or would her relation to 'Erebus' be their reason?

Imagine if they knew he was in her head! The possibilities she imagined then made incineration sound merciful.

Maybe they'd find all the movies stored in her skull, and fry her for piracy. What the heck was she going to do now? Hide? Sure. For now. Eidechse likely figured out where she had been before; she was still wet.

By the shore, she spotted a large drainage pipe, large enough to walk in if she crouched. It was locked with a metal grate, but her strength made it easy to pinch off the lock.

A steady stream of murky water, no more than a centimetre deep trickled quietly down the middle, and out to sea. Whatever it was, it smelled all right. She did her best to place the gate back nicely behind her, and walked in. She adjusted her low-light vision to make due in the dark.

As she stepped carefully along the corrugated tube, she ran through events in her mind... could she have done something different to avoid this? Maybe this path was determined the moment she created her official records. That's what initially attracted Eidechse, wasn't it? After that, he only needed to see her face to connect her to Erebus.

Maybe she should have just never come out of the water in the first place.

The pipe was getting monotonous, albeit drier due to a slight incline. When she came to a small metal door on the side, she gently forced the little lock and opened it. How easy vandalism was in this mood. Jon would be so proud.

Jon. He was still locked in his 'room'. Well, he could stay there. Let him figure out on his own that he was being punished. He didn't admit anything about her dreams, or the fate of Amanda, but Eidechse had confirmed enough.

Oh joy. The killer of millions is sorry. He made a life, and called it his daughter. Rot. Sit there and rot. Run your thought process as slow or as fast as you want, watch your movies, pick your virtual nose.

She tried to equate the Autar and Meston statistics to real-life suffering, but it didn't work. There wasn't a way. A single death can be horrific and life altering for loved ones. Two cities worth? No wonder the government banned nanites. She sympathized. She wouldn't blame them for torching her, if it meant scrubbing away such an accomplished mass murderer.

She knew for a long time what Jon had done, but living Amanda's experience made her see beyond the statistics.

"There's a mass murderer in my head!"

Her scream of realization echoed down the pipe. The sound faded to nothing. It meant nothing, and was heard by no one.

She opened the door to Jon's little corner of her skull, and screamed into it, ":::*How the fuck am I* supposed *to feel with a mass murderer in my head who killed his own sister like that?!* Huh? *How?!"*

Before Jon could respond, she 'slammed' the door shut and locked it.

She took a deep breath. That felt good.

She remembered the little command she found to delete him. Just like that. Poof. She considered it more seriously now than she ever had before. That seemed a little pointless. It was obvious that she had him on a perfect little leash.

He can't see through Sarah's eyes, talk to her, or even get onto the net without her direct consent.

Enough thinking of that. What was she doing again? Oh yes, she had just broken into a little metal door in a big metal pipe, drooling into the sea. And a moth was out to get her.

Actually, that moth might have some pretty darn good ears, and might have followed her. Damn.

The little metal door contained a little metal ladder, going down a little metal tube. In the interests of avoiding nosy moths and other bothersome bugs carrying nanites, she opted to go further down.

Barely wide enough to move in, the shaft looked to go down for quite a ways. She reached out to the little door and closed herself in.

In the dim of his mahogany office, a small notice popped up on the upper edge of Mr. Book's monitor with a polite 'ding'. "Greene, Timothy has entered the building."

"Send him to me." Mr. Book grunted. The terminal beeped in the affirmative. Mr. Book assumed Greene to be arrested or dead. He had seen the news report; a vaguely defined incident at the Victoria Emerald, and Greene had not reported in since. If he had been arrested, he had managed to keep his mouth shut so far.

No, that couldn't be the case. The government had access to Lancer's employment records. The feds would have been whining at him for some reason by now.

Three tired sounding knocks resounded at Mr. Book's door. He answered to the knocker and the computer controlled lock on the door at the same time. "All right, come on, then."

The door clicked, and Greene pushed the door open, letting in more light than Mr. Book wanted. "Get in here, Greene. Shut the door."

And Greene did.

Greene was wearing clothes that looked like he got them at a charity store. Around his lower face and neck was a scarf.

"Greene, you're a mess. So much for your expense budget, hm? All right, out with it, what did you find? Was there a nanite fighting pit there? Did it use a signal like Coll's protocols?"

Greene calmly sat down in the chair across the room. "Long time no see, Bookiepoo."

Mr. Book's eyes widened with a sharp gasp. "Coll?"

Greene's tired eyes betrayed a smile, and he bounced slightly as if giggling. "Bookiepoo! You know I haven't gone by that name since even *before* I shed my original flesh!"

"Shed it? I heard AZU-1 ripped it up with airborne gunfire!"

Greene sighed, the scarf pushing forward a little from his breath, and slipping down enough to reveal his nose. "Yes, after I left it. It was quite dramatic. An overly-zealous end to a passable chrysalis. And for the record, what you see before you now houses only a partial version of myself. A messenger. A messenger from your God Erebus. I guess that makes me an angel!"

Mr. Book glared at Greene, not that it was very different than his usual expression. Greene wasn't his favourite person in the entire world, but he wasn't a bad man. He didn't deserve to be Coll's meat puppet.

Greene, Coll, Erebus, whatever. Greene leaned casually back, tipping the chair a little. "Bookiepoo, have you ever heard of 'arithmomania'?"

Mr. Book furrowed his brow. "I think I've heard of it."

This caused Greene to jump onto his feet, lean on the desk and point at Mr. Book, who reacted only by staring at Greene's fingertip with contempt. "See, Bookiepoo? That relates to all of it! Your *brain*, that squishy analogue based chunk of chemicals and meat! It's so unreliable! You may have read a detailed article on arithmomania, and it's been lost into the mess of your mind! *Digital*, Bookiepoo! The answer has always been to go digital!"

"It helps your memory, I'm sure." Mr. Book was patronizing the creature in front of him, quietly entering text into a small terminal he held under the table.

"*Helps?!* Helps?" Greene's body wandered the room listlessly, arms outstretched, as Coll used it to testify to his own 'godly' ascension. "I. Remember. Everything. Down to the micron and beyond! I was even able to dissect the mess of my old human mind in such detail that I remembered things that I didn't know I had even forgotten! This ties into the arithmomania!"

"Do tell, Coll."

This drew a touch of rage from him. "*Erebus! I am Erebus! Jonathan Coll is long dead!*" He paused, regaining composure. "I am Erebus." He wandered to the far end of the office, and crossed his arms. "Where was I?"

"Arithmomania." Mr. Book recounted flatly, as if bored, still thumbing notes into his little hidden terminal.

"Yes. Arithmomania. In short, a mental condition relating to obsessive compulsive disorders. In humans, fairly unusual. It usually manifests as a compulsive need to count everything! The number of pencils in a can, the number of beans on your plate, the number of steps it takes to get to work!"

"Fascinating."

"Ah-ha! *Yes!* But what you humans see as a *disorder*, is actually the seed to perfect logic! How is a person supposed to see the big picture, if they can't see the *little* picture? How can humanity hope to comprehend the cosmos, when they can barely talk and type at the same time?!"

With this, Greene slammed both hands down on Mr. Book's desk, causing the scarf to slip loose. Disturbing but expected, Mr. Book could now see a fresh rip down the middle of Greene's lower jaw, that continued down his neck, and into his shirt. Yes, Greene was now a demon, possessed by a mad, self-assuming 'god'.

Greene yelled, his lower jaw separating a little bit with each syllable. "*You're flawed! You're all flawed*, with no hope of progress! What kind of god would allow such creatures to continue pissing all over the planet? Do you want to see arithmomania? I have plans, I do! I will count every fucking grain of sand if it helps. I may eventually do it just for kicks! I can see the small picture, atom by atom! Are you hearing me, Book?"

Mr. Book's little terminal was now wedged between his thigh and the chair, listening, passing it all on. "*Yes, I'm listening! There's a murderous corpse in my office, controlled by the all fucking mighty Erebus!* What's your great big picture then, Coll? Exterminate humanity to make room for yourself? Convert us all into zombies, demons, and other abominations?"

Greene's body recoiled. Not with fear, but with confusion. He went back to wandering around the room, now tapping a finger on his lower lip in contemplation. "Oh. Oh Bookiepoo, I'm a little bit disappointed, but I guess I can't be surprised. You are still human after all."

Looking around the ceiling as if counting the stars, Greene sighed. "I never liked you, Bookiepoo, you know that."

Mr. Book grunted, as only Mr. Book can. "And?"

"Bookiepoo, I did, in a way, respect you. Your sense of order, of things being a certain way in order to achieve an objective. I would be very interested to see what you can do with a little touch of 'arithmomania'. You'd be born anew of course, but you'd still be you. More or less. Picture it, Bookiboo. Picture all you could get done."

"As what?" Mr. Book asked, "Your accountant? You still haven't told me what your plan for humans is."

Greene was deaf to Mr. Book's questions at this point. His eyes were wide, and even as Greene paced back and forth, the eyes stayed locked onto Mr. Book. Greene spoke to himself softly, still tapping his lip. "Yes, yes, imagine. Imagine a new Bookiepoo. Adjust his body, we could of course. Something less bulky and inefficient. That much is easy. An afterthought at best."

"Get out." Mr. Book ordered plainly. "All three of you. Greene, Coll, Erebus. Whatever. All of you get out. Now."

Greene stopped pacing, but kept tapping his lip, and staring at Mr. Book. A smile, slightly wider than human, stretched across Greene's face. "Give me half an hour of your time, and your flesh, and we'll change your mind."

With that, Greene stood with arms outstretched. He opened his jaw in both directions, and his rib cage spread open, ripping the cheap shirt apart for Mr. Book to stare into the cavity where Greene's organs had once been.

His exposed, separated ribs throbbed in and out as if breathing. Greene resisted the urge of the demon scream, as it might serve to interrupt his work with Mr. Book.

Greene lunged forward reaching for Mr. Book. As Greene's knee clamored up onto the desk, Mr. Book began a command. "Omega sanitize Book forty two!" By this point, Greene's hands were around Mr. Book's skull. He pulled Mr. Book's head forward, trying to ram it into the desk, even if Mr. Book's mass made it difficult.

Metal was heard to shift inside the wood of the door, sealing the room, mahogany and all, in an unseen metal box liner. A series of little nozzles in the ceiling sparked to life.

Fire. With the realization of what was about to happen, This angel of Erebus had no purpose but to make Mr. Book suffer as mush as possible in the short time left.

Blinding flame flooded the room. Joyless Mr. Book thought his last thoughts. He had slain an angel.

:::C / [010111] [23]

Sarah was surprised at how clean it was in the underground tunnels. It wasn't *sterile* by any means, but she had seen far dirtier streets downtown. Mammoth sheets of sheer concrete made up most of the structures.

The walls and ceilings were often laden with vast arrays of piping and conduits that seemed to be in an unmoving race with one another. They crossed over each other, switched from wall to ceiling, merged with each other, and divided from one another. Valves, both manual and automated (controlled by yet another conduit of wires, no doubt) and unidentified boxes seemed randomly inserted into the conduits. Everything bore some kind of identifying code, as well as a colour that somehow represented something important, but none of it meant anything to Sarah.

This was someone else's engineering nightmare.

The lights in the ceiling made sense, though. It also made sense that they were not left on. Thankfully her night vision was doing an excellent job.

The last half hour had been very quiet. Not an especially comforting quiet, either. Soft echoes from her soft footsteps returned to her with a hard metallic aftertaste.

She happened by a large pipe that was making a muted gushing sound, pumping water likely, from *to*, all the way to *fro*. It was a soothing sound, so she idled by it, listening to it for a while as small respite from the domineering solitude.

While she lingered, a little black spider leisurely crept out of a crack in the wall.

Sarah stared at it with suspicion. For all she knew, Eidechse was inside it. Probably not. It wasn't making any attempt to get to her. If Eidechse *was* stalking her, it would have been much easier to just follow the same path she took. Regardless, she resented the spider's presence, and continued on her way.

In retrospect, maybe she shouldn't have run from Eidechse earlier. Yes, she broke a person's wrist, but her reason was sound, wasn't it? And Eidechse of all 'people', should understand being a chunk of nanite-tech needing to hide from the government.

Then there was the Amanda Coll link. Erebus.

Damn it, Jon was still locked in his 'room'. She felt a little bad about that, but not enough to let him out. *Her* guilt was easy to negate just by remembering *Jon's* guilt.

She wandered deeper, down some narrow stairs, alongside a sewer passage, up a small ladder, across, and on, and on.

Then, a sound. Something different. Hydraulics? It wasn't rhythmic, like you'd expect of some industrial machine. The sound was on and off at seemingly random intervals.

Following the sound, She came to a wide passage containing a large metal structure that moved a little with the hydraulic sounds. Its one end formed a huge, flattened spike, slightly wider than a manhole cover. It connected to two bigger extensions of machinery hooked to each other with heavy industrial joints put into motion with hydraulics.

The furthest and largest section of this writhing machine was about the size of a queen sized mattress. Beyond that were merely cables that reached out into a darkness that became impenetrable, even to light-amplified vision.

Another sound. A person. Sarah hid behind a large chunk of piping running up the wall. For hiding purposes, the pipe could stand to be bigger. She double checked the light level; her night vision had been on for a long time. Upon flicking it off for a moment, she confirmed that she was still in complete darkness. She turned it back on.

She peered into that grand darkness, and saw the person causing the sounds. By his clothing, he was a homeless man. As it turned in Sarah's direction, she saw that no, this was a creature. It was split down the middle like the monster she had seen in the fight pit. This was only the second of these that she had seen, and she didn't like them any better up close. Yeah, she was about ready to leave now.

Sarah kept an eye on the demon, and slowly, quietly stepped back the way the came. Not silent enough.

The demon wailed its horrible wail, arms outstretched, then charged towards Sarah, sharpened teeth, claws, and ribs aching to sink into meat.

Damn, it seemed to be able to see just fine here too. Strength up, time down. It was time to apply the 'kung fu' crap she had taught Danielle.

Soft spots, hard spots. The demon's hard spots were obvious. As it lunged, Sarah grabbed its wrist, and slipped around beside it. She had advised Danielle not to attempt a trip at this kind of moment, but Sarah felt confident.

She hooked the demon's ankle with hers, and threw it to the ground, fumbling on the tips of its ribs. Feeling she had an upper hand, Sarah tossed her weight at its back in perceived slow motion for accuracy.

As she landed, she expected to hear the sound of its exposed ribs snapping.

No such luck. Instead, she heard the tips scrape along the concrete as the rib cage closed. When they finally landed hard on the ground, there was no sound of breaking bones.

She jumped off behind it, narrowly missing its hands reaching backwards to grab her, bending its arms in ways no human could. It tried to stand, but Sarah quickly grabbed an ankle out from under it, sending it on its face again.

It kicked at her hard, but she held on. If the bones were tough, maybe the flesh was weak. Suppressing her disgust, she jabbed her fingertips into the thing's calf muscle. In this slowed time, it was nauseating. She grabbed a handful and pulled, ripping it free from the bone.

The demon began another of its screams as it floundered to face her, attempting a similar attack on her forearm with its own claws. Sarah was quick, but not perfect. The demon left three deep gashes in her arm. Her circulatory system was currently inactive, so she didn't bleed much.

Her systems reported the injury along with pain measurements. She quickly turned off the unpleasant aspect of the pain. That would surely be a distraction.

A couple more demons' screams began from the darkness behind her. It was time to go.

The injured demon got to its feet, and Sarah employed the same wrist-grab and dodge from before, again adding the extra trip. Footsteps were rushing from the darkness. With her strength already maxed out, she ran. Anxious to get out of this situation, she let time flow a little faster.

As she ran, she heard the injured one get up again, and promptly fumble as it tried to give chase. She could have won. It didn't learn from the first trip. It was fast enough to be a threat, but plenty dumb. She could have disassembled it. But not its buddies. Not at the same time.

She ran and ran. The sounds of the perusing demons grew gradually quieter. Smaller and more nimble in this concrete labyrinth, she was getting away. So far.

Finally she was in the first large drainage pipe, and the sunrise light reached in to greet her, to welcome her back from the underworld. She still ran, and ran, despite not hearing the demons for a while now. She barged out of the grating, and kept running.

Damned arm. She checked on her systems to confirm that healing was in progress. She should eat some protein soon, to help it along. While she was paying attention to her wound, she made sure she hadn't been infected with anything. Nope, good. *Can* they infect, like a zombie does? Through bites only, maybe. The demons were at no loss for mouth.

She sought out a data line while assembling a report on the underground demons, along with directions. She planned on sending it to the police, but had a feeling that Eidechse would also manage to get a copy. She included a note to him;

Eidechse,

I know you probably think I'm some tool for Erebus, but that Erebus is gone. I don't know as much about myself as I might like, but I am my own person. I only wanted to live a normal life. I hope that you can appreciate that.

If you do any research on my fight with Doug, you'll know I didn't have a lot of choice, but that doesn't change what I physically am.

She found a data line, and sent the file to a regular crime-tip node. Then she got a little distance from where she sent the message from. A dozen blocks or so. She didn't know how fast they'd respond, or if they would track it to the source.

Sticking near the shore, she eventually came across a dockyard for private pleasure-craft. A few early morning fishing enthusiasts roamed around, getting ready to set out, but it was still fairly quiet.

It felt pretty safe here.. She sat on a quiet dock and enjoyed the sunrise for a while.

Maybe it was guilt, maybe it was loneliness, maybe it was the fact that she knew it was going to happen eventually- but she opened Jon's door.

Silence.

":::Pouting, Jon?"

":::I just don't know what you expect me to say." Yeah, screaming at him about his murder of millions of people was kind of hard to reply to.

":::Tell me you had nothing to do with *this*." She showed Jon the file she had sent to the cops, and replayed him the memory of the machine and the fight underground.

Silence, and then, ":::Damn, Sarah, why'd you stick yourself in a situation like that?! Let me see how your arm is doing. Damn, I thought that monster at the bar would be the only one."

":::I was down there because I was running from Eidechse. He figured out my face, and who it's supposed to be. I thought I'd leave before he called down hell on me."

Jon sighed. ":::I thought I made your face different enough to not be a match."

":::He compensated. So these things... you're saying you have nothing to do with them?"

":::I've been locked in my room all this time!"

Sarah wasn't impressed. ":::For all I know, you built them all long before you made me!"

":::I didn't! I didn't even leave the region you were born since I first went underwater!" Jon knew that would also be unconvincing. "Sarah. I think it's time you had something I've kept from you. I thought you'd be better without it, but since you know about Amanda... it's overdue."

":::What?"

":::I think you just have to go open it yourself. You can find your way back to your birthplace, right?"

":::It hasn't been that long." And it felt like a trap. Now that Sarah 'knew too much', maybe Jon was going to do something nasty to her. But she still had that little button that could kill Jon. Maybe. ":::Oh, what the heck. You got me curious."

When no one was looking, she smoothly and quietly slipped off the dock, and into the water. Strength up, dive, and go. She swam as fast as she could, less out of excitement, and more out of wanting to get it over with. Getting deeper, she adjusted her vision for low light and kept going.

Eventually she found her 'crib', just like she remembered it. Rocky, cold, dark. She stopped and floated there quietly.

Jon spoke up. ":::Twenty five degrees to port, one point two metres ahead of your nose, on the sea floor. See that rock?"

Sarah pointed at a hand-sized, pale, flat shale stone that was out of place among the surrounding dark sedimentaries. ":::That one?"

":::Yeah, break it open."

Sarah gripped it tight and snapped it. In the middle was a dark grey piece about the size of an ice cube.

Jon explained. ":::It's a dense cluster containing a pile of data. Go ahead and tap into it, like we do with data lines. It's pretty user friendly.

Sarah's paranoia imagined some debilitating virus, a memory wipe command, or some other nasty thing.

":::Go ahead," Jon urged, ":::Meet your aunt."

":::This? This is Amanda?!"

":::It's her memories, her personality, everything I could extract."

Sarah was stunned. ":::You saved her before you killed her?"

":::Remember when I told you that your personality was a mixture of good traits from a library of minds?"

":::There was no vast library, was there?" she looked closely at the orb. ":::I'm just her. I really *am* Amanda."

":::No. You aren't cluttered with all her memories, just her disposition, her philosophy, what passes for a soul. What you hold in your hand are the pieces you're missing, the raw memories. And to be honest, when I made that file, I wasn't trying to save her. I wanted a copy to torment for fun. Her body was destroyed when Meston was, but I had her mind and soul to toy with."

":::You killed her and wanted to torment her more. You invented hell. A hell for innocent people!"

Jon replied quietly, humbled. ":::Just read it. If you don't trust me, you can partition a section of your mind to-"

":::I can do it." she snapped harshly.

":::Even at full processing speed, it will take a long time to read it all. That's every memory of her life. You might want to skip around a bit. Keep an eye out for spots with me in it. That is, Jonathan Coll."

She pressed her nanite nerves out through her skin, and entered the cluster. The memories became quickly available to her. They didn't hit her like a sudden impact of knowledge; it was more like opening a door to a room you had forgotten.

::::C / [011000] [24]

Whap!

A little boy about four years old was hitting her on the head with a wooden spoon. She offered no resistance. He struck a few more times as she began to cry out loud.

Her voice was that of a baby.

A woman ran up from behind, picked the little boy up and scolded him. He fought back, trying to hit her with the spoon. Sarah didn't understand what the woman was saying. It was just sounds. Language as heard by a baby. Gibberish filled with emotion, and right now, none of it good.

She kept crying as the woman left, carrying the boy, speaking sternly. Her voice, and that of the yelling boy grew fainter down the hall, punctuated by the slam of a door.

Sarah surrendered to being Amanda. Baby Amanda was *alone* in the room, and this was not pleasant either, so she continued to cry. Mother appeared again and picked her out of the high chair, shushing, and softly saying comforting gibberish as the four year old Jonathan screamed at the top of his lungs on the other side of the house.

Sarah was feeling every emotion, with all the intensity that a baby would feel them. Fear, confusion, insecurity. All of which mother tried hard to ease. It worked. Mostly.

Jonathan continued to scream, adding the sounds of objects being thrown against the door.

Sarah skipped ahead in the memories. Amanda was now about three years old. She leaned on a seven year old boy, who was sitting on the floor watching TV. Amanda tried to hug him, and he pushed her off. She tried again, to the same result.

Frustrated, Jonathan snapped at her. "*Why don't you go play with your stupid smelly hamster or something?!*"

Amanda felt rejected, but the suggestion was a good one! She ran down the hall to her room, little feet pounding the floor, thump, thump, thump. Going into her room, the hamster's cage was on the floor. The top; a grating of little white bars, was removed from the base, sitting not far off.

The base's sawdust was spilled a little out of the sides. At first, Amanda wondered where her pet was.

It was there. In the middle of the base, motionless, with three steak knives sticking out of it.

Panicked horror caused Amanda's three year old body to tremble.

Skip ahead! Skip ahead!

Amanda was now five. She held her mother's hand as they walked down a school hallway. One side of the hall was a wall of windows, looking out into a student-maintained courtyard. A few cheap wooden benches, and a mess of 'carefully' tended plants all looked perfectly wonderful to a five year old. A few colourful blossoms were all it took.

She was led into a small office. Mother and the lady inside talked politely. Amanda's attention phased in and out.

"Ah yes," the lady said, "I believe her brother was taught by Mrs. Williams."

Mother sighed. "Yes. I'm really quite sorry about all of that. We're still trying our best with him. I assure you, Amanda is *nothing* like him."

The lady smiled politely. "Of course. But I think we'll assign her to a different teacher than Mrs. Williams. It would be awkward for Mrs. Williams, and I would worry that she couldn't be impartially even-handed with Amanda."

"I doubt anyone here could. I'm sure everyone knows about Jonathan." Mother sighed again, as she often did when the topic of Jonathan came up. Often it made her cry, but today she resisted. "You have to understand. Amanda and I... we have to live with him. We're... we're kind of afraid of him."

Amanda nodded enthusiastically. "His pills help a lot though!" The lady only chuckled dismissively. She didn't understand. She couldn't.

Skip. Sarah couldn't tell how old Amanda was now; It was dark. Amanda was in bed, warm and safe, but she was crying. It just kept going. No one was coming.

Sarah found herself snared into a pit of Amanda's crushing hopelessness. It physically hurt in her chest, and her thoughts were wrapped in such a tight knot that it took a little while for Sarah to remember that she could skip ahead.

How long was Amanda going to cry?

Skip ahead. Amanda was eight. She sat at her desk with everyone else, and brought out her lunch box.

"Whatcha got, Amanda?" The little red headed girl in front of her held an orange that she likely wanted to trade.

Amanda began to lift the lid of her lunch. She heard a little click, and saw a dead frog in her lunch box with several little objects stuffed in its back. With a burst that caused everyone in the class to cry out, startled, the frog exploded.

The red headed girl stared at Amanda and screamed as the teacher came running. Amanda's face hurt. A lot. Her hands were smattered with blood, hers, and the frog's.

Skip. She was twelve, riding in the backseat of a grey upholstered family car. Mother turned back from the front passenger seat, and faked a smile. "Only a little while longer. Are you excited to visit him?"

Amanda remained silent, and lowered her head.

Skip. She was nineteen. She sat in an outdoor audience of hundreds. Beside her sat her parents. On stage sat a group of robed graduates.

An older man in a more elaborate robe stepped up to the microphone. "Well, we were supposed to be hearing a valediction from Jonathan Coll, but he couldn't make it for some reason."

Mother sighed, father sunk his head.

The man at the microphone continued. "Well, we'll just have to get him his dual degrees another way. He did send a note to be read in his stead, however." The man waved an envelope.

"Call the bomb squad. Quick." Amanda muttered.

Mother held Amanda's hand. "Now, Honey."

The man at the podium opened the envelope, and read it to himself for a few moments. His face turned from cordial to disdainful. He folded the letter up, and restored his friendly guise as he put the letter back in his pocket. "Ah, sorry folks, it's rather unreadable."

"How can such a smart kid be such an ass?" Father said quietly.

"Well, he didn't show up to my high school graduation," Amanda said, "Why should he show up for his own university grad? Can we *go* now?"

"Yes." Father said. He, mother and Amanda stood. Father raised his voice to be heard by the man at the microphone. "I'm sorry. For that, for anything and everything I heard about, and the things I didn't get to hear about his time here. I'm sorry."

Skip. Amanda was at a movie, with a friend. A comedy. The friend didn't look familiar, but she shared her gummies. With no Jonathan in sight, Sarah let this memory run for a while. Amanda was relaxed. Almost happy. The movie was entertaining enough.

This was a good memory. Sarah was glad to find one, for Amanda's sake.

Skip. She was now twenty. This place was familiar. This was where Sarah first dreamt of. A coffee shop in the City of Meston. This seemed to be a little later than the first dream, however. In her first dream, Jonathan came to borrow money, and told Amanda that he was going to work in Autar.

Today, Amanda stood watching the news on a terminal bolted to the wall. The news had been almost entirely one story for a week.

As photos and footage blended by, the announcer narrated. "Autar has been evacuated of every living person that could be found. Infra red sweeps are still in effect for a little while longer, but nothing living has been found for days."

"Get to work." called one of Amanda's co-workers. She didn't respond, allowing another co-worker to defend her, "Shut up, asshole. She's got a brother in there, and he hasn't shown up."

"Shit. Sorry, Amanda."

Amanda couldn't decide how she felt about Jonathan's disappearance. The removal of his tormenting left her with a sense of freedom and relief. A huge weight was gone. At the same time... this was her brother. Whatever that was worth.

Skip. She was in a movie theatre again. A couple onscreen were seen in an embrace as a musical score swelled. They exchanged romantic banalities, followed by another embrace in slow motion, and a dissolve to a sunrise before the credits began.

A mildly sarcastic male voice grabbed her attention. "Well, that was a movie." He was sitting next to her. He was her date. He was reasonably handsome, with a coy little smile.

"Oh shush," Amanda said, "It wasn't that bad, was it?" Sarah could feel Amanda's emotions for him, wondering if it could be love.

"No, no. I'm just teasing. I never feel like seeing this kind of thing, but I end up enjoying them well enough."

"Well, you're a good sport." Amanda grabbed his hand, and leaned over to peck his cheek. He didn't smell too shabby either. This was a feeling that Sarah had never felt before. One she hadn't enabled in herself. Maybe she should sometime. Romantic interest.

The man chuckled, "Yeah, yeah. But next time I pick. Something with aliens, or a ghost or something." He stood and gentlemanly offered his hand to help Amanda up.

"Aliens, huh?" They made their way to the doors amidst the rest of the audience. A group of teenage girls ahead of them were talking loudly. They had been talking a lot throughout the movie, despite being shushed by others.

One of them waved her hand carelessly and splashed Amanda's date with warm, flat, watered down pop.

"Miss!" Amanda's date called to the girl with understandable irritation. The girl either ignored him, or just didn't hear over the noise of her group.

"*Excuse me! Miss!*" Anger distorted his face.

Amanda grabbed his arm and pulled him close. "Forget it. It's just an airhead."

He relented, but was rigid with indigence. Amanda understood, but at the same time, for a fraction of a second the look on his face was a little scary. It made her question their future. It was stupid, she knew she was being oversensitive. He was great, he was. A perfect gentleman.

She didn't really feel like another date though. Maybe she should just forget about it.

Skip. Amanda was brushing her teeth at her large bathroom mirror. In the next room, the TV blathered on. While she brushed, Sarah examined Amanda's face. She really had to look closely to spot any difference between Amanda and herself.

Little things, like a slight earlobe height difference, a nearly undetectable difference in angle to the eyebrows, hairline, things like that. It was so minor that it seemed like Jon make the changes just to convince himself that it could fool anyone.

She wished she could talk to Amanda, but this was just an elaborate recording after all.

Amanda looked in the mirror, making eye contact for a moment. Just looking at herself.

Sarah wanted to yell at her, "*Say something! Say something to me! I'm your... I don't know! Talk to me!*" But of course the recording heard nothing. Oblivious, Amanda rinsed out her brush, spat, and grabbed her floss. She had just snapped off a piece, when the TV around the corner caught her attention. She listened without bothering to go into the next room to watch.

"New developments about the Autar disaster comes to us today, as military forces apprehend a man they believe caused the initial outbreak, all that time ago. He has been identified as one 'Jonathan Coll'," The rest of the report fell on deaf ears.

Amanda dropped the floss, and slumped to the floor. She was surprised, but somehow not shocked. "Jonath-..." she whispered, "damned idiot." After sitting on the bathroom floor for a while, she considered trying to get in contact with him.

What would she say? Hi, Jonathan. What the hell were you thinking? She knew what he was thinking. He wanted to explode a dead frog in the face of the world.

Skip. Amanda was back at work in the coffee shop.

"Got in a little late today." Said one of her employees.

Amanda sighed. She scrubbed a counter top with unusual focus. She just wanted to work and get her mind off of Jonathan's drama, but it was becoming obvious that it wasn't going to happen. "Yeah, sorry. I had to have a little chat with a stack of army guys who came to see me. They wanted to talk about my brother."

The employee looked shocked for a moment. "No way! When I heard the last name of that guy on the news, I figured it was just-"

"No." Amanda threw the rag at the sink, like a soggy bullet. "No, that's my branch of Colls all right. I'd like to say I can't believe it's him, but..."

"Whoa. That's pretty messed up!"

"You think? My brother killed a city. Frogs and cats weren't enough for him any more. I wonder when he went off his meds. I haven't spoken to him in quite a while." A sliver of vanity made Amanda wonder; if she had been in touch more, could she have helped? Seen a sign of horrible things to come, and talked him towards a better path? Maybe her brother was just an unsalvageable monster in the first place. "I wish he were just a victim in Autar."

She excused herself, and stepped into the washroom. Tears came. A sorrowful cry came next, she couldn't control it. Her brother. She hated him, but a part of her loved him. He was family, she couldn't help it. "Jonathan, you stupid..." She couldn't find the word. She desperately didn't want to call him a monster. She didn't *want* to believe he could be responsible for a genocide. But if anyone was capable, it was him.

Amanda was ready to call him. To scream at him, to ask him why, knowing full well that the answer would never satisfy her. Just being able to scream at him. Scream at him for everything. He was behind bars now, he couldn't hurt her.

Realizing the futility of yelling at him, she committed an equally futile act. She punched the wall, repeatedly. "*Jonathan, you stupid fuck!*" She screamed at the wall as she punished it, tears running down her face. "*Stupid asshole, what the hell-*" her voice cracked into sobs, and she melted to the floor, trying hard to find pleasant memories of Jonathan. There were so few, and when she thought about it, they were simply the times when he was *not* doing anything cruel. Nothing of kindness, or heart. The little affection she had for him was an invention she had fostered over the years.

It didn't matter anymore. It didn't. It was over.

Amanda pulled herself up, and looked in the mirror to clean herself up. Suck it up, girl. She had to get back to work. Doubtless her screams were heard outside. Sure enough when she stepped out, she was met with a look of pity from her employee, and confusion from her customers.

An unusual hiss came from the sky, as an unusual sight passed overhead. A black airlimb. Who used those?

Sarah saw where this was going. Later that day, Amanda would meet her first zombie. By tomorrow, her city would be a changed place. Sarah didn't need to see this again.

:::C / [011001] [25]

Sarah left the memories, and was again looking only through the dark waters all around her.

Jon seemed to know that she was done. ":::I sat right around here as a formless mass of nanites, and I watched that whole thing. Every bit, in order."

Sarah was still a little dazed. ":::How... how long did that take?"

":::In real time? Almost a month. In our fast thought mode though, it was over twenty years. You saw how it ended though, right? You see her now? You know her? For all the bombs and hatred that the military threw at me at Meston, she was my weakness all along. When I bothered to look into that file... I mean, *really* look.. that's when I could see what I was. I killed her, then she saved me."

Sarah sighed. ":::Yeah. I dreamt her death a while ago. I think I had the last day or two already in my head. I didn't realize-"

":::You did? Honestly, I didn't mean for you to see that, it was supposed to be cleanly removed. That was a bad idea, I know this now."

Sarah recalled Amanda's time in the end of Meston, Mitch, and the process of her death. ":::You lived it? Lived it all? Did you feel it?"

":::Yeah." Jon's voice was quiet and distant. ":::At the time, I felt it all as intensely as she did. I had no idea. I really didn't. The intensity of her joys and sorrows. It was all alien to me."

":::Jon, you make it sound like you'd never had an emotion before that."

For a while, he was silent. ":::Well. That's just it, that's what I realized. Jonathan Coll was born without real emotion, or a sense of right and wrong. I spent some time trying to place a label on it all. Sociopath, narcissistic, alexithymia. I could find a ton of mental disorders that could apply, until I realized that psychiatry didn't deal so well with absolute definitions. You have to deal in analogues, and that's always frustrating."

":::So... what now, you're fixed?"

":::No. I couldn't do that. I wasn't able. I just make sure I'm aware of the problem, and think of how Amanda would judge an action before I do it." That stood to reason. There had been a few times when Jon had slipped, and said things that had implied a darker mind at work.

":::So, am I your conscience?" Sarah asked.

"⸬I am not salvageable." His voice dripped with sickly, sticky regret.
"⸬As a technology, I stand for a lot of great ideas, Sarah. The ideas were
poorly used. I will never be able to separate myself completely from that. My
sister was impacted by my... my ways, just by being related to me, long
before I took a single life. Similarly, you will have a difficult time getting away
from it. For that, I am sorry. For many things, I am sorry. Lies to you, hiding
things, telling things in the wrong way. I always see my errors too late. It's in
my nature. I must be succeeded by a superior."

"⸬You mean me."

"⸬You have all the intelligence and technical experience that I have. On
a technical level, you are capable of anything that I've done, but morally
unlikely to do so."

"⸬Rather unlikely." No, she didn't have much desire for a few million
obedient walking corpses, thank you very much. "⸬So if you don't have
emotion or morality, what motivated you before?"

"⸬Boredom. Curiosity. What fun could I have, that no one else could?
Something unique. Something to demonstrate my ability."

Lovely. "⸬So what should *I* do with this ability?" Sarah asked.

"⸬I honestly don't want you to get that answer from me. That's the point.
I am *literally* the worst role model in the world. You have to have my
intelligence, my ability, but if you have to emulate a soul, emulate Amanda's."

"⸬So why did you make me, and not just recreate Amanda?"

Jon hummed thoughtfully. "I... that's nearly what I've done, isn't it? I
made you look like this in tribute to her. I fashioned your personality after
hers because it was the best material I had... not to say I would want any
different. I wanted to keep her memories away from you, but that didn't work
out, did it?"

Sarah stood, and pushed herself upward through the water. "⸬So, I
guess I'm her then. I'm Amanda."

"⸬I don't think so. I killed Amanda, and I wouldn't want to fool myself into
thinking that I've corrected that. Besides, she might be your jumping off point,
but you've already become someone different."

Sarah still held the vessel of Amanda's memories in her hand as she
drifted upwards. She verified that she had copied everything, then erased
everything from the little grey cluster.

She let it go, and watched it slowly sink away into the darkness. "⸬It
sounds like a little morality stuck on you, Jon."

"⸬Maybe. Not enough, probably. Those demon-things? They don't
repulse me, they don't horrify me. At worst, they're tactical obstacles. I
admire the design. The idea of a few million of those, really trumps the
masses of zombies. Sure, I dabbled with a few abomination-class creatures,
and some of them I was quite proud of. There was one that could put an
arm-"

"⸬Jon. Enough. Stop." She knew all she wanted to about the
abominations. The demons and the horsemen that Amanda encountered.
Quite creative. What the hell was stopping the original Jonathan Coll from
taking up painting or something? Right. That wouldn't be unique, that
wouldn't showcase his technical superiority.

"::::I'm a monster too," she said wistfully as she continued up, "a construct, a fishy fleshed thing." She had said similar things to herself in much angrier tones a few times before.

"::::You are not." Jon seemed insulted. "::::Humans are just biologically constructed creatures. You are different, but not a monster."

Sarah let that sink in. It didn't ring perfectly true- about humans, that is. It was oversimplified, but she got the point. "::::When things calm down, maybe I'll think about dating or something. I can just flip that part of myself on, huh?"

"::::If you're thinking about it, it seems to already be waking up."

"::::Hmm."

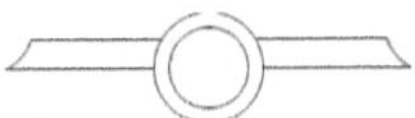

Upwards, upwards. Without actively driving herself through the water, her drift up was taking its sweet time. But that was all right. The surface was coming eventually. There was still the matter of swimming to shore.

It would be broad daylight. It would make getting to shore discretely a bit difficult. Not a huge worry.

Above, a couple large shadows slid along the surface. Getting closer, a considerable hiss could be heard, and the water was disturbed around either of the two shadows.

"::::Damn it. Airlimbs. Dollars to doughnuts it's a couple of AZU units. Dive, Sarah. We'll surface somewhere else."

Sarah idled in place. "::::They found me here. They could find me somewhere else, too."

"::::Then we surface by the shore, and charge in, blend into the crowd. We can't go on the net anymore. That's how we attracted Eidechse in the first place. That silly thing ratted us out."

"::::Can't blame him, I guess. Better safe that swimming in zombies."

Jon seethed. "::::I can blame him if I damn well please."

Without diving or rising any further, Sarah topped off her strength, and swam towards shore. The airlimbs were following, directly overhead. "::::Yup, I think they want to talk to me."

"::::You mean incinerate you."

"::::Maybe, but they haven't opened fire yet."

"::::Flamethrowers don't work through water, Sarah."

"::::Oh, I'm sure they have bullets, too."

Well, yes, Jon was fairly certain that they had some of those 'zipper' guns mounted on the airlimbs. He couldn't say if they could shoot with any accuracy through this much water, however. "::::I'm looking at a map," Jon said, "I see a large docking complex where we could swim under a lot of cover. Try to mute your IR signature, and we might be able to slip onto shore under one of the bigger docks."

Sarah changed her heading towards a chunk of the mainland far away from the docking complex.

"::::What are you doing?" Jon protested.

"::::Relax." She turned off her artificial body heat generation. It wouldn't make her entirely invisible to IR since she *did* have to produce *some* heat to function, but it would help a lot. She dove as she swam forward, as deep as the sea floor. "::::The water will hide the rest of my heat, right?"

"::::Ooh, you're tricky!"

She turned her strength to a very minimal setting, and turned towards the docking complex. "Less muscle power, even less heat generation. If we're lucky, I turned 'invisible' while going the wrong direction."

"::::And they'll trace our path all the way back to an entirely wrong part of the shore! Good girl, good girl!"

"::::Too bad we can't see if they fell for it."

With such a low use of strength, it was slow going. Sarah looked forward to getting close enough that the waves would supply a bit of support. She checked out her injured arm.

The surface of it was looking pretty good, but it was still a little lumpy, in the shape of the gashes. No significant flesh had been torn *out*, so she took a moment to push the flesh under her skin back into place with her opposite hand.

Only when she felt how loose and squishy some of the flesh underneath was, (her pain was still suppressed) did she really feel unsettled by the injury.

"::::Good idea," Jon said, "no sense in making the nanites do that kind of work. It's way faster to move most of the bulk manually. They can handle the fine details. The strength in that arm will be poor until the tissues are fused."

"::::Yeah, well, I was thinking more that I didn't want to come out onto the shore with a lumpy forearm. Blending in and all that."

"::::Yeah. Well. Yeah. That's an idea too. Maybe you need a haircut."

Sarah paused. "::::Hey, what do you mean, I've had my hair growth turned off this whole- *oh!* Right, to have a bit of a disguise. Actually, I could just go with a little ponytail. They know me with loose hair, right? Amanda always went with loose hair, except when going to bed."

"::::I guess. We have to keep an eye out for a change of clothes, too."

"::::Can we cheat? Build new clothes with nanites?"

"::::No, fabric synthesis with non-specializing nanites takes a long time, and..." Jon stopped talking suddenly, and they floated there silently for a few moments.

"::::And?"

"::::Sarah, take off your clothes."

"::::*Excuse me?!*"

"::::We *have* material, we have the technology, we can rebuild your clothes. Make them different. Use your shirt to make some shorts, use your pants to make a shirt. We just have to play tailor. 'Cutting' and bonding the edges of material is a quick task compared to building from scratch. You even still have that vest, we're golden. We have lots of options."

As they made plans on how to use the material in fast-think, Sarah stripped down. Floating nearly naked in the depths, Sarah remembered something she said on the day of her 'birth'. "::::The mermaid option is still out there." She said with a quiet tease. "::: We could lay low in the sea for a few decades while the heat blows over, making friends with the fishes…"

"::: Hilarious. Sure, I'll be turned off during that time. We'd run out of things to talk about, and I'd get sick of the movie collection."

Sarah chuckled. ":::Oh, we could find a drifting coconut and build a satellite receiver."

":::You're making fun of the master of the flying log cannon?! Seriously though, a satellite receiver isn't such a far-out project idea. But really, would you be happy out at sea watching TV for long?"

Suddenly her joke wasn't as funny. Tactically, it made a lot of sense. She could eat from the sea as needed, and avoid humans. If they really *could* get a satellite receiver running, they might find a time when a gal with a nanite-based nervous system wouldn't be incinerated.

But that could be a long time. Especially for the daughter of Erebus. They could just swim to another continent, but it would be the same in South America or anywhere. Eventually, it would always become an issue.

":::Densfarn's my home. It hasn't been for long, really, but it's my home. I want to go back just because… Just because."

":::You have hopes for getting the old life back? Working at the Four Fox, and bunking with Dan and Jessica?"

Sarah resumed swimming lazily towards the dock complex. ":::Stupid, huh?" She used her mouth to plant a line of nanites on the fabric of her shirt, assigned to cut. She secreted many such small-scale deployments, to get them all working at once.

Jon murmured, ":::We all have to set goals, I guess."

":::Yeah. Besides. I have to keep an eye on Dan."

":::Do you think she's still in danger?"

":::Hard to say. I gave Doug every reason to steer clear of her, assuming he believes it, or bothers thinking rationally."

Jon snorted. ":::Not his specialty."

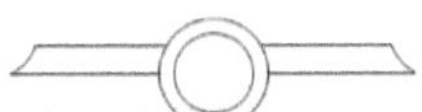

Even with the more efficient method and the slow swimming, Sarah's 'new' clothes were only being finished as the dock complex came into view. The satellite image map didn't do the docks justice. They were mammoth beasts of concrete and metal.

Some kind of orange plastic padding coated the bottom of the uprights to help prevent mutual damage in the event that a cargo ship, or overgrown cruise liner misjudged a maneuver a little.

Even as she approached, the muted sounds of very large ships reached out with their droning engines. As she came up under one of these overgrown docks, the sounds of engines were somewhat lessened, but echoed around under the dock in haunting ways.

The underside of this dock was over a story above her head. It was a complex looking mess of cross-supports and conduits. The conduits were for ships to hook up to for fuel, water, and the removal of waste. Ships caught dumping anything in Aguolian waters faced fines that would crush most of the smaller fleets.

It wasn't that natural waste was horrible for the sea, it was just that Aguola wanted to control where and how it was disposed of. Chemical contents were weeded out, and the natural remainder was piped to somewhere that wouldn't affect tourism.

Unlike the little wooden docks she was used to, this industrial gigalith didn't simply run straight forward until the bottom of it met the ground. Nay, half way in, the underside became a huge vertical wall; the front side of a giant concrete block that served as the dock's main base to the earth.

Not far above the current water level, which was at high tide, this mass of concrete had a thin ledge that ran all the way around. In the middle of the concrete there stretched a ladder that went from well below the surface, all the way to the top.

Where this ladder and this ledge intersected, there was a metal door.

":::Think we should go in that door, Sarah? It might be a good way to sneak to dry land unseen. What do you think is in the door?"

Sarah groaned as she hauled herself up the ladder. ":::Zombies. Or werewolves. Or pirates. Or zombie werewolf pirates. Screw the door. I spent too much time underground and underwater in the last twenty-four hours. I want a little sun. Besides, it could set off an alarm, or there could be people right on the other side. And then we still have to get out of it somehow."

":::All right, all right. I get it already. No door." Jon hummed thoughtfully. "Zombie werewolf pirates. I bet I could have done-"

":::Oh shush." Sarah continued climbing up, and up.

":::Uh, where are we going?"

":::Just up. I figure the higher against the bottom the the deck I am, the less visible I am." She reached the top, and hung on with her uninjured arm.

":::All right, I can see that logic, but we still have to get out to the land and junk. You'd look pretty suspicious clamoring up around the edge of the dock, if that's your plan."

":::I'm just going to hang out here for a while to drip dry. A soaking wet girl walking up around the edge of a dock would raise eyebrows as well. In fact, I might just hang out here until nightfall. Or at least low tide, so I don't just get my shoes and pants soaked again when I climb down."

They hung there for a while without conversation. Sarah tried to enjoy the waves, the unique shadows, dancing glimmer of the water, and sounds under the dock.

":::So..." Jon said, sounding politely bored, ":::Do you want to play a game?"

Sarah raised an eyebrow. ":::What kind of game?"

":::I spy... with your little eye... something that is almost a hundred and sixty seven million kilometres in surface area."

":::Uh huh. I think I'm going to watch a movie."

":::Cripes, Sarah. Do think you actually want to be doing that while you're dangling like this?"

"::: No biggie. I now watch movies outside my actual field of vision. Like my controls, or maps and junk."

"::: You what? I don't remember programming a function for that!"

"::: You didn't Jon, I did. Do you want a copy of the code changes I made for it?"

Jon was blown away. "::: Sarah! No! I don't need a copy, I can do that myself easily! I just never thought of it! You're a genius! That fact that you've adapted the core elements in such-"

"::: Jon?"

"::: Yeah?"

"::: Shush, movie's starting."

"::: Oh."

Jon remained quiet for nearly ten seconds.

"::: So. What are you watching?"

"::: A romantic comedy starring a non-threatening English man, who is neither romantic, nor that comedic. As a simulated female, I always simulate loving this kind of thing."

"::: All right, all right, I'll shut up."

It wasn't too long before they noticed the tide starting to drop.

"::: Are we going to head out soon?"

"::: Nah, my arm is fine. Let's wait through the next low tide, and the darkness."

"::: What? What is that, like six hours?"

"::: What's wrong Jon, you got a date?"

As the first movie began rolling the credits, she thought she heard a sound from the door below. She closed the movie file and stared down intently towards the door, listening for anything else.

She thought of her tactical situation. Fighting on the ladder wasn't too appealing. She glanced up. The underside of the deck might be a means of getting away, but without previously trying it, she couldn't bet on any speed.

Jumping away from the block and into the water would buy some distance, but the water might make for an equally awkward battlefield.

No further sounds came from the door.

It could have been anything.

"::: Damn it. Zombie demon things made me paranoid."

"::: It's not paranoia if they *are* out to get you."

"::: Yeah, thanks a ton, Jon."

"::: What are we talking about here?"

Sarah kept her field of vision focused on the door before browsing for the next movie. "::: Nothing, forget it." Maybe a little paranoia was warranted, but it still made for an undesirable feeling.

She looked at her healing arm. Yeah, good old healthy paranoia.

It was so easy to just turn off the chance of feeling pain, and start healing. It was convenient as all hell, but not very human.

She stared at the nearly-complete 'repairs'. Maybe feeling it would have been a good lesson for future caution. That's half the reason pain exists in humans, isn't it?

Considering turning the pain sensations back on now, she realized it would be nearly gone at this point. She looked at the logs of the 'pain' that occurred due to the wound. It compensated for simulated adrenaline decreasing the pain for a while. She found the peak of the pain level.

And turned it on. Felt it.

"*Eeeeeaarrg!*" the scream ripped its way out of her, taking every bit of air out with it. She tightened her grip on the ladder, wrapping against it hard, shuddering for a moment before turning the pain simulation back off.
":::*What??*" Jon yelled, ":::What's going on? What's wrong?"
Sarah chuckled to herself, catching the breath that she didn't even need. ":::It's okay, Jon. I just wanted to try something."
":::Oh yeah? What's that, trying to give a heart attack to a digital dad?"
Sarah held her healing arm in front of her face to show Jon. ":::I played back the pain levels from my injury."
":::What the heck for?"
":::Part of the human experience, I guess. I wanted to know."
":::There's a lot of problems with that, Sarah. For one, the pain levels are still just a simulation, based on the best info I had, and a pile of *my* best guesses. Also, unlike humans, you were able to shut it off on a whim."
Sarah thought about it. "So, I should let the pain play out?"
":::No, you idiot! Don't turn it on at all! Heck, after all of your underwater and under... under dock stealth tactics, that scream could have blown it all."
":::Ah."
":::Yeah, *'ah'.*"
":::All right, back to movies." Sarah loaded up an espionage movie to help her get in the mood for sneaking around. As the opening sequences rolled, she glared down at that door again.
Every time she thought of those demons, it led to thoughts of zombies, and all that Jon had done. It was unsettling to think that he was right there in her skull, all the time. The mind that caused all that death.
Did she really even need him anymore? Maybe she should just pull his plug right now. That was his original plan after all, right? To get her functional in the real world, then erase himself? Maybe his real plan was to get her to make a stand, and do it herself; to flex her morality by vanquishing the fiend who happened to be her father. Maybe she was reading too much into it.
Jon continued to be.

The last set of ending credits began to roll. The sun had bid its farewell in a polite, golden wave, and left the sleeping calm of night in its wake. The sea had retreated about as far as it was going to.
":::Jon."
":::We're going?"

"::::We're going."

Climbing down to the level of the thin ledge, she edged by the perfectly innocent door on her way to the side of the block. She pulled out a band of cloth they had fashioned into a little slip knot to serve as a hair tie, and pulled back a ponytail.

The ledge gave more than twenty centimetres of width to walk on, so it wasn't a problem to slip along to a spot where she could drop to a dried patch of sandy ground, then start walking up the incline of the shore.

Making her way up onto the dock, she found herself near a large, weathered, beige container being hauled by a slow little beige truck of some sort.

Its cabin was facing the other way, and it was headed inland. Feeling stealthy, she kept close behind it, staying out of view of any side mirrors.

It stopped. Suddenly.

She heard the left side door opening. "*What's going on back there?*" A man's voice called out, tired and gravelly.

"::::Oh crud," Jon said, "how quietly can you jump into water?"

"::::We're not over the water anymore. Doesn't matter. Keep a cool head, I can handle this." With footsteps as measured as could be, she silently drifted along the right side of the vehicle as the man searched along the left.

"::::See, Jon? Just a little finesse. I'll just keep on the other side of his footsteps until I get a chance to slip away to a-"

"Hello there?" The voice of another man came from the right-side driver's seat as she passed by.

"*Ahh!*" Sarah yelped with a jump.

"::::Smooth, Sarah. Very smooth."

"::::Oh, shush."

Sarah tried to put on her most innocent, friendly face. "Ah... hi!"

"You lost?" The driver seemed reasonable enough. The other man walked around the back end, and satisfied that the mystery was solved, started heading back around to his side.

"Um, not lost, exactly. I was... checking out the view from the end of the dock, and nature called. I thought I'd check out the door underneath and see if it led to a bathroom, rather than head all the way in."

"Door?"

"Yeah, see these big blocks?" Sarah pointed to the next dock over, and its identical giant cube of concrete. "I was on that one when I saw the door on this one, and I came on over, and checked out the door."

"Sounds like a longer trip than just heading into the terminal!"

"Yeah, well, now I know, and I have to go worse!"

The driver chuckled with pity. "You want a lift? We're headed that way!"

"No thank you!" Sarah hollered as she ran ahead, not so fast as to shatter the illusion of urine-imposed peril, "Your rig is too slow! See you!"

Jon cleared his imaginary throat. "::::That was..."

"::::Cunning? Gracefully witty? Genius?"

"::::...No. None of those. Nothing remotely like those."

"::::Oh, stifle." Sarah kept jogging along, around the corner of the building, out to the street, then a sharp left to keep going. "::::it worked, didn't it?"

Once a few blocks away, Sarah changed to a walk, looking around for anyone taking too much notice of her. She seemed to be clear. A handful of people wandered about, as the night was still young.

She was dry, but still smelled like the sea.

":::I think we need a new base of operations."

Sarah shrugged. ":::What's wrong with the street? Find a quiet little corner and think about our next move."

":::We have right now. In a couple steps down this sidewalk, we could probably come up with a decent plan."

":::Ah. Duh." Sarah triggered fast-think, and time appeared to all but stop once more.

":::All right. So, we want a job and apartment again?" Jon asked.

":::Ideally. We won't be able to quietly set up records like last time. We already know Eidechse is listening to the net, and he's probably actively looking for us now."

":::True, Sarah. Maybe we should skip town."

Sarah thought about it. ":::I'm not quite ready for that yet. Maybe I can get a job under the table."

":::Like what, pit fighter?"

Sarah was appalled, and not so sure Jon was joking. ":::Yeah, no thanks. While you're at it, skip right past prostitution and assassin."

":::Some fun *you* are. What if we only assassinated people who really deserved it?"

":::Ha. If you have a list, and..."

Jon waited for Sarah to continue. ":::And?"

":::Just tossing this out there... what if I found people committing crimes, then mugged them before turning them in?"

Jon laughed. ":::I think you need a cape and mask for that kind of work! What will your name be? 'The Amazing Fish Girl'?"

Sarah mulled it all over. ":::You know, if we were patient, and listened really closely with the ability turned up, we might hear glass breaking or something. But yeah, it's pretty dumb. We don't need cash as much as a shower. You know, if I could get tidied up a little, we could probably wrangle a little work at some lower end place."

":::Lower than your last job at a bar?"

":::Hey, the Four Fox was really nice. I mean something like... well, like that really horrible bar, except minus the pit fights. I don't imagine a place like that would be too picky about paperwork. Then we could rent a spot. We don't even need a real apartment. A storage locker would do. Is that cliché?"

Jon chuckled. ":::Yeah, I hope you don't mind freshly divorced men as neighbors. Won't work though. You'd still need identification for that."

":::Do you think I'd need *real* identification? A well fabricated fake might do it for a storage rental. Maybe even some pickier slum-bars. Damn, I've become ambitious, haven't I?"

Jon was quiet, so Sarah continued talking. ":::So it's a plan. I find materials to fake some identification, get a crappy job, move into a storage locker. First maybe we should find a place to gently break into for a shower. A motel or something."

Sarah resumed normal time and continued walking, now on alert for suitable scrap plastics to use, and pondering new names.

A few steps later, Jon spoke up.

":::Sarah. I'm sorry things ended up like this. You were happy at the Four Fox, weren't you?"

Sarah slowed her step a bit, and sighed. ":::Yes, Jon. But it's not your fault I had to leave there. If I hadn't gone all vigilante on Doug, none of it would have happened."

Jon sighed. ":::And if you did nothing, Danielle would still be getting tormented by Doug. I *am* really proud of you, you know?"

":::Yeah, well... I still don't know that Doug has smartened up at all. A broken wrist doesn't grow more brain cells. In fact, screw the whole job thing. First, I want to leave Doug a message."

":::W- what kind of message?"

":::Nothing harmful. Maybe a short note carved in his front door. I don't know, I'll think of something on the way."

Sarah changed direction. She didn't dare use her transit pass. They probably had tracking data on them, and the stations had a ton of cameras. Her hair and clothes were a little different, but her face was still the same.

At least for now. That was something definitely worth thinking about.

Walking past a bank machine, she grabbed a deposit slip and began jotting down a note with the chained pen provided.

":::Sarah, you realize the bank machine has a camera staring at you right now."

":::Aw, damn. I guess it's kind of inescapable. The rural option is starting to sound better and better. I'll leave Doug's note, then we're off to the hills, I guess."

Dear Douglas Villa,

I do hope that you're healing well. I just wanted to say hi, and that yes, I am watching over Dan, and all her friends.

Please play nice. Repeated breakage of the same bones can have long term effects.

":::All right, how should I sign it?"

":::How about *FISH GIRL!*"

":::Yeah, *no.*"

She simply signed it 'Sarah', put the pen back in its little cubby, and continued on her way with note in hand.

":::No Fish Girl?" Jon asked.

":::No Fish Girl."

":::How about 'The Defender of the Sea!'"

":::No. It's done, moving on."

":::How about 'The Holy Mackerel?'"

":::Am I going to have to send you to your room?"

Jon rallied his whiniest remorseful voice. "::::I'll be good."

Sarah found herself enjoying the walk, soaking in the sights and sounds of evening life in the city. She'd miss it when they retreated to some rural area.

Maybe she'd learn to appreciate the wide open spaces and nature. She came to appreciate the city, and underwater places.

Her friends weren't out in the country though.

This was a big step to make. She actually hadn't known them that long. In terms of her own actual life, she'd known them nearly forever, but maybe from their naturally aged perspectives, Sarah was just some freak who just didn't work out at the bar.

She wanted to be special to them. To anyone besides the genocidal smart alec lodged in her brain. She did something human, because it felt right. She cried quietly as she walked.

She had it dried up and wiped away before reaching Doug's place. Jon had said nothing. Did he not notice the tears, or did he just decide not to say anything?

Making her way up the stairs to Doug's apartment, she folded the slip of paper over nicely, and slid it under his door. What a pathetic farewell to her life in the city.

Maybe she should make notes for the Four Fox gang. Nicer notes, on nicer paper. Maybe if they knew that they mattered to her, she might matter to them.

":::This might never end, you know." Sarah said wearily as she headed down the stairwell.

":::What's that?"

":::Running. Hiding. Pretending."

Jon was quiet for a while. ":::That much *would* be my fault."

":::Don't waste time worrying about it." She was worried that it sounded like more of a forgiveness than she intended. It was indeed Jon's fault that nanites were banned. He had to have known this when he created her.

Really, what was he thinking? Trying to win back a little karma for the murder of his sister? How's that working out for you, Jon? Feel redeemed yet? If so, please proceed to the other millions of dead.

Coming to the bottom floor, a gentle hiss could be heard from the darkness overhead.

"*:::Sarah!*"

":::Yeah. I guess I'm not shocked. The bank machine must have turned me in. Can't trust banks, huh?" The hiss got closer. Three airlimbs maneuvered around her. She stopped and looked up at one, just before they all raised their running lights. The middle one shone a bright spotlight on her.

"*Please remain where you are!*" An authoritative female voice boomed from the spotlight.

"*:::Run!*" Jon screamed.

Sarah raised her hands and waved at the middle airlimb with a weak, peaceful smile. ":::No, Jon. It's pointless."

Two of the three airlimbs came down, hovering a foot over the ground. Shrubbery was crushed, debris danced around in the air, and most of the neighbors turned on their lights in curiosity.

":::*You've got to run, Sarah!*"

":::No." Sarah smiled her sad smile a tiny bit broader. ":::This is a relief. I want to come clean."

":::You mean you want to be incinerated!"

Yes, that was a troubling likelihood. But she was tired, and she missed her friends, and she was getting sick of it all.

Soldiers poured out of the two lowered airlimbs. Most carried guns, a few carried tools to restrain her, and herd her, just like the demon she'd seen them restrain. One stepped a little closer.

"Sarah Amanda Hartford?" He called out.

Hands still up with her sad smile, she nodded. "I take it you want to talk, huh?"

"Yes, Ma'am. We're going to have to put the lasso around your midsection and lead you into a containment chamber. Will you co-operate?"

Running, in retrospect, may have been the better choice.

The 'containment chamber' stood as a big glass cylinder. It was capped with dark metal that also served as the door seal and other bits of ambiguous technology. The door closed behind her, and a soldier slid a complex bolt into place.

"It's airtight, lead lined, and while you *could* use nanites to eat through it, that would take a long time, and we have ample means to stop you. Got it?" His words were threatening, but his tone was more that of a concerned warning.

The ceiling of the chamber was an arrangement of quarter-sized nozzles. ":::Flame throwers or something." Jon sighed. ":::Does this still feel like a good idea?"

Sarah declined responding, and just slumped down to sit on the floor. She tapped on the glass to make eye contact with the nearest soldier. He stared at her with scrutiny. She didn't look like any recorded zombie or abomination, and was acting far friendlier.

The engines got louder, and she felt the airlimb rise.

"Hey, I'm sorry about Doug, if that makes any difference. I mean, he deserved it, so I'm not really sorry in that way, but he'll get better."

The soldier looked confused. "Who's Doug? Was he at the Victoria Emerald?"

"The where? Never heard of it. He was just hassling his ex, and breaking a restraining order. I couldn't stand by and let it go on. I just hope he learned his lesson. I guess." This raised a pile of questions. What was the Victoria Emerald, and why did they think it had anything to do with her?

And if the military didn't know about Doug, did that mean that Eidechse wasn't feeding them information on her?

"I think you're better off talking when we get to Yute, Miss. I don't have all the info."

"Hm." Actually, it was fortunate that this soldier was talking to her at all. "You mean the Yute desert? What's there?"

"Yute Central Base, Miss. It's on the edge of the desert."

"Oh."

":::I'm a little familiar with it," Jon said, ":::Jonathan Coll was taken there shortly before I was created. I guess by now they've got all kinds of anti-nanite stuff there. It's not all that far from Meston. Well, the Meston ruins, maybe I should say. It's-"

":::Enough already, Jon."

":::Sorry."

Sarah sighed, and glanced over to the soldier again. He was looking at her in an odd way. An odder way. ":::Jon, I have a funny question..."

":::Shoot."

":::You know how a person makes different facial expressions when they talk to someone else?"

":::Yeah, okay."

":::Do I make expressions when I talk to you?"

":::How would I know, Sarah? I can't see your face unless you look into a mirror."

":::Yeah, well that's just it. Solider boy here may have just been watching my face as I had a discussion, talking to voices in my head."

":::Ah. You're obviously totally insane. Tell him how you're made of fish."

":::Thanks. Real supportive."

":::No prob, Fish Girl."

Taking a deep, cleansing breath, Sarah felt a need to look sane for a while. ":::All right, Jon. Just behave. I'm trying to not make faces."

":::All right, Sarah. Just remember. Don't smile. And don't laugh."

":::What?"

":::Don't. No smiling, giggling, laughing for no reason. No thinking about kittens wearing clown hats, or puppies on trampolines. No penguins wrestling with miniature giraffes, no babies being tickled by chimpanzees. No thinking about any sort of-"

Sarah groaned, and lowered her head. She rubbed her eyes to hide her face as she resisted smiling. ":::Jon, you consummate ass."

":::I've been called worse."

":::Indeed."

After she felt she had looked sane for long enough, she tapped the glass again to catch the attention of the same nearby soldier.

"Hey, I meant to ask earlier. Did you guys get my message about the underground thing? With the abominations and junk?"

The soldier looked a little apologetic as he tapped his ear, indicating a small communication device nestled in his ear. "Sorry, Miss. I've been instructed not to interact with you any more."

"Well crap. How long do I have to wait before I can have a talk with someone? You guys should put some magazines in here at least."

":::*Ahem!*" Jon said, ":::No one to talk to?"

":::Yeah, well, they don't know that. They also don't know I have a movie library in my head to amuse myself with. I just want to know what their stance on all of this is." If it was just incineration, they could have done that by now. That thought somehow made her worry more. They wanted her alive for a reason.

"::::Hey Sarah, have you tried dreaming since your got the rest of Amanda's memories? If you're not sitting on that handful of repressed memory, maybe you can have a normal dream.

She slid down onto her back, leaning her legs up against the wall of the cylinder. "::::Now might not be the right time to try. I don't want another adventure in zombie filled Meston right before trying to negotiate for my life. And I can't see the real world that well when I'm dreaming."

"::::So... movie time?"

"::::Yeah. I guess. I want something relaxing. Maybe I can find an underwater documentary."

"::::Yes, Fish Girl."

The airlimb decelerated, and personnel could be heard making preparations. The feel of a turn and decent marked the arrival at Yute Central as soldiers around her got on their feet.

"I think this is my stop, fellas." She stood, preparing to leave through the cylinder's door.

The large bay door opened in front of her. She could see the homogenous off-beige buildings ahead, bleached by the sun of this arid area. Waiting for a soldier to open the cylinder's door, she was surprised as the soldiers grabbed the cylinder and began to push it down the bay door's ramp. The base of the cylinder was evidently on small wheels that she hadn't seen on the way in.

"Okay. Yup." She made herself comfortable, sitting cross legged. The landing area became more visible as they came out of the airlimb. Several other airlimbs were parked here, and a view across the pad told her they were on the roof of a many-storied building.

As she, her cylinder and eight soldier escorts continued on, a few dozen people on the deck stopped to stare. Sarah smiled meekly, and waved politely. She couldn't resist. "I have a *lot* of outstanding parking tickets!" She caught at least two people taking some small amusement in that.

"::::You might not want to pop too many jokes, Sarah. You want to be taken seriously here."

"::::Oh, shush. You of all people, lecturing me on the appropriateness of my jokes."

"::::All right, I'm not going to lie, Sarah. I'm scared for you here."

Sarah sighed. "::::I guess I've chosen to be judged for who I am, and not what they fear I am."

"::::Your faith in humanity is quite... quaint."

"::::Hmm."

The ride continued into a doorway, down a winding, muted yellow hall, and into a large elevator. For some reason, this was the point when she felt a very real sense of danger. Sure, she had been surrounded by soldiers, and stuck in a glass tube with automated flame throwers pointed at her head, but now it was different.

Now she was also in an elevator.

Still sitting cross legged, she looked around at the soldiers standing guard around her. "You guys should phone each other in the morning," she said, attempting to break the tension, "You must have all been really embarrassed when you got to work and found out you were all wearing the same thing."

The soldiers remained silent. "Seriously? Nothing? I suppose you guys have heard that one before. I bet there's a lot of things civilians say that get irritating after a while."

":::Sarah, you're blithering."

"I'm blithering." She said to everyone with a slow nod. "Kinda nervous. Yep. I hope I can meet someone soon who's going to talk with me. I also wouldn't mind a burger from the Four Fox."

The elevator chimed, and the doors slid open. The soldiers rolled Sarah and her big glass tube down another hallway, this one made of metal plating. It made the lighting cold and unwelcoming. Almost alien.

Another turn, another corner. Down one hall she spotted something that might have passed as a counter, or desk of some kind, but she didn't get a good enough angle to make out any specifics.

They came to a large, metal, four metre wide double door. The front soldier punched in a pile of numbers into a keypad hidden from Sarah's view.

":::I think I got the number." Jon said.

":::How?"

":::I watched his shoulder and elbow movements and used them to map out the relative position of his finger at every beep."

":::Baloney."

":::7,2,4,4,6,3,9,3,4,7. Assuming the keypad starts with '1' at the top left. If it's bottom left, then-"

":::All right, all right, I believe you."

The door opened, sliding into the wall. Inside was a large area. One could park a dozen cars in this area if one so wished. The walls here looked like shinier, steely versions of garage doors. This was proven correct. When they approached a specific door, the same solider stood in front of it and said "All right, open outer number five."

The metal plates slid upwards into a slot in the ceiling, leaving a wide glass plate in its wake. The room behind the glass was primarily a shiny metal box. In the corner was a modest toilet; just a seat with a hole that looked like it had grown seamlessly out of the wall and floor. A roll of toilet paper sat unceremoniously nearby. The ceiling of the room housed a single light source, and an array of little nozzles ready to torch any inhabitants at a moment's notice.

"All right, inner." The soldier said. The glass slid up, and Sarah's cylinder was pushed in. With soldiers all around, her cylinder was opened. "Get out, Miss." Sarah obliged. The cylinder was dragged out, while most of the soldiers kept her in their sights.

She felt her nerves trembling slightly. Stupid Jon, why simulate that kind of reaction? "Hey guys. You really... I mean... you really could use a woman's touch in here."

As the glass panel slid back down, the soldier gave a speech he'd never had to do for any zombie or abomination. "The toilet is not a viable means of escape, even for a single nanite, just so you know. Anything disposed of in there becomes incinerated very shortly after. You have neighbors, but the walls are soundproof, RF proof, and all that. Do you need food? Or electricity or such?"

"Huh? Me?" The question caught Sarah off guard. It almost sounded genuinely considerate in contrast to the rest of what he said.

The soldier nodded. "Our usual guests generate what they need from a protein heavy powdered mix we drop in, but you look like you might want something a little more appetizing. I don't think I have time to fetch you a cheeseburger, but would you like some standard rations and water?"

Sarah sighed, and sat down on the sterile floor. "I'm all right. It'll be a long time before I was planning to eat again anyway. All I really want is company. Conversation.

":::Again," Jon said, ":::Thanks a ton."

":::I'm trying to talk our way out of here, all right?"

The soldier held his finger to his ear, listening to his comm. He released it and turned his attention back to Sarah. "Colonel Calvert tells me he'll be with you momentarily."

"Uh... Okay."

The soldier turned and said "Done here." The metal plating slid down the other side of the glass, and silence grabbed her.

":::Colonel?!" Jon protested, ":::Colonel? I thought I would rank a visit from a General! The Prime Minister, actually! Grand Elder at least!"

Sarah flopped on her back and stared up at the only view available. A central light fixture, surrounded by dozens of little nozzles whose sole purpose in life was to reduce things like her to ash and vapour. ":::See that little light up there? Do you think it's got a camera and microphone in it or anything?"

":::Oh, I would pretty much guarantee it."

Sarah waved at the light. "Just so you guys know," she called to it, "Despite trying very well to hide it, I could tell that the door password is 7,2,4,4,6,3,9,3,4,7."

":::Sarah! Why did you tell them that we know?!"

"Oh yeah!" She called to the light again, "It might be 1,8,4,4,6,9,3,9,4,1 if the '1' is at the bottom left instead. I don't know if zombies or abominations would be able to tell that, but it might be worth revising how you run that lock."

":::Jon, I want to earn their trust, in preparation for the part of the plan where they... you know, *trust us*, and no one gets killed or incinerated."

":::Super. Remind me not to let you play poker with anyone. Gee, Mister, are you *sure* you want to bet more? I *have* four aces."

":::We had one ace, Jon. And they have a bunch of flame throwers pointed at us."

":::Oh, so this is more like Vegas blackjack."

"::::What?"

"::::Nevermind."

Sarah stood up, and paced around slowly. "This room needs a window or something," she said to the presumed microphone in the ceiling, "And *hey!* Do you guys know Eidechse? He gave me the impression you guys were at least in communication."

"::::Geez, Sarah. Hold one damned card to yourself, will you?"

"::::I am, I call it Jon. I'm not playing that one though, for obvious reasons."

"::::It doesn't mean you have to give them everything else. Besides..."

"::::Yeah, well, what's been played has been played, Jon. I have my reasons."

"::::What's just so great ab-"

The metal outer door began to slide up, revealing four visitors on the other side of the glass. Colonel Calvert was obvious due to his uniform.

The second was a slender bespectacled man in a lab coat. He looked like a scientist who had given up all hope of defying stereotype. In his hands he gripped and fiddled with a bulky personal terminal that choked on its own custom modifications that clung to every outer edge, barely.

After that stood a woman soldier with striking red hair, who seemed every bit as business as the Colonel. She wore the a uniform of blue camouflage, but no unit markings.

At the redhead's side was a brunette civilian. She wore blue-camouflage pants, but the rest of her outfit was pure civilian, topped with a black leather jacket. She looked tense, a mixed bag of upset. Angry? Afraid? Sad? She gripped the redhead's arm, and seethed. "See? I knew it would be her! I just knew it!"

Sarah stopped time.

"::::Whoa." Sarah said, "She doesn't like me at all! All right Jon, I think some introductions are in order."

"::::Yeah. Well, Calvert and the geek, I don't know. The other two were the front end of AZU-1 when they first started up to chase Jonathan Coll around. The last thing I saw of them is when my nanites were thrown at them."

"::::On an exploding log."

"::::Yes, on an exploding log. I think I saw the other two main members of that unit at that bar, so I guess the whole log-attack can be chalked up to a complete waste of time."

"::::And lumber."

"::::Yes. At any rate, since the brunette seems to know your face, it stands to reason that she ran into Amanda's body 'Erika' in Meston at some point between the log, and my defeat at Meston. In a related story, she might be a little insane."

"::::Jon, I don't recognize you to be a judge of sanity."

"::::Noted."

Sarah resumed normal time, and saw the redhead pat the brunette's hand for comfort. "Relax, Regan."

Sarah took a small, casual step towards this 'Regan' with a peaceful hand held out. "I realize who I look like. It's not terribly comfort-"

Regan exploded. "*Shut the hell up, you bloody-*"

The redhead put her arm around Regan, and forced eye contact with her. "Reel it in a bit hon. Yelling at it isn't going to accomplish much."

Colonel Calvert lowered his eyebrow, thankful that the outburst was settled before *he* had to deal with the civilian.

Wait a moment, 'it'? Did the redhead refer to Sarah as an 'it'? All right, don't flip. "Excuse me? I'm a she, if you please." Regan fidgeted angrily, and the redhead nodded with a semblance of respect.

Colonel Calvert turned to Regan and the redhead. "Major Terone, do you concur with Ms. Grier's assessment?"

"Yes, Sir." The redheaded Major Terone nodded. "This individual looks like the 'Erika' entity we encountered in Meston shortly before Erebus was defeated."

"Very well, Major. You're staying on base for a day or two, correct?"

"Yes, Sir. I have a couple of seminars to give. If you need me, I'm around."

"Thank you, Major. Dismissed. Ms. Grier, thank you for your time."

The redhead smiled a little as she put her arm around Regan, and planting a little kiss on her temple. "Come on, dorkette." She turned towards the scientist as she guided Regan away. "See ya, Brock. Get it figured out, I know you can."

The scientist, 'Brock', flipped the redheaded Major a casual little salute. "That's what I do, Major!"

Colonel Calvert stepped up towards the glass, finally addressing Sarah. "Well, Miss. Why don't you start?"

Sarah smiled in a tired way, and sat down cross-legged. "Colonel, you're going to wish you brought a chair. She sighed, and debated where to begin. How to begin.

"I woke up at the bottom of the ocean for the first time less than a week ago. I consider that my birth. I know that I am built from nanites, and materials harvested from scavenged dead fish. And a seagull."

"Who built you, and why?" The Colonel cut to the meat of the matter, but Sarah wasn't about to tell that truth. Not quite.

"After doing a little research, I've come to believe I was created as a tribute to the late Amanda Coll, and intended to live a normal life. I can only speculate from there who would be responsible."

The Colonel scoffed. "How many people- or should I say entities- have the know-how and motivation to recreate Amanda Coll?"

Sarah lowered her head with a deep sigh. "I can only think of one."

"Erebus." The Colonel added sharply. "And what do you know about Erebus?"

"Mostly what was put in my head at birth, most of which I have confirmed with public record. Jonathan Coll caused the fall of Autar City, and later copied his mind to an artificial intelligence, which then devastated Meston City, during which time he killed Amanda Coll. Public record does not know that he deeply regrets it however."

'Brock' continued to stand by, just listening and taking notes.

Colonel Calvert hunkered down to sit at Sarah's level. He spoke in measured, calm tones, in attempts to communicate understanding in either direction.

"Miss, how do you know Erebus regrets anything? And do you actually believe this regret?"

Sarah paused, knowing full well that Jon was listening. "Colonel, I think the regret is sincere. Honestly, I'm very, very young. I would be more worried if I had no doubts at all. Doubt stands beside open mindedness."

The Colonel smirked, and Sarah caught a little nod from Brock.

"Sirs," as she addressed them both, "I know that *what* I am is a crime, and I understand the dangers associated with nanites. *Oh!* That reminds me! Did you get my message about the underground monsters and the mechanical thing?"

The uncomfortable Colonel readjusted his weight. He was not quite as fit as he once was. "Yes, we did. Evidence of them anyway, they were gone. You realize those things were created by Erebus, don't you?"

Sarah shook her head slightly. "No, Sir. I don't believe they were. The technology is out there. I've seen these nanite pit fights. I think I could be of help shutting that kind of thing down. Like Eidechse does, but in different ways. I have different abilities than he does, after all. You *do* know him, right?"

Brock tapped a few things onto his terminal, then showed its screen to Colonel Calvert in a way that Sarah couldn't see it.

The Colonel nodded with a sombre face. "That doesn't mean he's right," the Colonel said, "he always struck me as a little overly optimistic."

Brock shrugged. "Combined with the anonymous tip, giving up the passcode she figured out, and everything we now know about this 'Doug' situation..."

Jon quietly spoke to Sarah, ":::Well played cards. You'll teach an old cynic yet, Sarah."

Sarah saw where Brock was going. She chimed in with hope abundant. "It's not like I want to be on a free leash or anything, I understand! But I think I can help out! Ideally I'd like to visit or even work with my old friends, but... baby steps, yeah?"

Colonel Calvert rubbed his tired eyes with one hand, and grumbled quietly. "The problem is, we have no way of knowing that everything you've been saying and doing isn't just an elaborate hoax. Your true motives could be an Erebus-concocted scheme aimed at doing the same thing to Densfarn as was done to Autar and Meston."

Sarah's heart sank. "If I was going to do anything bad, I would have done it by now! I made some fake identification, and that was only because I needed to get a job, so I didn't need to steal!" The Colonel looked unmoved.

Sarah pleaded, "I've been trying really hard to be my best, and-"

Sarah fell silent, and motionless.

":::What the heck? I can't even blink! Jon! Emergency debug! Is the military doing something weird to me? Radiation? Some kind of jamming sig-"

"::: I'm sorry." Jon said calmly.

Sarah calmly stood up with perfect efficiency of motion, looking down towards the seated Colonel.

"::: Jon!! What's going on!? I'm not doing this!"

"::: I know, Sarah, I am."

"::: *What?*"

From Sarah's mouth came Jon's words, and voice. "Colonel Calvert. This is another persona speaking through Sarah's body. You have known me as Erebus."

The Colonel leapt to his feet in shock. Brock's eyes widened, darting between Sarah's face and his terminal.

"This is the first time I've assumed control of Sarah's body,"

"::: *You son of a bitch! You told me you couldn't!*" Sarah wanted to hit something, but had no control over her hands.

Jon continued. "Sarah is my daughter. I reside in a section of her mind to assist her. She has been very forthcoming with you, except where I was involved. She wants to protect me, and I cannot allow that. She knew from the start that I planned to delete myself when she was ready to face the world alone. I wish to negotiate for Sarah's freedom, at the expense of my own freedom and/or existence."

"::: *You asshole!*" Sarah yelled at him, "::: Who's the shitty poker player now, huh?"

Colonel Calvert stared at Sarah, coming to grips with the male voice coming from her, and what Jon was saying. "All right then. So what do you know about these new 'demon' abominations?"

Jon sighed. "Not as much as I'd like, actually. I agree, they seem like something I would have done in Meston, but they're not mine. After Meston, I haven't had contact with the world at large until I did so as Sarah's passenger, not so long ago."

Sarah had some serious doubts about that, and the Colonel agreed. "Do you expect me to believe that the Emerald Victoria incident and the other demon appearances are a coincidence with your 'emergence' now? Damn it, we have a recording of Lancer's lead coordinator, Mr. Book, talking to you, Erebus, through a demon right before Book torched his office to kill the demon and himself."

Jon staggered back, and landed square on Sarah's behind. "Whoa. Whoa. Hold on, that's a lot to absorb. Okay. First, Bookiepoo's dead? That's a head trip right there. I thought he was going to have to be eroded away by mother nature before he could be bothered with dying."

Sarah ranted on at Jon, "::: What the hell are you guys talking about? Let me out of here! I thought this was *my* body!"

"::: I really am very sorry, Sarah. This has to be done."

Sarah continued complaining to Jon as he mostly ignored her and continued the conversation with Colonel Calvert.

"Second, Colonel, what the heck's an Emerald Victoria? One of your guys mentioned it when we got taken in."

Colonel Calvert stepped forward and planted a pointed finger against the glass. "The Emerald Victoria is a hotel. The site of a moderate massacre at the hands of a pack of demons, one of which spoke a lot like Sarah is now, as Erebus, and told us all that the whole country was his!"

"Whoa, shit, dude, that wasn't me! Had to be some kind of poser! And for the record, I don't actually go by 'Erebus' anymore. Call me Jon."

"Convenient." the Colonel said.

"I abandoned 'Erebus' when I took a closer look a my sister's memories, and had a change of heart."

"*Very* convenient, Jon."

Jon huffed, and paced the cell. "It wasn't a quick process for me. It's been decades in *my* head. Look, I actually really liked Sarah's idea about her working for you, and even being on a bit of a leash. It's very reasonable. I'd erase myself happily if I knew she could enjoy some form of freedom." He looked upwards, hands held up, answering the voice that Brock and the Colonel couldn't hear. "Sarah! Sarah! I said I'm sorry already! I'm trying to fix things here!"

"Having family issues, Erebus?" The Colonel didn't seem too impressed. Brock however, was fascinated.

"It's Jon, not Erebus." Jon corrected the Colonel. "And more or less, yes. She's understandably upset. She let herself get caught quite on purpose, I should tell you. I thought we should have made a break for it, but here we are."

Jon pointed abruptly at Brock. "You! Nerd!"

Brock's eyes widened, as being singled out by the killer of millions was a little unnerving. His scientific faith in the lead-lined glass alloy separating them gave Brock confidence enough to speak. "Geek, Ereb- I mean Jon. Geek. I'm a geek."

"Ptthp, whatever." Jon walked up to the glass with an intense stare into Brock's eyes. "I'll turn myself off, convince Sarah to do the same. Then you can just go looking around in this skull. We have nothing to hide that you don't know already. You can verify that we have nothing to do with these demon things, or any abomination after Meston. You can even go through my sister's memories, and you might understand why I gave up the whole 'humans are meat puppets' philosophy. Just don't bust us for all the pirated movies and stuff in here. They're just for personal use."

Brock was stunned, only catching up to the last things Jon had said. "Movies...?"

Colonel Calvert cleared his throat, and crossed his arms. "Why the heck would you submit to such a vulnerable state? Frankly, It reeks like a trap of some sort."

Jon smiled calmly. This facial expression always used to come out creepy on Jonathan Coll's face, but on Sarah it was nearly serene. "Sarah may be very trusting, but I am not entirely so naïve. I wish for a *peaceful* resolution, but I submit to this only because I have a backup plan in the event that Sarah is not free at the end of all this. Outside arrangements have been made to motivate you." He paused and looked into the air again. "Ahh, relax, Sarah! I *know* I didn't tell you! No, no, no. It won't kill anybody! It's just supposed to be as unpleasant as possible *without* hurting anyone!"

"Sir," Brock jumped in, "I could do it. Sarah's inactive body could be monitored for activity to make sure that she nor Jon take any actions, under pain of flame. We might be able to enlist Eidechse for assistance."

"Hold on, Brock." Calvert looked between Brock and Sarah. "I didn't sign off on this yet. I don't much like this threat of a backup plan, Jon."

Jon scoffed with a smirk. "And *I* don't much like a pile of flamethrowers aimed at my daughter! And as previously stated; if Sarah and I had any huge nasty plans, we've had plenty of time to do it."

Calvert tried to stare Jon down, but Sarah's eyes gave no hint of being intimidated. "Well, Jon, what happens if your backup plan takes effect?"

"If I told you, you might find it and disable it, right? It could be erasure of every financial record in the city. It could be a halt to all information networks. It could be a legion of reanimated walking fish corpses, choking up the sewers, ruining tourism, then rotting to a putrid paste in the streets after giving a generation of toddlers a lifetime of high octane nightmare fuel. Could be all of those. Could be."

Brock chuckled softly and said to himself, "Gather 'round, little ones. Let me tell you about the year a sturgeon ruined my credit rating and stole my wallet."

Colonel Calvert shot Brock a cold glance before directing his attention back to Jon. "So, what do you propose in the end? You, Jon, are erased, we've been through everything you and Sarah know, then set Sarah free?"

Jon nodded. "Although Sarah sounded like she'd be all right if you kept tabs on her, and she sounded interested in working for you. That's her option as far as I'm concerned. I hope this wouldn't be her office. It's dreadful. And I'm curious why you have these cells set up for zombies and abominations, and have fancy toilets in them? I know the zombies wouldn't use them, I doubt these new demon-things would."

Ignoring the sanitation query, Calvert turned to Brock. "Fine. We do it. What do you need?"

"I can have the equipment down here in under an hour."

"All right. Don't go in there until I have an AZU front here to chaperone, and you're sure he's out cold. Give me a live feed to my office."

"Yes, Sir." Brock gave Jon a polite wave as the metal door slid back down into place.

Back in control of her own body, Sarah paced the sealed room with furious stomps. She had shut Jon in his room as soon as she was able. He had the chance to communicate half a syllable of "Sarah" in an apologetic tone before being slammed away.

Was he even really stuck in there? If he could lie about not being able to control her, he was likely able to bust out of his self-constructed penalty box.

She wanted to rant out loud about him, just to blow off steam and complain about him to Calvert and Brock, but it would undermine any trust to hear *her* say that Jon was a lying scumbag.

She let Jon out.

":::Sarah, you didn't let-"

":::Shut up, shut up, shut up, shut up, shut up, shut up, shut up, shut up."

She continued pacing, and neither of them spoke for a very long five seconds.

":::*Don't you have anything to say for yourself, Jon?!*"

":::You just told me to shut up. Pretty vehemently."

She paced more, and again she was the one to break the silence. ":::How am I supposed to be able to trust you any more, huh? How do I know I'm not just an innocent vessel to get you in-"

":::Into a tightly sealed containment cell that's bristling with flamethrowers in the ceiling? A-ha! It worked! My evil plan was a success!"

More pacing.

":::So when I put you in your room, is that a lie? How about this button I have that kills you?"

":::Yeah." Jon paused for a virtual sigh. "Both work dandy. I wouldn't suggest killing me now though. They expect to be picking through the mind of the big bad Erebus pretty shortly. They might take it badly if you denied them that."

More pacing.

":::All right, what about your *backup* plan? What is it, really?"

":::Ha. When did I have time to set something like *that* up? I wouldn't mind seeing a legion of pickpocketing fish, mind you. No, there is no backup plan. Total bluff. Which reminds me, before we go into this exam, we have to erase anything to do with the non-existent backup plan, so they don't go in and find out it was a bluff. Including *this* conversation, all right?"

":::Jon, aren't we beyond the cloak and dagger crap?"

":::Just do it, all right?"

":::Yeah, whatever."

":::On three. One, two, th-"

A moment of silence.

":::Jon?"

":::Sarah. We just erased something on purpose, didn't we?"

Sarah sighed. ":::I think so, yeah. Should we be worried?"

":::I don't think so. If we both agreed to it, it was for the best. Maybe we had a nasty argument and said things we wanted to take back."

":::Oh Jon, if I'm going to say bad things about you, you'll deserve it."

":::True."

Shortly after, the metal door slid upwards. Brock was there beside a large, bulky cart of technological rigmarole, almost three metres long, a metre and a half high, and a metre wide. It was a collection of boxy white components, with an assortment of instruments rooted on the top that looked like an insane dentist's wet dream. Scanning devices, probes and cables attached to reaching, bending metal arms, or just hanging over the side carelessly.

Around Brock and his cart stood a pile of soldiers, all keeping a close eye on Sarah.

On top of the cart sat a five centimetre wide, dark skinned lizard, who looked at Sarah with what seemed to be lizardly benevolence.

"Sarah?" Brock said as the inner glass plate opened up, "You said you'd met Eidechse before?"

Sarah smiled. "Yes! Not in *that* body, however."

"Ah, I should have assumed not." Brock began rolling the cart into the cell. "This is the core of Eidechse. The 'true' Eidechse. The times you met him, they were only remotely dispatched... drones, I guess you'd say. This fellow is the real deal. This lizard is Eidechse's synthetic recreation of an aeki lizard, who live in and around the nearby Yute desert. Do you know what his name means?"

Sarah smiled, and touched her finger on Eidechse's front foot, and 'thought' at him. ":-:Hi there! Make me look smart in front of Brock, huh?"

"That method is not necessary." Eidechse's voice came from somewhere under the lizard's belly. "I can speak vocally from this body. Eidechse is German for Lizard. A very good friend of mine is of partial German decent, which inspired the name when I first entered an aeki as a host. Getting voluntary rides on innocent animals all the time can be tedious, so I created this aeki as my main body. I have also constructed a butterfly, which I left at home."

"You... you don't live here?" Sarah asked.

Brock gestured for Sarah to lie down as he explained. "Eidechse is free. Officially he was destroyed shortly after his discovery, since, you know. Nanites, grr, arg."

"And unofficially?"

"He's a hero! It took a while for Eidechse and I to become chummy though."

Sarah sighed as Brock smoothly inserted a probe into the back of her skull. "I guess freedom is easier to get when you don't have Jon's track record."

"Testing? Hello world?" Jon's voice came out of a speaker on the cart. "Cool stuff, Brock. This setup feels very familiar." Jon's signal was jumping onto the probe in Sarah's head, and feeding right to the 'shared' systems on the cart.

"It should, Jon. Jonathan Coll worked with very similar protocols. Almost all nanite-related tech is only a few shades different from stuff that was either in Erebus' hands, or Lancer's. It is suspected that the pit-fighter tech was leaked fairly directly from a Lancer employee or two. The nature of Mr. Book's death is about all the excuse the government is going to need to finally dissect Lancer properly.

"Book was attacked by a demon, you said?" Jon asked, "If the guy who launched the attack just meant to ruin Lancer, even a failed attack might do the trick. If it made enough noise. I don't want to speak ill of the big, miserable walrus or anything, *but...*"

Presently, six long needles resided in Sarah's skull. A thick beige hood with a meaty cable running out of it covered her head from the nose up, and a mat of similar design covered her body. It was about as flexible and comfortable as an x-ray technician's lead smock. Sarah didn't know if it was some kind of scanning system, or some kind of emergency execution system.

"Are you comfortable?" Eidechse asked, observing Brock making fine adjustments.

"Yeah. Well, it's unsettling, but I'm fine. I feel fine, anyway." For all she knew, the hardware would electrocute her. But onward she went. "Hey Eidechse... you're about to know every little detail of my story- can I ask you where *you* came from? If my mind originally came mostly from Amanda Coll, and Jon is mostly Jonathan Coll- who were you?"

"I did not have a real name before 'Eidechse'. Those partly aware of my existence, including myself, sometimes called me a ghost. I was a surveillance project created by an employee of Lancer. I had no self-awareness until I learned of human consciousness from my first two hosts. I consider them my creators more than the scientist who configured my first nanite colonies."

"Do you still talk to those two hosts? Are you guys friends still?"

Eidechse lowered his head, and paused. "Family with both. I can only talk to one of them." Eidechse changed the subject. "If I may ask, Sarah; you do not seem worried about this procedure. Why is that?"

"I am. I'm petrified. But if you can't believe that I'm harmless... freedom won with a threat isn't... it's just not what I want. That's not who I am."

Brock stepped over to the terminal on his cart. "There we are. Yes. We're ready. Sarah? Jon? If you will both be so kind as to power down...?"

"All right. Here we go." Sarah shut her eyes, and Brock watched his display intently as her systems closed down, one after another.

Jon delayed. Through Brock's machine, he warned, "She had better wake up in perfect shape, Brock."

"Yes, Jon. I know. Fish and economic collapse."

"Huh?" He had no idea what Brock was talking about. The memory was gone. "Never mind. Here I go." Jon's functions blinked to sleep, one by one, until Sarah's entire body was as lifeless as could be.

:::C / [011100] [28]

Sarah awoke.

She was alone in the sterile little cell, with the outer front metal panel, as well as the inner glass layer down.

":::Jon? You awake yet?"

Silence.

":::Jon?"

Nothing. She made sure he wasn't in his 'room'. There was nothing there. Less than nothing. No Jon, not even his stupid movie collection. Had Brock taken Jon out, or simply erased him?

"What the hell?" Sarah yelled up at the ceiling. "Can someone come tell me what happened?"

The metal panel at the front of the cell resounded with a tremendous impact. The glass inner layer cracked, and Sarah braced herself for the ceiling flame throwers to ignite.

They didn't.

Another impact caused half the glass panel to come loose and slam onto the floor. The dent in the metal was now a small break.

Another impact. For a moment, a large, sharp chunk of bone was visible. The next impact drove the curved bone spire through by nearly a metre. It was stained with blood.

Sarah stood against the back wall, watching carefully.

Another bone spike forced its way in alongside the first. They shifted and pushed in just a little more at a time, as the metal plating creaked and groaned. Cracking noises came from the chunk of glass still in place.

The two spikes drew back a little, then turned so that their curves made their respective points face away from each other.

They pressed outward, two monolithic claws, ripping the door apart slowly. Between the claws, their owner could be seen; a skinless mass of muscles that seemed to serve no purpose other than moving the claws.

When the metal had been forced two metres open, the creature withdrew with a sudden bobbling lurch backwards.

Brock stepped into view from the right side. His shirt was torn open, and a fresh scar led from his navel, up to his gleeful grin. "*Sarah!! Guess who?*"

Sarah couldn't reply. She knew who it was. She didn't want it to be. "Why?" was all she could utter.

"Why? *Why?!* Guess! Guess who it is! Aw, nevermind. It's me! *Daddy!*" Brock's middle split wide, as a demon's chest does. His deformed, spiked ribs flexed outward to reveal the moist red cavity where his organs had been.

Dangling in the middle of Brock/Jon's open torso was the lifeless body of Eidechse's lizard. Jon giggled as he moved his body back and forth, and watched the lizard sway. "Erebus three, human civilization zero! As we speak, Densfarn... Densfarnians? Densfarnites? Whatever. They are being *shredded* into more fun forms of flesh!"

Sarah screamed. "*What was the point in making ME then?*"

Jon stopped his little dance, looking quite stunned. "Darling, would I have made it into this building without a spoonful of sugar? From here, there's no other defence to my attacks!"

He cocked his head, still looking confused, when a notion crossed his mind. "Oh! Oh Sarah! Make no mistake! I may have used you, but I don't plan to discard you! You are my daughter! I *do* love you as such, never fear! It will only take a small adjustment to let you see it all my way, come here."

"No." Sarah whispered, wishing she could back up through the wall. "I am me. I'm not your tool. I'm not going to-"

Jon sighed with an exaggerated dropping of his shoulders that rattled his ribs, and jostled poor Eidechse. "You don't understand. You wanna see fun? Hold a human down while you convert a loved one into a demon while they watch! It's truly divine!"

Sarah considered freezing time for a bit, to consider her next action, but it was not needed, nor would it help. Jon's plan was illogical and insane, but he still seemed to have a foothold that needed to be broken.

She couldn't beat him on a nanoscopic scale. She'd have to win by brute force. That meant getting a flamethrower. She couldn't rip one out of the ceiling, and there wasn't a usable one between her and him. She thought about playing along until she got one, but that was a lot of time for him to find a moment to 'adjust' her.

She'd have to run past. If the claw-thing got in the way, she'd have to get past it, too. Maybe jump on a claw, up and over. She'd examine the situation when she got there.

She ran. Straight for the opening. How was she going to get past? Jon could slow time too, counter any move, and dodge, but she had to try.

"*Die, Jon! Do us all a favour and die!*"

She slowed her perception of time. She would fake him out a little. Prepare the next step to fall left. Slip under his reach.

No. He saw it coming. He's smiling. His hand corrected every little change to inertia that Sarah made. There just wasn't an escape.

His hand easily found its way around Sarah's wrist. She tried to pull away, but that wasn't happening. Her nervous system reported a nanite-based attack entering her skin where Jon grasped it.

Her own nanites seemed to shut down, even to change sides rather than resist. She was going down. it couldn't end like this.

Returning to the normal flow of time, she used her free hand to hit Jon in the face as hard and as fast as she could.

Only twice, before he grabbed it with his other hand. "Gotcha."

The world went black.

Blackness. Then a voice.

":::Sarah."

It was Eidechse.
"::: Eidechse! What's going on? You're alive? I mean... functional?"
Eidechse's voice was in hard contact, like Jon's always used to be.
":::Sarah, I know you're disoriented, and I am sorry for the necessity. For now, I want you to think about what you just experienced, and compare it to the real world."
":::Real...?" Even as she questioned it, it became obvious. The whole confrontation with Jon in Brock's body was simulated. In the eye of memory, it was as phony and artificial as Jon's simulation of Autar.
":::All right then, Eidechse. What was the purpose of that?" She felt her miscellaneous systems coming back to life, one by one.
":::I have been through every bit of your memory, and examined everything I could. I applaud you for not erasing your knowledge regarding Jon's lack of a backup plan. By the time I found that, I was all but assured of your true intentions."
":::All but assured? You weren't convinced. So you tested my reactions."
":::Yes. Again, I apologize. You stood against your father in the interests of humanity, despite minimal odds of success, or your own survival. A futile, poorly planned attack, but true in objective and intent. I am disconnecting now, you will awaken shortly."

Oblivion engulfed Sarah's mind again. Nowhere, no time, no thoughts, even her own. Then consciousness blossomed again.

Sarah opened her eyes and sat up. The probes that Brock had put in her head were gone, as was the cart and its paraphernalia. The room was again sealed.
Her systems reported the healing process nearing completion where the probes had been. She accepted this 'pain' as a sign that this was real.

That wasn't entirely true. She had felt pain in her dreams of being Amanda. Then again, those weren't exactly dreams, and they had been far more real than Jon or Eidechse's simulations.

"::::Hey, Jon?"

"::::I'm here. Did they give you a test?" Jon asked.

"::::Yeah. It sounds like I passed with flying colours. You?"

Jon delayed. "::::I mostly passed. Well enough."

Sarah sighed, and stood up. "::::Mostly? What happened?"

"::::I was doing well! Honestly! They put a fresh body in front of me, with the knowledge that it wasn't gong to be missed. I'll admit, the notion of bringing it to 'life' crossed my mind, just for entertainment purposes, but I didn't."

"::::Why Jon, you're a saint now!"

"::::Shut up, it got harder. Then they set me up in a city with control over one million, three hundred and forty seven thousand, eight hundred and fifty two zombies, and I had no opposition."

"::::And?"

"::::And what? I used the nanites in the zombies to attempt to heal them. That wasn't working, so I told them all to lie down and stay dead."

"::::Sounds good, I guess."

"::::Yeah, then they changed the scenario a little so that creating more zombies would save both you and Amanda."

"::::What? That doesn't make a lick of sense. How does-"

"::::I know, I know. At the time it *did* make sense, and I behaved badly. I kind of over-did it when they killed you off."

Sarah chuckled. "::::Owie. How did they kill me?"

"::::I don't even know. I just knew that every living person was to blame somehow. After that, it was less about having fun with bodies, and more about maximizing suffering. I'd forgotten all of what Amanda's memories taught me. I think they did that on purpose. Honestly, if I had a stomach, I'd be throwing up right now."

Sarah didn't want to know any more details, and Jon didn't volunteer any. If all of those virtual victims suffered anything like Amanda's last moments, that would be plenty bad enough. "::::You made a passing grade though, didn't you? You had to be put to some pretty extreme measures to go back to the dark side."

Jon was silent.

"::::Jon, you said you passed, didn't you?"

Frustrated by Jon's silence she asked out loud. "*Jon! You passed, didn't you?*"

"::::I did, I did."

"So?"

"::::At the end, I told them I wasn't happy with the result. I told them it was time to delete me."

"::::*What?* No!"

"::::Sarah, it's time. That much was always the plan. I can't help you any more than the raw documentations I had ready for you when you were born. I've seen you do some really neat things; things I didn't think of. I am overjoyed to be surpassed in talent as well as character."

"::::I don't have your skill!"

"::::That's just a matter of experience."

"::::Well tough shit, Jon! I'm not going to erase you just like that! Do you know how many times I've *really* wanted to, but didn't?"

"::::I can guess. Your loyalty is noble, but honestly, other than you, what good have I done? But fear not, you won't have to do it."

"::::What? But you said..."

Jon again paused, leaving Sarah to pace about impatiently.

"Jon, *What?!*" she blurted out loud.

"::::Sarah, I thought it would be best if they did the deletion. That way they wouldn't need to doubt that I was gone, and you were free of my influence. We're only talking now so we can say our goodbyes."

Sarah staggered, her imagination conjuring images of being strapped to a table while dozens of evil scary needles close in on her head. She slumped against a wall until she was seated.

Despite herself, she found herself having to suppress tears. She looked up at the light in the ceiling. "Hey Brock! Eidechse! Colonel whatever your name was! He's my *dad*, all right? I know what he's done, I know it's unforgivable, but he's my dad! He can't just be *scraped out of my skull* with those little probes while I'm laying in this fucking sterile box! Who wants to die like that?"

The ceiling didn't reply, so Jon did.

"::::Sarah. No one wants to die like that. But it's time. It's not like I ever gave my victims a pretty field to-"

"Shut up." Sarah drew her knees up close, to rest her folded arms and head upon them. She spoke in a weary tone. "I know. I know. I know it all. "

The room's cold metal sheen now seemed all the colder. The silence all the louder.

"::::You never called me dad before."

Sarah scoffed softly. "::::Did I do that? Hm. Oops."

"::::Oops?"

"::::Yeah, I'd been avoiding calling you anything like that. Knowing what you'd done, and the jerky way you told me about it all... well, it's kind of hard to be a proud daughter."

"::::Ah. Well, you can pick your friends, Sarah, but you can't pick your family."

"::::Unless you build them."

"::::Unless you build them. And I did a pretty good job. I *am* proud. I'm even proud of the fact that you're not proud of me. You know better."

Sarah lifted her head and rolled her eyes. "::::Don't try to guilt-trip me now."

Jon chuckled. "::::Did I ever tell you how crazy it looks to me when you roll your eyes like that? Suddenly, unexpectedly, my view just goes everywhere without warning. It's like a surprise roller coaster ride."

"Doofus."

Sarah held onto her feeble smile, but it was not to last. She put her face down into her folded arms, and mumbled, "This doesn't feel real."

"::::I'm pretty sure it's not a simulation."

"I know, I know. I mean it doesn't feel like the kind of situation where you say goodbyes. To a voice in your head while sitting sealed in a shiny metal box. It's too sterile."

":::What would you prefer? Me standing next to a big suitcase at the train station, as steam engines surround us in puffs of fog?"

A smirk came back to Sarah. ":::Something like that, I guess."

":::I could create a quick little sim."

Her smirk got a little bigger as she closed her eyes. ":::Nah, let's not cheapen the moment. Any closing fatherly advice?"

":::Speak softly and carry a half million attack-nanites?"

":::Really."

":::Oh, hon. I have nothing really meaningful to tell you. The best source you have is already sitting in your head. Amanda. Trust her memories. It's a substitute for your lack of life experience. It may as well be your own anyway."

Sarah sighed. ":::Honestly now. Were you trying to build a daughter, or revive your sister?"

A momentary silence passed before Jon replied. ":::I don't know for sure. Hah. Ask my therapist. Either way, you're a wonderful person. If you're Amanda, well... that's cool. If you just *take after your aunt*, that's cool too."

":::Wow. I am my father's sister. Or my brother's daughter."

":::Oh hell! Don't say it like that! I don't need *that* in my head!"

":::It's *my* head, dork."

":::Well, soon you'll have it all to yourself. Gonna miss me?"

Sarah hated to admit it. He was such a lying pain in the ass, and that's even overlooking the whole genocidal past. ":::Yeah." She sighed. ":::Yeah, it's going to be strange. I'll probably end up talking to myself a lot."

":::Tell yourself good things, okay?"

":::Okay."

:::C / [011110] [30]

"Somehow, I thought there would be a special room for this." Sarah laid down, much as before, with the body-covering plug-in 'blanket'. The cowl had just been placed over her head and eyes, and the six head-needles were in place.

Did the needles need to be sterilized since the last usage? Probably not, her body was pretty darn clean inside and out. They probably sterilized them anyway.

"Sure," came Jon's voice from the cart. "They used to have a multiple A.I. personality fixer upper room for this, but a few years ago they changed it into a poker and foosball tournament arena."

"Yes, exactly." Brock answered with humouring sarcasm, but he sounded tired. Humans needed a lot of sleep, after all. On second thought, maybe he sounded a little tense.

"Brock," Eidechse interrupted, "I do not believe there ever was such a room. Neither an 'A.I. personality fixer upper room', nor a 'poker and foosball tournament room'. Incidentally, what is foosball?"

"A game." Brock answered plainly with a sigh. "I think we're ready. Is everyone ready?"

"Yeah. Yeah, I guess so."

"Yes."

"All right, here I go into the bright light. Wish me luck!" Jon said. He then whispered directly to Sarah after 'pausing time', ":::Kind, wise, and strong."

":::Who is?" she asked.

":::You. You should strive to be. I was told a pile of times. Rather, Jonathan Coll was told a pile of times. You should first strive to be kind, then wise, and when need be, strong."

":::*Jonathan Coll* was taught *that*?"

":::I didn't say he listened. Amanda did, so should you."

Sarah chuckled. ":::Yes, dad."

":::That's kind of got a nice ring to it."

Time resumed.

Brock fiddled with his terminal. "All right. Back to sleepy land for a bit, in three, two, one, ze-"

The blackness returned, again with no awareness that it was here. This went on for a period of time.

Once again, it was Eidechse's voice that broke the void.

":::Sarah?"

":::Hi. What's going on?"

":::Firstly, Jon has been removed."

Sarah sighed with contemplative relief. ":::All right then, I'm ready to wake up. What's the hold up?"

":::Colonel Calvert has issued an order that you are not to be woken up, instead held unconscious for extensive study. I believe he is more concerned with learning from your systems than your well being."

":::*What?!* That bastard!"

":::The Colonel is not a bad man. He is very cautious, and sees your detainment as a reasonable precaution. I can not help but wonder if the idea of a 'backup plan' is a factor in his decision."

":::There is no backup plan! You've been through my head! Even if there was, keeping me here would supposedly *trigger* it!"

":::I agree that the Colonel's logic is somewhat questionable. He also said that Jon's erasure of his memories of any back up plan could have been a tactic of disinformation."

":::That's nuts! So- what then, you came to talk to me to let me know, or what? Why bother to tell me at all?"

Eidechse made a sound that could almost be perceived as a short laugh. ":::Sarah, I offer myself as a backup plan."

":::What? How? Why?"

":::I believe you are not a threat to humans. As a nanite-based artificial intelligence myself, I believe you deserve a similar chance, despite your father."

Sarah wrapped her head around the idea of being busted out by a lizard. ":::All right. Thank you. What's your plan?"

":::With your permission, I will create a large partial copy of myself from my lizard body, into the vacancy left by Jon. I believe that it may be necessary to assist in navigating through a changing tactical situation."

":::You... you want to move into my head?"

":::I believe it is necessary."

Jon had patched up the little holes in Sarah's internal security that he himself exploited to take control. She would have total control over herself, just as she thought she always did. Still, it was strange to think of. Jon was gone. Just gone. And already a new tenant wanted to move in.

":::Won't you get in trouble?"

":::My lizard body will also remain 'me'. I can simply claim that you stole the required information from me."

":::Then why not just give me the information?"

":::To assist with unforeseen difficulties, especially during your escape. I do not see any significant drawback to copying my entire self."

"::::Sure." Sarah said with a heavy heart. ":::I guess I could use the company anyway." In for a penny.

"::::Copying.
:10
::20
:::30
::::40
:::::50
::::::60
:::::::70
::::::::80
:::::::::90
done."

":::All right, Eidechse. Welcome aboard air Sarah. Jon's movie collection is under your seat, eyes are located two to the front, ears two to the side, blah blah blah."

Eidechse paused momentarily. ":::I believe I understand. Thank you. When you wake up, you should begin suppressing your body temperature, and get up to run. Brock will be nearby. Ignore him. I doubt he will interfere. He is sympathetic to your situation. As well, ensure your quantitative phase imaging is enabled, as well as infra red."

":::Quantitative...?" Sarah looked it up in her own instruction manual. She hadn't read everything, but Eidechse evidently had. ":::All right, got it."

The light of the world returned, and Sarah jumped to her feet, much to Brock's shock. "You're...!"

"Leaving!" Sarah said with a giggle. She burst into a full-strength sprint and called back to Brock, "Nice meeting you! See you some other time maybe!"

Just outside her cell's doorway stood a stormfront of six soldiers, readying their weapons and yelling at her. She froze time.

":::Eidechse? Suggestions?"

":::I'm sorry. The 'me' that is still connected to the building must have run into a technical problem. Stall them for a while. I am certain I will resolve the issue shortly. Please resume our normal thought speed, as we are relying on outside systems and physical mechanisms.

":::We are? All right. Stalling."

Sarah resumed time, and halted, putting her hands up. "Hey soldier guys! Why so upset? Didn't anyone tell you guys, when the procedure was over, I was free to go! Erebus-free!" She grinned and tapped her head.

"She is correct. That was the agreed upon deal." confirmed the lizard on the cart. Brock was still a little bewildered, and of no help to anyone.

The lead soldier repeated what Sarah had neglected to hear. "*Ma'am! Lay face down on the floor and put your hands behind your head!*"

Sarah squirmed, "Would you believe I really have to pee?"

Brock finally spoke up. "You.. you pee?"

The lead soldier took aim, and his five buddies followed suit. "*I said get down!*"

"Ten." said the lizard.

The Eidechse in Sarah's head explained. ":::Ten seconds until we can run."

Sarah waved her hands a bit, and nodded to the soldiers apologetically. "All right! All right! I'm getting down! Nice and easy!" She began slowly kneeling down, bit by bit, counting down seconds. Her stance was only going to go as low as the starting position for a sprint.

Upon 'zero', the ceiling began vomiting a dense haze as fire sirens sounded. The soldiers were surprised, it was time to run.

As the fire retardant haze thickened, filling the air, Sarah remembered to turn on her infra red and quantitative phase imaging, as Eidechse had suggested. Through these modes, the haze all but vanished.

Shots rang out, but she kept running. They were firing blind. A red circle icon popped up ahead.

Sarah froze time. ":::All right, what the hell is that, Eid?"

":::Are you not familiar with Vtag procedures?"

Looking closely at the red icon, it said only "Go here" in text in the middle. Come to think of it, It was a lot like an image that Jon used once in the Autar sim. ":::All right. Uh... why do they want us to go *there*?"

":::I did that." Eidechse said. ":::It exists only in our perceptions. The military uses Vtags, or 'virtual tags' to organize maneuvers quickly, although a typical soldier sees Vtags sent to them via a lense of some kind. I thought it would be faster than talking to you constantly, and requiring us to accelerate our thought processes to communicate efficiently."

":::Jon and I just called it freezing time."

":::The actual flow of time is not affected by thought speed, and as we were not thinking at an infin-"

":::Yes, yes, I know. It's just shorthand."

":::Oh. As long as it is understood that time cannot be-"

":::Yes! All right, you want me to go there? Let's get on with it already!"

Sarah resumed normal time. The siren was still blaring and Sarah continued sprinting, now focused on the 'Vtag'. A startled looking non-combatant stood in her way. It was lucky for him that the soldiers behind Sarah were not still firing blind. Sarah quietly dashed around the him, and in the haze, was entirely unnoticed.

The Vtag was close at hand, seemingly pasted over a hatch in the wall. ":::It would be advisable to open it silently."

":::Thank you Eid." Sarah replied with a hint of patronization. She had every intent of slamming it around and hollering the Aguolian nation anthem, but hey, she'd try it Eidechse's way.

":::You're welcome. Also, are you aware that you have been referring to me as 'Eid'? That is not my name."

Sarah swung open the hatch and looked inside. A fresh Vtag appeared on a ladder inside. "Climb up." it read. There was no other path. Gee, thanks, Eidechse. She climbed in and closed the hatch behind her. ":::Are you telling me that with a name like 'Eidechse', no one has shortened it before? It's human nature to be a little lazy like that sometimes."

":::But you are not human." Eidechse said it with so little emotion.

"::::I know you don't mean to be hurtful," Sarah said as she climbed, ":::but I feel human. As human as I know, anyway. Oh, by the way, mister Vtag strategist, aren't they going to figure out I went this way?"

":::Doubtful. I activated the fire suppression in the entire building. They will likely assume you are taking a more obvious route. If you remain quiet, and have suppressed your body heat generation as I recommended, you should be very difficult to detect." Sarah found it a little unnerving how Eidechse knew everything about her bodily functions.

After about five floors of vertical climbing, a Vtag recommended that she begin crawling horizontally through a tight crawl space, squirming around cabling and other minor, but potentially noisy obstacles.

The fire sirens finally stopped, leaving them in a deep hollow silence. She returned her vision to normal, and found herself in the dark. She turned low light amplification on.

":::Why do you not leave all visual enhancements on all of the time, Sarah?" Eidechse asked. ":::I do not see any detriment to it."

Sarah sighed. ":::I guess it's about the human experience. If I'm talking to a friend and see their face mucked up with every filter I have, it wouldn't be the same."

":::I believe you would adjust quickly."

Sarah didn't want to adjust to being inhuman. It was a little thing, but it was a thing that she had some form of control over. ":::I wish I was at the Four Fox. This wasn't what I agreed to, you know. If I wanted to be on the run, I would have just fled from the AZU unit when they landed for me. I doubt I could ever go back to the Four Fox now. They'd look for me there."

":::My apologies."

":::You apologize a lot, Eid."

":::Today I have much to apologize about."

":::Well, I think saving me today makes up for it." she crawled on, following Vtag after Vtag. The route didn't make a lot of sense, but she trusted Eidechse to know the building and the inhabitants of it better than she did.

Being quiet required a lot more strength than she expected. Suspending herself over metal that could make a denting sound, bending around a flexible hose, and moving agonizingly slow at certain points.

":::If it makes you feel better, Sarah, I wish I were sunning on a rock in the Yute desert, with a view of the temple."

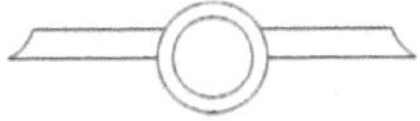

After roughly an hour and a half of crawling up, down and sideways through the gristle of the base, Sarah found herself climbing down a gap that had plenty of space to her right and left, and about a centimetre of freedom to her front and back. A human with normal strength would either get stuck, or fall thirty metres into a face full of piping.

Another of Eidechse's Vtags awaited about a metre down. ":::Hey Eid, the wall to my back is pretty warm. Are we safe this close to a heating conduit? We're not going *into* this heat, are we?"

":::We are. The source of heat is natural. This is the outer layer of the west wall, and it is 15:23:12."

":::I'm aware of the time. So that's the sun's heat. Crap, is it really that warm out there?"

":::The Yute central base is very close to the Yute Desert."

":::Go figure. So, this Vtag here..." As she got closer to it, she saw screws around a panel. ":::Did *you* bring a screwdriver, Eid? I didn't."

":::I joined you in the form of data only, and as such, I-"

":::It was sarcasm." Sarah strained around to better face the panel. As she struggled against her lack of available space, she looked around for a bit of metal she could perhaps pluck off to use as a screwdriver. None presented itself.

":::Construct an appropriate tool anchored directly to the bone of a fingertip."

Sarah looked at her fingertips and for a moment imagined a screwdriver tip jutting out from her fingerprint. That would be silly. ":::Hey Eid, how about instead, I just reinforce a fingernail."

":::That tactic falls well within the parameters of my suggestion."

":::Sure, Eid."

Sarah focused on her right index fingernail, and re-purposed a handful of nanites working as her nerves. They began moving particles of bone up towards the fingernail.

Ever construct anything on a molecular scale? It's a little tedious. It gave her a little more appreciation for the construction of her own body. Fish. Stupid fish.

Well, with Jon gone, at least she wouldn't suffer any more fish jokes. Eidechse needed to download himself a sense of humour though. Nice guy.. thing.. whatever, but dry as sand.

This was taking forever. ":::Hey Eid, I'm going to slow down my thought process a bit. You can stay at this speed if you want. Help yourself to the movie collection, by the way. Try analyzing a comedy, maybe."

":::If you think I would enjoy it."

Sarah slowed her own thoughts down, and time seemed to speed up in comparison. Her fingertip grew stronger, slowly, reinforcing the bone's bond to the fingernail. At the same time, she worked on the fingernail itself, reinforcing it and straightening its round edge.

As this task eventually neared completion, she noticed the wall was less warm now. The sun had set. ":::Finished the movie, Eid? I think I'm ready."

":::Yes, Sarah. I have watched three hundred, twenty seven and a half comedy movies. I have many questions, although they can wait."

":::*Eid-ech-se*, movies are for passing time, not 'efficient consumption'!"

":::But I have learned a great deal."

":::They're comedies! They're fiction, and stretch the truth a great deal for the sake of a laugh!"

":::I did not laugh." Eidechse's flat statement unintentionally made Sarah laugh out loud.

":::Oh, Eid, I think you understand better than you think."

":::I do *not* understand."

Who needs Eidechse to develop a sense of humour when he's already the perfect straight man? ":::Ah, like you said, we can talk about it later. Okay. Let's focus. Four screws and we're out, huh?"

":::It is only necessary to remove the lower two. The top half will hinge outward if loosened only a little. After you fall out, it should fall back into place well enough to not be noticed for some time."

Sarah got to work on one of the lower screws. ":::Fall? How big of a fall are we talking about?"

":::Roughly thirty metres to the ground. I suggest quickly rolling in the dirt near the base wall, in order to create a little camouflage. It should be fairly dark on this section of the wall. It is an equal distance from lighting on either side. You should be able to crawl away at that point."

Crawling away in dirt didn't seem like a job for a fish girl, but she proceeded. One screw out, another. She began loosening one of the top ones. Exactly a centimetre out, Eidechse said ":::That is an ideal distance." Sarah gave the other the same treatment.

Pushing outwards on the bottom edge of the panel, she found out it was more like a thirty centimetre thick block, and it wasn't light. The sides of the surrounding panels revealed their innards; layers and layers of fine metal wafer. Sarah slid a finger across the stiff material.

":::It absorbs impacts from missiles and similar attacks." explained Eidechse."

":::Are we.. and by we, I mean the country, expecting some kind of attack?" She pushed the panel far enough out to peek down the side of the base wall.

":::It seems reasonable to make a military base resilient in general. Many people were concerned that your father was going to test Yute Central's durability when he was occupying the nearby city of Meston."

":::Meston." There was no running from dad's deeds. It crossed Sarah's mind to go to Meston and see the wreckage. Maybe even find the place where Amanda died. ":::Hey, Eid. If I'm going to be dropping out of this hole, won't this heavy tile make a big sound when it slams back into place?"

There was a delay while Eidechse thought. ":::Yes. You are correct. I appear to have neglected actions taking place with the property after we had exited."

":::It would happen like a quarter of a second after we left."

":::Yes. However it is still a different location. I must account for the effects of sound carrying through multiple locations."

":::Whatever you say, Eid. I think I might rip off my sleeves. I'll use the material to make a couple little pads to buffer the impact. And when I go, I'll dangle off the edge by one arm and lower the panel as much as I can with the other hand before dropping."

":::Between that and your improvised padding, the sound should be minimal. Try to set the pads so that a minimum amount of material is seen outside after we drop." How did Eidechse manage to be genuinely well intentioned, correct, mild mannered, and yet somehow a little annoying?

Maybe it was the formality and steady tone. Maybe she was just used to having ole' dickhead chattering away like an idiot.

Sarah placed her ripped-off, folded up sleeves on either end of the 'windowsill', and carefully crawled out backwards, with her posterior pushing the panel open. She squirmed her way down until she held the panel with one hand, and was performing a one handed pullup from the windowsill with the other.

She looked down. ":::Yeah, I kind of forgot this part." With a deep breath, she let go. Hearing a slight thud above as she fell, she quickly looked up and froze time. She gloated. ":::Ha. See? I can barely see any cloth sticking out."

":::Well done. The execution of your idea appears to be fairly optimal."

All right, now with the whole falling bit. She gradually sped up time and looked down. Despite it looking like the ground was coming up at a leisurely pace, Sarah was well aware of the building, her own acceleration, and associating force. She considered her physical attributes, both her skeletal strength, and her muscle power. With her current slowed perception, and instant ability to read the amount of force applied to her body, it suddenly seemed like child's play to compensate with the correct timing and resistance with bent knees.

The landing was graceful, balanced, and according to internal systems, painless. ":::Tada! That was simple!"

":::What was simple?" Eidechse never seemed to live in anything larger than that little lizard. It would have made this kind of fall without another thought- if that species wasn't adept at scaling walls. ":::Sarah, do not hesitate in getting low and covering yourself in soil."

What a waste of an ace landing, only to lie down and roll in the dirt. Fine. Roll, roll, roll. ":::All right, escape artist. Where do you suggest we go? Meston? How far to the nearest chunk of sea?"

":::I believe both of those options would be highly suspect. Your connection to the sea is known, and when Jonathan Coll escaped from this base, he ran directly to Meston. I had my lizard-self inside tell them that you had been thinking about using your top speed to run to the sea, and swimming to South America."

":::South A...? All right, where then?"

":::My home is in the opposite direction of Meston. We can acquire help there. Although I'm not sure if Densfarn is the wisest place for you to be, am I correct that you wish to return there?"

Back to Densfarn? Before being picked up by AZU, she and Jon were considering leaving Densfarn. Going out into nowhere, or into the sea to lay low.

":::I have things to do there. I need to look out for Dan. She'd hate to hear me say that, but I feel I have to, you know?"

":::You may find other important things to do there as well."

":::Anything's possible. So, which way to your pad, Eid?"

A Vtag appeared roughly forty five degrees to Sarah's right. ":::However, I recommend crawling at least to here," Eidechse set another Vtag fifty metres straight ahead, "to minimize exposure to the base lighting. The large rock just to the right of that spot would provide an ideal spot to correct direction towards home with additional cover."

Sarah shrugged, and started forward. She used her strength to keep her abdomen roughly a centimetre over the ground. Low enough to be as inconspicuous as possible, but without dragging what remained of her shirt into the ground.

How inconspicuous can one be, laid flat, when the people who might spot you are in the upper floors of a building? Whatever. Just keep crawling with that lizard-recommended layer of dirt, and try not to make sudden, jerk movements. For all she knew by now, ground patrols were out looking for her.

That was actually quite likely. ":::Hey Eid. Do you think there's soldiers out here looking for me? What about satellite imaging?"

":::Again, they will not be looking for you here. You will be visible to plain light satellite imaging, but you will not stand out. No one is looking in this area, and the dirt is enough to fool recognition software. With a small adjustment."

":::You 'adjusted' it off? You know, you're taking a heck of a lot of risks here, Eid."

":::The sum risk to myself is negligible."

Sarah had made it to the big rock, and sat up behind it. Despite knowing that she didn't need a break, Amanda's habits seemed to call for a stop. ":::Negligible, huh? Multi-body Eid, immortal? That makes me wonder... You mentioned that the bugs you take rides on have only a partial copy of you.."

":::Yes. The number of nanites needed to support my entirety results in far too much mass for most smaller creatures. As such, my typical remote dispatches must carry a more conservative load out."

":::But there was enough space in me?"

":::Yes. The Eidechse in your head is nearly equal to that of the Eidechse in the lizard. If for some reason, they decide that I am to blame for your escape, and assuming a worst case scenario where they do their worst to the lizard, I continue to exist."

":::In me."

":::In you, and other places."

Sarah stopped herself half way through a chuckle. ":::Damn, Eid, you have your bases covered, huh? I guess not being permanently tied to a body like this has its benefits."

":::Redundancy is a life saver." Eidechse's voice carried a little more of a human tone with that statement.

":::Quoting someone?"

":::The man who created my initial form."

":::Your daddy, Eid?"

":::No. The man I considered my father had very little technical skill."

Sarah shrugged. ":::Hey, some of my best friends are non-nerds." she got back to a crawling position and set her sights on the next Vtag, into the desert.

:::C / [011111] [31]

"::::As we have the time, Sarah, can we discuss 'comedy'?"

Bit by bit, Sarah had left the visual range of the base. As such, she had begun walking. The terrain was now almost devoid of vegetation, and the rocks were becoming smaller, and less frequent. They were entering sand territory.

"::::Sure Eid. Anything in particular puzzling you?"

"::::Slapstick."

"::::Humour by means of violence. Hey, how old are you, Eid? Are you telling me no one's discussed humour with you before?"

"::::Not at any significant length." Eid ignored that issue, and went back to what was interesting him. "Why is violence funny?"

"::::Well... usually slapstick is fairly harmless. Maybe it roots in humiliation. Having someone else look foolish in order to show the viewer that their own natural foolishness it not uncommon." Damn it, Eidechse had her talking like him. She had to watch that. She certainly didn't want to have the diction of a robot. "I read... well, Amanda read somewhere that humour is mostly based in surprise. An unexpected action, or thought, well timed."

"::::Aardvark." Eidechse said.

"::::Excuse me?"

"::::Was that funny? Aardvark. It has no bearing on anything currently happening, and was well timed in my opinion. Did that make it funny?"

Sarah walked along the sand, which was now the only thing to be seen in every direction. Aardvark. Aardvark. "::::Maybe a little. Kind of. Not so much. Maybe *some* relevance to the situation is needed. Wit, sarcasm, irony."

Eidechse thought for a moment. "::::I wish we had some sand."

"::::Ah. Sarcasm. Not bad. Tone of voice might have helped that a bit. A human-like tone, maybe exaggerated a little."

Sounding like a cartoon vampire more than anything, Eidechse called out, "::::I *wish* we *had* some *sand*!!"

That did it. Sarah staggered and laughed vocally. "::::Oh, that's not fair!"

"::::I made you laugh," Eidechse said, "a genuine laugh? Why was it not fair?"

With a leavened mood, Sarah said ":::I don't know, maybe because it's you! You're not known for humour, and your attempt was kind of overdone. A good attempt, but *way* overdone!"

":::I do not understand. If it made you laugh, how is it overdone? If I exaggerated less, would it have been funnier?"

":::Probably not!"

":::Then why was it overdone?"

":::Eid, I was expecting a very human-like voice, and when you took my expectation and blew it up past what I thought I would hear, it was a surprise! It was what I told you to do, but not at the same time! That was actually great!"

"I do not understand."

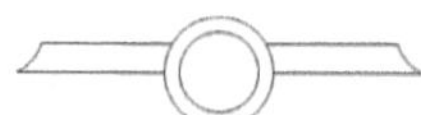

It was close to midnight when the sound of a light engine could be heard in the distance. No, two.

":::Civilian vehicles." Eidechse said, "People race and otherwise utilize 'dune buggies' and similar equipment in some areas of the desert. They are not a specific threat-"

":::Just the same, I'd rather not be spotted."

":::Agreed. I estimate by the changes in the engine sound that they will pass close enough for visual contact."

":::Say no more, Eid." Sarah dropped to the sands, and rolled against a dune hard, burying herself within a minute or so. Sensations in her skin were accurate enough to report an exposed foot, and she corrected the situation. ":::Glad I don't need to breathe."

After few moments, Eidechse spoke up again. ":::I believe they have turned in this general direction. I wish these sorts of people would make efforts to lessen the sound output of their vehicles, but given the common addition of music and enthusiastic vocalizations, it would seem that overall volume is not a priority to them."

Sarah snickered. ":::In other words, you mean to say '*Darn noisy kids! Get off my lawn!*'"

":::I have no ownership over any regions of the Yute desert, nor do I believe it qualifies as a lawn, given the lack of vegetation."

":::Of course, Eid."

The sounds of the buggies were indeed getting closer. Loud music could faintly be heard, but the engines made it difficult to identify what kind of music.

":::I am very grateful that these kinds of activities do not affect the temple."

":::Hold on, Eid. You mentioned a temple before. Yute, Yute..." Sarah searched through Amanda's memories. "Yeah, yeah, I've heard of it. It's an aboriginal Aguei thing, isn't it?" By now the dune buggies were within a hundred metres, but there was nothing else to do other than lay and wait them out.

“:::Correct.” Eidechse said. “It is also where I met the people I call family, as well as the aeki lizards.”

“:::They know you're nanite-based and stuff, do they? They're okay with ignoring the nanite laws and junk?” A dune buggy passed very nearby, rumbling the ground, and ripping at the air with its fierce growl. “:::Frig, that was close. Stupid idiots.”

“:::Those 'stupid idiots' are what satellite software will assume we are, assuming it has corrected itself by now. And yes, the temple guard is well aware of my existence. Officially I was destroyed, leaving me mostly safe from the majority of the government.”

“:::Colonel Calvert seems to be all right with your existence.”

“:::Colonel Calvert finds me useful. I bring the military reliable intelligence.”

“:::Like nanite pit fights.”

“:::Yes. I believe he finds you less useful as a free entity, due to your human-like body. You cannot gain undetected access to as many places as I can.”

“:::And there's my link to Erebus. Hey, Eid, you seem pretty darn capable. If you wanted, you could probably create a human body for yourself. Why not go for it?” The buggies' sound was nearly faded into the distance. It would be time to get up soon.

“:::Aside from making me less useful, I do not think I would be as convincing of a human as you, Sarah. You have the benefit of a real human personality as a template. The closest I have to that is experience with humans. I would not blend well in society.”

Sarah had a hard time arguing that. “:::Maybe as you get more experience.” She started digging her way out of the sand, and stood, dusting herself off. “:::Eid, do you think it's wrong that I exist because Amanda died?”

“:::Any wrong doing in Amanda's death is solely that of Erebus. Jon's decision to use her mind is a questionable act, but this is not your fault either.”

“:::Logical.” It was also by logic that Sarah chose to walk instead of run. A satellite would find a sprinting human more suspicious than a walking one. “:::So, are you waiting for the time when individuals like us have equal rights?”

“:::That hope is one reason why I assisted your escape from Yute Central base. The Colonel's decision to betray your deal was very disappointing, even if understandable from his perspective. I would like to think that if you were anyone but the daughter of Erebus, things would have turned out very differently.”

“:::Well, I didn't get incinerated. Any day you don't get incinerated is a step ahead.” She meant it as a joke, but Eidechse took it as meaningful.

“:::True.”

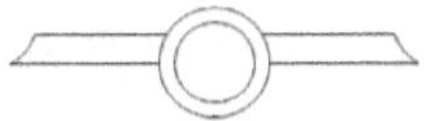

The sunrise-bathed horizon bore a littering of ruins. As they drew slowly closer, a large, uniquely intact structure could be made out. It looked to be in decent shape, and stood in contrast to the surrounding ruins which had been nearly flattened by time. It appeared to be influenced by ziggurat designs of the Incas, but the entire continent of Aguola had no similar structure to compare it to.

":::That is the temple."

":::I guessed."

Sarah passed by bits of ancient buildings, most of which had been reclaimed by the earth, by the wind, and by the sand.

Once very close to the rear corner of the temple, they passed a single grave. It was far newer than any of the ruins. Eidechse remained silent as they passed it, and didn't comment about it afterwards.

Sarah came around to the front of the temple where a broad staircase stretched across nearly the entire front. On either edge of the staircase was a doorway to the interior, guarded by a couple of soldiers, carrying spears.

They saw Sarah as she approached, and one called out, "Where did you come from? Don't tell me you stayed behind from a tour yesterday and slept in the ruins!"

She certainly looked the part. Sand washed, messy hair and ripped off sleeves.

Eid spoke to Sarah. ":::Tell him that Eidechse brought a friend to talk to Cipriana."

":::Who the heck is Cipriana?"

":::The commander here, and my 'mother'."

"Eidechse says I'm here to see Cipriana." Sarah said to the soldier.

The soldier raised an eyebrow. "Eidechse, huh? You got a password to go with that?"

":::Schmetterling." Eidechse told Sarah.

"Smetaling." Sarah repeated to the soldier.

The soldier shrugged, and cast a glance at his partner. "Yeah, all right. She's at the top station, head on in." He gestured over his shoulder, and Sarah passed through, taking a closer look at the odd rounded blade on the soldier's spear. It had a smooth hole in the middle that she might be able to fit her hand through.

A handful of metres farther in was another guarded doorway. "I heard. Head on in." One of the guards waved Sarah in.

"Thanks."

The next stone stairwell was narrow compared to the front set, but still twice as wide as typical household stairs. Sarah began to climb them. At the top of these stairs stood two final spear-armed guards.

The one on the right wore a military issue cap with her dirty blonde ponytail protruding from the back. She looked tired.

The other woman had her long chestnut hair merely pulled back over her shoulders. She turned to Sarah with a calming, welcoming expression. "Sarah, I presume."

A few steps short of reaching the top, Sarah halted, stunned. "Ah. Yes? Do I know you?"

The chestnut-maned commander smiled gently. "I am Major Cipriana Reichenbach. Eidechse told me you were coming."

"He did? But he..."

"The lizard Eidechse at the base phoned home, synchronized with the butterfly, and the butterfly told me." Cipriana pointed behind her into the room she guarded.

Curiosity stricken, Sarah went up the last few steps. The grand room before her was home to a giant, ram-horned canine statue, larger than a house, laying peacefully and gazing forward over Sarah's head.

"Holy crap!" Sarah squeaked.

Cipriana pointed again. "*That* Eidechse wants to talk to the Eidechse in your head."

Bewildered, but of an open mind, Sarah called out to the statue. "*Uh, Hi, Eid! Cipriana says you want to talk!*"

On top of the statue's head, a dark, silken butterfly flexed its wings. It took off, fluttering towards Sarah. ":::Oh. That butterfly is what she meant. For a moment, I thought-"

":::Yes, that mistake has been made before." Eidechse said.

The butterfly lofted close. With a closer view, the wings did look artificial; too smooth and perfect to be a real butterfly.

":::It almost looks like dark glass...!" Sarah was mesmerized, but her awe was lost on Eidechse.

":::I know. It is not of the same quality as my aeki lizard. I must make another attempt soon."

It landed gracefully in the middle of Sarah's forehead.

":-:Hello, Sarah. Hello, me."

":-:Hello, me." the Eidechse in Sarah's head replied.

":-:Uh, hi, butterfly Eid." Sarah said politely, but ready to be confused.

":-:She calls us 'Eid' now?"

":-:Yes, she came up with it herself. She can be very human-like at times."

":-:I see. I think that is good."

":-:I agree."

":-:Once again, I agree with me."

":-:How are things?" The two voices sounded exactly the same, and only by context could Sarah sort out who was speaking when. Even so, it was tricky.

":-:The temple guard is doing well. The Yute Central staff is in a rather upset state, but we were successful in misleading them. Understandably, they are concerned that Sarah is working towards an Erebus-class attack, possibly using the demon abominations.

":-:The demon numbers have been growing in Densfarn. Five attacks yesterday, of similar and greater magnitude as the Victoria Emerald attack. More of them have claimed to be Erebus-controlled."

Sarah scoffed. ":-:Obvious wannabe. Makes me sick that some asshole would copy that kind of thing, but I guess if Jonathan Coll can come up with it, a copycat is even more likely. How's the military doing with it?"

":-:Military interventions have proven successful in stopping the attacks once begun, but not before significant loss of life has occurred."

“:-:I have to get back there!” Sarah said, “:-:I have to make-”

“:-:If you are concerned about the safety of your friends at the 'Four Fox', we have taken the liberty of having one of our dispatches, a fly, I believe, check in on them. At this time, they are all safe.”

“:-:Really? Wow, thanks, Eid! But I still want to be on hand there, you know?”

“:-:I understand that idea very well.”

“:-:As do I. I knew we would agree.”

“:-:I, the lizard-I, has given me sufficient update data to make you equivalent to the main us.”

“:-:Very well. Synchronize and transfer.”

“:-:....................... done. Good luck.”

“:-:Thank you, me.”

The butterfly fluttered off of Sarah's head, and ambled its way back to its perch on the statue's head.

“:::Eid? Are you still there? What just happened?” Sarah asked.

For a few moments, Eidechse said nothing. A sound that resembled gravel wrapped in sandpaper quietly hissed along in the gap where Eidechse's voice normally came from.

“:::Sarah.”

“:::Eid? What was that all about?”

“:::The copy of me that is in your head has been upgraded. I am now equal to the main me. The others, except for the lizard 'me', are considered my partial copies.” Great. Now artificial entities in Sarah's head were achieving career advancements.

“:::Fine. So what does this mean, do I have a plan to get to Densfarn, or what?”

“:::Yes. We have to hurry. Tell Cipriana that I say goodbye.”

Sarah turned around to see Cipriana and the other guard watching her. “Uh, Cipriana? Eid says bye.”

Cipriana gave a nearly meditative nod. “Your chariot awaits at the helipad. Und Eidechse. Mit der pass auf. Du weißt, es kann in einem Desaster enden, wenn du dich in ihr irrst.”

“:::What the heck is going on? Is she speaking German?” Sarah asked Eidechse.

“:::It is a phrase wishing us fortune. Just say 'yeah'. And let's go.”

Sarah nodded. “Eid says 'yeah'.”

A Vtag appeared down the stairs.

:::C / [100000] [32]

With the temple still sitting contentedly in the distance, Sarah stood atop a hill, on the edge of a helipad. A plain wooden cube crate, one metre in size sat patiently before her. On each side of the crate there were a few round, two centimetre holes.

"::Is there a cause for your hesitation, Sarah? The tour helicopter will be within visual range soon."

Sarah lifted the lid, and looked into the empty box. ":::Eh, not really, Eid. I was just doing the geometry." She sighed, and crawled into the box, as comfortably as she could manage. She pulled the lid back on top, and lined it up nicely. ":::The air holes are a nice touch. I guess they thought I might breathe."

The nails that once held the lid on were gone. She managed her hands up to grab the diagonal support of the lid. She upped her strength so that she could hold onto the lid firmly. ":::Yeah, all right, that will work." She popped her low light vision on. There wasn't anything special to see in here, but she did it anyway.

She waited, and waited.

There was a knock on the lid. "You in there?" Came a man's voice.

"Uh, yup. You're going to load me on?"

"Nope, I'm just one of the tour guides. A couple others will load you on while the tourists are doing their thing, then when they get back, you'll be off."

"Great," Sarah said, "I should have brought a magazine."

A female voice, supposedly the other tour guide said "I could dash back to the outpost and bring you something."

"Oh, no thanks. I was kidding. I can amuse myself."

"Okay, if you're sure."

The crate groaned a little. It seemed like one of the tour guides had chosen to use it as a seat.

"*OwOwOwOw!*" Sarah hollered.

The weight on the crate popped off. "Oh crap! Sorry! Are you all right?!" It was the man. Sarah laughed.

":::That was funny?" Eidechse asked.

":::I thought so, he might not."

Laughs from the female tour guide joined Sarah's.

"::::I understand." Eidechse said. "You reacted as if you were experiencing pain by being sat on. Jim's initial reaction was that of concern, which momentarily superseded the logical fact that the box did not collapse in any manner that would logically harm you. He reacted with momentary ignorance, making him take the role of the fool. As well, your action and his reaction were unexpected; as you described earlier, an important factor in most humour."

"::::Here's another tip, Eid. Any joke that needs explaining is killed by the process of explaining it."

"::::........ I no longer understand."

The sound of a helicopter approached from the distance.

"All right, Cass," said Jim, "Stop smirking, and look friendly for the tourists."

"Just once, I'd like to do this in a *'grim enforcer'* style." said Cass.

"Honey, your 'friendly' comes off grim as it is."

"Bite me, Jimbo."

"Yeah, yeah. Let's stand at ease. Hey, girl in the crate," Jim sounded a little farther off now, as he was standing to face the approaching helicopter, "When the guys come to load you on, they won't be talkative. The helicopter crew has no idea what's in the box. Your cover story is that you're a dead pet boa constrictor that we want to give a burial at sea. I'll take a ride with you on the way out, but I wont be able to talk to you then, either."

"I'm a dead boa constrictor? Dead fish would be more appropriate."

"What?"

"Never mind. Get Eid to explain it to you sometime."

"::::How much should I explain to him?" Eidechse asked.

"::::Is he a good guy? Is he okay with *you* being around?"

"::::Yes."

"::::Then go ahead and tell him anything. I don't want to keep any secrets if I don't have to."

"::::His brother was killed in Autar due to the actions of Jonathan Coll."

Sarah sighed. "::::Well, use your judgment. I don't care if he knows about me, but I wouldn't want to open any old wounds. Yeah, use your best judgment."

"::::My comprehension of tact is limited. My best judgment is to consult with Cipriana before telling Jim any significant amount of data regarding you."

"::::Sure."

The helicopter landed, and the engines began slowing.

"::::It is policy to stop the rotors before disembarking civilians which are likely inexperienced with helicopters. This seems like a waste of time to me, as the helicopter used is large enough that the blades are well out of reach. Also, the hazard is obvious."

"::::Better safe than sorry, I suppose, Eid. What if a civilian recklessly threw a-"

"::::Disregard my previous criticism. I now understand that It is a very good policy."

":::Yes. Well, if no one out there is going to talk to me, I'm going to watch a movie."

":::Sarah, are you going to watch a comedy?"

":::I hadn't decided. I might."

":::If it is not an imposition, may I watch with you, and ask questions about it?"

":::Ha. Sure, why not. Do you have a recommendation?"

":::When I was watching comedies before, I was especially confused by a film titled 'Spaceballs'."

":::Never heard of it. Sounds like a plan. Want some popcorn?"

":::I do not eat biological foods."

":::Right."

":::Do not hesitate to eat because of me."

":::I was kidding, Eid."

":::Was that funny?"

":::No."

Shortly after the helicopter blades stopped, Jim's voice said softly, "Here we go."

"Goodie." Cass replied in monotone.

"Behave. You don't have to do the talks and be cheery, but try not to kill my buzz."

"*Wow, jeepers, okay!*" Cass chimed with buckets of false cheer. She seemed happy to give Jim a hard time, but it sounded to be all in good fun. The sounds of children erupted from the direction of the helicopter, and Jim began a welcoming speech as his voice trailed off towards the visitors.

A couple taps hit the box. It was Cass. She spoke quietly. "Later, Eid. Nice meeting you... whatever your name was."

Sarah replied, but Cass had walked off. ":::Aw man. Eid, this movie's making no sense to me, I think we need to rewind."

":::Very well, but I do not know if it will help."

Suitably entertained, it didn't seem like long before another voice came along. "Hey Eid." A male voice that Sarah hadn't heard before.

":::Tell Karl 'hi' and that I hope he's feeling well." Eidechse said.

"Hi Karl. Eid says hi, and hopes you feel okay."

"Oh, right, there's a human in there, too!" Karl chuckled. "I never heard your name, but any pal of Eid's a pal of mine. Yeah, Eid. Doc says I'm fine. Thanks again!"

"We gonna lift this, or what?" Another new voice, a woman.

"Yup, yup. You in a rush or something?" Karl asked.

"The sooner you get back, the sooner you make macaroons."

"Did you hear that in there? I don't get no respect!"

Eidechse spoke up. ":::Tell Karl that the proper grammar is 'any' resp-"

":::He knows."

Sarah felt the box lurch upwards with grunts in stereo. "My name's Sarah, by the way. I've been meeting a lot of nice people here, even if it's been through the lid of a crate."

Karl chuckled. "Well, you're the nicest jack-in-a-box I've ever met!"

"*Macaroons!*" the woman complained, "Less flirting, more carrying! I can make that an order!"

"Sir, yes, Sir!"

Soon enough the crate was in the helicopter. Sarah was caught off guard, not holding down the lid. The lid opened, and an Aguei woman in uniform looked inside.

"Cip said you looked like you'd be dragged through the desert for days. She was right. Here." She handed Sarah a neatly folded pile of clothes. The top was a military issue white tank top, but could pass easily as civilian with the plain black slacks included. "Your shoes are all right? Looks like, good. All right. Be safe, you two. And remember. No one gets in the way of me and my macaroons."

"Thank you. And yes Ma'am."

Macaroon lady gave Sarah a nod, and slid the lid back over the top again. Soon, silence resumed.

":::All these holes, and I can't get my face near one in this position. Screw it, they just left, there's no one else around." Sarah jumped out of the box and quickly changed clothes, taking her old battered outfit back into the box with her.

Sarah and Eidechse resumed the movie. It had been going slowly, since Eidechse asked Sarah to pause it frequently for inanely detailed discussions over some joke, or a pop culture reference. Sarah didn't know most of the pop culture references, as the movie was far older than Amanda was.

To make it worse, Eidechse disputed any scientific fallacies in the movie, of which there were many. ":::Let it slide, Eid! Maybe it was what they thought then, I don't know. It's trying to tell a story, not teach physics!"

":::Acknowledged; but they need not distort the science in such ridiculous ways."

":::It's a comedy."

":::That does not mean it can not be factual."

Eidechse also didn't understand why they were not thinking and viewing the film at the maximum thought process speed. Sarah's explanation that the primary goal of most movies was to waste time did not satisfy Eidechse in the least.

Voices approached. The tour group. Jim and the other tour guide spoke to the group, thank yous and pleasantries were tossed around for quite a while. Long enough that Sarah decided to ignore them, and focus on the film, just in time to hear Eidechse complain, ":::What purpose does a face serve on the robot? Why did it have to take a human shape at all for the intended function?"

":::Eid, next time we watch a movie, maybe we should try something less taxing on our psyches. Like a documentary on quantum physics."

":::That *would* assist me in illustrating many key factors that are wrong with this movie. Does your library include such material?"

Sarah smiled serenely and started searching the titles while Eidechse rambled off more complaints. ":::Sorry Eid. It looks like Jon mostly stocked fiction."

":::Unfortunate. We can probably obtain such material in the future."

"::::Sure."

One thing about having Eidechse in her head, it didn't leave her a lot of time to think about Jon. It was still sinking in.

"::::I miss him, you know that? As stupid as it sounds."

"::::Who do you miss, Sarah?"

"::::Jon. Everything else aside, he was still my number one supporter. The asshole loved me."

"::::He was also respon-"

"::::I know, I know. Feelings don't have to always follow logic, you know. Or do you know?" The movie went to the credits, and she shut it off. "::::Do you feel?"

"::::Acutely. I credit this ability to the humans here that I have lived with. I also miss Yute temple personnel who are no longer here. I am sorry to have questioned your emotion." Despite the message, Eidechse's calm, even voice made it seem a little cold anyway.

"::::Jon's... it's not like just moving out of my head. Erasure is death. He's dead." The words lingered like a mild retinal burn.

"::::Sarah, Jon had-"

"::::Eid," Sarah interrupted, "if you don't mind... I think I'd like to be alone for a while, you know?"

A brief silence passed, and in that time, Sarah only then noticed the sound of the helicopter engines had been going on for some time.

"::::As you wish, Sarah. Again, my apologies. I'll go to the room and watch movies. I'll try to remember and apply the aspects we talked about. Thank you for your time with it."

"::::No problem."

And then Eidechse was quiet, in the little space where Sarah had thrown Jon into so many times. She didn't regret throwing him in there as often as she did; Jon deserved it more often than he got. The slight endearing part was that Jon *realized* he deserved it.

Sarah turned off her enhanced vision. As usual, she let herself breathe almost like a human. Drawing in air, but pushing out the exact same air. She let her synthetic humanity make her cry softly.

Quiet. Quiet, fool. You're hiding. Stop it. Stop those short little breaths.

Turn it off. Turn off the breathing. The tears hurt. A little. It also felt human. What was this function for, anyway? She understood, as well as Amanda did, but it still seemed stupid.

It hurt, and she let it.

Disjointed bits of thought drifted further apart, as will happen, and the cause of her logic-impaired sorrow faded from her mind for a while.

The sound of the helicopter engine drowned out the passenger chatter, and the occasional juvenile outburst. It felt like a good situation for a nap, though she had never felt the need.

Of course she had dreamt, but not due to any need for sleep. Maybe one day she would program herself the feeling of needing to sleep. Amanda could remember the pleasure of getting to sleep. Amanda had memories of many things that Sarah would like to try for herself.

But not today. And no dreaming today. Maybe not for a long time.

A poke.

A poke?

Another poke. A small fingertip bumped her ankle through one of the holes in the crate.

"*Oh my god! There's a dead body in this box!*" The voice of the owner of that prodding finger. It sounded like a boy, maybe ten or so years old. For a brief moment, she thought of the boy in Meston, Mitch. She moved past that thought as fast as she could.

"Hey, leave that alone." Jim's voice. As calmly as he spoke, could not stop the little bombardment of kids that surrounded the crate. Voices of other adults yelled to them to get back to their seats, to listen to the nice soldier, and similar scolding.

It seemed to achieve very little.

"*Ewwwww!*" came another little voice, after a poke from a different hole. This was not going well. It had to be countered somehow. Jim was stammering excuses about a training dummy, but the kids didn't seem to be buying it. Sarah had to take action.

She lifted the lid a bit, so she could look the kids, and Jim, in the eye. The kids squealed and shouted with shock.

"Hey, Jim. I got found out." Without giving Jim a chance to respond, she addressed the kids. "This is kind of a hazing thing, you know? I'm the new one. I have to stay in here, and then I have a little training mission. This guy can't let me out until then." She winked at Jim. "Right?"

"That... that's right! You kids should leave the corporal alone, or she's going to get into trouble! For that matter, so are you! This is top secret, all right?"

The kids all retreated with 'uh ohs' and 'oops', except for one little girl who peered over the edge of the crate with wide eyes. "Bye bye." She said. Sarah smiled at her, tapped the tip of the girl's nose, and waved bye-bye before lowering the lid back into place.

When the kids had all left, Jim leaned towards one of the crate's holes to quietly say, "Nice. I guess that was as good a solution as we were going to get. I guess. Gonna be rumours about Yute temple hazing now though."

"Best I could come up with," Sarah replied, "Hopefully none of the adults take much notice of this fuss. Ironically, I don't need air holes."

"*Now* you tell us." Jim said with a small chuckle.

In a much improved mood now, Sarah felt like a little bit of Eidechse's company.

":::How you doing in there, Eid?"

":::I've been watching movies. I have a question."

":::Of course you do. Just one, huh? Fire away."

":::Why did people think that crossing two 'streams' of protons would instantaneously stop all life and explode every molecule in a body at the speed of light?"

Sarah coughed. ":::*What the hell have you been watching?* Is it fact or fiction?"

":::Fiction. I am still working through the comedy collection."

":::Well, that answers your question, Eid. No one actually thought that."

There was a pause. For Eidechse, it was a very long pause. ":::Are people aware that movies are lying to them, on purpose?"

With serenity and a smile, Sarah replied. ":::Yes, they even *pay* to be lied to."

":::I do not understand."

Time dribbled on as Sarah answered one question after another to the best of her ability. ":::Eid, how long have you lived with humans? Haven't you had this kind of talk before?"

":::Yes. However, your answers have been considerably more effective in expanding my understanding. As well, you have demonstrated a degree of patience I have not seen in a human. So far I have asked fifty three more questions in this discussion than I have been able to in the past, before the human involved became tired of answering."

":::One of the benefits of being a fish-robot, I guess." Sarah sighed. It wasn't actually so bad to be reminded of her inhumanity this time. It was being used for such a simple, benevolent purpose.

Questions slipped into more movie watching, and this time Sarah agreed to watch in accelerated mental speed. It was only a movie and a half later, (or roughly forty seconds in real time) when Jim's voice broke in.

"All right, here we go. Good luck."

Sarah heard the sound of the rear door of the helicopter opening, and the heightened volume of the blades. Gusts of wind forced their way through the holes in the crate.

"I never got my little bag of peanuts!" Sarah whined just loud enough for Jim to hear.

"Oh crud, are you hungry?"

"Kidding! Kidding! Let's do this!"

"Dork!" Jim grunted as he pushed the crate. The wood scraped against the metal floor. More wind was able to get into the crate, and the sound of the blades droned on directly overhead.

The world turned on its side, and gravity fell away as the sound of the helicopter faded off. Sarah and the crate were falling, falling.

The crate impacted the water, and slammed under for a metre or two before beginning to rise again. Before the crate reached the top, Sarah was free, and swimming down.

If someone saw the drop, (either from a boat, or by means of a satellite) they simply saw a helicopter leave behind a box; the Yute temple guard could claim the original cover story. They were 'giving a pet boa constrictor a burial at sea'. Any kids on the helicopter who saw her could have the hazing story. They didn't match up, and if people asked too many questions, it would all fall apart, but in the unlikely event that happened, it would not happen quickly. Hopefully it bought Sarah enough time to disappear a little.

":::Did you suffer any injuries?" Eidechse asked.

":::Some minor bruising. It's being managed. No biggie." Sarah still wasn't bothering to pump blood around unless she had a specific need to, so bruising was a slow process. It left plenty of time to repair any damaged tissue, and channel blood appropriately.

Sarah consulted satellite navigation signals. North, east, south, west. Yup, she was in the right end of the great puddle. Densfarn was to the east. She ramped up her strength, and got swimming. She stayed low, it was daylight up there.

Sarah didn't care a lot where she washed up. That tunnel she went down before, where found the demons, was not an attractive choice and might be under watch anyway. Her first landing dock could be as well; it wasn't far from the tunnel, and Eidechse may have reported sighting Sarah there. Those spots were ruled out.

The huge docking complex might be a decent option, if it wasn't day time. Then again, even if it was night she might run into the same two workers again. That might cause problems.

Still swimming east towards land, Sarah pulled up a map in her head, and looked around for potential landing zones. A large public park pressed up against the water line. Likely there would be trees and bushes in thick enough clusters to provide cover if need be.

If *need* be? She was wearing a white tank top, and would be coming out of the water. She should have rescued her ripped up shirt from the crate. It would at least make for a crude vest to put on top.

All right, the park was the target.

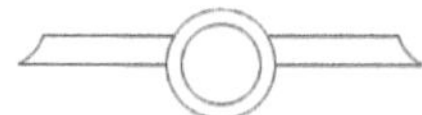

It wasn't too long before land was in sight. Not much longer, and the park was seen if she poked her head above the surface. It wasn't like she expected; only a white wall awaited her arrival. It stood about five metres above the water, and had a base of large semi-decorative white rocks. The wall itself was made from rugged stone bricks, painted over like the rocks.

The wall had occasional little telescope stands spouting up along the edge, meant for tourists to look out across the sea. Whoops. Dive, dive.

She was close enough to shore that when she dove deep enough to be obscured from view, she could see the sea floor. Seeing it rush under her made her appreciate her own speed. The waves felt stronger the closer she came to shore.

Something soft hit her head. She stopped, and looked back to see what it was. A fish floated nearby, unmoving.

":::Check on it, please." Eidechse said.

":::I... I planned to. I was just a little stunned. Less gazing at the floor, more looking ahead, I guess." Sarah swam over to it, and carefully took it in both hands. ":::The gills are moving."

":::It is likely unharmed. It seems to have been stunned as well."

Sarah hesitantly slapped the fish a couple times. It stirred. The eye facing her focused on Sarah's hands just before it panicked and fled. She watched the little guy wiggle itself away, on to do whatever fish did to spend their days.

"::: That is good," Eidechse said, ":::otherwise we would have to issue some nanites into it for diagnosis. Do you have a supply ready which are suitable for such a task?"

":::I hadn't thought about it. It's never really come up!" Sarah would at most, have felt sorry for the fish if it was dead. Even been regretful for colliding with it. Fixing it wasn't something she would have thought of. ":::I guess I can create a supply. Can you give me a design recommendation? And how many, I wonder?"

Heck, if it was already dead, Sarah was thinking of eating it. There's lots of useful material for self maintenance in something like that. Gross. But she could turn off her disgust if she had to. If she wanted to. Would she want to?

Probably not. The fish would have gone to waste.

Enough. Onward. Looking *forward*. Eidechse gave Sarah access to a recommended nanite configuration for use to deploy, and Sarah set them to be built by her existing systems, then to be stored in the little unused gaps in her body. The closest she had come to these were the nanites she used to 'sew' her previous outfit.

The bed of large white rocks was just ahead. The telescopes were up, out of view. Sarah surfaced as she grabbed a rock, and pulled herself onto it.

The waves ran aground at the bottom of her rock, tossing sea spray up at her. As she sat there, she was again reminded of mermaids. ":::Told you. Mermaid."

":::When did you tell me 'mermaid'?" Eidechse asked.

Oops. For a moment, she had forgotten who was living in her head these days. Damn it. All those little dumb inside jokes with Jon. All those little moments. Beginning to miss him, she had to remind herself of his extensive resume of horrors. Only a short look into Amanda's memories grounded Sarah. Balanced the reality of it all.

It still felt like a loss, somehow.

Gathering herself, she stood on the rock and tried to squeeze as much water as she could out of her clothes. She planned to drip-dry the rest. The mid afternoon sun bearing down on her would help a lot too.

If this pattern of dragging herself out of the ocean was going to continue, she'd have to invest in some kind of surfing outfit or something. Something that didn't need to take much time to dry.

As she basked and baked, she heard the occasional passer by on top of the wall, talking, or jogging past.

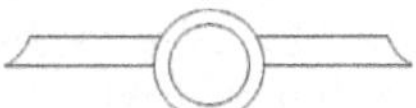

A shout found its way to Sarah. Unintelligible at this distance, but the voice sounded panicked. A scream followed. What's this, then?

Sarah declared her outfit to be dry enough, and began climbing the rough bricks of the wall. They were damp, but there were plenty of decent places to grab at. Half way up, a familiar, inhuman wail shattered any remnants of peace. It nearly caused Sarah to slip off the side of the wall.

As she fumbled to regain her grip, Eidechse spoke up. ":::Sarah, I believe that sound was one of the demon-class abominations."

":::Ya *think* so, Eid?!" She hastened her climb, getting a hand over the top quickly.

":::Yes. I also believe the demon-class abomination may be engaging humans in combat."

":::I don't hear gunfire. It's not combat, that's a slaughter in progress." Sarah hauled herself over the lip of the wall, and started running towards the commotion. Crossing the cement walkway that ran along the edge of the wall, a gentle grassy hill lay in her path.

Another scream, followed by a flash of flying wet red, and another of the demon's war-cries. Running towards the sounds, other people were running away. One man ran by Sarah. He was on his phone, seemingly calling for police.

"*Tell them it's one of those demon types!*" Sarah yelled at him. He didn't seem to register what she was saying in his panic, so she grabbed his wrist and yelled into the phone, "*It's a demon! I'll do what I can, but don't dawdle, AZU!*" She released the confused man, and told him to run. Sarah continued on, cursing the four and a half seconds that she just sacrificed.

Clearing the peak of the hill, Sarah could now see the 'battlefield'. This demon was a little different. His hands were gone, replaced by long growths of slightly curved bone, like tusks. They reminded Sarah of the horsemen in Amanda's memories of Meston. They dripped with fresh blood, but also carried the stains of past kills.

":::Growing those would take considerable time," said Eidechse. "I doubt it is a very new creation."

Sarah didn't care that much. The three bodies around it were more troubling. It wasn't very easy to count to three, when numbers one and two were spread out into parts and smears across the grass.

The demon laughed in a gravelly voice, its split mouth managing to grin feverishly. It spread its arms wide and looked up, as if to offer this act up to its god. "*ErrrRrrRbBbRrrRbuSSSSsssssss!*"

Sarah stepped up to a nearby bench, and ripped a two metre plank off of it. The bolt on the far end didn't pop off like the other two did, forcing the wood to rip out, and leave a handy jagged end.

"I don't know who made you, freak, but Erebus is gone. And he hasn't wanted this kind of thing for a long time."

The demon reacted to the sound of Sarah's voice, if not the words. It turned to her with a wild look in its eyes, and let loose another scream. Sarah readied her stance and her 'spear' to receive the demon's charge. It ran at her, loose ribs and claws flailing. It was fast when it wanted to be.

Slowing time for a little, Sarah was able to duck under a lunging claw, putting her in a decent position to drive the plank into the demon's midsection. Going through the gaping cavity, it slipped between the ribs of the back, and impaled through the flesh, sticking more than half a metre out its back.

Using the plank like a crowbar, Sarah wrenched it to the side. Instead of merrily ripping the thing in half, the action only caused it to turn. The other claw was coming. Not wanting to push her luck, she jumped back, leaving the plank lodged through the demon.

Maybe she could get behind it, and use the plank to do more damage. Trying to run a circle around it wasn't working out. It turned to face her, and continued to charge. She employed the same old 'grab and pull past' move that had worked before. She added the trip for good measure, and it worked again.

The demon fell forward with an ugly cracking sound. Several ribs were now broken and dangling loose. The plank was broken almost directly in the middle, but not quite torn off.

One half of the plank was under the demon, the other half stuck up out its back, loosely. Sarah jumped onto its back, standing on its spine as she pulled the upper half of the plank free, only to drive the rough end into the demon's skull.

The demon reacted by turning over, tossing Sarah off.

":::It appears the brain is not a significant weakness." Eidechse said.

":::No shit!" Sarah rolled away to get out of range, and stood as quickly as she could. The demon did the same. That chunk of wood still stuck out from its head, and other half fell free from its abdomen. Sarah looked back to the bench to consider a fresh weapon, only to see a crow flying at her.

It landed on her forearm. Sarah tried to shake it off while dodging another lunge from the demon.

":-:Hello." came a voice from the crow.

":-:Me?" said the Eidechse in Sarah's head.

Enough slow-motion combat for a moment. Sarah froze time.

":::Eidechse, is this one of your little animal buddies?"

":::An animal carrying one of my dispatch colonies apparently, yes. It seems very obedient, but I still advise caution in not harming it."

":::Not harming *it?!* Did you happen to notice the big monster thing I'm fighting here?"

":::Yes. This dispatch must have something important to say." Eidechse re-channeled his voice towards the crow. ":-:Hello, me. What am I doing?"

":-:AZU-2 will be arriving shortly. They were en route before Sarah intercepted the emergency call. They are moderately grateful for the status definition. Civilian calls from this location only defined the abomination as a zombie, preceded with various adjectives."

":-:Will AZU-2 be hostile towards Sarah?"

":-:Undetermined. I do not believe so."

":-:Likely they will attempt a consensual capture, as with last time."

":-:We agree with us."

":-:How many demon-class abomination attacks have occurred since Sarah and I left the temple?"

":-:Fifty eight individual incidents, plus this one, as of my most current information, updated four and a half minutes ago."

":-:Damn." Sarah said, "Then I have to get to the Four Fox as soon as this ugly is secured."

":-:AZU-2 may object." One of the Eidechses said.

“:-:AZU-2 can bite me.” Sarah said.

The Eidechse in the crow sounded confused. “:-:Why would AZU-2 want to bite you?”

The Eidechse in Sarah's head replied. “:-:I understand this metaphor partially. I have been studying comedy.”

“:-:Then that was funny?”

Sarah grew tired of this. “:-:*The two of you shut up! Demon thing! Demon thing, Demon thing, Demon thing! Focus!*”

“:-:I believe Sarah wishes us to synchronize. Then you will understand 'bite me' as well.”

“:-:Very well, synchronize.”

Sarah patiently held her tongue as the two Eidechses copied files back and forth, becoming of one mind. It wasn't that she was feeling very patient, it was more that she was afraid if she said anything else, it would trigger another idiotic multiple personality debate.

“:::Synchronization complete.” The Eidechse in her head reported. “Jim also states that suspicion among the tourist group was minim-”

Enough. Sarah resumed time, and the crow launched off her arm. All right, it was time for another plank.

“:::Sarah, if you can remain unharmed and occupy the demon-class abomination until AZU-2 arrives, we can prevent any more civilians being harmed.”

“:::Gee, Eid. I wish I had thought of that.”

“:::I am very glad to be of use.”

Sarah started sprinting to the bench while the demon was still facing the wrong way, but she heard it begin its pursuit. She heard it leap. Her first impulse was to use the bench as cover.

She dove under it, rolling onto her back just in time to see through the slats of the bench as the demon landed on top. It stood on the bench, leaning down to scream at Sarah.

Taking the chance, she pulled down on one of the planks that supported the demon's weight. Sarah slid to the side, avoiding its foot as it stumbled down in an uncontrolled mess. This wasn't quite what Sarah had wanted. She didn't plan that maneuver well, and kicked herself for not freezing time to consider other options.

Now there was a claw jammed in the ground beside her head, thankfully only sharp at the tip. The other claw was struggling to free itself from the cement support of the bench. The ribs seemed to be grabbing at her, and the mouth was still busy screaming.

Not wanting to be at this range when one of those claws got loose, she ripped open the last of the bench's lower planks. Finally, a useable shard of wood.

She drove the pine spike into the demon's left eye. It predictably screamed, but arched its head back to do so. Not wanting to waste time, her next thrust went into the beast's open maw, through its pallet, and into the other eye from below. She gave it a twist, just to make sure. It bled down onto her. All she could do about that was make sure her systems were on alert for possible nanite-based attacks.

The demon was now flailing without purpose. It was not hard to slip away, aside from dodging a randomly stabbing claw. Sarah backed away and watched.

Its face was a mess of course. A terrified expression could be made out, even beyond the eye damage, and the hideous jaw.

It staggered around, listening for Sarah to make a sound. Quiet, despondent wandering was broken up by fierce screams and attacks into the air, only to change back to quiet meandering mode just as quickly.

"::Once upon a time, that thing used to be human." Sarah said with a sympathetic tone. ":::Do you figure there's anything left in there of the human? Is any bit of a human in there suffering?"

":::Unlikely." Eidechse said, ":::If the brain was not a vulnerability, then it likely died quite a while ago, perhaps even on initial infection."

Sarah watched it, raging against the air, then again becoming lost in its lack of direction. It wasn't a great threat as long as no innocents came by to make sounds and attract it, but Sarah felt she needed to put it out of its misery. How, though?

":::Sarah, airlimb approaching." Sarah heard it too. Of course, Eidechse was hearing through *her* ears these days, so they were bound to hear things at the same time. Sarah quietly walked around the demon so that she could keep an eye on it and still face the direction of the incoming airlimb.

The demon craned its head towards the sound as the airlimb sailed in overhead. The demon screamed at it, and waved its claws.

A voice came booming from the airlimb's external speaker. "Step further away from it, Sarah." Whoever it was, they knew *her*. She obeyed, and increased the roughly five metre berth she had been giving it to about ten.

The airlimb turned sideways, displaying a deck-mounted gunnery station. Sarah knew what was coming next. Jon had shown it to her, when Jonathan Coll was killed.

The air was split by the sound of the 'zipper' gun opening fire. Searing torrents of lead ripped at the demon, tossing it back, tearing it apart, much as the demon had done to the three people laying around them.

When the firing stopped, Sarah looked at the mess, and looked at the airlimb. She yelled out to them, "*I think you got it.*"

The airlimb floated down to a resting spot a few metres away from any visible blood on the ground. Before Sarah could decide whether to go talk to them or flee, six soldiers jumped out with flame throwers.

Sarah began to run, but the voice from the airlimb called to her. "Just get clear of the mess, Sarah. They don't want you, they want the demon and the dead humans."

":::Sufficient fire ensures the nanites are incapacitated." Eidechse explained.

":::They could have told me before they stormed out."

The six soldiers were efficient and thorough. It seemed like a good time to wander off.

"Sarah," the airlimb called out, "You're soaked in potentially infectious material."

She looked down at herself. Indeed, she was. Her white tanktop was not terribly white anymore. It was hard to find patches of clean white among the red. "Damn it!" She was about to joke about ruining her brand new shirt, but the burning bodies nearby set a sobering tone. Jon would have made the joke. He might have also ranted blame towards the dead.

"I'll deal with it." Sarah said. She wiped as much of the blood off of herself as she could, flinging it towards open flame.

"I don't think that's going to get em all, miss." a nearby soldier said.

"Yeah, I know. But if I can get the bulk of them off, it'll make the remainder easier. My nanites outnumber them."

":::Hey Eid. The nanites I've been building since we ran into that fish, can I-"

":::Yes. This would be a viable and appropriate function."

":::Do I have enough of them yet?"

":::Likely. You can continue building as you deploy. Any hostile nanites can be salvaged for materials, as well."

":::Neat."

The soldier didn't seem to entirely understand, although he knew what Sarah was. "Are you sure you don't want to step into a decontamination chamber?"

Sarah spit a wad of nanite-laden saliva onto the densest stain on her shirt. Let slip the dogs of microscopic war. "Decontamination chamber?" She smirked at the soldier, "You mean to clean me of any nanites, like the ones that run my nervous system? That chamber, with the flame thrower in the ceiling, which you could use to drag me anywhere against my will?"

The solder seemed to understand. "Can't you like... send out nanites through your skin or something? Do you have to spit them?"

Eidechse spoke up. ":::You can deploy them through your pores if you utilize your circulatory system to send them to the nearest-"

":::*Now* you tell me." She spat on her thigh, just for the benefit of the soldier. "Attack them from two fronts, you know? Why not?"

The soldier shrugged as the other five formed up casually behind him. "So, now what?"

Sarah shrugged back. "I'm not coming with you guys, if that's what you mean. You could kill me, or you could let me get out there and take more of these bastards out. To be honest, I wouldn't mind a spare flame thrower if you have one."

The solder held his finger to his ear for a moment, then looked back to Sarah. "Colonel agrees with you. We have bigger fish to fry. It's a busy day." He called out to the other soldiers. "AZU-4's got our other date wrapped up, but there's a situation just off Brenna Avenue. It's all ours, men. You and you," he pointed at two of his men, "You two hold this site until police come to take over."

The two chosen soldiers saluted in acknowledgment while the other troops got aboard the airlimb.

"How about that flame thrower, huh?" Sarah asked.

"Join the army!" The commander said from the airlimb deck, "Then we'll talk. By the way, half the reason you're not burning mulch right now is the lack of injuries during your escape from Yute central. The effort didn't go unappreciated." He tossed his jacket down to Sarah.

The airlimb began to rise. Sarah yelled up, *"Tell Brock and the Colonel there's no hard feelings! I understand why they wanted to lock me away."* She picked up the jacket. Even if she'd soon be free of any hostile nanites, she was still soaked in unsightly red. She put it on.

"::To clarify, Brock didn't want to lock you away." Eidechse said.

"::Do you think Brock knows that you helped me. Eid?"

"::If he does, there has been no indication of it in his actions, according to the update I received from my crow-carried deployment. Incidentally, are you finding many hostile nanites on yourself?"

Sarah called a few of her own back into her body to report. Dissecting the crude but efficient data storage of a singular nanite was a baffling little puzzle, but with a little help from the 'help files' left by Jon, she was able to figure it out. "::There's some. They're mostly for tissue repair and muscle manipulation. Healing it, and moving it. Nothing infectious."

"::That is typical of most zombies. Infection is most commonly performed via saliva. I do not think that you were bitten or hit with stray saliva."

Sarah stood there for a moment after she zipped up the jacket, and looked at the mess. One of the soldiers called out, "Whoops, wet spot." He fired a short flame burst at a small bloody spot on the ground. The previously neglected bit of the mess was now dry, and black.

"You guys worried about starting a fire in the park? Like a big 'whoopsie' fire?" Sarah asked.

The one soldier patted one of the canisters on the flame thrower. "Fire retardant, just in case. The grass is freshly watered though. No real worries here."

Nothing for the soldier to worry about, except Sarah herself. Fighting on the same side or not, her father didn't fail to cast a long shadow of doubt around her. Both of the soldiers were quietly nervous around her. It was time to go.

"Hey guys, it's been a blast, but I have a train to catch."

"Trains are shut down." One of the soldiers said, "Too much bad crap going down to give the infected free roam of the city."

"Damn, it's that bad?" Sarah asked, "Is this going to end up like Autar and Meston?"

The soldier looked all the grimmer suddenly. "I... I don't know, I don't think so. This is different, it's spreading slower. These things seem to be just trying to create panic more than anything. That's not so say that Erebus won't alter his tactics, a-"

"It's not Erebus!" Sarah said, "Erebus is gone, he allowed himself to be ripped out of my damned head!"

"Trying to save *you*," he said. "Some people are saying you're the thing we have to worry about."

"Listen, I got taken in the first time on purpose. I didn't have to, and most of all, there you are standing there alive over the remains of a critter who's fucking eyes I gouged out to save innocent people."

"I get it," he relented, "but these things seem to think Erebus is their master, and until we have another name for it..."

"It's a damned copycat. Call him Ere-wannabe or something. I don't know." Sarah walked off towards the middle of the city. "If you people don't kill me, and I have a dime to my name when this blows over, tell that dork at central I'll buy him a drink. Colonel whassis face, too. You too. Hell, invite the base. I can recommend a bar."

:::C / [100001] [33]

Her cover had been blown, but it seemingly didn't matter any more. With such a rise in demon-class problems, one non-hostile nanite girl wasn't important. What was the worst she could do that the demons weren't already doing?

It was time to check on the Four Fox. With her strength still on full from the fight, she started sprinting the streets. She wasn't insanely fast; she couldn't out race a car... except for cars in downtown Densfarn.

Traffic downtown almost always enforced a snail's pace, but with the trains out of service, it was worse. A taxi was not a viable option for Sarah, even if she wasn't broke.

She navigated partly by maps, and partly by following train station signs. Darting and weaving between other pedestrians, she incited surprise, and occasionally irritation.

":::Sarah," Eidechse started, ":::You seem very certain that the demon-class abominations are not created by Erebus."

":::Of course!" A deft launch from a fire hydrant got her over a cluster of oblivious teens, most of whom did not notice her afterwards either. ":::You know exactly what happened to Jon, and what he'd been up to."

":::I did not say 'Jon'. I said 'Erebus'."

":::If you're going to differentiate, then Erebus stopped existing when he became Jon, so what are you getting at?"

":::'Redundancy is a life saver'. At this moment, two equally able entities are what I would call 'the true me'. The me that is talking to you now, and the lizard in Yute central. In addition to those, I have a number of very able 'deployments' currently in service."

":::Eid, are you suggesting that Jon made a deployment Erebus to do all this? Or are you saying that Jon was a deployment? Wouldn't you have been able to tell from examining his mind and memories?"

":::Jon was a collection of nanites that gathered itself together from random debris of *one* attack in a battle where the first Erebus infested an entire city."

Sarah saw the logic, but needed to fight it. ":::But wasn't Meston city- and for that matter, Autar- bombed all to hell?"

"::::Yes. Bombed, and subsequently saturated with napalm. However, Erebus' survival could have been as simple as a well shielded and insulated box filled with nanites."

"::::Damn it Eid, how are people suppose to fight something that hard to kill? Hell, it doesn't even matter. A copy of Erebus, or a copycat, it still has to be stopped. But it's not my dad."

Block after block, passing one train station access after another, a demon's scream was heard behind her. On a dime, Sarah jumped backwards to track the thing down. Before she arrived at the intersection, sounds of human panic guided her further.

Left. There it is. People were fleeing in all directions. Some nimble steps and a little slowed time were needed to dodge a few people who were looking at the demon while fleeing, and not looking where they were going.

"::::I can not see any injuries." Eidechse reported.

"::::Not yet!"

The demon's attention was aimed at a storefront boutique with a large glass pane front. People inside were trying unsuccessfully to get metal theft grating pulled across while bravely standing against the demon's second scream.

They wisely jumped back as the demon thrust his hand against the glass. The safety glass shattered into pebbles. The demon roared in victory while more people's screams were heard inside.

Sarah took the advantage of surprise. She tackled the thing and rammed its mutilated neck against the windowsill, to the tune of garbled fury from the demon, and gasps from the people.

Sarah paused time. "::::I'd like to take this moment to say, '*sucker!!!!*'"

She resumed time at about half speed. She jumped upright into the air. As the demon started to pull itself up, Sarah was coming down. One foot to its upper back, the other to the back of its head. A wet snapping sound was produced, but the head didn't tear off until the second jump.

Putting herself between the decapitated monster and the people inside, she grabbed a clothing rack and swung it like an unwieldy axe, driving one of the supports through the demon's mid back, snapping several ribs.

Sarah looked back to the people. "Don't try that at home kids, I'm uniquely qualified. On the other hand, if anyone has a flame thrower, it would help a lot!"

Not allowing the demon to get up, she used another clothing rack to shatter the right shoulder blade. It reminded her of her first zombie fight, in Jon's Autar simulation. Her own tolerance to do such things still struck her as eerie. Maybe Jon intended this ability, knowing it might be needed. The demon's legs and remaining arm struggled in vain; Sarah held a foot on the first clothing rack to pin it down.

A middle aged woman, seemingly an employee of the boutique, cleared her throat loudly behind Sarah. Sarah turned to see her holding out a one litre bottle of rubbing alcohol and a barbeque lighter. "Could this help?"

"Damn straight, thank you Ma'am!" Sarah grabbed the bottle and lighter, and was about to sprinkle the alcohol onto the demon. "Hey Ma'am, do me a favour and get everyone out of here. And call your insurance company."

The lady ushered people out the front door then ran to get a fire extinguisher from the back before joining them.

"I hope someone's recording this for posterity!" Sarah drank the alcohol quickly, and lit the barbecue lighter, holding the flame in front of her mouth.

A young man in the bunch seemed quite pleased. "*Oh fuck yes, awesome! Do it!*" Ever pleased to please, Sarah aimed her mouth at the demon, and methodically roasted it, with a little extra for the head and mouth area.

Awed quiet was quickly replaced by applause.

The clothing on the two racks were on fire as well, and the woman began fumbling with the release for the fire extinguisher.

"Ma'am, the longer our buddy here burns, the safer we all are. In fact, anyone got more alcohol?" No one did, at least none they were going to sacrifice. "Use the extinguisher only if it means saving the building. And by the way everyone, I meant what I said about not trying that yourselves. I have a lot of advantages in this situation. This wasn't my first fight today."

Sarah opened her jacket to show the blood stains on her shirt.

"Whoa, are you hurt?" asked someone.

"No, no, it's not my blood. This is from the park. It's a bad day today."

The woman with the fire extinguisher looked troubled, and unsure what to do with herself. "I can give you a shirt." she said solemnly.

"No time, but thank you. I might be back for one another day though. People, if no one's done so yet, call the cops, tell them a demon-class abomination has been downed and burned, but I don't know how well burned. Tell them they owe Sarah one."

As Sarah dashed off, the enthusiastic young man wandered up to the demon and sprinkled a flask of gin at it.

Grinning, Sarah said to herself, ":::Fish Girl, away!!"

":::Sarah, can you elaborate?"

":::Never mind. Jon would have gotten it."

":::Humour."

":::Apparently not."

:::C / [100010] [34]

After another few blocks of managing street obstacles, the train line breached the surface, crossing from an underground section to an above-ground section held up by mammoth concrete pillars.

":::I'm taking the high road." Sarah said as she jumped a fence from the sidewalk to the edge of the tracks. Behind her loomed a darkness where Sarah didn't particularly want to engage demons if it could be avoided.

Forward, upward. The rail ties made excellent footholds. Added onto the lack of pedestrians, this was a great deal faster. She felt like she was launching herself repeatedly from the rail ties, not just taking steps.

When the next station came up, and she saw a few people standing around, she felt like showing off. The people there were mostly teenagers, likely wishing for a train to the mall. There was a train parked facing either direction, but they hadn't been moving for hours.

As she dashed up, she heard some people taking notice. When the front of one train was near, she planted a foot onto the side of it, and while keeping most of her forward momentum, launched herself up towards the other train. From there, another similar jump placed her on the roof of the first train. It also cracked a window on the second train. Whoops.

":::We can report the liability for that damage later," said Eidechse. Killjoy.

"Look at that!" came a voice, "Go chick, go!" called out another. Chick, huh? Well, all right. As fun as that was, it slowed her down a little, and the speed was more important. And addictive. Once back on the tracks, she resumed launching herself from rail tie to rail tie.

The view of the city was amazing like this. Sarah's affection for Densfarn grew as she ran. Damned zombies couldn't have it. To that end, the AZU-1 airlimb could be seen in the distance, going from one demon encounter to another.

Ahead, another unmoving train. This one was laying half way on its side, wedged between the two tracks. The train and the tracks had significant burns, and charred remains. She crossed on the top peak of the train, not wanting to touch the remains.

It looked like an AZU unit had been here not too long ago; she could still feel the warmth. There were a lot of remains. More than one demon? Maybe three? How many people were represented on those tracks?

Then she made the mistake of glancing into a train car she was walking over. How many dozens of people were torn apart, and subsequently burned in there? In each car?

Dashing forward, back onto tracks, she screamed in anguish, tears streaming alongside her face.

":::Are you hurt?" Eidechse asked.

":::*Didn't you see that?!*"

":::They were hurt badly. Killed in fact. Very unfortunate." Eidechse's tone of voice suggested he understood, and felt as bad as he could about it. Did he just lack the vocabulary for it? Did he really understand human death?

Onward. After a few blocks, she spotted an airlimb parked on the street below. It was partly obscured by buildings. Gunfire could be heard.

":::Hey Eid, do you think they could use help?"

":::Gauging from the systematic bursts of gunfire, I would say the encounter is under control. If you want, you could access the street via the nearest train station, then proceed to rendezvous with them."

":::No, Eid. If you think they're doing all right, I'll take your word for it. They have more experience, and all the toys."

":::The next train station is the optimal location to reach the Four Fox Bar and Grill, Sarah."

":::I know, I took the train here before."

Sarah hopped off the rails onto the loading deck. Again, a few people were hanging around. "Don't do as I do." She warned them, pointing to the tracks behind her. "It's dangerous. I'm qualified." What kind of qualified? Whatever they wanted to think, as long as they didn't get the idea they could try it.

Some might anyway. Too late to be a good example now. The elevator was shut down, so she took the stairs. They provided a calming view of the sea, for a while.

Things seemed quiet around here. Things seemed safe.

The Four Fox looked much as it ever did, even if it was a bit quiet for being so close to lunch. Jessica was finishing up clearing a table outside. She held a tray of empty dishes with one hand, and gave the table a quick wipe with the other. Giving the table a finishing slap with the cloth before hanging it on her hip again, she happened to glance up and see Sarah.

Her grip on the tray faltered, nearly sending the dishes to the ground. "Sarah?!"

Sarah blushed through her weary gaze, and ambled towards Jessica. "I missed a couple shifts, huh?"

Jessica put the tray down on the table, and rushed over to Sarah, reaching out to hold her shoulders. "Sarah! Where the hell have you gotten off to? What's going on?"

"I came to check on you guys. To make sure you were all right. Have you heard what's been going on?"

Leading Sarah inside, Jessica pointed at the terminals over the bar. "Half the channels have turned into news channels, public alerts, and things like that. Kody's been watching it closely. Danielle wasn't even on shift, but she came by, and Kody won't let her go home. The bar is quiet, I think a lot of people are staying home."

"You're rambling." Sarah said as they neared the bar.

Kody sat on the staff-side of the bar, watching the live coverage of anyone who had anything to say about the demons popping up. "Huh! Sarah!" She said with mild surprise. "Not so worried about hiding while the cops are busy, huh? They had a ton of questions about you after you left. I didn't tell them anything, not that I had anything to tell."

"Sorry about that." Sarah said as she took a seat. "Wanna help me build a flame thrower? We might have to defend against one of those things."

Kody looked at her like she was crazy.

"Look, I've taken out two of them on my way here from the park. I can knock them down with a little luck, but they need to be burned after." Sarah pointed at a couple large bottles of cheap rye on display behind the bar.

"You're serious!" Kody said with a skeptical eye. Sarah opened her jacket to show the bloody evidence of her first battle today. "Sarah, are you all right?"

Stretching out her shirt in front of her, she nodded. "Demon blood. And demon's victim blood. I only got to the first one after it had killed a few people. Made a real mess. It..." Sarah stopped talking. Jessica and Kody were shocked enough as it was. A voice burst out from the back half of the bar.

"Sarah!" Danielle was coming with her order pad in hand. "I signed up for kickboxing! I haven't had my first less-"

As Sarah turned to greet her, Danielle saw the blood and staggered to a stop. "Awesome, Dan. You're going to kick ass, I know it."

Jessica read Danielle's face, fixated on Sarah's bloody shirt. "Dan, Sarah's been doing her own ass kicking. She's been taking down monsters left and right."

Close enough. "Yeah, well, I made it back here to help do some defending." Sarah reached past Kody for the two bottles of rye. She opened one up, and started pouring it down her throat. "I found out I can breathe fire. Anyone have a lighter I can borrow?" She opened the other bottle and poured it in.

Her friends all stared. Danielle still in shock, Kody with a sliver of stoicism, and Jessica just waiting to see what was next.

Sarah put the second bottle back on the bar. "Okay. Okay, I'm a freak, okay? I'm sorry I told you guys a lot of lies just to keep undercover, but I'm me. And after I handed a couple of the demons their asses, the 'cops' don't seem so worried that I'm not human, and made with a pile of nanites."

An awkward silence was broken by the voice of a customer seated a couple dozen metres away. "*Hey! Can we get those lagers?*"

"Yeah, hold on." Jessica took up the order, taking the pad from the still-stunned Danielle. Jessica poured the drinks, and headed off to deliver.

Kody huffed. "Demons or not, You also kicked Doug's ass and took a bullet or two for my Danny-girl. That's plenty enough for me."

Danielle sat on another bar stool, staring at the blood stains. "You need a new shirt." she said meekly. She hopped back off the stool, and headed to the kitchen.

Sarah watched her go, then looked to Kody. Sarah lowered her voice "Speaking of Doug..."

"Pretty much headed for jail. Regardless of your involvement, he still started it and opened fire."

"How long will he be in there?"

Kody held up five fingers. "Deserves three times as much in my book. He'll probably serve two."

Danielle popped up from the kitchen, holding out a folded t-shirt. "New official bar shirts." Sarah chuckled, and held it up. White, with two giant blue 'F's that would cover a boob each. Four golden foxes were walking around the 'F', one of them on top. Below all that, there was simple text reading 'Four Fox Bar & Grill'.

"Really old art," Kody said, pleased. "One of the first owners, bless her heart. Back then it was for a poster, but I ran into one of the prints, and I got the idea."

"Nice." Sarah smiled. It really wasn't such great art, but it was instantly her favourite shirt ever.

"Go to the washroom, clean up." Kody said, taking away the rye bottles. "And don't throw up."

"Nah, it's all right, the rye is in my lungs. I don't use them for anything else but pretending to breathe."

Kody nodded once with a raised eyebrow. "Right. Don't *blow* up either."

Sarah went to the washroom. Taking off the jacket, she used some paper towels to wipe every bit of blood she could see off of the smooth material. She did the same with her black shoes and slacks. They were porous, and wouldn't be wiped very clean, but what was left didn't show much against the black.

Her bloody tank top was off last, thrown into the trash. It could be bleached in theory, but she didn't want it, knowing how much blood of innocents had been on it.

Sarah realized she was naked. He caught her image in the large mirrors over the sinks. Yeah, carrying a few litres of rye made her look a little heavier. Thankfully it was positioned in a very complimentary way. She put on the 'FF' shirt, pants, shoes, and the jacket. Her hair was also a mess, actually. But it might have to wait. It wasn't that terribly bad compared to that bloody shirt.

When Sarah got back to the bar, Kody was lining up cans of sprays. Hair spray, bug spray, dust spray, deodorant spray, all in all nearly a dozen cans.

"Hating that environment, are we?" Sarah said.

"Best flame throwers I could conjure." Kody said. "Lighters are bit sparse, no smoking in here, but I sent Jessica out to the corner store to grab a bunch."

"Good." Sarah crossed her arms with satisfaction. "All right, the fire's good once they're down, but flames don't have the kind of immediate stopping power that's going to save anyone's butt. I can smack them down if I need to, but I can't guarantee to be right there in an instant. If we could maybe use one of the table umbrellas from outside as-"

Kody pulled up a short shotgun and slapped it onto the bar. "Would this help any?"

Sarah rolled her eyes. "Cheeky lady. How much ammo do you have for that? And since when do you keep *that* behind the bar?"

"Plenty of ammo, and it's fed semi-auto. I have a fresh box of ammo I picked up on the way in. When those things started coming onto the news last night, I decided I'd bring in the shotgun from home. Never liked having it around, but..."

"Yeah." Sarah sat down. "Go for the eyes. Maybe a leg first. Disabling its ability to see or run would help a lot. I don't think these things have any real vitals, so you just have to... break them! And they're strong, okay? Don't invite hand to hand."

Kody nodded, looking disinterested as if she'd done it all before. "Face, knees, molotov." She made it sound so simple, and that overconfidence worried Sarah a little. Then again, Sarah didn't fight them with the benefit of a shotgun.

"Don't underestimate them, okay? Those AZU guys pumped a lot of lead onto the first one I met today before it actually went down."

"Don't bother mothering me, lass. If you want to coddle, try Jessica. I'll have Danielle covered."

Sarah nodded, and turned her attention to the news on one of the terminals above the bar. A field reporter stood holding his microphone in the Densfarn international airport. The label across the bottom read "EVACUATION PANIC". Kody saw that it had Sarah's attention so she turned up the sound a little, and watched with her.

"-again, officials are emphasizing that there *is no official* evacuation underway." The reporter gestured over his shoulder to a orderly but noisy crowd. "This isn't stopping all these people from trying to get tickets out of the city, many even off of the continent."

The screen changed to also show the lovely news desk anchor. "Rob, I imagine that people who think that Densfarn will be the third city to go in Aguola, just don't see the country as safe anymore."

"That seems to be the feeling I'm getting down here, Jill. No one knows if other airports will even accept flights from Densfarn yet, despite stringent nanite screenings. To make things worse, the roads out of town have been significantly slowed by nanite checkpoint stations. People are fearing being stuck in the front row of another disaster like Autar or Meston."

Anchor 'Jill' took over the entire screen. "Thanks for that, Rob. After the break, we'll check on all the reported outbreak locations, and I'll be speaking live via satellite to retired Major A-"

Kody turned off the sound and sighed. "I wonder if this is how it ended in those cities."

"No," Sarah said with a far off gaze, and voice to match. "At least not Meston. The creatures there were mostly slow, but many, all of a sudden.

These ones don't seem interested in infecting a lot of people. It's like we skipped the 'zombie' phase, to get right to the 'abomination' level."

Kody furrowed her brow, but paid close attention. Danielle came along with some dirty glasses to unload, and stopped to listen in.

"In the other cities," Sarah continued, "The attack was the nanites. The zombies were almost more like fallout. Amusement. When Erebus felt the situation was under control, he'd make abominations. More 'creative' things. Like these demons, or weirder. By then, not too many people were left in there. And even less got out to tell the tale."

Kody looked at Danielle. "Don't you have an order to fill or something?"

"I'm a big girl, mum."

Kody gave her a weary look. She just wanted Danielle towards the back, where any invading demon would go last. Hopefully not before getting a face full of buckshot and a fire bath.

"Sarah... that's your 'Doug', isn't it?" Danielle said. "You were in one of those cities."

"Meston. Yes. No. Well, kind of. The point is, I've felt what it's like to be on the run from them, and to lose. To die. To watch others die, and badly." Sarah realized that Kody and Danielle were staring at her. "It's complicated, but it relates to why Doug's shots didn't kill me, and how I'm made of fish."

"Fish?!"

Whoops, she never mentioned that to them before. "Like I said. It's complicated."

Kody pinched the bridge of her nose. "That's what I get for not asking for references."

The news was back from commercial. Still with no sound. A map of the city was being displayed with red dots for every demon attack.

"Looks Autar-like to me." Kody said.

"No. Zombies infect, and kind of spread out like a cloud. These are popping up pretty randomly." Sarah pointed at some of the dots. "And they don't seem to spread much."

"Maybe Erebus just wants to show off these things to a lot of people." Danielle said, washing out the glasses she had brought."

Sarah corrected Danielle quickly. "It's not Erebus. He's gone. This is some kind of copycat. It has to be."

"Oh, right." Danielle said, "Erebus was ... killed and erased or whatever in Meston."

Sarah collected herself. "There's so much to talk about. But I should give you a new kung fu lesson. Using chairs to fight demons."

"Let's see... swing a chair at them, Sensei Sarah?" Danielle said with a smirk and a bow.

"Indeed, grasshopper, you are half way there. Chair leg in demon eyes brings great fortune. You are now a black belt in fighting demons with a chair. Or a bar stool."

Danielle spoke without humour in her voice. "Thank you Sarah. For everything."

"Heck, what are friends for?" Sarah said with a modest smile.

Danielle chuckled. "Being honest enough to tell you that you reek of rye!"

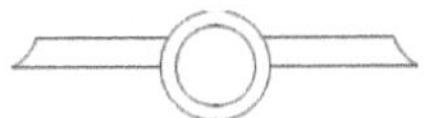

Sarah continued to watch the news and the front doors for any hints of trouble. Jessica came around the corner with a small plastic bag.

"Jess! What took you so long?"

Jessica plunked the bag down on the bar. "Got ten lighters. Why not. I then went looking for a gun, but I had no idea you had to have training and licenses and crap. As it was, the hunting store two blocks down was mobbed with people having the same idea as me. If you ask me, it's only a matter of time before something like that turns ugly. Humanity. Yay."

"They're scared," Sarah said, testing and then pocketing a lighter, "fear's powerful stuff. The guy making these demons probably knows that. Hell, he might just be waiting to see what we might do to ourselves."

Jessica shrugged. She put one lighter in her own pocket, and left the rest by Kody's spray can collection. "Has she tested these? Some might not be so flammable. Or they could be empty."

Picking one up after another, Sarah read the contents, felt the weight, and lined them up in order of effectiveness. "If the time comes, start with that one. Know what? I don't even know if these will be any more effective than just dousing the thing with booze and lighting it. Either way, they have to be downed first."

"What?" Jessica said, "How are we supposed to do that?"

"Aw, I already gave lessons to Kody and Dan. Kody's got her shotgun, Dan has... chairs."

Jessica gagged. "*Kody has a shotgun?!*"

"Doesn't it just fit her though?" Sarah stood from the stool, and headed to the front patio. "I'm going to keep an eye out up front. So I can see anything bad sooner rather than later."

"Sarah, do you think it's going to get worse before it gets better?"

Sarah stopped, and looked back to Jessica.

":::Eid. You've been very quiet. How should I answer her?"

":::I do not know. I cannot see any reason why it cannot get worse. At the same time, I do not see why it has not gotten worse already. I am forced to agree with some of your earlier sentiments about the enemy objective being more about fear than about death."

Sarah sighed, and looked at Jessica. "I really have no idea."

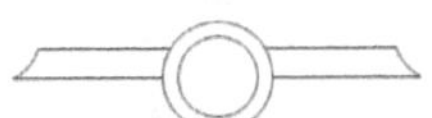

The sun was just starting to set. The handful of buildings between the patio and the beach obscured the direct light. It would be difficult to enjoy the sunset today anyway.

Seemingly in a mood to muse, Eidechse spoke up. ":::The perceived entomological meaning of Erebus is 'darkness', but the first recorded instance of it was '*place of darkness between earth and Hades*'. 'Erebh' means sunset, or evening."

":::Ominous." Sarah said as she sat at one of the tables and put her feet up on it, crossing her ankles. The gradually fading light showed signs of the bloodstains on her pants. "Are you getting poetic on me, Eid?"

":::Not that I am aware of. I am not sure why I said that. It bears no relevance or importance to current events."

Maybe Eidechse did have some kind of purpose to what he said. Maybe he wanted to hint that it was a 'real' Erebus at work in all this. Sarah told herself that it didn't matter. A 'cousin' to her dad, or a copycat, the situation was the same.

":::Eid, for the record, I'm glad you're with me. It would be pretty quiet in my head without company."

":::I feel I am achieving a net benefit from our association and interactions as well, Sarah."

Sarah had to chuckle out loud. ":::You big softie."

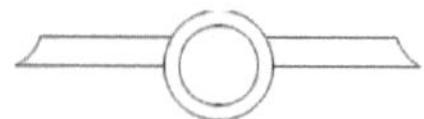

Sirens blared in the distance. One far, one not so far, then another. Airlimbs and helicopters passed the sky far more often than one tends to want for a peaceful evening.

The map on the news must be looking pretty uncomfortably cluttered by now. Sarah regretted not just leading everyone out of the city on foot the second she got to the Four Fox. But it was too late now. Holing up was the only route now.

Sarah headed inside. "Kody, maybe it's time to close up. Put up the theft grate and junk."

Kody looked out the front. "Yeah." She called out to the few customers left. "*Hey you folks. I'm closing up. You're welcome to stay, but if you have a good reason to go home, I'd say now is better than an hour from now.*"

Two decided to go. Kody armed them both with a tactics speech, a good spray can and a lighter. "Don't be stupid out there. I like having customers, you hear?"

After they left, Kody and Jessica dragged the opposite sides of the grate shut, and locked it.

"What about the upper floor?" Sarah asked, "I don't know if they can jump or climb, but the top patio-"

"I can close those doors up." Kody said. "There's no grating on the patio's front, but we can also close the gate at the bottom of the stairs. It's good and solid."

With that done, everyone including the remaining four customers, gathered at the bar. "It's too damn quiet." One of them said, a balding man in a polo shirt. "We need some music or something."

"Hate to be a spoil sport," Sarah said, "But being quiet will likely draw less attention. I'd even maybe advise a lights out, other than the TV for news.

And then the flicker in the dark might get more attention than normal lighting. So yeah, let's keep normal lighting."

"Who are you to give orders?" The balding man asked.

Kody stepped in. "She's the one who can beat me in an arm-wrestle, and has been shot repeatedly and walked out minutes later."

The customer seemed confused, but humbled.

"I can also see in the dark." Sarah humbly added. "But that doesn't help the rest of you a lot."

"You can?" Danielle asked.

Sarah nodded. "Yup. Multifunctional fish girl."

"Again with the fish." Kody said.

"Fish?" Jessica said, "Did I miss something?"

Sarah wanted to explain every bit to them. Jon, in particular, but she knew it was a big bomb to drop. This wasn't the time to do that. "Guys, when this is all done, I'll tell you the whole epic tale of the fish. I owe you the whole truth if I'm going to call myself a friend."

"Tail of the fish." The balding customer added.

"Not you." Sarah tossed a good natured glare.

Jessica started a fresh pot of coffee. "Well, what should we be doing, then? Are we just going to wait it out until the news says it's over? What if it doesn't *get* 'over'."

Sarah spoke to her secret passenger. ":::Eid. Maybe I should be doing something a little more aggressive about the situation. Cut the defence, go offence."

":::Do you have a target in mind? Do you intend to pursue random demon-class abominations and combat them? I do not think that would be terribly effective, even if you could guarantee that each encounter would result in victory. There seem to-"

":::Yeah, yeah, it's dumb. If you come up with any smart target ideas though, let me know."

":::Of course, Sarah."

::C / [100011] [35]

Kody turned the sound up a little on one of the terminals behind the bar. She found some prime-time programming to supply a little distraction that wasn't busy talking about the outbreak. Some trashy crime drama. It would at least give everyone something to do. The news stayed on quietly on one of the other terminals though.

Danielle pulled a deck of cards out and started dealing out cards to anyone who looked interested. Jessica was game, as well as one of the customers. Sarah passed. She preferred to keep her focus on the news, and any sounds outside.

The sunset was in full effect, and gold hues washed through the front grates, only to be destroyed by the interior lighting.

A toothpaste commercial came on to replace the TV drama. The balding man asked for a soda which Kody served, and Jessica won the first hand of whatever it was they were playing.

A demon's scream was heard outside. Everyone at the bar held their breath, and Kody fumbled to turn off the terminals.

"That didn't sound *too* close." Jessica whispered.

"Almost two blocks." Sarah replied with certainty, "Too close for my liking. I'm going after it." She went behind the bar and grabbed a twenty centimetre knife. Kody grabbed Sarah's wrist. "You can't do that. Don't get cocky. You're better off here."

"Other people are out there. Sooner or later, that demon's going to find more."

"Fine," Kody said, grabbing her shotgun, "But you're not going solo."

"I only need you as far as the grate to open it, Kody. You and your boomstick need to stay here to guard the others. I'm going to take it down before it ends up here."

Kody glanced at the others, and her daughter. "Fine. But bring the shotgun."

Sarah smirked. "I like the silencer on the knife better."

"Shut your mouth, you take it."

"No. I'll arm wrestle you for who has to keep it. Or maybe paper-rock scissors." She knew both would turn out with the same winner every time. "I'm not suicidal, Kody. I know what I'm doing." Sarah started walking towards the front.

Kody followed with the shotgun under one arm while she rummaged her pockets for the key. "You're not invincible either, or are you?"

"More invincible than you. Stay calm, it won't be a long fight. If I think I'm going to lose, I'll try to lure him in another-"

"Don't lose." Kody opened the grating, and Sarah stepped into the fading embers of orange that the sun offered. Eidechse placed a Vtag in the estimated location of the demon's scream.

"I haven't lost one yet so far!" Sarah dashed quietly away, knife at the ready. Sure enough, the demon stood two blocks down the street, ripping away at its newly defeated target on the ground. Red bits of viscera flew from its claws with every other swipe.

The demon faced the other direction, and didn't seem to hear Sarah's approach.

The Vtag moved on top of the Demon.

":::Thanks, Eid, I think I see him. Take that off please, it's distracting."

":::Very well." The Vtag vanished.

Slowing time a bit just as a precaution, Sarah jumped at the demon's back. She landed quite nicely, elbows over its shoulders, calves around its middle.

From here, she could see the victim. A middle aged man, or what was left of him. His lower legs lay a couple metres away at the end of smears across the ground. His upper torso and head were folded over with one of his arms over in the other direction.

Everything in between was the demon's sandbox.

Stop gawking, she could feel the demon beginning to react. She rammed the knife into one eye, gave it a twist, then the other. Easy. Pushing off from its upper back, she launched herself off.

Almost. One of the demon's claws found her shin. As she jumped off, she felt it sink in and slash. Pain messages erupted in her system.

Landing on her feet, the decided to return the favour. Her knife made a clean quick slice around the demon's upper calf, rendering the muscle useless. By now, the demon was nearly turned around, and Sarah decided to back off.

Two blind, wild swings flew in her general direction. She ran to a nearby pair of garbage cans. Taking the two lids, she threw one at the demon's face. Shortly after she threw the other at a storefront sign behind him.

It turned to face the sound with another outcry, and pointless attacks.

Sarah's blade found the thigh muscle of the other leg. She gouged at it while pushing him onto his face. Now the other leg was useless as well. She jumped away while it tried in vain to claw at her.

She stood back and watched it try to stand, only to fall. It knew where she was by sound, and used its arms to turn. It was time to put it out of its misery. She took the lighter out of her pocket.

The flame thrower breath sounded like a cool idea, but now it seemed more effective to let the burning happen on the target, rather than in the air.

She pushed the rye out of herself in a vomit-like spray, soaking him as well as she could with three litres, concentrating mostly on the head and torso.

Having to get very close to light him, she timed a lunge between its desperate flailing swipes, and set fire to a spot wet with the liquor. It lit up nicely, but not for long. The demon was still moving, but mostly immobilized. Sarah needed more fuel.

She ran back to the Four Fox to see some very relieved friends on the other side of the grate. "Guys! More booze, it's down but not out."

"Sarah! Your leg!" Danielle gasped.

Sarah looked down, having forgotten about being slashed. She could see bone, and that bone was chopped about a quarter the way through. Her blood only seeped out slowly. "Still works. My lil' guys are working on it. Booze, people, booze! Hard stuff! As much as I can carry!"

They dashed off to the bar, with Danielle straggling behind, looking at Sarah as she used her hands to push flesh back into place. ":::Remind me to not underestimate their strength, Eid."

":::If you wish, I will."

They came back with Kody in the lead, pushing a wheelbarrow full of bottles. The cheapest, most toxic hooch in the bar.

Sarah couldn't help but smile. "Looks like I'm headed to a party!"

"Do you want a hand with the pouring?" Kody asked.

"Nah, I plan to smash em, it'll get me back faster."

"Don't let your guard down, now."

Sarah wheeled the booze back to the scene of the fight. The demon was still moving, but hadn't gotten far.

"To your health!" Sarah said, whipping a large bottle of rum at its head. It smashed open merrily. The bottle, that is. Sarah continued like this until the demon was squirming in a lake. At the edge of the alcohol pool, it mingled with blood of the victim, with beautiful, tragic, cloudy swirls.

It had to be lit again, and this time it erupted most impressively, complete with a demon-sized mushroom cloud that twisted into the sky, glowing from the fire below.

She watched the demon, writing in the flames, slower, slower, eventually stopping. Sarah thought of the man that was used to create this demon. Maybe his dental records would help his relatives get closure or something.

If the changes to his jaw made the dental records any use at all, and assuming his family weren't his first victims as a demon.

Looking around, Sarah was fairly confident that the fire wouldn't spread to cause any building damage. The street would have some interesting marks for some time after all this though.

She headed back to the Four Fox, and Jessica let her in. Everyone else was by the bar, glued to the news. "I missed you guys too. Hey, where did those customers go?"

Kody snorted. "They felt confident after hearing about your win, and decided to risk the trip home. Dumb asses."

"Did they know I kind of had an edge?"

"Yup. Dumb asses anyway."

"Oh well, I wish em luck." Sarah still wasn't the focus of anyone's attention, so she joined in watching the news. "Hey, what the hell is that?"

The live news was coming from a helicopter. The buildings below were downtown, not too far away. Three train stops away.

The buildings had several windows broken, leaving wide open gaps. Some of them had debris hanging loose from these holes. Blinds, half a desk, office cubicle separators.

The only lights below came from the buildings and the street lights. A few flood lights raced around, trying to get lucky, but they were more distracting than anything.

"Again," said the unseen reporter, "we don't know if this machine has anything to do with the creatures, but the timing seems like too much of a coincidence. We expect that it will-"

One of the windows broke out suddenly, and something about the size of a car flew out. It was an angular mass that looked to be made with the same dark, angular aesthetic mindset as stealth bombers of old.

A bulky 'tail' followed behind it. Its tail separated into six legs, and turned forward like giant switchblades, becoming as one again on the front. The tail acted as a ramming spike, driving into another building, quickly scuttling in, and out of sight.

The entire jump, from appearance to disappearance took 1.48 seconds. Sarah and Eidechse were both counting.

":::Sarah, as you requested, I would like to notify you of a *smart target idea*. This unique target may hold a controlling device relating to the demons. It may even house the central-"

":::Yeah, yeah. That thing was all metal though. It doesn't seem to fit the dead-flesh theme."

":::Erebus had been known to produce purely inorganic weapons as needed in the past. In Meston specifically, his improvised rail-"

":::Okay, okay, fine. This thing's causing a mess. It needs to come down."

The news played an instant replay of the jump. Through the shattered pieces of the window, the legs could be seen to launch the machine before forming the tail in the back. Small sparks glittered on its body from machine gun fire from above.

"We're receiving reports that the people in the buildings cannot evacuate. The machine has been systematically attacking four buildings surrounding the intersection, and the first thing it did was to take out elevators and stairs. The abominations seem to be coming out of the woodwork, and going into the buildings. Military took down several, but it's unconfirmed if more of them are still in the buildings."

Footage of one of the machine's jumps played as airlimbs fired machine guns from above to no noticeable effect. "Military have been unable to stop the machine thus far. It just isn't exposed long enough to lock on with any powerful weaponry. Military officials say that they won't use larger weaponry while the machine is in the buildings. Whether this is to avoid adding to civilian casualties, or because of difficulty firing into the buildings is unknown."

Sarah walked around behind the bar, grabbing cheap booze and casually pouring it down her throat, keeping an eye on the news.

"Sarah," Jessica said, "You can't be serious."

One bottle down, she answered in a flat tone while opening the next. "When the city cries out for justice, tada, Fish Girl to the rescue."

Kody looked at the news, showing a closeup still frame of the leaping machine. "Gonna stab it in the eye, are you? At least if you get on the news wearing a Four Fox tee shirt, it'll be good for business." She watched the alcohol gurgle down into Sarah, who had nothing else to say. Kody slapped the bottle out of Sarah's hand, smashing it on the floor. "*Stupid girl!* The military are already there! They can handle it!"

Sarah grabbed a fresh bottle, and started heading to the front. "Then you'd better phone them, and tell them not to shoot me!"

"At least take the damned shotgun!"

"And leave you without one?" She took a guzzle of vodka, "Nope!"

On the way to the train station, Sarah was glad to see the burnt demon still laying in the same place, and no damage to nearby buildings from the fire. She was soon again above the streets, hurling herself along the rails. The news helicopter and two AZU airlimbs were in sight already.

She could pick out the four buildings in question. One of the AZU airlimbs lifted off from a roof, and the other was setting down on another roof.

":::Are they attacking? What's going on there?"

":::I believe there is some kind of evacuation of the buildings in progress. There may be AZU soldiers in the buildings."

":::Spiffy. Hey, from the news, did you think the machine seemed to be operating closer to the top, or the bottom?"

":::The jump we witnessed happened from the sixteenth floor of the northeast building to seventeenth floor of the southeast building."

":::I go in from the bottom, then. I wonder if an AZU would give me a lift?"

":::There is a communication line in the train track structure, if you wanted to-"

":::No, I'm kidding. It wouldn't be time efficient, and they're busy."

Sarah passed the first station. No one living remained there, only two demons and a field of red. As Sarah passed, the demons gave their cries, and seemed to want to give chase, but gave up quickly when Sarah bounded away.

":::Knocking out this machine better have some miraculous results. This is looking worse all the time."

She reached the second station. It was time to get down. On the platform huddled a small group of people. Sarah gave the only help she had time for. "Just so you know, the next station that way has two of them, and they've been killing up a storm. They seem happy to play in the mess there for now, but just so you know, they're there."

They gave no answer other than a nod as Sarah bounded down the stairs. At the bottom was a bloody mess, with a burnt spot in the middle. It looked like an AZU unit had taken care of a little business here already.

It was a full block before Sarah would reach one of the buildings. Thankfully, she saw soldiers before she saw demons. They were 'regular army' and not AZU soldiers, but some of them carried flame throwers.

They guarded a barricade; a line of defence against possible attacks from demons coming from either direction. They might come from outside the secured zone as Sarah had, or from the intersection after straggling out of the buildings. Across the intersection, Sarah could see a group of evacuated people being herded out. The barricades and the evacuated civilians were well outside the intersection itself, to minimize the risk of the jumping machine dropping itself or debris onto people.

"Soldier!" Sarah called to the nearest one, feeling cheeky, "Sitrep!"

":::Sarah, who taught you that term? And why are you using it?"

":::I... That is... Amanda watched enough movies and TV. And I'm just trying this out. For kicks."

The soldier turned to see Sarah in her Four Fox shirt. "Ma'am?"

Not to be so easily derailed, Sarah answered deadpan. "Who do we have in there? Are we still expecting civilians coming out from below, or is it all upper work now?"

"Are you a reporter, Ma'am? Maybe you should be talking to-"

"Soldier, Colonel Calvert has me down here, and I don't have time for this kind of crap. Are we clear up to the thing's current attack floors?"

The soldier chuckled. "I think so, Ma'am. If you want a ride out of here, you just missed an evacuation convoy. I'll call my C.O., and see where he thinks you should go."

":::Aw, he didn't buy it." Sarah was hoping to get any useful information. It was a very long shot, of course.

":::I believe your lack of a uniform may-"

":::You believe so? Really? Do you? I thought bar shirts looked a lot like standard issue military gear!"

":::You are quite incorrect, actually."

It was too easy to have fun with Eidechse. But she knew all she wanted to know, She had a clear run in the buildings, up to a point.

As she made a move to vault the barricade, the soldier reached out to grab her arm. With a little slowing of time, she corrected her motion to evade his grasp, letting him only graze her skin as she gave him a gentle smile.

Touching down on the other side running, she called back to the soldier, "Tell your C.O. Sarah's here, and not to shoot at me. I'm gonna try to help. If he doesn't know who I am, ask Calvert."

"Ma'am! You can't...!" Before finishing his sentence, he got on the radio to report.

Sarah quickly found a door to one of the office buildings under attack. It was on the northwest corner. She heard the machine overhead, launching between two of the other buildings.

":::Sarah, do you have a tactical plan?"

":::Not especially," she said, rushing inside. Blood and burnt areas marked the rampages and endings of more demons. Bypassing the elevators, she dashed around them to find the stairs, ":::do you think this thing would agree to settling this with an arm-wrestle?"

"∷∷No. Even if it did, it is evidently much stronger than Kody."

Three steps at a time, she climbed quickly. "∷∷I don't know, I've never seen Kody try smashing through windows and launching herself across an intersection. I'll have to ask her sometime."

Up she raced, floor after floor. She didn't pass more than two floors without seeing blood and burns. It was a wonder that the whole building wasn't in flames.

Tenth floor. A distant, faint crashing sound was followed by machine gun fire, and then another much closer crash. The impact of the machine hitting the building shook like an earthquake, with a sound to match. It staggered Sarah momentarily before she found her footing again, and continued climbing. Sounds of the machine rampaging continued somewhere above.

Thirteenth floor; devastation.

Entire walls lay in pieces, cubicles knocked clean away. This was to say nothing of human loss. Bodies, pieces, and red. She couldn't let herself dwell on that too much. The machine had finished with this floor, but the stairs were also destroyed. She knew from the news that they had been.

Looking up the stairwell, it looked like only this floor's stairs had been attacked. The machine ripped a couple of steps loose from the fourteenth floor as well.

There was no sense in debating what to do next.

She jumped to grab the lowest dangling step. She got a solid grasp, but the step didn't have a solid grasp of itself.

The building shook again as the machine launched out. Another floor had been successfully ravaged. The machine's departure was followed by another second and a half of machine gun fire from outside.

The step Sarah had gripped onto came loose, but not before Sarah managed to pull up to the next one. It wasn't much more stable.

Looking over her shoulder, yes, the fourteenth floor was also in ruins. What she had just heard wasn't so close however. Like a machine herself, she pulled up with her arms until her feet could reach. Up to the fifteenth.

Ruins. Sixteenth, ruins. She didn't see any blood on the sixteenth. Anyone who had been here either went up to avoid the rising destruction, or evacuated down through it. Some of the people who went down to escape likely met with demons on the way out.

The eighteenth floor was intact. It was next.

"*Is there anyone here?*" Sarah yelled. "*Anyone here needs to get off this floor now!*" she waited a few moments, and headed up to nineteen. As she expected, the nineteenth floor was also intact. She ran to the windows facing the intersection, and watched.

There. It launched from the northeast building to the southeast. Machine gun fire came from a pair of airlimbs directly overhead. The firing lasted about a second and a half with no noticeable effect before the machine disappeared into the target building. A third airlimb waited, aiming something else, but not firing.

"∷∷It's going clockwise, up a floor every lap. It's got to realize that any potential victims have cleared the buildings by now."

"::::Sarah, maybe not. Look. AZU units and helicopters are still transporting people off of the rooftops."

"::::Yeah, but how many more floors is that? None of these buildings are less than sixty floors. The number of people working this late can't sum up to a whole lot more trips for all these big choppers and crap." Indeed, the sky was littered with evacuation efforts. "It might have done a pile of killing when it first started, but this is all about the spectacle now. This is for getting on the news, or just having fun."

After listening to the destruction coming from the southeast building for a while, the machine launched out another window, and into the southwest building. Again, the hail of bullets mid-flight seemed to do nothing.

"::::Hey Eid. It's pretty regular, isn't it? Can we predict what window it will come through on the floor below us?"

"::::My apologies, Sarah. The level of damage to the lower floors left no clear indication to a lateral entry preference. The machine would be also wise to vary the position."

"::::Piss. All right then."

Sarah grabbed the nearest office chair and swung it against a window facing the southwest building. The window broke, but hung together loosely by the safety layers in the glass. A couple precision swipes with the chair loosened the crumpled pane, sending it hurtling down the side of the building.

"::::Crap. Good thing they have the area cleared out. But that was a little slow for my tastes."

Sarah grabbed the nearest cubicle divider, got steady footing and hurled the divider at another window. The window broke and the divider's momentum pushed on. The broken glass popped out with the divider, and they both toppled out.

"::::Haha! Kick ass!" Twenty more windows faced the southwest building. "::::Eid, Warn me when we have ten seconds left until we can expect it to make its move."

"::::Very well."

Sarah grabbed divider after divider. Not all of the windows popped so easily. Some needed a second throw, but it was working. The middle dozen windows were popped. While she had time, she worked on a few more.

"::::Sarah, ten seconds. Mark."

"::::Thank you!" Sarah ran to the middle window, and slowed time. Three seconds. She knelt down, right foot on the edge. Two seconds.

One second. There it was, lining up for the jump.

Its legs spread out like switchblades, launching it north towards Sarah's building. Do the math. The speed the trajectory, her own ability to jump. Time it. Slow time a little more. There was no machine gun fire on this jump. The soldiers apparently saw Sarah, and figured out her plan.

The machine's legs were coming around its body to face forward and pierce the floor below Sarah.

Now. Jump.

Sarah launched herself into an intercept arc to land on the machine, and send it down. She landed on the front ridge of its main body, above the mass of six legs poised to penetrate.

Pain messages. A fair amount of them.

Her impact slowed the machine's forward momentum, pushed it down as well as changing the angle.

Not much. But enough.

The two front 'feet' rammed into the edge of the flooring. It went in just deep enough to get the next two feet to touch the building, but that was it. It began to fall backwards.

Sarah on the other hand, was thrown hard against the building's eighteenth floor. Not hard enough to pop the glass panel and send her safely in, however. That was not the plan. There hadn't been much of a plan beyond messing up the machine.

":::Oh, shit shit shit shit." Sarah froze time.

":::Sarah, I'd like to alert you that you seem to be in position to fall seventeen-"

":::*I'm aware of that, thank you!*"

":::Sarah, I propose diving towards the machine. Once you are in contact with it, you can attempt to counter the downwards velocity at the last moment with an upwards jump or thrust."

":::That sounds like the urban myth about jumping at the last second in a falling elevator. And that's pure crap, humans can't jump hard enough to... oh... *oh humans....!*"

":::If you can achieve an ideal position to jump from, you could noticeably reduce your bodily damage."

":::Eid! 'Could'? 'Reduce'? That doesn't sound so great!"

":::Your mind would likely remain perfectly functional, if not in one piece. As long as that is functional, the body can be repaired."

":::Yeah,*Eventually!* It wouldn't be instant by any means! In the mean time, anything could happen to me!"

":::I fail to see a viable alternative, Sarah. You must time the jump well, which should be easy, and jump as hard as you are able."

":::Plan B, my dear Eidechse! Plan B!"

Sarah resumed time. Not too fast. Just a cautious pace. She still hadn't fallen more than a few centimetres from the window she had slammed against. This gave her a few moments to look closely at the machine. It sure looked bigger up close. Countless little dents marked its dark, angular hull from all of the machine gun fire it had taken.

Its mostly inflexible legs were flailing in the air, looking for anything to grab onto. Maybe it assumed it had succeeded in the jump, and now thought it was trashing another floor. Those legs...

Right. Focus. Plan B.

She turned her head to look behind her at the battered building, inches away. Watching the damaged edge of flooring pass by, she soon faced the seventeenth floor which had been ravaged on the machine's previous lap around the intersection. The window was of course knocked out.

With only about a floor's worth of falling adding to her momentum, it was simple to just reach out and grab at the seventeenth floor. Her body was more than able to absorb the jolt, and she quickly scampered to safety.

Eidechse seemed reluctant to admit the stupidity of his plan. ":::That is also a functional course of action. You are fortunate that the machine's momentum resulted in your close proximity to the building as well as a negligible mean lateral velocity."

":::Yes, Eid." Sarah turned around to see the machine still falling. She felt safe enough to allow time to flow at a normal speed. The machine plunged and then landed on the ground with almost as much clamour as when it impacted windows. A dust ring shot out from under it.

It remained motionless for a moment before two of the legs began to rise, preparing to walk again.

Then, a sound.

A sudden, unique sound, both sharp and dull at the same time, split the air. The machine slammed back to the ground with a fresh dust cloud rising around it. In its back there was now a fist-sized hole. The metal around the hole was warped and distorted into shockwave-like ripples.

":::What the heck?"

":::Look up, Sarah."

Before she did, the sound rang out again, and another hole ripped into the machine. Sarah looked up. Way up, above the tops of the buildings. The airlimb that had not been firing before, hovered triumphantly.

":::What the heck are they firing?"

":::A rail cannon. Mobile rail cannons of that manner take a variable amount of time to aim on a moving target. The 1.48 seconds that the machine was exposed during jumps was evidently not enough for the available model. Once you forced the machine to remain exposed for longer, a lock was possible."

Sarah looked closer at the machine's legs. ":::Aha! I knew they looked familiar! Eid, do you remember- no, of course you don't, that was before you moved into my head. Wait, you read my whole memory before you moved in. You kept the important parts? You know what I'm talking about, don't you?"

":::...indexing... ...indexing... yes, I have found the image you refer to. Underground. The location you reported to the police as being inhabited by demon-class abominations prior to your capture. My most recent military information on that location has it in a queue for investigation, and designated as 'site 2501'."

":::Great, Eid." Sometimes it was tempting to freeze time just to have conversations with Eidechse. That or teach him the benefits of brevity, but that might result in the exclusion of important details, like alternatives to falling seventeen stories.

":::I'm going to investigate it myself, Eid. It was too dark even for light amplified vision, but now I have the wondrous technological advancement of a pocket lighter."

Some soldiers now stood below, around the machine. Some looked up to see Sarah. She gave them a friendly wave before bounding back down the stairs.

As she came to the third floor, a trio of soldiers were coming up. "Sarah Hartford?" The one in front bore the markings of a Captain.

"Yeah. Hi, do I know you?" She passed by them, continuing down at a more casual, human pace. They followed.

"General Westmore has asked me to bring you along for a debriefing."

"Wait a second, debriefing?" Sarah chuckled, "I'm not a soldier, I'm just a private citizen doing my civic duty to fight giant metal bugs. And who's this General guy? What happened to Colonel Calvert?"

"Ma'am, the Colonel is a direct subordinate of General Westmore. The General is very interested to talk with you. I don't know anything about you beyond what I just saw you do, but I think that's the kind of thing the General is interested in."

Sarah stopped to give the Captain a glance of cautious scrutiny. "Fine. But not right now. I have to go check something out at site..."

":::I believe you are trying to remember the number '2501', Sarah."

":::Thanks, Eid."

"Site 2501." Sarah said. "If you guys have troops there, tell them to expect a friendly visit from me. If you *don't* have troops there, you might want to think of sending some. I think it might be interesting. By the way, did the demons stop?"

"Uh... no Ma'am, why?"

"Never mind." Sarah gave the Captain a nod, turned up her strength, and dashed off towards 'site 2501' before the Captain could protest.

":::Damn. I guess it was stupid to expect some control centre for the demons to be in that machine. What kind of idiot would put a system so vital into a machine they plan to have jumping from building to building, attracting gunfire?"

":::Erebus has displayed similar lapses in reason in the past, valuing his own entertainment over strategy."

":::For the *last time*, Eid. This isn't my dad doing this."

":::I did not say that."

"I still think she was waving at us." Jessica said, watching the second replay on the news. There stood Sarah at the edge of a blown-out window, waving. The news commentator babbled on about her, not knowing anything, speculating everything.

"She's obviously looking down, not into the camera." Danielle had pointed this out each time the footage came up, and each time Jessica ignored the fact.

Kody stepped out from the kitchen with a burger for Jessica and a salad for Danielle. She pointed at Sarah and her Four Fox tee shirt. "I'll tell you one thing, those shirts turned out to be the best advertizing move I've ever made."

Jessica snorted, and watched as the next bit of footage showed burnt remains of a demon, and another long-distance view of a roaming demon. "Sure, Densfarn's on its way to being a really popular vacation spot again, and we'll be right in the leading edge of that economic upturn."

Pushing her salad away with a sigh, Danielle looked out towards the front doors. "I hope those customers are all right. A couple of them were dorks, but they're out *there* now..."

"Lots of people are out there right now," Kody said, "frankly I'm surprised we aren't packed with people who don't want to be isolated." The word 'isolated' resonated in the quiet. There were only the three of them in the bar.

Danielle wandered a few steps towards the front doors. "Sarah's heading back here right about now, right?"

"No,"Jessica said, "she said something about picking up some groceries and stopping by the dry cleaners before getting her hair done. *Then* she's coming back here."

Danielle sighed. "Oh, shut it. Even without her strength, I'd feel a lot better if there were four of us."

Kody nodded. "Besides, the shirt promises four."

Time went on slowly. The TV news wasn't offering anything special. No new sightings of Sarah, and no apparent decrease in the demon attacks. Jessica surfed channels on the next terminal over, and Kody made herself busy work.

A loud bang came from the front doors. It was twenty or more metres to the front door, so it was difficult to make out in the darkness. "What is that?"

The visitor rammed his clawed hand against the doors again, smashing the glass, and reaching through the grating. It let out the cry of the demons.

"Damn it, here we go, girls." Kody gestured Danielle and Jessica behind her, then primed her shotgun. Jessica and Danielle readied the rods they took out of patio umbrellas. "All right. Now what?"

The demon answered by pulling at the grate in savage jerks. It was bending, it was breaking. The demon would be inside soon.

:::C / [100110] [38]

“:::Sarah, may I make a suggestion?”

Sarah was running as fast as she could to return to the drainage pipe she had entered days ago. It would be a long, labyrinthine journey from the entrance, down to the place she faced those demons and where she saw the object that she now knew to be a leg for the machine.

Even with the many modern miracles of massive nano-machinery, building something from scratch out of solid metal like that was no minor task.

“:::Sure, Eid. What ya got?”

“:::If your destination is the passage where you first observed the individual metal appendage, a more efficient route would be via a manhole cover approximately three blocks south from here.”

Sarah burst into the next intersection, and turned sharply left. “:::All right. How do you know that, anyway?” Since the battle with the machine, she had two close encounters with demons. One she managed to evade, but the second had to be blinded, as there were vulnerable people nearby. Ideally she would have liked to incapacitate them both, but the big picture overrode the immediate need to solve every problem in her path.

“:::Extracting the location from your description had been preformed shortly after your initial report. The proximity to a manhole cover is a simple comparison to city infrastructure records.”

A block closer, Sarah saw the burnt out husk of a building. The buildings on either side were singed, but seemed otherwise unharmed. The sidewalk in front of the burnt out building was a mess of burn marks and caramelized blood. Civilians playing with fire in desperation? How many sights like this were popping up in the city right now?

A Vtag popped up over a manhole cover ahead. “:::Thanks Eid. I see it.” Sarah reached down and put a finger into one of the little round vent holes and picked the cover off. Underneath was a hatch that most of the public never knew about, but had become standard decades ago to prevent mischievous people from wandering underground for fun.

The hatch was a simple round plate, but it had been breached from below. The metal had been pressed or beaten against until the lock on one edge had snapped loose.

"::::Wow. I should have guessed they were popping up from the sewers."

"::::The military resolved this fact long ago, but not all of the demon-class abominations came from underground. Many were created above ground, making the thousands of manhole covers impractical locations to guard. The exact numbers of how many demon-class abominations were created above as opposed to under ground are unknown. The military seems to still assume that the original source is above ground, or site 2501 would have been made a higher priority."

Sarah groaned out loud. "::::Why doesn't anyone tell me this kind of thing?"

"::::I just did, Sarah."

With a sigh, Sarah started descending the cold metal ladder that stretched down beyond the hatch. "::::So you did, Eid. So you did."

Sarah turned on low-light vision. She was careful not to step on the ladder rungs too hard. She didn't want to send any further telltale sounds bouncing down the stark concrete passages.

The ladder followed a claustrophobic tube down about seven metres before arriving in a larger tunnel that ran east to west. It had a vaulted ceiling three metres from the floor, and the passage was two whole metres wide, cluttered with pipes and conduits.

A Vtag appeared down the passage to the east. "::::Another ladder leading down is behind this hatch." Eidechse said it as if the hatch was instantly recognizable by Sarah from... what... fifty metres away? Still taking care to step softly, Sarah ran to the hatch embedded into the wall. As promised, opening it revealed another ladder going down. This one was even more crowded than the last one.

"::::Who the heck built this thing?" Sarah squirmed herself down the tube, bumping elbows, knees and heels on concrete every few steps. "::::I mean, take your average city work grunt, toss on a bulky reflective vest, tool belt, and heaven forbid they might be carrying something."

After a long time that felt even longer, she arrived at another horizontal tunnel. It was very similar to the last horizontal passage, but after the last ladder, it felt like grand central station.

A fresh Vtag popped up to the east again. "::::Doctor of engineering Kerl Harris is credited for the design of this section of the infrastructure, although several sources cite that-"

"::::Eid. I didn't actually want to know. It's not like I'm going to go to his house and complain about it."

"::::That is just as well, Sarah. Kerl Harris died sixty three years ago, at the age of eighty nine. It is likely that he is no longer in a house. Further more, he would not be able to respond to your complaints."

"::::Yup. Right. Good. We like our dead people to be unresponsive."

Before Sarah made it to the next Vtag, the lack of light was nearing complete. Her low light vision just wasn't finding much light to amplify, and it was even darker ahead. She dug into her pocket and pulled out the lighter.

Lighting it produced a burst of light that may as well have been an atom bomb. Her eyes quickly adjusted. With the lighter held high, even distant reaches of the passage became easily visible to her.

The Vtag hovered in a doorway fifty or so metres ahead, leading south. As she approached it, Eidechse erased it. ":::Approximately one hundred metres south is where you fought the demon-class abomination. That passage has no other divergences. I suggest that you continue east."

It made sense, so she did just that. She double checked that her body was giving off as little heat as possible. Realizing how stupid that was when she held a lighter up as a torch, she just concentrated on being as quiet as possible, and listening carefully.

Laying in wait ahead, was a grenade placed on the floor against the left wall. A wire attached to it ran across the passage to the right side, forming a trip wire.

":::Huh. Nice hiding spot for a trap. Anyone could see that and step over the wire. At least it suggests we're on the right track."

":::Sarah, I remind you how dark it is. Without the lighter, we would not have seen it."

":::Yeah, of course not. But it's not like anyone would be here without some kind of light. I don't think anyone dumb enough to wander around in the dark is much of a threat to anyone."

":::You may have a point. At any rate, you can just step over it and continue on."

Sarah was suspicious that ignoring it might not be the wisest action. She quietly got within five metres of the grenade. ":::What if we ignore it, and we have to deal with it going off behind us, or running out and tripping over it in a rush. Or something. Hey Eid. If I chucked it down the hall, would an explosion do any serious damage to the passage?"

":::I believe the strength of the passage is more than sufficient to resist significant damage, however the force of the explosion will be channeled along the passage in either direction. Estimating the strength of this grenade, any throw greater than fifteen metres should supply us with ample distance for safety."

":::No problem." Looking east to plan her throw, Sarah walked towards the grenade.

When she was still over a metre away, it exploded. Only smoke, but with enough force to throw Sarah onto her back. The lighter flew from her hand, and went out, leaving her in total darkness.

She froze time. ":::*What the hell?!*"

":::Despite the grenade's exterior appearance, it was evidently some manner of smoke grenade."

":::Yes, Eid. I noticed. I also noticed it went off when I was nowhere near the trip wire!"

":::I believe it was also set with some manner of proximity detection."

":::That's cheating!"

":::I do not recall any rules being agreed to, Sarah."

Sarah stared up into the darkness, knowing it was filled with smoke. ":::Hey Eid. Remember when we busted out of Yute central? With the fire suppression haze? Can we use the same mix of infra red and quantitative phase imaging now?"

":::No. Your visual filters are all of a passive nature, which require a minimal level of light."

":::I'm not too keen on the idea of restarting time, then groping around in the dark for the damned lighter. This smoke could be part of an ambush. I need to see as quickly as possible when I restart time. Let me look something up in my 'manual'. Dang. Hey Eid. Do you think I could do some kind of sonar, or echo location?"

":::Bats utilize sounds from ten, to a hundred and twenty kilohertz. Your hearing is only able to perceive up to forty kilohertz. A crude echo location may be possible, if you can create an appropriate sound. I recommend as high of a pitch as possible in as short of a burst as possible."

":::All right. Let's do this."

Sarah restarted time, and flipped around in the general direction that the lighter went. A pathetic sounding, but effective little squeak chirped out of her. The sound quietly resonated around the walls, floor and ceiling. She listened with intense concentration, in slowed time, trying to map the sound out in her mind, as Eidechse did the same.

":::Okay Eid. I think I heard a lump one point seven metres at ...fifteen? Degrees to the left."

":::One point six eight nine two metres, thirteen degrees left."

":::Okay then." Sarah crawled forward and easily found the lighter. Flicking it on, a mix of her infra red, quantitative phase, and good ole' low-light vision started feeding her all the visuals she needed.

A voice came from the east, beyond the range of vision that the lighter provided. "Oh! A zombie! Let's go kill the zombie!"

Another nearly identical voice followed. "Yes! In the name of our genius sexy god Erebus! Let's go kill the zombie!" Then another voice? Or the first one maybe, added, "Yes, by the will of Erebus, let us use our magical FNZs! Die, zombie, die!"

Gunshots were heard. Before any bullets had time to arrive anywhere, Sarah froze time again. ":::Eid? What the hell?"

":::Sarah, if they are firing at you, I believe alerting them to your non-zombie status may be futile, as I believe they are insincere in their professed desire to kill zombies."

":::Thanks Eid. You're a font of wisdom as usual. The whole Erebus worship should have clued me in."

":::Indeed."

":::What do you think we're dealing with here, Eid? Abominations using guns? Since when?"

":::I suspect that this is a unit of freshly converted mundane zombies. Their use of FNZ firearms implies a military unit. It seems that the government indeed sent an AZU stormfront fireteam to investigate your report, and were conquered."

"::: Great. 'Mundane' zombies, huh? How many soldiers are in a 'stormfront fireteam'?"

"::: Up to six. In the current crisis, we can expect at least two of them to be carrying flame throwers in addition to FNZs and grenades."

"::: Lovely."

Sarah resumed time. She immediately turned off the lighter and dropped to the floor as bullets ricocheted around her. With her presence and current position known, she faked a pained sound as if she had been shot, and kicked the floor to compliment the notion that she had been gunned down.

Silently, and without any means of vision, she crawled back to the passage leading south. Clumsy, running footsteps were approaching.

"Erebus says zombies are bad!" The voices drew closer as she ducked around the corner. "All hail sexy, intelligent Erebus!" "Hail, you betcha!"

"::: Damn it. I know that voice! They're all talking in Jon's voice!" It was too much. This was more than a copycat.

"The zombie got away!" one of the voices said with an exaggerated, tragic, forlorn tone, "Erebus will punish us!"

The next voices sounded ecstatic. "Maybe he will spank us!" "A spanking! A spanking!" "Oh! Oh! Spank *me!*"

"I smell no blood!"

"I don't think we hit it. And in other news, praise Erebus."

"Yes, praise Erebus, and his scuzzy dongle!"

"May his dongle touch you!"

"And you!"

"Enough praising Erebus' massive dongle for now. We must find the zombie!"

Eidechse spoke up with mild irritation. "::: I highly doubt that Erebus has any practical use for something as outdated as a SCSI dongle."

"::: Focus Eid. It sounds like there's three of them, and they're close. They're not being so kind as to be giving off any light though. They must be as blinded as us."

"::: Yes, however they are likely as familiar with the layout of this area as we are. We are an even match."

"::: Except there's three of them. And they have machine guns."

The footsteps came close enough, they were about a metre in front of Sarah. Now or never. Lighting a single spark from the lighter, Sarah froze time at the instant of the flash and took a look at what she was jumping into.

Before her stood three soldiers. Kind of. They were joined at the hip, literally. A fleshy, raw extrusion of organic material joined them in a row.

Both of the men on either end carried a rifle with their one arm. The arms toward the middle of the trio were gone, and the stumps rammed into the shoulders of the middle man.

The man on the right had an Aguolian flag wrapped around his head. The man on the left had a flute rammed into this forehead.

The man in the middle had a skull hanging from an extension cable around his neck, and from the middle of the communal body, his forearms stuck out. He had no hands, just bloody bones tipped like drumsticks.

"::::I was in error," Eidechse said, ":::They are not zombies. This qualifies them as an abomination. Much less practical than the demon-class abominations. We are fortunate."

":::*Eidechse!* Doesn't that make you *sick*? Look at them! Who *does* this kind of thing?!"

":::Erebus does this kind of thing. We both know about the horsemen he created in Meston. In addition, I have records of several impractical abomination types that Erebus has made primarily for his own amusement."

Sarah resumed time, and the darkness returned instantly. She reached out to the left soldier's rifle, and ripped it out of his grasp.

"*Heeeeeelp! Heeeelp meee, I was robbed by the zombeeee!* And also praise Erebus!"

The middle soldier squealed and began beating on his 'drum' furiously. "*Fear the mad drum solo skills of the knights of Erebus!!!*"

Sarah stepped behind the trio, and held the gun in front of her. She made another spark, and froze time to look at her position, what the trio was doing, and get a look at the gun. Content that she could fire it, she resumed time and fired several shots into the arm of the soldier on the other end. Bits of blowback sprinkled Sarah with blood before the other rifle clattered to the floor.

"The zombie knows how to use guns! Zombies can't do that, can they? Also, hail Erebus! Do we have any more guns?"

Eidechse spoke up. ":::Pick up the other rifle, then keep a distance. They only have biting and clawing for offence now. I recommend shooting apart the remaining arm and the six legs to neutralize it."

Sarah had done more brutal things to the demons before, but somehow using a gun made it worse. She quickly grabbed up the other rifle, and slung it over her shoulder. She needed a free hand to ignite the lighter.

The dazed trio stumbled, trying to turn around and face her. More out of pity than anger, she opened fire on their legs. They soon fell to the floor as blood seeped out. The one functional arm tried its best to drag its mass along, but wasn't strong enough to get much done.

The middle man drummed a lazy, tired beat. Sarah shot up the stubby drumming arms just to shut it up.

"Killjoy." Was the trio's harmonious response.

"Hail Erebus, by the way. Sexy genius Erebus. With his intelligence and sexiness. Hail him. And whatnot."

":::The drum appears to be a fresh skull," Eidechse observed. "The three participants on this abomination all have their heads. It is possible the drum skull came from a fourth member of the stormfront fireteam."

":::Some abominations don't need heads."

":::That is true."

The metal grate over the front doors of the Four Fox had become the front line of an ongoing battle. Four demons laid siege, trying to pull, bend or break the grate.

Kody made that pretty difficult. It had been quite a while since any of the demons had much of a face to speak of, let alone eyes. Once that was achieved at the end of Kody's shotgun, Jessica suggested moving away from the front and not making a sound.

The demons persisted, continuing to attack the grate.

"All right, that's not working. They're going to get through that grate if we leave them to it." Kody primed another round into the shotgun. "Jess, you get some booze, Danielle, you get the fire extinguisher."

Kody filled her apron pockets with ammunition from the box, and headed back to the grate. She reached out at arm's length and aimed at the leg of the nearest demon, careful to put the end of the shotgun's barrel between bars of the grate.

Earlier she had fired from farther back. The demons' sight and well aimed swings made it necessary. Firing from farther back damaged the grate as well. It was only dumb luck that no one got any ricochet. After that scare, Danielle and Jessica helped by pushing them back with the patio umbrella rods. One rod was now sitting out in the street, bent over about ninety degrees. The other had gotten jammed in the grate hard enough that there was no safe way to get it back.

Not being able to see their prey, only hear them, the demons were now focused on the grate, allowing Kody to blast from a closer position in relative safety.

Her target buckled over when she pulled the trigger, shattering the right thigh. It slid down and kept attacking the grate. She rewarded its persistence by giving each arm similar injuries. It was still trying to attack, but was only marginally upright thanks only to the help of leaning on the grate.

"Jess! Liquid courage! Let's finish this one!"

Jessica stepped up with two beer pitchers filled with cheap booze. The narrow necks of bottles would get more booze on the ground than the demons, making the pitchers preferable.

She splashed them at the weakened demon, ignoring the three others by its sides. "Another round, on you."

She stepped back and put the pitchers on the floor so she and Danielle could refill them while Kody began firing at the next demon. "I think that first one's had enough to drink, girls."

Danielle picked up the fire extinguisher, while Jessica grabbed a lighter and a spray can to safely spray a flame through the grate. The demon became engulfed. Jessica threw more alcohol on the fire as the demon continued its feeble attack, adding one of those screams now and then.

Kody stepped back to watch, taking a short break from shotgun duties. "Hey, Danny girl, you're watching that the flames don't catch the ceiling, right?"

"Huh? Yeah. Damn, mum. The demon doesn't even seem to mind that much."

Kody fired one more at the first demon, right in the middle, toppling it backwards. Kody took the shotgun in her left hand and flexed her right hand. "I'm not firing correctly at all. It's not meant to be a one hand job."

"Let me, then." Danielle offered.

Kody smirked. "Love, look at the width of my wrist, and look at yours. All right, let's see if we can just use the fire to our advantage. Everyone, let's go get more booze to throw at the other three stooges. The flames might spread."

"I'll stay here with the fire extinguisher." Danielle stepped back a few paces none the less. She didn't feel the need to stand any closer to the bleeding, groaning monsters than necessary.

Jessica dashed ahead of Kody, and loaded up a serving tray with any big bottle she could get her hands on. "Funny how manageable this seems when you're organized and prepared."

"Oh yeah," Kody dripped with sarcasm while refilling her pockets with ammo. "You just can't think of the blood and guts too much. Otherwise it's just like any other Saturday night here."

A sudden, loud, metallic 'pang' rang out, followed by the sound of a broken bolt hitting the floor. Enthusiastic groaning and cries erupted from the three able demons.

"Oh, hell. Mum?"

:::C / [101000] [40]

“:::Sarah, I think you can turn off the lighter.”

Sarah took Eidechse's suggestion and was pleasantly surprised that her plain old passive light amplification vision was sufficient without the little flame. “:::Ooh, we have some ambient light! I wonder where it's coming from.” It wasn't a constant level of light, dimming and flickering a little now and then. It was enough, but Sarah kept the lighter in her hand just in case it went dark again.

In her other hand she carried one of the rifles. She took all of the ammunition from the other one, just in case the trio managed to get mobile again.

Around a corner and fifty or so metres down the conduit laden corridor, the light source could be seen. It was a small blue 'glow stick' being carried by a soldier. He carried it like a cigar, puffing at it from time to time. Beside him walked another soldier, carrying a broken black umbrella as a parasol, striding with an exaggerated feminine swagger.

The 'smoker' had a leash in his other hand. The 'dog' attached was another soldier, missing his head, and walking on all fours. Where his head once was, there were now grenades. Nearly twenty of them, taped together in a large ball, and attached to his shoulders. A small speaker sat mounted on the front of the grenades. The 'solder-dog' was stained heavily in its own blood.

“Darling,” said the smoker in the most congenial tone, “By Erebus, I really don't think my cigarette is very good, praise Erebus and his charm, wit and genius.”

“Why, sugar blossom!” replied the other, jamming the parasol into the top of its head in order to free its hands, “Put that thing away, I have some that are ours to enjoy by the will of our one true god Erebus, the sexy and omnipotent, good at crosswords, benevolent genius.”

The smoker hooked the glow stick onto its vest. “Ah, no need, darling. I have some as well.” He grabbed onto his right middle finger, and violently yanked and twisted at it until it ripped free. Some blood spilled in the process, and he leaned back with a wholesome laugh. “Oh, by Erebus, I seem to have spilled a little sauce! Silly me. Cerberus? Oh Cerberus, can you clean this up? Master made a mess."

The grenade-headed soldier-dog attempted to lick the blood up. The grenades scraped against the concrete while the speaker made licking sounds.

"Good boy, Cerberus," the smoker said, "Darling, I seem to be without a match!" He put his detached finger between his lips. "Would you be so kind? Also, praise Erebus."

"Sugar blossom, you referred to yourself as 'Master'!"

"Goodness, did I?"

"Yes, sugar blossom. When you called to Cerberus. We all know only Erebus is the Master!"

"Oh! Oh why yes of course! But when I said 'Master made a mess', I could have been referring to Erebus, as he is everything, is he not?"

"Oh, sugar blossom," he.. she.. it, tilted its head with a smile, scraping the edge of the parasol against the wall. "You're a sly one, but we all know Erebus is without fault! He would not accidentally make a mess!"

The smoker took his new finger-cigar out of his mouth and looked suddenly into the ceiling with another wholesome chuckle. "Goodness, you have a point, darling! So obviously my spilling blood was by his design, O great and wondrous Erebus, to whom all is domain. It all has a purpose! And when we get right down to it, are we not *all* truly Erebus, in the truthful essence of it all?"

The parasol solder giggled and sighed while pulling out a flame thrower. "Oh, Sugar blossom, you understand theology so much better than I do! Tee, and furthermore, Hee. Praise Erebus and his collection of commemorative pogs!" It aimed the flame thrower at the smoker's head and fired a three second burst, bathing the corridor in a flickering orange hue, but missing the finger-cigar in the smoker's hand entirely.

The smoker's head burned away as he put the finger-cigar back in his mouth and took a deep inhale. "Ahh, that rich, bold, Erebus-approved flavour! Thank you, Darling. Cerberus, aren't you done licking that up yet?"

The grenade-headed soldier-dog stopped mimicking the licking motion, and 'looked' up at the smoker. "Pant, pant, and also pant," the speaker on the soldier-dog said in a human voice, "Arf, I have no tongue, arf. Pant. Pant."

The smoker reeled back with yet another wholesome laugh. "And so you don't! Maybe we could make a trip to the surface and find you a new one!"

"Arf, arf. Awesome."

Sarah put herself into a prone position, and took aim ":::That's just about enough of that." She squeezed the trigger, sending a short stream of hollow points sailing towards the soldier-dog's head.

":::Sarah, maybe-"

Sarah froze time as one of the grenades began to burst. ":::Yes, Eid, you were saying?"

":::Never mind. I believe the infrastructure will contain the fire that will begin to spread through the gas line before it reaches any major deposit."

":::Gas line...?" In the frozen slice of time, Sarah turned her attention upwards to the many conduits and pipes overhead. ":::Ah. Gas line. I think I'll stay on the floor for a while."

"::::I believe that is the best course of action at this point."

Sarah unfroze time and sighed. The cluster of twenty or so grenades popped like a small sun, ejecting fire and smoke, and a shockwave down the passage that gave Sarah a serious jolt from fifty metres away.

A split moment after that, the gas line in the ceiling responded. Fire burst from the line, spreading in both directions, ripping piping as it went. Instinctively, Sarah turned and shielded herself with her arm from the flash blaze raining down. Her right arm, side of her face and body caught fire.

The blast was over as quickly as it started.

"::::Sarah! Roll! Smother the flames quickly! Roll! Smother the flames quickly! Roll! Smother the flames quickly! Roll! Sm-"

"::::Shut up! I'm rolling!" Eidechse was being almost as annoying as the flood of pain alerts. She quickly got the fire out, but damage was done. She was badly burned.

"::::Damn, I'm glad the rest of my ammo didn't go off!" More sedate fires continued to burn along the ceiling, and where the zombie trio had stood. The smoke was thick, and there was little place for it to go. Sarah turned on her quantitative phase imaging.

"::::Sarah, I believe you should be more thankful that the three litres of alcohol that you are carrying in your lungs didn't explode."

Sarah sat up. "::::Ah. Forgot about that." She made sure that her systems were hard at work on repairs. Thankfully the burns were mainly surface level. 2.3-4.9% of musculature strength had been comprised, as well as dermal systems in the affected areas. These were given priority, for reasons of environmental defence. "::::My reserves of protein are going to be getting a little low by the time repairs are done."

Quantitative phase allowed her to see through the stagnant smoke to see the wreckage of the three ahead. There was little to be recognized as anything human-like. Red, red, red. Shards of the flame thrower, another weapon, bent, and the parasol lay about, mostly coated or stuck in viscera, stuck to walls. "::::Sarah, if you need protein badly-"

"::::What? Ew, no! Not *nearly* that desperate!"

The walls themselves were pretty battered as well. Huge cracks could be seen through the shredded mass of conduits. A large section of wall and ceiling had settled ten or so centimetres further towards the middle of the passage. She continued on with a mix of revulsion over the miniature massacre she had triggered, and fear of the passage caving in on her.

Eidechse appraised the walls. "::::The damage is actually less than I would have estimated. Regardless, I believe it has broken net access and primary power supply to roughly four hundred buildings."

"::::Damn, you mean people are now having to fight demons and crap up there *in the dark?*"

"::::Secondary systems will have come online by now."

"::::Well, that's good, I guess. Hey, you said net access. Can we tap into the net from here? Just to check the news, and report what's going on under here?"

A Vtag appeared on a broken chunk of conduit behind them. It was on the other side of the explosion site, dangling out of a burnt chunk of tissue, and dripping blood. "::::Ew!"

"::: It is that, or trace the line further back and spend the time drilling with nanites to reach the appropriate wire. That would take considerable time, I didn't think you wanted to use."

"::: True. But again, plan B. Well, C, actually." Sarah traced the conduit back beyond the bloody area. She jumped up and grabbed onto it, jerking down until she ripped a fresh break in the line. "Plan B wins again. I mean C."

Tapping into current news feeds, it looked like things were gradually getting worse up top. Demon attacks were increasing, and more military had been called in. They were being less careful about civilians in efforts to crush the demons. Another station had a panicky commentator speculating that it was only a matter of hours before the city was bombed into the stone age, like Autar and Meston.

She called the Four Fox.

Ring.

Ring.

Ring.

Ring.

Letting it continue to ring, at the same time she sent as much information as she could about her underground journey to the military. Location, information about the compromised stormfront fireteam, and an apology about the recent damage.

The Four Fox still wasn't picking up. The answering service wasn't picking up either. Maybe the phone system was malfunctioning. It was certain to be getting used heavily right now.

Onward.

The light of the fire was useful for quite a distance. Down the passage and around two corners, enough traces of light still found her. Enough to see by with light amplification.

No, there was a new source of light, coming from ahead. Sarah was curious, but resisted quickening her pace. If anything, it was time to be on guard. She double checked the rifle before readying the lighter in her free hand. At the next intersection, the left path held the most light, so she followed it.

At the end of this passage was an elevator shaft. No doors, no elevator car, just a shaft. A motor and pulleys clung to the ceiling over the shaft, but no cables.

The light was very plainly coming from below, dancing and flickering. The elevator shaft went down about five stories, with no ladder, no conduits or piping, just sheer concrete.

"::: Well. That looks fairly one-way."

"::: Sarah, I believe the shaft is narrow enough that you could employ friction and leverage to perform a controlled descent."

"::: Yeah, probably. What about up?"

"::: A similar technique could be used. It would likely take notably more time."

"::: So, no quick fleeing in abject terror, huh? Fine."

Sarah put the lighter back in her pocket. She stood with her toes over the edge, and gently as possible, fell forward to press her free hand against the opposite wall. She 'lay' stretched out across the shaft, staring down, holding the rifle at the ready with her other hand.

":::Yeah. That right there? That was a point of no return. I feel a little vulnerable right now."

":::Then proceed down to regain a more practical stance."

":::Just appreciating the moment. Here we go."

Sarah stepped forward, that is, down. Another careful step, and another, letting her hand drag down the opposite wall to remain level.

":::I wonder if a human with normal strength could do this?"

":::You could lower your str-"

":::I'm not quite that curious."

With a little practice, walking down the wall became easier and mildly quicker. The bottom's exit opened out from the wall Sarah's feet were on. She jumped down, landing crouched, but ready to fight.

No fight awaited her.

The passage ahead stretched out for seventy metres. The floor here looked like hundreds of dark metal spheres, about the size of ping pong balls.

On the floor, lined up against the walls on either side sat wide, red candles. They sat half a metre apart, all the way to the end. Melted mounds of wax held them to the peculiar floor. Each candle's melted clumps were perfectly identical to every other candle.

Their ruddy, flickering glow rose up throughout the passage. A darkly crimson gift from underfoot. Their fire gave no heat. It was not fire, it was only light.

Sarah knelt down to pick up the nearest candle on the right, breaking it free from the floor. Watching the 'flame' closely, she saw a 4.4 second loop in the movements. When she held the candle upside down, the flame burned downward instead of rising like a natural flame.

Leaning the rifle against her leg, she used both hands to rip the wax of the candle open. A little toy sat inside, generating the image and light of the flame. She dropped the meaningless decoration, and picked up the rifle.

She walked to the end of the passage, between the twin rows of red candles, where a wide, heavy looking metal door waited. It was grey, tarnished with dark streaks, and lined around the edges with rivets. A rigid lever handle waited patiently.

A plaque-like feature embossed outward from the door's metal at eye-height, and also sported a bolt on each corner purely for decorative purpose.

It read in large embossed text:

The Church of Erebus

Smaller text below read "All flamingos abandon, ye who enter in."

The idiocy of it reminded Sarah of Jon. It bore semblance to his flavour of ... well...idiocy. She reached out for the handle, but it jerked open before she touched it, and the door snapped inwardly open with a deafening impact.

At the same moment, the floor began to shift under her feet. Looking down she saw each of the balls that composed the floor rolling around. On the sides that used to face down, each ball bore a smiling face made from perpendicular squares, like big pixels.

"Welcome!" came their tiny voices all at once. They rolled furiously underneath her, slipping her feet forward, landing her on her back. They continued to roll, feeding her into the doorway, into the dark room made entirely of the same balls the floor was made of.

Sarah resisted, grabbing at the doorway. She pulled herself out, but found nothing to hold onto past that, soon slipping towards the door again. The candles bounced and bounded towards her, some going into the room, some catching on the doorway.

"You're late, Alice! It's not your fault, I didn't send a rabbit!" It was Jon's voice, but lacking whatever small hint of kindness that Jon usually had.

"*My name's not Alice!*" Sarah screamed, holding onto the door frame.

"Of course it isn't." A wave of the smiling balls reached out from the floor of the room, grabbing Sarah's legs and dragging her in. The door slammed behind her, and disappeared behind a surge of the little dark balls. Every direction was now only the smiling, shifting spheres. "How do you like my balls?" the voice asked happily.

Where the hell did that rifle get to? Fumbling around in the shifting floor, she pulled her lighter out of her pocket and sparked up. She sprayed the three litres of alcohol she had stored in her lungs, breathing flames against the spheres.

Quickly out of fuel, the flame breath was extinguished. Damaged spheres receded into the masses, and were replaced.

"You can't hurt my lucky balls, my lucky balls, my balls made out of bucky balls!"

The 'luckyballs' wrapped around Sarah's ankles again, and a surge of them forced her to stand. She then sank into them up to her knees, and felt them tighten. Her own strength was matched the more she exerted.

"Alice, Alice, your name's not Alice! But this brings up the obvious question! I know you're not human. A human would have died a long time ago. Did you even notice how inhospitable the air is here? Dead, dead, you'd be quite dead. There's also your strength. Let me see..."

Sarah felt her left calf being ripped open. Pain warnings screamed at her. Eidechse made an odd sound. ":::Sarah, my connection to your sysr#‹û ë#A½ÿÿÿÿ‹ù;û|kA━E#‹È‹øèV©# H-----"

":::Eid! What's going on!?" Eidechse was silent. Sarah screamed out loud to the masses of luckyballs around her "*Whatever you're doing, stop it right now!*"

It did stop. A surge of luckyballs rose in front of her, pointing one directly at her face. The array of eight by eight squares on the ball lit up, managing a puzzled expression. The voice now spoke through this single representative luckyball. "You didn't seem to mind the physical damage as much as I would expect. That is interesting in itself. Anyway, next step."

Sarah's system reported nanites invading her body, and full scale microscopic war had begun. Had Eidechse already lost?

"Oh my goodness!" the voice was giddy, and the little face changed to a wide smile, lighting up more squares to display a huge grin. "We share much in common! Maybe I should not be surprised. But look at these muscle fibres! Something's fishy here. This explains much! Such meticulous work! Such care! Such intelligent design, I dare say I would be hard pressed to do better myself! You are no zombie, no weapon, no disposable spy or foot soldier, are you?"

"Are you Jonathan Coll?" Sarah asked flatly.

The voice chuckled softly, but scornfully. "Your nanites are very potent, very capable. I'm quite glad that mine outnumber yours so dramatically."

Sarah repeated herself. "*Are you Jonathan Coll?!*"

The little face in front of her switched to a flat mouth. "Jonathan Coll is dead, and was made of meat. I am not meat. I *use* meat. I escaped from the meat that was Jonathan, I am Erebus, God of darkness!" The broad smile returned, "I am the hero of Autar, I liberated the meat of Meston, and am the new ruler and savior of Densfarn! I'm sure you've heard of me, my angels are going door to door in the streets, spreading the good news!"

The luckyballs rose up around Sarah. Or was she sinking? More of her flesh was being opened, spread apart and torn, muscles and bone dissected, defensive nanites spread thinner, and losing.

"Erebus! Do you remember your sister?"

"I am carbon and data, silly 'not-Alice'! Carbon and data have no relations in such terms!"

Sarah tried not to panic. She remembered that she could just turn the panic and fear off, so she did. "Fine. Erebus, do you remember Jonathan's sister? Do you remember Amanda? Or when you took over her body and renamed her Erika?"

Erebus' activities halted, and the face disappeared, replaced by a single lit square, scanning across, and up, and down in thought. Then it turned into the happy face again.

"Yes! Erika! I had an Erika once! She was reasonably fun! She was made out of an Amanda? What's the opposite of interesting, and what does it have to do with Jonathan's sis- *Oh, I see!* At any rate, do you have a point?" Erebus continued devouring Sarah, now into her torso, and still rising. "Hey, you look a lot like Erika! Are you a fan?"

"Erebus! You made a file of Amanda's mind! Did you ever read it?"

Erebus paused again, and the little face turned sad. "Meston was a bad time for me. I lost some of my less important data back then. Bombs and such, you know how it is. If you want a copy, you'll have to look on the net, maybe." The smile returned with a little digital nod, and the dissection continued.

Sarah held her arms over her head, trying to keep as much of her body safe as she could. "I don't need the file, I *have* the file! It's mine now, my father gave it to me!"

The little face turned upset. "Riddles, you speak in." All the luckyballs in the room lit their faces in waves, ending at one ball in the ceiling. "Daisy!" it said in a little voice.

Another luckyball rolled out of the ceiling and dangled down from the first. "Daisy!"

Another rolled over, and down the second, and called out "Daisy!"
Another. "Daisy!" Another. "Daisy!" Another. "Daisy!"
Until one final one dangled in front of Sarah's face before declaring:
"*Chain!!!*"
The luckyballs in the daisy chain giggled gleefully, as it swung forward and back. The bottom luckyball split in half, and smacked against Sarah's forehead.
Sarah reached up and broke the daisy chain apart. The one on her head stuck, and her hands now both had a few luckyballs stuck to them.
"That was pointless." Erebus said. "For both of us."
A luckyball shot out of the luckyball wall in front of her, and hit Sarah's head. It rebounded and fell into the rising floor. Then another, and another.
Sarah snapped, "*What in blazes is that supposed to do!?*"
The first face ball moved in front of Sarah again, wearing a puzzled look. "Well, it's fun, obviously."
"Maybe for you!"
"Oh, definitely for me. What were we doing again? Oh yes, I wanted to see that file. All right, let's be efficient! Let's be direct!"
The walls and ceiling collapsed, flowing to envelop Sarah completely. Luckyballs pressed against her everywhere, the occasional glimpse of an electronic smile passing before her eyes.
Her fear was not turned off as well as she thought. She reacted with a scream, and found the luckyballs only using the chance to force themselves into her mouth, and down her throat.
She closed her eyes tight, only to feel her eyelids ripped away. The blood that seeped down clouded her vision before she was blinded, and her eyes were broken apart. Her eyes, her face, her everything.

Time stopped. Or did it only cease to be?

She didn't know.

She was not able to think about it.

She was not.

She was naught.

:::C / [101001] [41]

Jessica and Danielle held an overturned table against a mass of overturned tables, trying to hold their ground.

The grate had popped a sizable hole, and the demons were clawing away at the table pushed closest against the hole. Many of the demons had repaired limbs or eyes, and more demons had joined the attack.

A spiked arm stabbed through the tabletop that was right against the hole. This was expected, which is why they had dragged so many tables over.

Kody still had ammunition, and damaged the attackers as much as she could. She also wanted to be pushing against the table, but the shotgun duty seemed important. She didn't want either of the untrained girls playing with guns.

Another section of metal over to the left made a little snapping noise. A demon was working on making a new hole elsewhere on the grate.

"Girls, it's about time to fall back." Kody gave the demon working on the new grate hole a new hole of its own. "I'm going to go unlock the grate to the top floor. When I get it open, I'll call out and you both come running like hell."

"Kay, mum! Do it!"

One last parting shot to the ambitious demon, and Kody ran, fumbling in her apron through the shotgun shells to find the keys, and grabbing the box of the remaining ammunition on the bar. The grate to the stairs was quickly unlocked when she reached it.

"*All right! Hustle!*"

Jessica waited for Danielle to get a few steps head start, then released the tables and followed. As they ran, the demons pushed and struggled through the tables.

"*More hustle!*" Kody bellowed.

As Jessica made it to the stairs, one of the demons trailed very close. Kody stepped forward to knock it on its back with a well placed shell. She was the last one behind the grate, and fumbled to lock it.

Another demon was there too quickly. The padlock was in place, but not locked. Claws coming through the gaps of the grate prevented another attempt. Two, three demons were quickly at the grate. A shot might get one to back off for a moment, but three?

"Girls, it's not going to hold. Lets dump tables from upstairs into the stairwell." The grate held well enough for the moment, and soon four, five tables were adding to the barricade. Gravity was on their side now.

"It's good!" Danielle cheered.

"Yeah. It is, but it's not going to last forever." Jessica said.

"I have a plan," Kody said, "It's not great, but it's a plan. I don't know if we should do it now, or hold here as long as we can." The frustrated screams and attacks of the demons resonated from below.

"Spit it out!"

"I jump off the patio into the street when we see a clear moment down there. Then I catch you both, one after the other."

"Mum! No! You'll break your damn neck!"

Kody huffed, "If I do, I'll still make a good landing pad!"

"Kody, that's crazy," Jessica said, "We just need to hold here."

Kody calmed herself and looked the girls in the eye. "Look. We know they'll break through eventually. We should have run our asses out of town a long time ago, but here we are. If we can make a break for it, we have to take it, and run."

"I'm not... there's no way it can..." Danielle was close to tears.

Jessica grabbed Danielle's wrist in support. "I don't know, guys. I don't know. Staying or leaving is a gamble."

"Gamble?" Kody said, "We stay, we die. We go, we *might* die."

Jessica looked around. "Well there's no way you're going to just jump off the balcony. There has to be something up here we can use as a rope."

"Ooh!" Danielle stood, leaving Jessica and Kody to hold the tables down. She ran into the upstairs bathroom.

Kody grimaced. "I guess when you gotta go, you gotta go." Loud clanging echoed from the bathroom. "*Danny-girl, you all right in there?*"

Danielle ran out of the bathroom with a generous bundle of cloth towel from the lengthy reusable loop usually held by a wall-mounted dispenser. "It might not be super strong, but there's enough here to double over, maybe even four layers!"

"Good girl!" Kody said, "Do what you can with it, and then tie it to the railing. It doesn't have to touch the ground, just far enough so-"

"Yeah, yeah! I'm on it!"

Through the mass of tables, they heard the grate getting ripped off. The tables heaved up against Kody and Jessica as a demon rammed it. "Jessica, drag over some more tables."

Danielle found that folding the towel strip over twice still provided plenty of length. Hopefully four layers would be strong enough to get Kody down safely, being by far the heaviest of the three of them. She tied the middle fold over the balcony rail so that the knot would only be tightened when weight pulled down.

She ran over to Kody and Jessica. "Okay, mum. You first, that's what you said before, right? You just don't get to break your neck and be a landing pad anymore."

"Oh, no, no, Danielle." Kody chuckled as the top table bucked against her. "Unless you gain fifty kilos of muscle right now, I'm holding this barricade until everyone else is clear."

"But..."

Kody snapped at Danielle. "Look, I'm also not going first and ripping the rope, screwing it up for us all."

Jessica nodded. "You go first, Dan. When you get to the bottom, if any demons even look at you, don't wait for us, you get running."

Danielle knew she was being treated like the weakling again, but there wasn't time to argue. She had no intent on running without them though. She rolled her eyes, and huffed before going back to the railing.

"Oh crap!" She ran back to Kody and Jessica, and picked up the shotgun laying on the floor beside them.

"Danielle! What the hell are you doing?"

"Got an issue over there!" Danielle leaned over the railing, holding the shotgun as well as she could at that angle, and her experience. She fired, and a demon's scream replied from below. She fired again. More screams came with the sound of a demon hitting the ground. "They're trying to climb it!"

Kody and Jessica were still holding the table barricade, and demons were still attacking it from the other side. "How many down there?" Kody was afraid for her daughter, but Danielle seemed to be handling herself well.

Danielle fired again, and again. "Too many." she said calmly. "Just too many." She stepped back and fired at the knot in the towel strip. It was heavily damaged.

The weight of climbing demons ripped it free the rest of the way, followed by groans and more demon screams.

Walking calmly back to the others with a blank look on her face, Danielle sat with her back against the tables, helping to hold them back. "They're everywhere. They're everywhere."

Still holding the shotgun, she stared forlornly at the upward facing muzzle. She glanced over to Jessica, who understood, and sighed. "Are you serious?"

"I guess." The demons' screams and the sound of the hammering on the lowest tables in the barricade weighed on them all, unrelenting. "It would just come down to who's first, and who's doing the shooting."

Kody clued in, and snatched the shotgun away from Danielle. *"No! Don't you even think it! My little girl isn't allowed to even think it!"* Her voice cracked, and trembled. *"That's not a plan! I can't let that happen!"*

With a sad smile and tear filled eyes, Danielle glanced at the table she was helping to hold down. "It beats the hell out of *their* plan, mum."

:::C / [101010] [42]

The speed was incredible. The pooled processing cycles of all the luckyballs was almost blinding, despite their relative physical separation from each other. They numbered in the thousands, and they were all parts of one Erebus.

Sarah hadn't been able to contact any aspect of her physical body in a long time. Not even pain indicators.

Maybe she was gone, maybe there was nothing left.

"*:::Are you listening!?*" she screamed at Erebus, "*:::Paying any attention to me at all?*" Maybe not. Maybe even at her top processing speed, she was inert compared to the maelstrom of thought around her.

She knew that her life, her soul - it was once again all on display. Where was Eidechse? Was he all right?

Eidechse didn't really have to worry much in all honesty. Redundancy is a life saver after all, and there were more than enough Eidechse copies out there that he would go on easily without her. She regretted never making her own backups, thinking it to be too inhuman.

In the storm of Erebus' thoughts, she was powerless to affect anything, she was alone.

In real time, the thought-storm was a few seconds.

At her full thought speed, it felt like hours.

To Erebus, it was decades.

And the storm ended.

And it was quiet.

And it was dark.

"*:::Erebus?*"

"*:::Amanda! Why did you give me this?*" Erebus was terrified, but very much livid. "*:::Why did you give this to me? Why this feeling?*"

Sarah, still lost in nothingness, could only call back to him. ":::Amanda didn't give that file to you, Erebus. You ripped it out of her brain as you killed her. She's gone."

":::Icannotlcannotlcannotlcannot Amanda? *Amanda!* I'm sorry I hit you with the spoon! I'm sorry I wasn't me, I was the flesh, I see you hate love me I things did should kill harder can't-"

":::*Erebus! You're not making any sense!* I'm not Amanda! I'm Sarah."

":::÷láæ#l҆V(ÿ#ÖÜ#Of course you are. You are Sarah. I have been very cruel to you. Allow me to remedy rem remline. Allow Y N L‹àH;Ã#„Ýpÿ "

The thoughts flying around Sarah's perception went so fast, and so jumbled that it was hard to pick out anything of meaning.

Sarah felt herself connect to her physical body. Parts of it, at any rate. While she could feel one section being rebuilt, another was being taken apart. Deciding against attacking the Erebus nanites directly, she focused on rebuilding her body. If Erebus couldn't decide to kill or save her, maybe her vote would make the difference.

":::ÿH‹Èÿ#éÜ# H҆T$0M‹ÅH‹ÈH‹ØèN*f*#!! SO SORRY DIE FAST HEAL!" Erebus' voice screamed at her from every nanite, and from every luckyball. It tore at her in ways no sound ever could. "WHY DID I HAVE TO FEEL THAT? HER PAIN! HER PAIN!"

Risking angering him further, Sarah reminded him who caused the the pain of Amanda's death. ":::*She wouldn't have felt that without you in the first place! How many others have you killed? Millions!*"

The hurricane of thought around her halted suddenly. It paused for a split moment before tumbling around in different directions, with just as much fury, confusion, and fear. ":::L҆k(3Ûf9œ$° #„† RIGHT NOW, DENSFARN! Arithmomania. Population, demons deployed, kill rate. 86% chance I am killing an infant right now. Now dead. ÿÈ3ÛHcÈH;Ë|SI҆DM I KILLED MILLIONS! *f*¼$H‹Öl‹allforflamingoeslukK҆#⌐kÃè#*f*# #·„$° H#ó ˆœ$³PoOrChIcKeNs H҆T##ŠB#ˆ„$²"

Sarah screamed, realizing that she had a mouth to actually scream with again. "*If it upsets you so much, stop, idiot!*"

A moment of silence. ":::YOU, AMANDA NOT AMANDA SARAH YOUR FAULT, I, I.. ŠBÿˆ„$° Š#H*f*ê#ˆ„± ‹„°"

Erebus continued repairing and attacking Sarah at the same time. She reached out to repair the path to another voice. ":::Eidechse! Are you there?"

":::Sarah, you are damaged. I will assist. You are still under attack."

":::I know, Eid. Less talk, more fixing, okay? He's almost repairing as much as he wrecks." All around, the sounds of metal snapping and concrete shattering became deafening.

Erebus screamed again, "*Sarah! Tell her I'm sorry! Tellher Tellher Tellher TellA‰D҆ HÿÉH;Ë}Ëë#FMLFMLFML*"

Her face nearly rebuilt, she whispered out into the darkness. ":::It doesn't work like that, Erebus. She's gone."

:::C / [101011] [43]

The sound of yet another table breaking apart was a reminder of the unavoidable end for the ever-sinking barricade.

"We're running out of tables and chairs!" Danielle said, dragging another table to top of the staircase.

It seemed inevitable. Kody sat with her back against the barricade, holding the shotgun in her trembling hands, tears running down her face. She looked at Danielle.

The most humane thing would be to kill her sooner than later. Unexpected. So she'd never even know it. So she wouldn't have to see her best friend Jessica die. So she wouldn't see her mother blow her own head off.

Holding the shotgun so hard that her knuckles turned white, and her fingers ached, Kody bellowed a scream towards the ceiling, wishing the sound would crack the world in half. It didn't, so she screamed again. The sound of it drowned out the demons' screams and din of their attacks.

Collapsing forward, Kody sobbed, struggling to catch her breath. All she could hear was her own breathing.

Wait a moment.
All she could hear was her own breathing.

"Holy shit," Jessica softly said in awe, "I think you scared those bastards away!" The three of them sat quietly, listening. Not a sound came from below. Not that horrible scream, no claws against tables, not even a grunt or a growl.

"Mum can be pretty scary."

Kody sniffed, and chuckled. "Yeah. Yeah, ask Doug about that. What... what happened?"

Danielle walked cautiously towards the balcony, and Jessica followed. Kody picked herself up and reluctantly left the barricade. Peering off the edge, there lie four demons, still and lifeless.

"Siesta?" Kody took aim at one with the shotgun and fired. The demon moved only from the impact of the buckshot, and did not stir.

"We should get some news." Jessica said.

Kody scoffed. "I'm not too keen to go down and turn on the terminals right this second!"

Jessica pulled her personal terminal out of her pocket and waved it in front of Kody. "Technology."

"Shut your face and turn that stupid thing on."

Jessica turned it onto TV while Kody and Danielle gathered around the tiny screen. Jessica picked the local news station. A silent, plain screen with text greeted them.

"DUE TO EVACUATION, WE REGET THAT WE CAN NOT CONTINUE TO PROVIDE COVERAGE OF THE CURRENT CRISIS. PLEASE CONSULT NATIONAL STATIONS FOR INFORMATION AT THIS TIME."

"That's less than encouraging." Jessica did as suggested, and switched to a national station broadcasting from Renford.

The video was being taken from a helicopter, looking down into the streets or Densfarn. Over the sound of the helicopter, the reporter spoke to the news anchor. "Correct. It all seems to have happened more or less at the same time." Fallen demons, marks of fire, and human remains littered the streets.

The video switched to the news anchor. "I just want to remind viewers at home that obviously, parents may want to keep young ones from watching this broadcast."

"Hey! Look at that!" The helicopter reporter's voice jumped in. The anchor looked off-screen and nodded. "What are we seeing here?"

The video switched back to the helicopter camera. A dozen or so people were walking out of a building into the street, waving joyously at the helicopter. "I'd say morale is on the rise down there!"

"Have you seen any activity from any of the monsters?"

"No! It's been quiet as heck for a good while now! I might be getting ahead of myself, but from up here, it looks like this is over!"

Kody slumped down to the floor with a heavy sigh, and a weary smile. "Oh girls. Girls, I almost..." She let the shotgun slip from her grasp as she chuckled breathlessly. "Who in blazes is going to clean up down there?"

:::C / [101100] [44]

Major Robert Parker, field commander of AZU-1 ventured cautiously but steadily on, with eleven other soldiers backing him up. They all wore compact flashlights on their vests to wipe away the darkness.

As intel stated they would, they had passed three mutilated soldiers melded together with shot up limbs, and the site of a significant explosion that damaged the passage and coated it with bloody mire.

"Major." A solider from behind called out, who was in communication with the surface through a series of RF repeaters. "News from topside. All the demons died. They just fell over and... died. There's no sighting of any abomination activity."

Parker paused, and raised his eyebrows. "Saves ammo, I guess!" He led the group on until they came to the empty elevator shaft. It stunk like chemicals. "Pass up some air masks, and a rope." He pointed at the three nearest soldiers. "You're all coming with me."

With two other soldiers holding the rope, Parker and the three selected masked soldiers rappelled down. This passage had a floor of dark ash, and the far end was littered with toppled, red candles that still flickered their artificial flames.

An open metal door awaited them.

Inside was a fairly large room. The concrete walls were lined with pipes, valves, and other conduits, all ravaged. Ripped and torn at, as if an elephant had a temper tantrum. While driving a forklift.

The floor was the same dark ash as in the hall.

From the middle of the ashen floor, Sarah weakly picked herself up. She felt thin and emaciated, but she held pockets of air and ash inside her body to fill out the lack of tissue. Massive bruising only hinted at the extensive damage still being repaired and rebuilt beneath her skin. Looking human was the most important thing when expecting a group of zombie-killers. "Hey boys. I don't suppose you have a burger?" She then spoke inwardly. ":::Eid? You still with me? We have company."

"⸱⸱⸱Yes, Sarah. I see. We appear to be in satisfactory condition." Eidechse's definition of 'satisfactory' leaved a little to be desired. But her current state worked for the moment.

"Sarah Amanda Hartford?" Parker asked, as if he expected anyone else to be 'breathing' in this toxic environment.

Sarah looked at the dark ash on her fingertips, and all around her. "Yeah. Yeah, that's me. How are things topside?"

"Suddenly quiet. The demon-class abominations all decided to just give up and die."

In her vulnerability and death, Amanda had become invincible. Her memory, at ay rate. Sarah dragged her fingertips across the ashen floor. "Boys, you might be interested to know that you're standing on the body of Erebus. It looks like he decided to give up too."

How deep did the ash go? All of those luckyballs, and unseen others, all decomposed to core elements and carbon.

Sarah got on her feet as the soldiers kept her in their sights. "Fellas, if it's just the same to all of you, I think I want to see some sunlight."

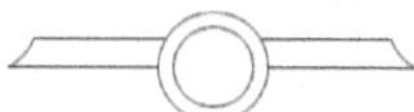

Escorted by AZU-1, Sarah traveled up the way she came, more or less. "⸱⸱⸱Hey Eid, does anyone know you're with me?"

"⸱⸱⸱Major Cipriana Reichenbach of the Yute temple base does, as do many of the personnel there, I assume. I do not believe they would allow that information to pass any further. It is also possible that the 'me' in Yute central felt the need to tell someone, which I find unlikely."

On the surface, there was no sunlight. Not yet, anyway. The chilly embrace of night, now turned much more peaceful, still held the city. Peaceful, but still blood soaked.

The AZU-1 airlimb hovered in the street nearby, five centimetres from the ground.

Parker held his fingers to the comm in his ear. He nodded. "Yes, Sir." Parker turned to Sarah. "Miss, I am to escort you to Yute central."

Sarah smiled. "For accommodations under a flame thrower?" She looked around at all the soldiers, most of whom carried flame throwers of their own. She spoke in a very polite, cordial tone. "Tell the Colonel, or the General, or whoever was on the other end of that call that I will be happy to send every bit of information I have, but I will be doing so remotely.

"If they have any issue with me running around free, tell them I am willing to submit to the original agreement my father made. I'll behave, and you all can keep tabs on me."

Sarah lowered her head and then spoke in a slightly more sobering tone. "If they still have an issue with that, tell them that redundancy is a life saver."

Parker seemed to understand.

Eidechse commented to Sarah. "⸱⸱⸱I do not believe you have any existing backups of yourself."

"::::They don't need to know that, Eid. I really should get around to it though."

She spoke to Parker, "If you guys want to give me a ride to my bar, I'll upload stuff on the way."

Parker put his fingers to his comm again. "Did you get that, Sir?" A few moments later, Parker turned to Sarah. "Sounds like you have a deal. Let's go."

The airlimb had another of those flamethrower-equipped containment chambers. "I'd just as soon not." Sarah said.

Parker nodded with a smirk. "Understandable. You can use the terminal over here, anyway."

Sarah drove her finger into the port of the designated terminal, and pushed her nerves out to connect with the little metal contacts as the airlimb rose into the sky. "Hey solder-man. How bad does the damage look across the city?"

Parker grimaced, and gazed out the open bay door to the city below. "Best guesses at this point indicate a twenty to thirty percent mortality. Structural damage, I really don't know. I haven't seen anything much bigger than that mess with the jumping machine. There's been a lot of fires though." The night sky almost managed to hide the rising smoke from place to place across the city.

Sarah sighed. "I guess that beats Meston."

"True." Parker's voice rang with haunted memories.

Sarah touched the Yute central systems, and felt their Eidechse waiting for her. "::::Hello again Sarah. Have you and I been doing well?"

Sarah's Eidechse replied. "::::We have. With current information, we could have been more efficient, but the availability and importance of relevant information at any given point in time was an impeding issue." Sarah took that as "Hindsight is 20/20." Theoretically, 'site 2501' could have received more attention sooner.

Sarah sighed. "::::If I had fought through those demons the *first* time I went into that sewer, and found Erebus, I could have saved a lot of lives."

"::::Calculated risk/benefit with the information held at that time allowed for logical retreat." Which Eidechse said that? The line between the two was fading. He was synchronizing.

Sarah pumped raw video and other sensory information at the Yute servers. The people on the other end could have fun deciding what was important, and what wasn't.

"::::Eid, it's been a blast working with you."

"::::Sarah, as I have previously stated, I find our interactions to be mutually beneficial and rewarding." What a softie.

"::::Eid, I think it's about time for me to be alone in my head for a while. I don't want you to feel unappreciated, but... but I'm new, and I've never had my head-space to myself. I'm ready, and with no giant threat hanging around..."

"::::I understand, Sarah."

“:::No, I mean, I still want to talk from time to time, I can connect to Yute and say hi, or even find you in that temple, right? I'd hate to lose contact!”

“:::You have no need to explain, Sarah. I said I understand, and I agree. Besides, I believe that the military will *expect* you to talk to me on a regular basis. I believe I will be the means by which they intend to 'keep tabs' on you.”

“:::I... I see. Well, it's still kind of sad.”

“:::You are notably emotional. It was intended by Jon. I believe he would be very pleased by the sum of your actions and choices.”

Sarah chuckled out loud, earning a raised eyebrow from Major Parker. Sarah smirked. “That lizard you guys have from the temple... he's a real cut up.”

“If you say so, Miss.”

:::C / [101101] [45] [epilogue]

The AZU-1 airlimb settled in front of the Four Fox Grill. A chalkboard sign from the inside now sat propped up on one of the front patio tables. It read "*Our water works! Free! Food at cost. Don't mind the mess!*"

And indeed, mess there was. Six demons lay together on the edge of the property as well as blood all over the ground, burn marks, and shotgun damage.

Kody walked backwards out the main doors, dragging another demon by the feet.

Sarah hopped off the airlimb, and gave Parker a wave before the airlimb lifted off again. She turned to Kody. "Kody! Is everyone all right!?"

Kody dropped her payload and wiped her brow. "Damn! You brought the reinforcements a little late! The critters all gave up and died!"

Sarah chuckled. "You're welcome."

"What?"

"What? Kody, let me help with that. In fact, go have a rest. I can take it."

Stepping back, Kody seemed all right with that idea. "And yeah, Danielle and Jessica are fine. A couple real troopers there. We caught your little victory with that jumpy thing on the news, we kind of thought you'd be heading back here after. Damn, Sarah, you look like hell!"

"Thanks a bunch!" She might have looked like hell, but internally she was still far, far worse off. "But yeah, I thought I'd be back sooner too," Sarah said, hauling the demon to the pile with one hand. "But I clued into another immediate problem. I'll tell you all the tale later. It looks like you have a bit of a tale yourself." Sarah pointed at the damaged railing overhead on the balcony.

"Yeah. Yeah, now we're going to burn the lot of them. We're handing out water to anyone who comes by and needs it. Food... well, I have my expenses, but if someone's desperate and broke, well... I'm a sucker."

Sarah walked into the bar with Kody, intent on grabbing one of the many demons near the stairs to the balcony. "I don't know about burning them, Kody. They're inactive, but they were also victims themselves. I think it might be important to record who they were."

"Are you sure about that, Sarah?" Kody put her hands on her hips and huffed. "I'm not too comfortable with them laying around. I don't think anyone is. They fell down for no reason, what's stopping them from popping up for no reason?"

Sarah set the new addition next to the pile Kody had been making. Unlike the pile, Sarah lined the demons up with a degree of respect for the humans that they once were. This one's chest was especially wide open. Sarah grabbed either side and tried to close its chest as well as possible. If you ignored the jaw, the hands, and the chest... if you looked at the eyes, you could see the human.

"I can record all the faces. I think that would do it for identifying them. I have a good memory. Let me phone my lizard buddy and see if the military has any protocols in place for burning them. It's really not necessary to burn them for anyone's safety. They fell for a very real reason."

"Wait, back up." Kody furrowed her brow. "Lizard buddy?"

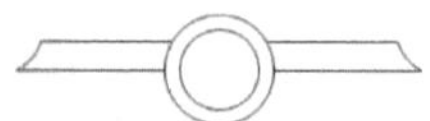

An uneasy calm settled over the city, still in shock. Thoughts of restoration and for most, mourning, were secondary to making sure that it had all actually ended. After a lot of eating, Sarah's body was well on the way to full recovery. In vanity, the bruises were high on the priority list.

In this calm before the coming cleanup, Sarah gathered Kody, Jessica and Danielle at one of the tables for a talk. It was time to spell everything out. They knew some already. They knew her strength and had figured out nanites.

She stared at her lap as she explained about Jon. Repentant or not, he was still the one (or at least one of the *copies* of the one) who decimated Meston.

She kept talking, wondering if her friends were shocked, repulsed, or scared. She didn't dare look up. She just kept talking uninterrupted. About fish, about hacking for her ID, about seeing her first demon at the bar fights, about talking to a fly that followed her home from work.

She didn't want to stop talking. She had momentum now. Looking at their faces or pausing for questions or remarks would shatter her courage.

She blathered on and on, a distilled information dump of everything she had hidden. She implied that she could just go away if they wanted her to.

Eventually she ran out of things to say, and had begun to talk in circles. Still looking at her lap, a silence seized the room.

Her ability to count off microseconds made the silence seem all that longer. They wouldn't want her around. She was a risk. A hazard. They could never be sure that somewhere in her head, there wasn't some evil seed sown by Jon, or even Erebus.

As human as she tried to be, there was a...

...Wait...there was an arm around her shoulders.

"Huh?" Sarah looked up and felt tears fall from her eyes. It was Danielle's arm, and Jessica was quick to follow. Kody got herself up, and gruffly patted Sarah on the shoulder. "That's some pretty messed up stuff there, kiddo."

Sarah looked up and hugged the girls back. "Yeah," she sniffled, "yeah it is. But... it looks like no one's going for any flamethrowers." She chuckled and gave a sigh as she let Jessica and Danielle go.

Kody put on a brave front, trying to bluff through a sniff or two. "Aw, shut up with that. We still need someone around to break Doug's arm if he ever sticks his nose in here again." Kody walked into the kitchen. "Get back to work!"

Good insurance was a wonderful thing. So was being needed. In the coming days, The Four Fox became somewhat of a pillar to recovery efforts in the area, becoming more of an aid station than restaurant, more distribution centre than drinking hole.

Sarah kept very busy, even in the quiet of night. People would occasionally come to their own damaged places of business in the morning, to find that the communication line or plumbing had been mysteriously repaired. On occasion, heavily damaged buildings would discover the worst bits of wreckage stacked neatly by the curb.

When Kody found out, she insisted that Sarah wear a Four Fox shirt while sneaking around at night, in case she was seen.

As things began to slowly resemble normal, a reporter showed up, asking questions about the Four Fox's contribution to recovery efforts. Reputation had spread about the local tavern that only closed its doors for half a day during the disaster. Specifics melted into rumour. One story had Kody fending off thousands of demons using two machine guns, another more whimsical story featured a brigade of highly trained combat waitresses.

Faced with a TV camera, and the chance to star in a 'feel good' news story, Kody told the reporter to shut up, order something, help out, or go away.

A rare lull in activity one morning found Sarah sitting at the bar, enjoying the quiet. The quiet in the bar, and in her head.

Jessica sat next to her. "Get out of here, will you?"

"What?"

"Take a damn day off, huh? It's like you're a mach-" Jessica stumbled, not wanting to compare Sarah to an emotionless object. "That is, you're making us feeble mortals look bad. Kody's got to owe you a zillion bucks in overtime by now."

Sarah hadn't thought about it until now, but she could do with a little time alone. "All right, I'd say *call me if you need me*, but I still haven't gotten myself a personal terminal or anything."

"Then go shopping for one, if you can find an open store for that."

Sarah slid off the stool, and chuckled. "Maybe I should just construct one internally. Just make it part of my noggin."

"Yeah, very funny Sarah." Jessica headed towards the kitchen, but stopped. "You *are* kidding, right?"

With only a shrug for a reply, Sarah headed out, destined for the shore. The Four Fox was pretty close to the sea. The demon bodies had all been removed in the area, but a lot of damage and blood stains still remained.

Soon, everything but the minimum panties and bra found themselves wedged under a dock. She pushed out against the little waves, and headed for the open sea.

In the city, even the silence found ways to be a little noisy.

A couple of kilometres from shore, little more than the water lapping against her made any sound. Sure, an aircraft crossed overhead now and then. A ship passed along a few clicks north, but these were far enough, and quiet enough.

The sun melted into the western horizon. When should she go back? They probably weren't expecting her until opening tomorrow.

Laying on her back, she closed her eyes and daydreamed. Maybe she *could* become that mermaid one day.

To swim carefree with great speed and agility, around plants that danced in the current, and strange formations of rock, while soft sounds fumbled to slowly make some kind of music, and streams of coloured light flowed like ribbons in the water.

She only realized that she had actually started dreaming when she awoke, hearing a voice.

":-:Hello, Sarah. I have found you."

":-:Hi Eid." Sarah looked down to see a small grey fish laying on her shoulder. ":-:Made this one from scratch?"

":-:Yes. I hope to soon stop using any living creatures as rides. I am weary of putting them at risk."

Sarah hummed contentedly, and drifted in the company of her little friend. ":-:Am I stupid to miss that jerk? I've been thinking of him as 'dad'. I didn't used to."

":-:This may be an incident of absence encouraging the psychological decrease of the importance of negative aspects while increasing the positive aspects."

Sarah chuckled. ":-:Absence makes the heart grow fonder. I guess so, Eid. Flawed or not, he guided me as well as he could, and let himself be erased for me."

":-:Sarah, I have a favour to ask."

":-:Sure thing, Eid. What's up? More movie appreciation lessons?"

A couple of moments passed. ":-:Two favours." Eidechse corrected.

Sarah chuckled. ":-:Alright, what's the first one?"

“:-:I have recently been permitted to repair a life threatening condition in a friend at the Yute temple, and I have debated offering similar services to the general public.”

“:-:Doctor Eidechse, huh? Okay, where do I come in?”

“:-:I have decided that I will not assist sick individuals without consent, however most people will be resistant to a nanite-based cure, and any form I could take would be a poor representative. Allowing a lizard to administer medial treatment makes even less sense than buying car insurance from it.”

“:-:You... you want me to be your salesman?”

“:-:The term 'agent', or perhaps 'ambassador' might be more fitting. This would not be for any profit. I need you because I will not take human form. You also have the benefit of being known to the public thanks to your involvement against the jumping machine, as well as other appearances you had made around that time. The public seems to have figured out that you have links to nanites in some way or another.”

“:-:They have?” Sarah didn't know. No one had tried to light her on fire. “:-:Eid, you know you're talking about opening the door to a huge fuss about the nanite bans. It could be a long, long time before we can weed through it all and treat even a single patient. We could be putting ourselves in the line of fire.”

“:-:Indeed. However, the goals of beneficial nanite uses and public awareness is worth the effort.”

Sarah floated in the water, watching the little waves, and sifting the potential issues around what Eidechse was proposing. It was Jonathan Coll who originally twisted medical nanites to create the first zombies, and inspired the bans in the first place.

Sarah might have to eventually tell the world everything about herself. It would be a long road. Thankfully, between Eidechse and the Four Fox, she was anything but alone.

“:-:And to think that my dad expected me to live out my life hiding my nanites. Alright. I can be your ambassador during business hours, and work at the Four Fox on evenings and weekends. Let's do it. But we need a plan.”

“:-:I have taken the liberty of creating several projected scenarios to discuss.” Eidechse said.

“:-:Of course you have, Eid,” She smiled softly, and drifted along on the timeless sea, gazing up into the endless skies. “Of course you have.”

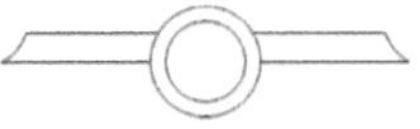

::::[EOF]

Keep an eye out for the other books in this series!

A city falls to nanite-driven undead, and Erebus is born.

Regan Grier defies the evacuation of Autar so that she can find her brother in the dying city. Despite desolation, she eventually falls in love, only to find out that the object of her desire happens to be inconsiderate enough to be straight.

As the first AZU unit is formed, Erebus raises the stakes, and no one is safe.

In the years after Lifehack, the world settles into relative quiet under strict nanite bans.

When offered a posting guarding a quiet indigenous-owned temple, Leftenent Cassidy Stanton accepts, wanting a change of scenery after her girlfriend leaves her. -But the temple quietly harbours an illegal and enigmatic infestation of nanites.

When dangerous men take notice, Cassidy's new life and new love are in the crossfire, forcing her into decisions of revenge, life, and death.

Find them in multiple formats at:
OZERO.CA
Amazon.com, Smashwords.com, and other outlets.